No Man's Land

No Man's Land

a novel

Duong Thu Huong

Translated from the Vietnamese by
Nina McPherson and Phan Huy Duong

HYPERION EAST

New York

Library of Congress Cataloging-in-Publication Data

Duong, Thu Huong.
 [Chon vang. English]
 No man's land / Duong Thu Huong ; translated from the Vietnamese by
Nina McPherson and Phan Huy Duong.
  p.   cm.
 Novel.
 In English; translated from Vietnamese.
 ISBN: 1-4013-6664-3
 I. Sino-Vietnamese Conflict, 1979—Fiction.   I. McPherson, Nina.   II. Phan,
Huy Duong, 1945–   III. Title.
PL4378.9.D759C4813 2005
895.9'2233—dc22   2004062911

PAPERBACK ISBN: 0-7868-8857-1

Hyperion books are available for special promotions and premiums. For details contact
Michael Rentas, Assistant Director, Inventory Operations, Hyperion, 77 West 66th
Street, 12th floor, New York, New York 10023, or call 212-456-0133.

FIRST PAPERBACK EDITION

10 9 8 7 6 5 4 3 2 I

No Man's Land

I

A strange, violent storm came one day in June that year.

The rain fell in torrents, steam rising in curls from rocks scalded by the sun. Icy water and hot vapor mixed to form a dense, smoky fog as an acrid, barbaric smell spread through air already heavy with the scent of dry tree sap and faded flowers, with the spittle left behind by birds in heat and the fragrance of the purple weed that covered the mountain peaks. Everything dissolved and merged in the flood.

Then, the rain stopped, the wind subsided, and water tumbled and swirled through the ravines, the stricken vegetation slowly lifting in the returning sun. From behind the clouds, the sun streamed forth, triumphant and conquering in the distant, intense blue of the sky. Like after a long separation, the blind passion of the earth and the forest flared, raking and burning everything that lay in the wake of their frenetic coupling. Butterflies, frightened by the light, scattered and hid in the crevices of rocks. Even the male bees abandoned their search for pollen. In the heavy, humid silence, only the banana flowers bloomed, their mesmerizing purple bursting into flames, as if yearning to take flight for the clouds.

Mien stood in the cave where she had taken refuge with all the other women from Mountain Hamlet. Feeling feverish, she touched her forehead, but it was icy. Her heart raced as she began to worry about her son: *Did he fall into that water urn? Maybe he got a stick in his eye? No, no . . . With a face like that, nothing bad will happen to him. Good and bad spirits alike will watch over him.*

She had stopped thinking about her son, but she still felt restless, anxious. Why? What misfortune lay at the end of the road ahead?

"That's enough," Mien said, breaking the silence. "Let's go home. It's just been an unlucky day."

No one spoke. The women stood in a group, clutching one another's shoulders, staring apprehensively up at the sky. This had been their first foray of the year into the forest to gather honey, but their bad luck had begun at dawn: As soon as they had started climbing the mountain, one of the women fell, twisted her ankle, and had to be carried all the way to the next camp. Then, after they had crossed just two peaks, the storm had hit. Now the ground was scalding, feverish. The footpaths were strewn with rotten leaves, and steam rose off flowers crushed and scattered by the rain, glued to the tree trunks. Little by little, everything began to exude a horrific stench.

"Let's go home," Mien urged. One of the girls in the group pointed to the mouth of the cave. "What? Do you want to be snake bait? Open your eyes! Look!" Mien kept silent. She didn't need to open her eyes wide to know that the place was crawling with snakes; they were slithering down the footpaths, leaping and darting from the treetops, ready to pounce. Above, the sound of lizards clucking their tongues echoed off the vaulted roof of the cave. Mien shivered and looked up. It was possible that a pregnant one, stifled by the heat, could leap down and bite one of them. A tall, corpulent woman who had been striking the plants in front of the cave with a stick turned to them and said, "Everyone get a stick. Just in case the snakes band together and charge at us."

Without a second's hesitation, the women all began to search for sticks to use as weapons. Then they stood back, still clutching one another, watching the glistening snakes slither down the footpaths, listening to the jagged sobs of the birds echoing in the distance. A dazed, numbed silence overcame them. They remained vigilant, waiting for the danger to pass, and yet they were as still as if they were asleep. No one dared say a word. As time passed, the sun slowly began to bake the tips of the rotting leaves and the trees gave off a nauseating smell as their bark shrank back in the heat. Stands of mud-spattered reeds at the edge of the stream straightened back into place, as slender and graceful as the blades of swords. The lilies swayed gently. Suddenly, a gust of wind rose, shaking the women from their dreamy stupor. They looked at one another. One of them threw down her stick and grumbled, "Another day lost! No use dreaming of honey. Let's just go."

Another joined her, sighing. "Yeah, let's go. It's already late."

And they all trudged back to Mountain Hamlet.

When they arrived at the edge of the forest, it was already dusk. The setting sun looked like crystal streaked with tiny fuchsia veins the color of wild roses. As Mien strode behind her friends, she felt the anxiety return, even more oppressive than before. She couldn't understand why from time to time her breath seemed to choke in her throat, or why her heart tensed, as if strangled by some invisible hand.

What's happening to me? Maybe Hoan has had some problem at sea. Maybe it was the storm . . . or even pirates. But they've been gone for years. Is he sick?

But none of these explanations satisfied her, and she kept walking, her gut twisting in pain, her heart racing, haunted all day long by the apprehension of some misfortune.

Mien's house stood on the road leading to the forest. It was one of the most recent in the village. Her husband, Hoan, had built their house at a time when the region had been deserted. But now a few young couples had settled next to them, making their home seem less marginal. Built into the side of a hill, the house was enclosed by a lush grove of orange and grapefruit trees. Farther to the west, the hills were ringed by coffee and pepper plantations. Here and there, Hoan had set up shacks with thatch roofs to store his pumps and to shelter the workers during their tea breaks. Their estate was the largest in the region; no one else had anything comparable. Hoan was both hard-working and clever. His pepper and coffee were always grown from the finest seed, the kind that required the best fertilizer and the most advanced technology, and that brought the highest price on the market. Eager to learn his techniques, all the planters in the region used to flock to his plantations, and after the harvest season, they would also clamor to be among those who rented boats with him to transport their products to the distant markets of Da Nang and Saigon. There wasn't a man in Mountain Hamlet who wasn't somehow indebted to Hoan. And Mien's women friends knew it. So when the group reached Mien's house and saw the throng of people at her gate and lining up all the way into the vast courtyard, they jostled each other, scrambling to get a look.

"What's happened? Why is there such a crowd in front of your house?"

"How should I know?" Mien replied. "I've been gone since dawn, too."

The crowd, buzzing like a hornet's nest, suddenly grew hushed when she entered the courtyard. Mien felt all eyes turn and settle on her, from the children to the old women, from her neighbors to people from distant hamlets. And their eyes gleamed oddly, at once curious and fearful, both defiant and threatening.

No one has ever looked at me so strangely . . . What has happened?

From inside the house rose the sobs and heavy sighs of a woman whose voice was strange yet familiar to Mien. A voice from her past, one she strained to recognize, from a time she had chosen to forget. People shrank back as Mien walked past. Contrary to custom, no one greeted her. Even the rowdy gaggle of kids stopped their playing and jostling and fell silent. In front of her house, clusters of men just back from the fields, bare-chested or still clad in their black, sweat-drenched shirts or military fatigues stained with rings of salt, stood gaping and talking among themselves.

Did they call a village meeting here while I was gone? . . . But the hamlet's admin-

istrative headquarters have already been repaired. They just replaced the tiles, changed the windows, and whitewashed the walls. The president of the commune even came with his briefcase to celebrate the inauguration.

While Mien was lost in these thoughts, the woman's shrill, ear-splitting lamentations suddenly rose again.

"Oh, my poor brother! Wandering in the jungle, along the river-banks, for all these years! The others were so lucky. They got their peace, their happiness. While you survived on moldy rice and eggplant."

The screeching voice grated on Mien's ears like a file against metal. As she stepped over the threshold of her house, shadows obscured her vision, blurring the individual faces inside. All she could see was a dense, tightly knit crowd of people, some seated, some standing.

"Mien!" a deep male voice called out to her.

Mien didn't recognize it. Surely it wasn't her husband's?

Hoan hasn't come back. His boats must still be out at sea.

"Mien!" the man repeated.

This time, Mien replied, "I'm here."

She turned toward the man's voice. Her eyes had grown accustomed to the darkness now. She could see a square, gloomy face, rectangular eyebrows, eyes sunken into their sockets, a vague flicker, the dying light of a bonfire.

"Mien!"

The man called to her for the third time. His voice was furious now, as if he was ready to smash something on the ground.

"Hello, sir," Mien replied, searching for a place to sit down. An old man, naked from the waist up, rose to offer her his stool. His bony, wizened hand settled on her shoulder, forcing her to sit down facing the man with the rectangular eyebrows, who continued to stare at her, tense, his wrinkled face and pale lips trembling, contorted by a nervous tic. On those pale lips, the tic reminded Mien of a face shrouded in fog that she still didn't recognize. She could almost hear it, a name echoing from the bottom of a chasm, lost somewhere in a black, icy pit, drowned out by the howl of the wind. Suddenly, the man frowned. A long sigh rose from the bottom of that abyss, stirring Mien's memory. A blurry, shapeless face glided past her eyes. Beads of sweat broke out on the man's forehead. His ashen lips trembled convulsively, gaping open. Mien felt her hands and feet go cold. Those open lips, those sad eyes, glistening under the thin lashes, she had seen them before one long-forgotten summer. Yes, summer, that season as fleeting as dying fire or the glow of dawn.

"Mien, I've come back."

The man leaned across the table, sweeping aside the half-empty teacups, and repeated, in an imperious voice, "I've come back . . . I've come back."

Mien extended her hand toward him, as if she were blind, or deaf, as if groping for the sounds. "You're back? You are . . ."

"It's me, it's Bon."

"I . . . You . . . are Bon?"

"Yes, I'm Bon, your husband."

The house went silent as a grave. The assembled crowd held their breath. Everyone waited for Mien to speak. As if delirious, she merely repeated what the man had said. "I am Bon, your husband. My husband?"

"Yes, it's me, Bon," the man replied, his voice muffled. Suddenly, he shouted, "I am Bon! I am back!"

Mien froze.

My husband? But Hoan is taking the pepper shipment to Da Nang. He promised to bring back a tricycle for little Hanh and silk for me. The night before he left, he asked me whether my favorite color was emerald green, purple, or canary yellow. Do you want anything else? he asked. No, I said, I don't need anything, that's enough. The sky is clear, the sea is calm. In less than a week my husband will be back.

"Mien!"

But Mien didn't hear him. She saw another face. A beaming, radiant face with finely drawn eyebrows arching over a wide forehead, a nose as straight as a Western man's, tender eyes, soft, warm, intoxicating lips.

"Mien, I'm back."

Now this man's voice was like a prayer, the hushed, muted whisper of the trees in springtime. The crude, bushy eyebrows rose again, the pallid lips trembled.

"Mien, I'm back."

Mien pulled her hand away. She understood; it was as if the voice had slapped the palm of her hand. They say that of all the parts of the body the palm retains sensations the longest, just as an elephant's ear holds the memory of the animal's seven previous lives. Only now did she fully realize who this man seated in front of her was.

She sighed, her voice listless. "Bon?"

"Yes," he replied. "It's me. I'm back."

Yes, he had been her husband once. The wandering soul that she had honored on the altar to "the hero who had died for his country" for so many years had suddenly been reincarnated in this sunburnt man with ghoulish skin and lips. Bon had come back. He was no longer the young man who had been her husband for the brief, fleeting space of a summer. Nor was he a wandering soul. No, he was something in between.

Night fell, shrouding the house. Mien retreated into the shadowy darkness. Someone spoke. "Light a lamp!" A hand darted out from somewhere, right under her eyes, seizing a candlestick from the table. "Quick, light the candles. But where is the lamp? Where are you, Mrs. Huyen?"

"She's outside. She went out with the little boy when she saw Mrs. Mien had come back."

"Lend me a box of matches. My lighter is out of fluid."

From the other end of the table, Bon spoke again: "Mien!"

It wasn't a prayer anymore, but a supplication. Mien could see his gaze, even through the darkness. It was like the face of a drowning man.

He's come back from the front. What woman would ever dare turn her back on a husband returning from war?

Mien knew that a ghost who comes back to the living is three times

as hungry for life as an ordinary man. The veteran returns to the special gratitude of the community and when he speaks out to claim his
share of happiness in this world, no one dares dispute or refuse him.
As a girl, Mien had witnessed the campaigns urging young girls to
marry handicapped soldiers who had returned from the war against
the French. At the time, she still lived in her village, her father was still
alive, and the sun still shone on their home. Their neighbors, an old
couple who were stonecutters, had a nineteen-year-old daughter
named Hien. She was the deputy secretary of the Communist Youth
League. So when the provincial Party leadership launched their campaign, Hien was one of the first to volunteer. She told Mien, who was
still too young to be wed, "I'm going to marry a handicapped soldier
so my family can repay their debt to the country . . ." She promised to
invite Mien to her wedding. "You'll be able to see the whole ceremony.
They say the Festival Room at the city capital is filled with pretty
lanterns. We're going to walk down red carpets, real velvet, not the
fake stuff we get from the seamstress back in Ly Hoa commune."

They had giggled with delight, dreaming of the day when Hien and
her new husband would walk down the aisle on that red velvet carpet.
Hien kept her word. Two days later, she invited Mien to come along
with her to the provincial capital to pick up her future husband. In the
village, a few other young girls had also volunteered. They woke up at
the crack of dawn and set off, arriving just before seven o'clock in the
morning. Just as Hien had said, the road was strung with red lanterns.
The wind snapped the multicolored banners that lined the Festival
Room; it looked like their village on a holiday. The "volunteers" were
the guests of honor, seated on chairs covered with red velvet. Wait-
resses dressed in traditional floor-length silk tunics served trays piled
with cakes and candies. Music played. After the salute to the flag, the
district Party secretary gave a seemingly endless speech. Still just a girl,
Mien had clutched the candies in blue and red cellophane paper
tightly in her hand; they were melting, but she didn't dare eat them.
She didn't understand a word of the secretary's speech, but the strange,

solemn atmosphere terrified her. Mien waited until the end before unwrapping the candies. But the secretary had barely stepped down from the podium when the president of the Women's Union strode to the rostrum. Her speech was even longer. When she finished, a group of children came forward with drums and bouquets of flowers, one for each of the young women who were to wed the handicapped soldiers. The drum rolls echoed noisily off the ceiling and the columns decorated with red paper flowers, thrilling the women's hearts.

Hien suddenly grasped Mien's hand; her icy palm and fingers were trembling. The drum rolls slowly subsided. Then, from a back room, stretchers were brought out, streaming with more rainbow-colored paper flowers. The handicapped men lay hidden under sheets, only their heads showing, their faces carefully made up with rouge and lipstick. The president announced that the district cadres had meticulously studied the résumés of the handicapped veterans to match them with the volunteers, so that the couples would be formed according to rational criteria, with each individual's age, family status, and temperament taken into account. Then she pulled a list out of a bag slung over her shoulder and in a booming voice read off the names of the brides and the grooms.

Hien was to be married to a soldier from a neighboring commune who was three years her senior. The man was an orphan, so Hien would be entitled to bring him back to live in her village. Mien saw Hien pale and cling to her friends. The other girls were just as white. They watched, panic-stricken. Hien dug her nails into Mien's arm and didn't let go until the minute the president read out her name.

"Dao Thi Hien . . ."

Hien jumped. The president stepped toward her, took her hand, and led her up to the stretcher that would be her fate.

"Here is your man . . . Dao Thi Hien, I trust that you will joyfully repay your debt of gratitude to this soldier who has sacrificed his life for our country."

"Yes . . . joyfully," Mien heard Hien stammer. After that, they lifted the man lying on the stretcher into their Jeep. Hien tugged at Mien's arm, silently begging her to come along on the drive to the soldier's home commune. The soldier had lost both legs, his left arm, and half of his right forearm. He wiggled his stump enthusiastically, bumping against Hien and Mien in turns, as if to stroke or gesture in friendship. The new couple exchanged their first words in the car.

Mien's memory of the experience, though distant, hadn't faded. She had visited Hien right up to the day her father died, the day she had to leave her village in the company of her little brother and sister. She still remembered how Hien had resigned herself to her marriage in the spirit of duty.

One day, Hien had confided in her, radiant with joy: "You know, today he ate two bowls of rice. One more half-bowl, and I'd be happy. The traditional medicine doctor from Ly Hoa commune came by to visit yesterday. He told me that his thing is still intact. One day I'll have a child, too!" Mien was too young at the time to understand Hien's sex life. But later, every time she thought of it, she shivered in pity for her friend.

Five candles flickered in the candelabra that stood on the table. The three rooms of the house were as silent as a tomb. Her head bowed, Mien sat wringing her hands, rubbing her icy palms back and forth, unable to warm them. Outside, in the garden, the wind subsided. A leaden silence. She wasn't alone; the villagers who had gathered sat dazed, stunned. After a time, a man behind Mien rose and spoke: "Listen, Bon . . ."

A white shirt. Pants the color of faded grass. A black leather briefcase hanging from the arm of his chair, just behind his back. Mien recognized his floating, blurry face; he was president of the commune. He continued, "Listen, Bon, you must rest, get your strength back. We'll decide everything later. As I told you, Mien remarried two full years after we received your death certificate. So all moral obligations were fulfilled. Your wife is in no way guilty."

A wizened, dark-skinned woman jumped up. "Oh, so my brother is guilty?"

So it was Ta. Mien now recognized the woman who had been lamenting earlier, her shrill voice rising and falling, as if she were chanting. Ta was shorter and tinier than Bon, but they both had the same tanned skin and bushy eyebrows. Now, Ta was showing her claws, ready to sacrifice for her brother, the Vu family heir. The president was a kind but stern man. He shot Ta a condescending glance and swept his hand outward dismissively, as if to prevent her words from soiling his shirt.

"Mien is not at fault. Neither is Bon. The war is the only guilty party."

When he finished speaking, he turned back toward the assembled crowd. "You've all been here visiting Bon for some time now. Please return home. We must leave our hosts in peace, let them rest and discuss matters privately. The commune authorities will do their duty by Bon as they have with all the other veterans. I hope everyone will help Bon in the spirit of the proverb 'The healthy leaves protect the torn leaves' and 'He who drinks from the river remembers the source.'"

Everyone heard what the president said, but no one moved or stood up to go. They were all waiting for the last act, the one that would be performed in the manner they expected, in keeping with the traditions that lived on in their memories, their imaginations, and their hearts. Turning to Mien, the president spoke again in a solemn voice, at once distant and heavy with implications: "Neither the state nor the Party interferes in the private lives of citizens. You and Hoan are both honest, law-abiding people. Now, circumstances force you to make a choice. You are the only one who can determine your life's course. We hope you will reflect before making a final decision. As you know, Bon gave his share of blood in the war against the Americans to liberate our country. We owe our peace and prosperity and our country's sovereignty and independence to the sacrifices of soldiers like Bon."

And then he picked up his black briefcase and left.

The crowd traipsed after him.

In an instant, the house fell back into an uneasy silence. Bon and Mien were alone now. He gazed at her passionately. The flicker of the candlelight illuminated his desire. Mien shuddered. She lowered her head, but she could still feel the lust that flashed in his eyes. He was just a ghost, but one who drank tea and could hunger for a woman. The horror of it made her skin crawl.

"Mien, are you . . . well?"

"Yes, yes . . ." Mien stammered.

"Mien, did you miss me?" the man asked.

In her confusion, she stammered something inaudible. She didn't dare lie, but she didn't dare tell the truth. The lustful glimmer in his eyes terrified her. Minutes passed in silence. Incapable of holding back, Bon leaped across the table and grabbed the face of the woman who, fourteen years before, had been his.

"Mien . . . I missed you . . . I love you."

Mien shrank back. She wasn't brave enough to use her hand to push aside Bon's face as it moved toward hers. But as she shirked to dodge it, she felt his hot, feverish breath on her face. And she gasped from the fetid odor wafting from his mouth. Tomorrow, the day after, for weeks, months, years, maybe even forever, she would have to live with this unbearable breath, with this man who had long since become a ghost in her heart.

"No, no!" Mien sobbed, hiding her face in her hands. Tears wet the cracks of her fingers, and she fell to the floor.

Bon pulled back and sat hunched over and silent.

Mien didn't look at him. She knew that he would stay there, patient, tenacious, day after day, month after month, more stubborn than anyone in the world. And everyone would take his side, do everything to help him reclaim her. The president had said that Mien could choose her future, but these were just platitudes. After the speech, everyone would vote for Bon. Bon the veteran. Bon the wanderer. Bon the martyr. Bon the hero, the man who had given his youth to their country in the war of national liberation. The man who had borne every sacrifice.

The villagers had their reasons. Mien could understand. She also respected Bon. But why couldn't they understand her? She loved Hoan. Her life, her soul, and her body were all harmoniously linked with her new man. She didn't love Bon anymore. Their love had been snuffed out, dissolved by time, before it had even had a chance to bloom. How could a woman sleep with a corpse, with a man who had one foot in the grave?

But Mien knew that no one would give her a moment's thought, that her questions would remain unanswered.

At about eight o'clock that evening, Auntie Huyen returned. Standing in the middle of the courtyard, she cried out to Mien: "Why are the two of you sitting in there like temple statues? Are you planning to skip dinner?" Then she strode up the three stairs of the porch and into the house.

"Where have you been all this time, Auntie Huyen?" Bon asked.

"I had to take the little boy to play. Being cooped up in the house makes him restless." She opened the door to a room on the left, facing Mien's room, where she usually took a nap with little Hanh. As she pushed back the door, she murmured, "That's odd, where did the lamp go?" She searched the room and emerged holding a flashlight.

"We need more light. I can't see anything in the courtyard or the kitchen. I almost slipped in front of the gate." As she walked out to the kitchen, which they had built in a small shack next to the house, she turned on the flashlight, sweeping the courtyard littered with rotting leaves. A few minutes later, two lamps were lit. Auntie Huyen set one on a low wall covered with flowering vines and hung another in front of the kitchen. Then she called to the two of them, "Mien, like it or not, you've got to eat something."

"Yes."

"The little boy is sleeping. Do you want to leave him at my place tonight?"

"No, no," Mien said, jumping to her feet. "I'll take him now."

"No, it's not necessary. Wash your face. You have to compose your-self so that you can prepare a proper homecoming meal for Bon. Af-ter all, he's come a long way. I'll bring Hanh back after the meal. I'll take the flashlight so I won't slip."

She spoke in a terse, measured voice, meting out her words like beats on a monk's wooden tocsin. She turned and left, the beam of her flashlight bobbing to the rhythm of her gait, then fading in the dis-tance. Mien stood up, reached for a towel that hung from a string un-der the eaves, and walked toward the well. Weeping, she filled a tin pail and plunged her face into the cold water. Her breathing brought bub-bles to the surface. Finally, her sobs subsided. She wiped her face and went back into the house.

"Do you want rice or porridge?" she asked Bon, just as she used to ask him every day at nightfall. She spoke in a calm, cold voice, as if the past fourteen years had been no more than a dream.

Bon hemmed and hawed, as if he didn't understand. As if these daily questions that he had missed for all these years had fallen on deaf ears.

"I'd like—I'd like—" he stammered, then looked up at her. "Whatever you like. It doesn't matter."

If Mien had looked into his eyes at that moment, she would have seen the tenderness that had overcome him. She would have seen not just love, but also submission; not just desire, but terror; and more than anything, the fear of an infinite loneliness, the kind that makes a human being weak and cowardly. Lurking behind these tangled emo-tions, she would have seen the flame of a summer's passion fourteen years earlier. A brief flicker that time hadn't extinguished, but rather had transformed into a raging inferno.

But Mien didn't see Bon. Her gaze didn't settle even for a second on his face, or on his body, or even on the space that surrounded them. As soon as he had spoken, she turned and hurried outside to the kitchen, where she knelt by the well to wash the rice, swishing and shaking the grains violently in a sieve. Then she lit the fire and hung a pot over it. When the water had reached a boil, she raked aside the coals and walked toward the chicken roost. Opening it, she thrust her hand in, grabbing haphazardly at whichever poor beast happened to be closest. Then she locked the cage back up, bound the bird's feet with some hemp string, and crushed it, wings and all, under her foot. She grabbed it by the neck with one hand and twisted with the other. Two brief jerks, and the bird went limp. Mien poured hot water over the carcass and began to plume it. Once this task was finished, she pulled a few chunks of bamboo from an earthenware jar and chopped them into thin slices with precise flicks of her wrist. The slices fell rhythmically into a nearby basket. When she was finished, she dumped the contents of the basket into an aluminum pot. She filled it with water, and set it, too, on the fire. The flames surged again. Sap fizzed and crackled on the branches of kindling.

From inside the house, Bon watched her, watched how the fire lit her glassy eyes, how they stared at something in the distance, somewhere beyond this world. Her movements terrified him; they were so precise, so determined, so mechanical, like the gestures of an automaton, a body whose soul was elsewhere. Mien stirred the pot of bamboo slivers that hung over the fire. Steam rose, hiding her face. When it dissipated, Bon could see the taut, hard muscles of her neck and cheekbones. Her face was like a stone mask, without the slightest crack.

Mien, you have so completely forgotten me these past fourteen years. You probably don't want to remember anymore. How could you forget that first night . . . the white moths that fluttered around the lamp in our bedroom. The next morning you gathered them in your hands.

Bon suddenly felt dizzy with fear. How would he kiss this face now, those tightly pursed, icy lips? He poured himself some more tea and swallowed it in one gulp. The scalding liquid warmed his blood and heart, steeling his resolve.

Perhaps she has forgotten. Perhaps she hasn't. Fourteen years is a long time. She has lived with another man. They have a son. Women fear change. They don't want up-

*heaval in their lives. I must learn to wait. Spring will come, the seedlings will grow
again through the ashes. It's like the sergeant used to tell me: In war it is the soldier who
perseveres who triumphs. In life as in war, then. For life, too, is a battle.*

This thought helped Bon regain his calm. He poured more tea and
emptied another cup. From the courtyard came the rushing of water.
Mien was rinsing the bamboo after cooking it. He saw her shake the
basket before she disappeared with it back into the kitchen. In the moment the fire had illuminated her face, he had felt his optimism disappear. Mien's stony face reminded him of a deserted space strewn with
invisible, unexploded bombs. A minefield. How could he hope to take
refuge there?

*No, no, I mustn't let these sinister thoughts get the better of me. Maybe it's a symp-
tom of my periods of depression, when I lived in the jungle, or all the bouts of
malaria, or liver problems. When the blood dries up, the heart twists and chills, the
soul turns dark, shadowy, I've made it back to my birthplace, this village. After all the
years of killing, famine, and illness, I must reclaim my lost happiness, I have to, whatever the price.*

Bon remembered how they had once launched the military campaigns, how the officers and soldiers had clutched the flagpole in their
hands and sworn: Until victory! Their shouts had boomed and echoed
through the jungle, no longer human voices but the thunderous chant
of some deity.

The memories flooded back, inspiring him. He vowed to launch a
new campaign, but this time it would be for himself, to win back all
he had lost. Until victory.

2

As the night deepened, moonlight shimmered even brighter on the tips of the trees. Their leaves, still rain-drenched, glistened like copper mirrors, reflecting and scattering sparks of light across the windswept courtyard. Mien stared out at the eerie play of leaves and light, the odd, mysterious shapes they conjured. A swarm of fireflies suddenly dove and plunged into the foliage, unexpectedly illuminating patches here and there, with each new gust of wind. This was Mien's own garden, yet she had never observed it as carefully as she had tonight, as if for the first time, just as she was about to lose it.

Mien knew that she had to leave her spacious home, and return to Bon's dilapidated shack, a place she hadn't set foot in for fourteen years. The shack was all he had to his name, and by deciding to return she had also chosen to accept his sad lot.

As she boiled water for his bath, she watched the embers and the ashes that rose from them, floating and drifting above the fire. *Why?* she asked herself for the hundredth time. And each time, the answer shot back at her, sudden, unequivocal, unwavering: *There is simply no other way. I must go back.*

The answer had come right after the commune president's speech, the moment he picked up his briefcase, turned, and strode from the courtyard. It was as if his back had become an official decree, a signboard covered with a scrawl of black letters, words bound together as tightly as barbed wire. And at the bottom, a red stamp, an official seal. She couldn't remember if it was round or square. All she knew was that this decree would change the course of her life. The seal was the symbol of power, an order that no one could disobey.

Her rebel heart had protested more than once.

It's only my imagination. No one gives me orders. No one has the right to tell me to give up the happy life that I lead. My marriage with Hoan was made in heaven, blessed by everyone.

But each time, the answer was the same.

My first marriage to Bon was also blessed. The gods always compensate for injustice. He who returns from the front is the winner. All I had to do was look at the faces of the crowd that surrounded me to know that.

Though she was seated in front of the fire, Mien felt frozen and clammy with the sweat that streamed from her shoulders, dripping in icy rivulets down her spine. As if she were being pushed underwater. Not a single boat within reach. Not even a plank of wood. Her desperate heart told her that she belonged to Hoan, that she would never be happy without him, that he was a talented, noble man. She had had the rare luck to meet him in this life; it would be folly to leave him. Mien knew that her heart spoke the truth, but she was too weak, too isolated in this small corner of life. Beyond her, outside this hamlet, the vast world belonged to others. It was a world teeming with people. Millions of people.

First, this world belonged to a whole battalion of well-aligned soldiers that marched toward her, wave after wave, in camouflage. Then to her distant ancestors, whether they were dressed in coarse hemp canvas or silk, clad in oak bark or brown tussah, whether they shaded their heads with regal parasols or bound them in simple black turbans. And finally, between these two crowds—the veterans and the ancestors— she faced her contemporaries: the president in his starched white shirt; the Party secretary in his faded green soldier's uniform and ragged top that hung out over his pants; the smartly dressed teenagers in their gaudy flowered and metal-studded T-shirts; the women of the hamlet in their drab black everyday pajamas. They all stared at her with accusing, vindictive eyes.

The soldiers spoke first. Their voices thundered over the infinite waves of troops, like echoes against the stone walls of deep caves. *You're not going to abandon our brother, are you? We fought against the invaders, sacrificed our youth, and spilled our blood. Our bodies, bones, and flesh are buried in that black dirt, decomposing there, nourishing the lush crops in our fields. Do men lucky enough to return alive deserve to be rejected by their loved ones?*

Then a single, old soldier in the first row lifted his head, his searing gaze bearing down on her, his voice at once mocking and imperious: *So, my beauty, answer me! You're not going to deprive our comrade of his share of happiness, are you?*

He squinted his eyes and bowed before continuing his march, his face masked by camouflage leaves. Then came a second soldier, and a third and a fourth. The next two were even older, with thinning beards and voices booming and rumbling like thunder. The battalion continued to advance, repeating the same question, over and over: *You're not going to abandon our brother, are you?*

Mien's knees went weak as this terrifying refrain merged with the thunderous military march, drumming in her brain. The soldiers' threatening looks were both a warning and a mute vow of retribution. Mien couldn't reply, nor could she plug her ears. She couldn't dodge the dagger-sharp gazes of these unfortunate wandering souls who clung to their thirst for life as they unleashed their rancor on her, a hatred born of countless, still-seething regrets. As they proceeded with their sinister march down the long road of another endless campaign, they spoke in chorus, their voices lamenting and echoing a cruel drum roll that summoned her, the accused, to mount the scaffold.

The flames of the kitchen fire danced in Mien's eyes and in their blazing light she thought she glimpsed the flames of executioners' pyres, where once, long ago, criminals had burned to death. And beyond this inferno, she saw the ancient courts of wartime, of the first primitive winters of humanity, when men first banded together to master fire, living in tribes in caves.

When this army had vanished in the distance, the crowd of ancestors strode gracefully forward, gliding toward her, their black gauze turbans, silk tunics, and ankle-length skirts swaying silently. In the luminous space, their long, flowing sleeves rippled and fluttered in a ghostly shimmer of funereal purple and inky black. At dawn, a milky, pallid light began to pour slowly over the rotting forests.

So, my child, have you reflected? A human being must know how to sacrifice in the name of loyalty. A good, upright woman must first master virtue before all other learning. To comport oneself in accordance with the Rites is very difficult, but she must. The gods created woman to be the pillar of her household, to pass on humanity and reason to future generations in her very milk. A woman who does not learn to sacrifice herself is a woman without nobility and without virtue, who will never fulfill her duty.

The old women who weren't busy chewing betel nut listened in silence to the sermons of their elders. Then they lifted the four panels of their silk *ao dais*, turned their backs on her, and exited with heavy strides. The wizened elders with their flashing eyes spoke slowly and lugubriously, each of their icy words taking flight like some malevolent bird. Then, leaning on their staffs, they turned to the foggy shadows of the east. Their sad, grave voices clapped rhythmically, like the beating of wings in a cavern whose walls answered back, over and over again, in haunting, tyrannical echoes.

This ancient crowd glided like a procession of clouds toward the horizon, the rippling white trousers of the men fondling the undulating, silky black skirts of the women. Then came the living. Loved ones and strangers alike rushed toward her like a tide, besieging her on all sides. Suddenly their faces turned hard, cold, and implacable. Terrified, Mien recognized them all; these were her neighbors, the same ones who used to beg antibiotics for a child stricken with pneumonia, a bit of honey for their aging mother's cough, a hose to water their fields, or even a bit of spare cash to buy groceries. The same people who had once been so friendly, or so fawning, now eagerly donned judges' masks. Bon's return had suddenly reversed their roles: From now on, she would be the one to plead and beg, to submit to their judgment. The richest woman in Mountain Hamlet had fallen from grace; she now stood accused before this Tribunal of Conscience.

So, now do you understand where your duty lies? Or has luxury and good fortune blinded you so that you turn your back on your husband in his moment of need? Don't forget all the families who sent their children to war. Bon shares the fate of all the men who sacrificed their youth on the front, who paid with their lives so that we could live in peace. In Bon's loss there is a share of the pain of all our loved ones. We stand with him . . .

Mien was surrounded by them—near and far, along every road, in every courtyard, even inside her own home. They interrogated her with their eyes, their gazes like arrows at the tips of sharp spears that plunged into her, stabbing at her flesh. Mien suddenly remembered watching a hunting dog lie in wait an entire morning for his prey. She had admired the animal's determination and tenacity. Those who besieged her today had the same gleam in their eyes. Theirs were animated by the frenzied, lascivious anticipation of those who spread their nets with delight, eagerly waiting for the perfect moment to close it on their prey.

There was simply no other way. Fate had voted for Bon. She would die if she tried to resist. She had no choice but to return to the faded love of a ghost, a man condemned to wander at the edges of a vast cemetery.

Mien remembered the flame trees that ringed the hills at the edge of the road that led to the forest. Back then, she was just a frail, skinny young girl. One day, when she and her friends went out to gather wood, the other girls had pushed her into a small stream and then run off, giggling: "Just try to get out!"

"Hey, Mien! Do the doggy paddle to get back to shore. Tomorrow I'll teach you the breast stroke."

The girls never guessed that their little prank would be the turning point in Mien's life. Mien didn't know how to swim and was terrified of the water. Her father had often taken her to Trang Nguyen Lake, just a few rice fields away from their house, where he spared no efforts in trying to teach her to swim. He used to throw her in the water with a rope around her waist. Superstitious, he forced her to let a dragon fly bite her navel. (There was a saying that anyone who was bitten would immediately be able to swim.) Once, he even tied her to a small dinghy. Nothing worked. It was as if in a previous life Mien had been a sea monster exiled for thousands of years from the watery depths, and now, in her human form, she refused to return to the site of her past unhappiness. After many failed attempts, her father finally gave up. "This daughter of ours is probably going to spend her entire life in the mountains," he sighed to her mother.

He died a few years later, but his prediction came true. After his death, Mien, as the eldest, decided to go with her siblings to live with Auntie Huyen in Mountain Hamlet. She had never guessed that even here she would have to face the currents. Mien's friends thought she could swim well enough to get to the nearest bank. They just wanted to have a good laugh. But Mien had slipped and fallen right into the heart of the current. The streambed wasn't deep, but the bottom was treacherous and strewn with slippery, algae-coated rocks. Mien hopped from one rock to the next, falling into deeper and deeper water, and drifting farther and farther from the bank. She tried to gather her courage and grope her way out, but she kept swallowing water, drawing it in through her nose. She began to feel dizzy and her eyes clouded over; she couldn't cry for help anymore because her mouth and nose were underwater. Just as she thought she would be pulled under, a young man appeared, a bundle of wood slung over his shoulder. It was Bon. He quickly leaped from rock to rock, dove into the icy water, and dragged Mien to safety. It took her a long time to emerge from her dizzy spell. Bon helped her blow the water out of her nose and cough to clear her lungs. When she was out of danger, he showed her how to massage her nostrils and temples to fend off a chill. She remembered how he had stayed with her on the bank above the stream until her clothes had dried and she had fully recovered.

"You were really scared, huh? Tomorrow I'm going to teach those girls a lesson."

"Oh no! Please don't!"

"Why not?"

"I don't want them to hate or resent me," Mien said. "Let's go home."

They got up. Bon stared at Mien's neck, admiring her skin. "Your skin is so white."

"What do you mean, white?"

"As white as cotton. Even your wrists are white." Bon laughed and recited a popular poem: "'I spoke and took your wrist / Who gave it such whiteness, such a curve?' May I hold your wrist?"

Mien blushed. Bon noticed Mien's adolescent breasts, rising and falling under her damp shirt.

Their love story had begun that afternoon. As for the days that followed, Mien couldn't remember much. They used to meet under the flame tree at the base of the hill where the road to the village was lined with reeds and pineapple bushes. Whenever the flame trees bloomed, they knew the pineapple was ripe. Bon liked to nuzzle the nape of Mien's neck greedily, like a pig plunging his snout into a trough of bran. Though they were the same age, Bon made her promise to call him "Elder Brother" after they were married, just as all the other young wives called their husbands. During the war, marriage was like a duty or a prize that the villagers offered to the young men before they went off to war.

"Tomorrow, I'll take to the road; tomorrow I leave for the front . . ."

This song was on the lips of every young girl and old woman in the village. The Party's village committee usually designated the master of ceremonies; and adolescents, often barely fourteen or fifteen years old, were called in as witnesses for the husband. For the bride, the witnesses were only slightly older. They all wore clean, chaste clothes. The boys were well groomed and the girls all wore flowers in their hair. Bon was the last young man in their village to be married. And exactly forty-two days after their wedding, Mien recalled, he had left for the front.

How did I live after that perfunctory wedding? I know I left Bon's place the day after he left for the front. Ta was awful. I couldn't stand her sordid, shabby ways. But that's all I remember.

Mien searched her memory, questioning her past. But aside from the image of the flame trees the day she nearly drowned, Bon had left no real mark on her heart.

Mien reached her hand through the window and grasped a branch of the orange tree. The leaves were chill and damp with mist. She knew every orange tree in their garden, from the lime-whitened trunk to the number. The Bo Ha varieties came from up north, and she and Hoan had purchased the Malaysian orange trees in the south. These trees were the fruit of their sweat, hard work, and hope. Just like this house, the pepper trees, and coffee plantations that covered the surrounding hills. Like the cement reservoir behind the kitchen, the well and its clear water, the peonies, the ivy in the courtyard, the hyacinth bushes in the corner of the garden, the birthwort plants that climbed the length of the wall. Everything here bore the mark of a happy life. Everything spoke of love and hope.

Why has fate put me in this horrible situation? I've never hurt or deceived anyone. I've never exploited anyone or made money at anyone else's expense. Did I contract some debt to Bon in a former life, a debt still unpaid in this one?

Mien shuddered, knowing that no one would ever reply. She would have to leave the gentle world of her life here, and travel back in time to live with a strange shadow amid the ashes of a love that had grown by the roots of an old banyan tree some fourteen years ago. She knew she could drown there a second time. But she had no choice; she knew that she had to jump, to accept the hand that fate had dealt her.

· · ·

It was nine o'clock at night. The glow of the yellow moon passed through the bars of the window, falling across Bon's face. The light made him open his eyes suddenly, even though he had closed them only for appearances; he wasn't asleep. Bon propped his hands behind his neck and looked up at the sky. Under his hands, this strange, opulent wooden bed felt as cold as stone. The bed was made of four types of ironwood and it was as smooth as porcelain or polished black marble. The moonlight shone on the intricate mother-of-pearl designs inlaid at the corners: bunches of grapes, daisies, a unicorn, a phoenix. Each motif seemed to come alive, glittering in strange pink, purple, and ivory reflections.

Back in the other room, Mien was bustling about, tidying her things. From the sound of it, she must have been folding clothes. The doors of the closet creaked repeatedly, opening and closing. Bon didn't dare call her or knock. That was another man's room, the place where Mien had made love to him, where their son slept. Bon had tried to banish these thoughts many times, but they always came back to torment him.

But I, too, have slept with other women. Why this jealousy?

You're envious of a woman, and she's the woman you love. Are you worthy of calling yourself a man, let alone a soldier?

I don't care. I'm just a person. I want my share . . . I was Mien's husband. Why do I have to suffer like this?

Your rancor is meaningless. Your wife is innocent.

I know, I know she's not to blame. But why doesn't she make any effort to fill the emptiness in my heart? She doesn't even try to share the silence, this endless loneliness that I've had to bear for the last fourteen years. She brings my platter of food, lights the lamp wick, and then leaves me to eat by myself, all alone, while she washes her hair. Then she goes off to her room with her son. She won't even look me in the eye anymore.

Each fit of jealousy like this seemed to distill a bitter sea in his soul. Was Mien sleeping? How could she be such an ingrate to him? Despite what had happened, they had once shared the same bed. Fourteen years ago. How many days and months of longing was that? He was like a man who was parched after crossing the desert: Now that he was right at the edge of a spring, he didn't dare drink from it.

Maybe she's fallen asleep. Women and children usually fall asleep after crying.

Bon froze, rigid, on the bed, his hands on his stomach, his ears peeled, waiting for the faintest sound from the other side of the wall. But all he could hear was the pendulum of the clock swinging, marking time in the silence. He watched the trickle of light wash over his chest and creep down his stomach. He hoped something would happen, but nothing did—aside from the buzzing of the insects that grew louder and more insistent as the night deepened.

A half hour later, Bon heard the little boy crying softly.

"Come now, sleep my child." He heard Mien consoling him, gently singing him a lullaby in a hushed voice.

She's not asleep. She's holding her son in her arms, completely oblivious to me! As if I were some homeless person who's come to beg food and shelter for the night!

Suddenly Bon sat upright and jumped off the bed. Shame had made the blood rush to his face. He ran to the door and knocked. "Mien, Mien . . . come out, I have to talk to you."

Mien didn't reply.

Bon reeled, dizzy with rage. Everything around him spun and grew darker. He banged on the door with his fists, shouting: "Mien, Mien! Do you hear me?"

"I hear you," Mien replied, her calm voice falling like a cold shower on his anger.

He froze in front of the door to her room. After a moment, she continued, "Go sit at the table and light the candles."

Bon lingered there a moment, unable to control a violent surge of desire. He was waiting until she moved past the door, just to be close to her, perhaps to smell the scent of her skin, to feel her breath graze his cheek.

"Light the candles," Mien whispered.

Bon felt his face burn. He turned and moved toward the table, then fumbled for the box of matches. After he carefully lit the candles, he heard a key turn in the lock. A latch was lifted. Mien pushed open the door and then closed it behind her.

"Sit down," she said, pulling out a chair facing Bon at the opposite end of the table. Bon sat down, his heart racing.

Why am I obeying her like some puppet? No, worse, like some domestic servant? What right does she have to order me around?

He stood up again. Not knowing what to do, he paced back and forth in the room, his hands stuffed in his pockets, exactly like his sergeant once had. He could see his reflection in the mirror on the tea chest and in the windowpane: a thin, dark-skinned man with a worried face. Unconsciously, he moved toward the large mirror that hung on the wall, raised his eyes.

Sit down.

The five candles flickered, their light darting almost as if from human eyes. They appeared to dance and shudder and multiply all the glasses and objects in the room into hundreds of other eyes. The entire house seemed to Bon as resplendent and solemn as a temple, or a place of worship; and the woman dressed in dark green silk, seated at the end of the long table, appeared suddenly like some great lady, noble and utterly strange. Bon was terrified.

It's only Mien, the shy little girl I pulled out of the stream, the woman I've made love to. The one with the beauty mark on her left breast, I know that much.

He moved closer to her, took just a few steps, purposely holding his arms akimbo as if he didn't care. But suddenly he felt awkward and sat down facing her again. All this while, Mien gazed out the window, her arms crossed. Even after a long silence, she still hadn't even turned her head toward him. Her rosy cheeks glowed in the candlelight. On her temple, just at the tip of her eyelashes, Bon noticed that a tiny, chestnut-colored mole had grown and darkened to a black dot.

"Speak, Mien, speak!" Bon shouted in a hoarse voice.

Mien still stared out the window illuminated by the golden moon. "You're the one who wanted to speak to me. I'm listening."

But Bon didn't know where to begin. While he chased thoughts around in his head, searching for a way out, desire overcame him. He imagined himself undressing her on the bed, awash in moonlight, devouring her milky skin, making love to her as he had dreamed of for so long.

Unable to find a logical beginning, he spoke hurriedly, in short bursts: "We are husband and wife, we *were* husband and wife. We cannot..."

But Bon no longer knew what to say. He lowered his head and fell silent. Mien said nothing either. She seemed tired and annoyed, and she kept staring at the moonlit window. A mayfly plunged into the candle. She struck a match and relit it.

The clock on the wall marked time with a dull ticking. Mien finally broke the silence: "Fourteen years ago, we were husband and wife. But I'm married to Hoan now. The village and the commune recognize both these facts. I married you after we had posted the banns. But my marriage to Hoan was also recognized by an official stamp after they posted the banns. And now you come back. What do you want?"

Her voice was tinged with contempt. Bon realized that he was the one being summoned, asked to make the honorable choice.

No, no, I don't care about honor. I need to hold the woman I love in my arms. I need her. Honor? The word has a nice ring to it, but it's just an illusion.

He cleared his throat. His hands shook, and then the trembling spread to his body. Mien had the right to choose between him and that man. The village and the commune were his firm allies, but she alone had the power to decide.

"Mien, I love you. All these long years, I've never forgotten you for a single day. How could I know that I was taken for dead?"

Mien kept silent.

Inside Bon's humiliated soul, chaotic, jumbled voices rose: *Courage, soldier! In your situation, another man would have already given up. In this world, anyone can make a living and find a decent wife. Why not be a man of honor?*

No, no. I don't care about being a man of honor. This woman is all I have left. I must win her back, whatever the price.

But she's married. She's happy. You can't destroy the home she's built.

I'll build her another house. I'm still young. We're the same age. With time, we'll have everything . . .

Are you dreaming? She already has the largest estate in the region, the biggest plantation in the province. How are you going to find the means to rival what this man has given her?

If I hadn't been a soldier for all these years, I could have made a fortune. I'm strong. I can read, and I've got a diploma just like he does. I love Mien. And this love will help me triumph over all the obstacles.

But what if she doesn't love you anymore?

Bon didn't dare continue this interior dialogue. He knew that Mien already belonged to another man, but his heart refused to accept it.

The crowd is on my side. They don't support this guy who has already taken advantage of his good fortune. People's envy and resentment will be my allies.

Jealousy and resentment were indeed part of the villagers' basic cast of mind. The mediocre and the petty have an indisputable advantage over those with honorable motives, for they know no laws or principles, and no lie or act of treachery is beneath them. Laws formally recorded had no value, no binding power, compared to the invisible, unwritten law of the village. Bon knew that this power—real power—was on his side. This was a fruit that had ripened in his absence, the reward for his fourteen years of deprivation and suffering.

Why should I give up the reward society has given me when I sacrificed my youth?

So you want to take advantage of your situation to force the woman you love to come back to you? That's shameful, dishonorable.

Yeah, but you can't touch honor, can't grab it like a woman and hold it in your hands. As for my dignity, I used it all up during the war.

That was it—he had decided. Bon knew that a man's destiny was forged in a single instant, a moment that lasted only the time it took to blink, or for the wind to change. He wasn't going to fake being a man of honor; he couldn't. At the edge of this cliff, he had to hang on, even if he had to scramble and grab at the reeds, bite the dust, even if he lost everything else . . . He couldn't lose Mien. His heart raced like the drum roll calling his unit to battle.

Mien suddenly looked at Bon. She picked up a copper rod at the base of the candelabra and brushed aside the ashes. Then she spoke slowly: "All right. I will do my duty for a man who has done his for his country and his people. I'll go back to your house and live with you. But I'll need a week to gather my things here. Hoan will be back next week. In two weeks' time, I'll move everything to your place—to your room. Tonight, stay here as a guest. But don't try to touch me. Here, in this house that I share with my husband, I will not tolerate any indignity."

She rose to her feet and added, "You can leave the candles burning. Just put them out before you go to sleep."

She turned, opened the door to her room, and closed it. Bon could clearly hear the key turn in the lock, the harsh, dry click of the latch. He bit his tongue, telling himself: *There. It's done. I'm lucky to have even that. I must wait. Time will give me back what it has taken. Like the sergeant said, In this life, it is he who is most persevering, most stubborn, who wins.*

Bon snuffed out the candles and stretched out on the bed, his hands folded over his stomach.

A ray of light filtered out the door from Mien's room. He watched it and dreamed of the lamp scattered with moths, of a lilac branch swaying, of the milky white clouds of a miraculous dawn.

3

The young men of the village had gathered at Bon's house at dawn. Big, burly men, specially chosen by the commune. They were a Communist Youth League volunteer team sent to help handicapped veterans at harvest time, or with heavy labor. Bon wasn't handicapped, but his family was so poor and so isolated that the Communist Party had decided to mobilize a team to repair the house before Mien moved back in. The men brought their own food for breakfast. All they asked for was a good cup of tea before starting work. Luckily for Bon, the night before one of the elders had given him a first-rate packet of northern tea. It was a rare luxury for these mountain people, who ordinarily drank only green tea or a cheap herbal *woi*. When Bon served the tea, its heady perfume and amber color drew sighs of admiration.

"Uncle Bon, I don't know what rank you had in the military, but today you're a nobleman with twenty-five troopers at your service. Just give the order!"

"I propose that the Party change Bon's title from 'uncle' to 'elder brother.' After all, Bon is just over thirty. Calling him 'uncle' makes him seem too old."

"True! After all, once this house is repaired, Bon will be ready to welcome his wife back and have a few kids. Calling him 'uncle' will bring him bad luck."

"Excuse me, comrades, but even great uncles and great grandfathers are capable of siring. Didn't Old Phieu have a son at sixty-nine? Like they say: The older the oyster, the more precious the pearl."

"That's easy to say. Who can compare to Old Phieu? He has a clan of eighty or ninety. Several times a month he chooses the friskiest young goats, butchers them, and drinks the blood mixed with alcohol. As for the penis and the testicles, he steams them with a concoction of medicinal herbs from north and south. And when he does, the whole village reeks of the stuff!"

"What an idiot! Southern and northern medicinal herbs are totally different. How can you mix them?"

Bon listened attentively to the young men debating these matters as he prepared tea. Their conversation piqued his curiosity. There was so much to learn now that the war was over; he had been isolated from village life for too long to be able to reintegrate easily. As a soldier, he had learned all kinds of skills: how to handle weaponry and dodge bombs and mines; how to stab in hand-to-hand combat; how to dress and bandage wounds; even how to detect enemy tracks and distinguish between different types of terrain in order to dig trenches or bury land mines. But now he apparently needed to acquire skills like preparing medicine from goat genitals, or mixing medicinal herbs.

Who knows? Maybe I'll need this recipe one day. It's uncharted territory I may need to explore.

Bon felt anxious, but he tried to reassure himself.

There's nothing to fear. I'm still young. With patience I'll learn everything I need to. My schoolteachers once had high hopes for me. Mien will be back in another week. I'll have a home just like everyone else.

Once the group had finished their tea, they all scrambled to their feet. "Now you can make full use of our strength, dear general! Then, we've got work to do in some other hamlets."

As the men got down to work, Bon struggled to weed the garden. He had decided to plant basil first, remembering the scented water Mien had used to wash her hair at that man's house. It was an infusion of dried citrus rinds mixed with basil and grapefruit flowers. Bon's garden was too small to plant a grapefruit tree, and if he wanted to plant basil he would have to do it quickly. He didn't have the means to build a fancy house lit with candles like that man had, but he would make up for it with his love and devotion.

Bon plowed the garden for two hours straight, until he felt fatigue overcome him and he decided to stop. A volunteer group of young women had come to help out, too, and they were now rinsing and preparing rice for lunch, noisily shaking it in wicker baskets. The communal authorities had launched a charitable campaign on his behalf and had approached all the wealthier families to ask for rice and food to feed this team of young workers for three days. Old Phieu had donated sixty pounds of rice and half a goat, and another villager, Mrs. Gia, had donated two rows of cabbage from her vegetable garden. All Bon had to purchase was salt, fish sauce, and a bit of lard to cook with. As Bon's sister had nothing to offer, pots, pans, and dishes had all been borrowed from the neighbors. This was humiliating for Bon, but he had no choice. The night before the young people had come, he had approached Ta to ask for help in the kitchen; after all, it was her house, too. But she had just shaken her head: "I've got debts to pay. I've got to go work."

Bon knew that no one could persuade his sister to help. Ta was a crude, vulgar woman who was the subject of many salacious jokes by the men. She lived like a weed; she grew wild, oblivious to gossip and contempt. The heavens had endowed her with a rapacious, almost bestial sexual appetite that had withstood the ravages of age, time, and poverty. When she was just fifteen, on a trip to gather firewood, Ta had met a woodsman from distant Thanh province, up north, and had brought him home to live with her. By that time, their parents had passed on, and Bon, who was still busy with his studies, worked hard to make a living. He could neither influence nor stop his elder sister. So they divided the house in two. Ta and her lover took two rooms, leaving Bon the small back room. At the time, he remembered thinking, *I don't need this lousy room. I'll pass the university entrance exam and go live in town.*

Ta and the woodsman had moved in together immediately, without bothering to get married. The communal authorities resigned themselves to the arrangement and looked the other way. But the villagers of Mountain Hamlet, thrilled by the scandal, flocked to Bon's house to gape at the woodsman from Thanh province, as if he were some curiosity. The man was only twenty-five years old, but built like a bear, with a hairy chest and neck and huge, tanned shoulders rippling with muscles. In the space of one day's work, from dawn to dusk, he could rival three local woodsmen at the saw. He wolfed down two huge bowls of rice with fish and chilies at each meal, but never touched meat or vegetables.

Sometimes the village elders of the hamlet would warn Bon: "Watch your sister. That man will put her in the grave within three or four years."

"The son replaces the deceased father as the pillar of the family. Tell your sister to watch out. The lusty male exhausts the female. She should be careful . . ."

At the time, Ta was petite, even thinner than Bon. The villagers feared she would die young because of the woodsman with the tiger's back and the bear's build. But it turned out to be the skinny woman who felled the giant. After two years with her, the man became sickly. His bulging muscles disappeared into his sunken shoulders. The hair on his chest and neck turned gray. In their third year together, they had a son. Ta was radiant; her skin glowed and her eyes sparkled. But her lover wasted away and could no longer compete with the other woodsmen. He had to rest, and be urged on several times a day by men the same age.

In the summer of their fourth year together, they had a girl. By that time, the woodsman couldn't even hold a saw anymore, so he became a carpenter. At the end of that same year, he came down with a chronic wheeze. As if he were a mountain spirit, this muscled giant suddenly shrank to a skinny, trembling reed. Every evening his eyes glazed over with fever and he would be racked with a violent cough.

He died the following summer. Ta didn't even have the means to provide the food for the funeral guests. It was wartime. The body was wrapped in plastic sheeting and a reed mat and buried.

After the woodsman's death, Ta had three mouths to feed, but she was still as gluttonous as ever. She sold their furniture, the tea chest, and the bed. But during wartime, none of this had much value. A few wealthy villagers bought the furniture from her, as if it were a bet with heaven, and stashed it away. When Ta had nothing left to sell, she borrowed money and traveled down the coast to buy marinated fish, re-selling it to the Van Kieu minorities, or the Laotians on the other side of the mountainous border. She left her two ragged, famished kids in the care of an old lady called Dot, her only remaining relative. Each time she left, she would be gone for months on end. And gradually her absences grew longer. Whenever she returned, she seemed even more voluptuous, more beautiful.

After three years of mourning, Ta was like a mare in heat. She pounced on widowers, and any man at odds with his wife was fair game. But the men of the village loved to gossip about the nefarious effects of Ta's sexual appetites; they believed that sleeping with her was literally fatal, so they avoided her like the plague. In the end, the heavens granted Ta a husband, but this time around he was an old man twenty years her senior. Found guilty of incest, he had taken flight from a coastal province before landing in Mountain Hamlet, where the authorities had allowed him to build a shack, clear land, and plant pepper trees. He was old but well preserved, and even had some money.

For Ta it was a good marriage. But her children were unhappy. The boy was thirteen and the girl just twelve. Once, the man threw a pot of boiling water at the boy. He managed to dodge the pot, but it left one of his legs badly burned. Two weeks later the boy fled with his sister. No one ever saw them again. The villagers thought they had left for Thanh province, perhaps to seek shelter with their dead father's remaining family. Ta didn't even try to find her kids. Nor did she seem to mourn their absence.

She had become pregnant again and bore her aging husband a son. When the baby was just one month old, a tiny Van Kieu man appeared in the village. He was dark, clad only in a loincloth, and carried a huge basket on his back. He spoke clumsy, broken Vietnamese, but when he saw Ta, he hugged her in his arms and burst into sobs. They spoke in a chaotic dialect, incomprehensible to the villagers. The villagers suddenly understood the reason for this wild woman's long absences. This man had no doubt been her lover during the three years of mourning. She must have promised him great things for him to make such a pilgrimage across mountains and streams. While she chattered with the Van Kieu man, her husband appeared. He let the man cry all he wanted, and then he grabbed him by the neck like a chicken, punched him, and tossed him out.

Ta bore the old man two more children. Then he died. Now, she was raising three kids alone, a girl and two boys. None of them went to school. They lived like animals.

Bon began to hate his parents.

You've left me with such a heavy burden, such shame. How could you bring such a disgusting, debauched woman into the world?

But he realized that this wasn't fair. His parents were just fleeting shadows now, clouds of dust. In this world, as in the world beyond, they were powerless. Just like him. Today, the villagers had come to fix up the house he shared with Ta. Any other decent woman would have stayed home to help with the cooking.

What shame to be of the same blood as such a creature! But no one can change his fate, or that of his clan. Whatever happens, Ta is my family. The same blood flows in our veins.

In fact, when their parents were still alive, they had known moments of happiness. Bon remembered the evenings gathered around the cooking fire with Ta, munching on grilled corn with honey. How he used to sit on his mother's lap, while Ta bounced on his father's knee. He remembered the aroma of the hot corn rising from the pan. His mother would hand him a fistful, and each time she leaned over to scoop some out of the pan, she would sniff his hair or kiss his cheek, saying: "My sweet boy, my treasure. Someday, when you grow up, you'll build a big, tall house for your mother. You'll repair and tend to the graves of our ancestors and bring honor to the Vu clan."

She must have uttered this refrain hundreds of times, his father gazing on, dreamily, his eyes brimming with love.

"Uncle Bon, come see!" a boy suddenly cried out.

Bon jumped up and strode into the courtyard.

"Uncle Bon, do you want us to separate your room from the rest of the house with a wall of bamboo or of brick? If it's a brick wall, we'll use the bamboo for the roof."

"Have you counted the bricks?"

"Yes. If we pack them like ants, there'll be just enough for the wall. But if you can make do with a bamboo partition, we'll enclose the garden with a brick wall, about two yards high. You think about it for a few minutes. We're going to take a break."

The young people were seated or sprawling on the roof, with the teapot and aluminum cups beside them. Bon glanced at the shoddy courtyard under his feet. Tufts of wild spinach and weeds poked up between the crooked bricks. The bricks had turned gray and the mortar was crumbling and dusty.

I won't be able to make anything of this courtyard. Even for pepper or coffee, I'd need a cleaner, smoother patch of land.

Then he turned and looked over the roof of the house. The three rooms were open to the elements. If he separated his room with a bamboo partition covered with newspaper, like he had fourteen years earlier, would he be able to have any privacy with Mien? On his wedding night, leaving an oil lamp on had been enough to start a fight with Ta. He imagined Mien setting foot in the dirty courtyard, entering the dark room with its dusty, smoke-stained wooden walls.

Such poverty. Such humiliation . . .

Both a curse and a complaint rose in him. When he was barely eleven, he had had to work gathering firewood to pay for his school supplies. He had dreamed of the city, of finding a brighter life, far from this poverty. But now, even after the war, he was still struggling. Even these bricks had been paid for out of his veteran's pension. The Party committee of Mountain Hamlet had donated the mortar, the lime, and a few leftover materials of mediocre quality, but salvageable. After Bon had paid for everything he had just enough money left to buy a new bedcover, as red as the flame trees and dotted with peonies as big as rice bowls. He would use it when Mien returned. Those peonies would help him regain his lost happiness.

Bon walked over to the young people. "Let's do the wall to the room in bricks. I'll take care of the courtyard later."

4

Hoan overheard the terrible news by chance, as he was walking up the bridge to the dock. His nephew was unloading merchandise there when a friend shouted to the boy.

"Tuan, hey, Tuan!"

Hoan's nephew looked up. One of his friends, an adolescent boy, was running toward him, his hair mussed by the wind.

"Hey, did you hear the news?"

Tuan set down a box he was lifting. "Are you blind? Can't you see we've just landed?"

"Your Uncle Hoan is about to lose his wife."

"What?"

"The other husband, the one they said died a long time ago . . . he's come back."

"You fool. How can a man who's been dead for more than ten years come back?"

"You're the fool. You'll see." The boy started to turn and run off, but Tuan grabbed him by the neck of his sweater and yanked him back.

"Hey, hey, sorry, we shouldn't quarrel like this. What's this all about?"

"The other day I was driving my Honda toward Mountain Hamlet to visit my cousins . . ."

Hoan was standing at the end of the jetty. The two young men had no idea that he was listening. When Tuan saw him, he pinched his friend and they both fell silent. Hoan walked slowly down the pier until he reached his nephew.

"Tuan, you load this merchandise onto the motorcycle."

Tuan ran off hastily to get the bike in a parking lot near the quay. About ten minutes later, he came back astride a large motorcycle. Without waiting for orders from his uncle, he started to tie up the packages of merchandise. Hoan glanced at the kitchen appliances that he had bought on their trip. One box contained a blender for mixing fruit. In the summer, Hoan loved to drink fruit juice with crushed ice. His garden was full of fruit trees, but he still planned to plant a few avocado and apple trees, so he could have the whole variety. The hamlet had had electricity for several years now, so the generators were no longer needed to irrigate the plantations or to operate the heavy machinery. Hoan also planned to buy a refrigerator and a television in the city, so he and Mien would be able to enjoy all the comforts of city life from their home in Mountain Hamlet. He glanced at another box, the one that held the tricycle for his son, Hanh. The last box, carefully bound and marked with a red "Fragile" arrow, was filled with new porcelain crockery. He had searched every department store in Da Nang to find it for Mien. He knew how she loved to serve on fine china. She couldn't restrain this childish passion and their house was already filled with all kinds—pure white and flowered, multicolored, and even gold-rimmed Kiang Xi porcelain decorated with tiny fairies, like day lilies. And then there were the blue porcelain plates, imitations of Chinese antiques. Hoan aimed to satisfy Mien's every desire, as if she were not just his wife, but also a little sister and a daughter. Her happiness was the source of his own.

"Uncle, should I hang this on the handle?"

"Yes."

The little bag made of fake brown leather held new silk clothes and nightgowns for Mien. Hoan had spent hours in the Han Market, following the city women around, watching carefully as they bargained and chose their dresses, so that he could find Mien's size and buy her the right clothes. He was no womanizer, but he had had enough experience to discern what a beautiful woman's face owed to nature and what she owed to the artifices of makeup, silk, and jewelry. The love he felt for Mien was tinged with adoration, with awe of her breathtaking, natural beauty, and with the pride of a man who knows just how lucky he is. How happy he had been when he had packed the nightgowns in his bag, imagining his wife trying them on, one after the other, in front of the mirror. He would be there, the first and the only one to contemplate and appreciate her beauty.

Now, it was all over. And without the slightest warning or signal.

Why have the heavens cursed me like this? I've never harmed or betrayed anyone. I've never stolen or turned my back on anyone who came to me in need. I lived so many unhappy years before I found my happiness.

"It's ready, Uncle."

Tuan had finished binding up his packages, checking all the knots. He started Hoan's motorcycle. Hoan got up and brushed off the dust on his pants.

"Are you planning on walking?"

"Yes, it's just a short stretch of road."

"Tell your mother that I'll be back in a few days."

"Yes, travel safely, Uncle. May luck be with you." The boy stammered, unable to meet his uncle's eyes. Hoan jumped on the motorcycle.

Hoan's hefty frame was intimidating and other vehicles moved out of his way, bumping up onto the edge of the road. As he drove down familiar streets on the way back to Mountain Hamlet, his heart raced.

Oh misery! Are the heavens blind or do they take pleasure in sowing injustice on earth? There are no gods. Just men. This lofty blue dome over our heads is just an illusion. Darling Mien, you are the only person in this world who sees me. You are my sky, my heaven in flesh and blood. Please, please don't leave me!

Just the thought of it made him shiver. As he did, a wheel of his motorcycle hit a rock, and he smashed into a milestone before skidding onto the gravel on the road's shoulder. If he had gone any farther he would have fallen right into the lake. Sweat streamed down his forehead. He took off his helmet, pulled out a handkerchief and wiped his face and neck, his eyes and his glasses. The shimmering surface of the lake below, with its thousands of tiny waves, seemed like a mocking, hypocritical smile. Hoan gazed intensely at the liquid mirror for a long time. Blood rushed to his head.

That was a close call. A few more inches and I would be dead. What am I doing? I don't have the right to die. My son is still too young. I can't condemn him to an orphan's life. I had a happy childhood. My father loved me so much, spoiled me so. Now it's my turn. I can't let myself give in to this.

He turned back to the road, picked up his helmet, which was set on the back of the motorcycle, and put it on. As he buckled his belt, he saw his father's face, the tiny wrinkles at the corners of his eyes and nose when he laughed, a face filled with love and compassion. His father used to watch him like this, on the nights when they sat by the beach at Dong Hoi, on the rainy mornings when they played chess on the low bench made of amboyna wood. And on the long, winter nights when he would take Hoan in his lap and tell him stories about the Knight Yeu Ly, or the love story of the beautiful Ngu Co and the brave Hang Vo, or the legend of the Trung Sisters. These happy images suddenly flooded his memory in a swirl of sounds, colors, smells, and flavors.

I have to raise a little boy, make a man out of him. Even if I lose Mien, there's still a piece of real life left, a happiness I can grasp.

Hoan checked his helmet and belt one last time and then got back on the motorcycle. A convoy of trucks suddenly roared past. Hoan stared at the cloud of swirling dust they left in their wake.

I'm going to lose her . . . Why did I sense this when I first heard the news? Why did I accept it as a fait accompli? For now, it's just a rumor. She's still at home waiting for me.

He would have to hear it for himself, even if it was so. He was a mature man, seven years Mien's senior. He didn't have the right to act impulsively.

Hoan had been lucky to be born in Dong Hoi, with its perfect beaches and charming old houses, tall and straight as bamboo. His house had opened onto the street with a shop front, like all the other city houses. In the back, they had a storage area for merchandise and the bedrooms, and at the very back, a courtyard garden enclosed by a high stone wall. Everyone who lived there had a garden, even if it was only a tiny one. But Hoan's family had a lush garden and the walls that enclosed it were covered with climbing roses and cacti. The scent of the flowers mixed with salty sea wind was a melancholy aroma for Hoan, one that always made him think of both meetings and partings. The name of the town was in itself a sigh of yearning: Dong Hoi! Ho, sea to the east! A name filled with sadness, nostalgia, and the distant echo of waves. Once, the poets had called it the City of Roses, in memory of the great poet Han Mac Tu. It deserved the name. After the rains, the chill dawn seemed to exhale the intoxicating scent of roses.

Hoan's family garden, like all the neighbors' gardens, was filled with rosebushes and cacti. But they also had persimmon and custard-apple trees and a miniature mountain covered in moss that stood next to a stand of green bamboo. On the days when they prayed to heaven and earth, or observed the ceremony for wandering souls, they used to set trays piled with food around the tiny mountain, then place sticks of incense in large ceramic pots at the base of the bamboo. Hoan's mother, dressed in an *ao dai*, would kneel and chant prayers. His father was always seated behind her in a wicker chair, his arms folded, gazing up to the sky and then down at the ground. He was a schoolteacher and his salary didn't measure up to the thick wads of bills his wife brought home from her shop, but he was still the boss, the master of the household. Hoan remembered the melody of an old Swiss cuckoo clock, a music that had ushered in the morning all throughout his childhood. When the music stopped, Hoan's father would always put the coffee on to brew. His mother and one of her nieces would prepare breakfast in the kitchen while the two children got ready for school. At the time, they lived under a regime that had a radical interpretation of the dictatorship of the proletariat. So Hoan's father's coffee-drinking was considered a vestige of his petty bourgeois class background, even though their breakfast was no more than rice noodles with a bit of bouillon or wheat noodles cooked with onion leaves.

Hoan remembered hearing his mother plead with his father: "How can you forget the Land Reform Campaign and the Campaign to Reform the Bourgeoisie? It wasn't so long ago, you know. The government can launch another campaign at any moment. We're lucky to have a few friends in high places. But that's the only reason they allowed me to keep my job after the collectivization, so I can earn this pittance. I know they're still watching us. Please, I'm asking you, stop drinking coffee."

But each time his father would reply calmly, "But we're good people. Our family has lived honestly for generations. We have nothing to fear. I like to drink coffee and I shall continue to drink it. I am not going to change my habits to suit the mandarins who would prefer that I sip herb tea or water."

Hoan's father was frail but stubborn. Meticulously groomed, he liked to wear cologne and well-pressed clothes and his hair was elegantly combed back. He always held his head high, a regal air about him. But all this refinement was at odds with a fearful, impoverished society; Hoan's father stuck out amid the dirty, hungry masses, amid the heads bowed over bowls of watery *pho* in the grim state cafeterias, like livestock from numbered feeding troughs, eating from tin spoons that had been clipped to prevent theft. Hoan sensed that his father exaggerated his rituals and grooming habits as a kind of silent challenge to society. But people pretended not to notice—perhaps because he was a respected teacher, or perhaps because he was spared by fate. At home, he maintained a peaceful, harmonious atmosphere, but he was strict. Respect was like a religious rite, and generosity was a fundamental virtue. Human destiny was taught through each sip of water, through each mouthful of rice. During this peaceful period of their lives, the scent of cactus flowers and roses soothed their souls, kept them apart in a pure, clear space, from which hypocrisy and cowardice had been banished. His father's spirit prevailed over their family life, so none of the filth and pettiness of the outside world passed their doorstep. He ordered his wife and niece not to speak of the dark, vulgar happenings of society in front of Hoan and his elder sister. Raised in this manner, Hoan grew to be the kind of young man his father expected him to become: intelligent, hardworking, and generous. But Hoan's father was often hopelessly idealistic; he never dreamed that his son would fall into the traps laid by the hypocrisy of a world he had managed to keep at bay.

At age twenty-two, Hoan was tall, muscular, and as dashing as a film star. He quickly became the heartthrob of all the young girls in their town. Every time he set foot on the volleyball court, female bystanders suddenly became passionate fans. Whether they thronged to the playing fields cheering noisily, or cowered whispering in the yard, all the local women were mad about Schoolmaster Huy's only son, "the prince in white socks"—this was the nickname they had given him, though he didn't know it. But Hoan didn't pay much attention to women. After he passed his university entrance exam, he was impatient to leave for the nation's capital up north. Sensing his anxiety, Hoan's father let him tear the pages off the family calendar. Once, he said, smiling, "You're not as much of a homebody as I thought. I guess it's me who has gotten older . . . and more fragile."

Unable to restrain himself, he reached out and stroked a lock of hair on Hoan's forehead. Hoan stood silent, petrified. He wanted to put his arms around his father's neck, to embrace him, but he didn't dare. He had grown up. A head taller than his father, he could no longer lean his cheek up as he had as a boy. Nor did he dare lean over to kiss him, like you would kiss an inferior. In Hoan's heart, this thin, fragile man remained a giant, and he wanted to preserve this image forever.

. . .

But his father's handkerchiefs were never put to the use he had intended and the train that should have taken Hoan up north never left the station. One evening, a week after that memorable afternoon, Hoan went off to play volleyball, as he always did. On the way back, he was caught in a rainstorm. A summer shower carried by the sea wind darkened the sky into a dense vault, and a curtain of rain as heavy as a waterfall tumbled from the clouds. Everyone ran for cover. Hoan waved good-bye to the other team members and then headed for home along the houses bordering the street, running under the roofs to keep dry. In no time, however, he was soaked from head to toe. At the first intersection, a woman appeared in a doorway and called to him: "Hoan, Hoan, come over here."

Her shrill voice carried even over the noise of the rain and the howling wind. When Hoan brushed the water from his eyes, he recognized the manager of the store where his mother worked. Standing in the doorway, an umbrella in hand, she kept shouting to him from the other curb. Finally, he walked over to her.

"Come on in, quickly, you're going to catch a cold, it's very dangerous," she said, pulling him into the house and leading him directly to the bathroom. "Take a bath. You must be careful not to get a chill. Here's soap and hot water."

Hoan was stunned. He had never taken a bath at anyone else's home, let alone a stranger's. And now he was in this woman's bathroom. Mrs. Lan, the manager of the state store, insisted. "Don't just stand there! Take a bath, quickly, before you catch cold."

Hoan couldn't refuse. He grudgingly entered the bathroom and locked the door. He had barely removed his wet clothes when the woman knocked loudly.

"Hey, Hoan, open the door, I've got dry clothes for you."

Hoan jumped. At his house, only his father was allowed such familiarity. He opened the door a notch to let the woman's arm through.

"Thank you, Auntie, that's very considerate."

"No need to be polite. Your mother and I work together, you know." Her voice was syrupy and seductive. In fact, his mother had known Mrs. Lan for a long time, but his family didn't like her. When the shop was nationalized, Mrs. Lan was named the manager of a dozen saleswomen, including Hoan's mother. Of all the managers of the state stores and production communes, Mrs. Lan was the most well dressed; she was also the best at giving speeches and the most skilled at wielding her power. Her husband, vice president of the town, was also an old friend of the provincial Party secretary. She could always count on the man's backing, and everyone knew it. At the time, Hoan and his sister were too young to understand what private property was. They didn't feel much resentment when they saw their grandparents' shop pass into new hands and suddenly fill with a crowd of strangers. But they understood clearly that vulgar, cowardly people were now in charge. Every day, they could see how the manager looked down on the salespeople, ordering them about, especially their mother. Mrs. Lan's every word and gesture showed a deep satisfaction with her position of power over others. The older Hoan got, the more clearly he sensed this, and so he had always avoided her on his way home. But now that he was a tall, eligible young man, she had begun to smile and try to socialize with him. He had always found a way to rush past, making some excuse so she couldn't strike up a conversation. But now this sudden rainstorm had brought him through her door, into her bathtub, and even to wear clothes she had given him with her own hands.

The warm bath did him good, all the same. He felt better in dry clothes. As he left the bathroom, he clucked his tongue to himself. *Well, it's not so bad. I'll think of it as a debt and pay it off.*

In the meantime, Mrs. Lan had made tea. "Please, have some tea and chocolates. They're from the Soviet Union." She unwrapped a chocolate and continued, "A gift from a friend of my husband who just got back from Czechoslovakia. No one in this town has tasted any yet."

It had been a long time since Hoan had tasted such delicacies, which were considered too extravagant for the impoverished society in which they lived. The hot, fragrant tea was truly delicious. He emptied cup after cup as he listened to the woman hold forth on one topic after another. He found her less offensive than he had expected; she was outspoken and clever with words, and she knew how to pepper her speech with popular jokes and anecdotes. Her sharp insights gave spice to her otherwise long-winded stories. They chatted until nightfall. The streetlights dimmed. Her husband came home. Mrs. Lan invited Hoan to dinner, but he declined. "I haven't asked my parents for permission. Next time . . ."

"Okay, but a promise is a debt, and you owe me."

"Yes, that's what my father taught me, too. Thank you, Auntie."

Hoan told himself that he would come back a few days later for dinner when he returned the clothes. But the next day, as he was coming home after volleyball, his mother handed him a letter:

> My dear Hoan,
> Even though it was the first time we talked, I already feel great affection for you. I asked your parents for permission to have you dine with us this evening. Nothing fancy, just a family dinner. I do hope you won't refuse us.

At the bottom, a florid signature: Lan.

Hoan felt anxious. This overbearing manner, this gushing expression of friendship, was distasteful to him, alien to the reserve he had been taught to cultivate. "What did Mrs. Lan say?" he asked his mother.

"Nothing but compliments."

"Why did you accept for me?"

"We didn't accept anything. She said you had promised to dine at her home."

"Yes, but not this evening. I wanted to wait a few days. I've got to find a gift to thank her for her hospitality the day I got caught in the rain."

His mother sighed. "I couldn't refuse the letter."

Hoan went to find his father. The schoolteacher was reading in the garden. He seemed to sense Hoan's presence and turned.

"What's the matter, my son? Are you feeling embarrassed about this?"

Hoan kept silent. His father continued, "Before asking our opinion, she claimed you had promised to pay her a visit, that you had really appreciated the hot bath and that you had both enjoyed a good conversation."

His father tried to console him: "Don't worry, it's nothing serious. You can understand her wanting to host you. Lots of women with daughters to marry off would love to do the same. They just wouldn't be so brazen and manipulative."

Hoan stammered something, unable to explain to his father the sudden fear that had seized him. He didn't know why, but he felt terrified, as if a snake hidden in the grass was watching every step he took.

The schoolteacher continued, "Go on now. We don't care for these people, but we can't avoid them altogether. Well, it's your decision. From time immemorial it has always been the man who has asked for the woman's hand in marriage, and not vice versa. However modern our times, it will be hard to change this custom."

He smiled mischievously and joked, "Well, I guess my son is quite sought after!"

Hoan laughed and went in the house to change. He thought of wearing a short-sleeved shirt, but his father advised him to wear a long-sleeved white shirt.

"And wear your gray pants. With people like this, it's best to dress conservatively, older than your age." His father then asked him to change out of his sandals and into a pair of leather shoes.

"Are there any other formalities you require of me, father?" Hoan asked.

"That'll do. You can take the box of cakes on the table. I asked your mother to buy them for you."

Hoan took the box of cakes, tied in a red ribbon, and headed out toward the manager's house. When she saw him arrive, she squealed like a child: "I knew it. Schoolteacher Huy's son is a man of his word!" The house reeked of perfume. The manager must have sprayed the walls because the air was saturated. The chairs, the cushions, even the tablecloth stank of a cheap, Chinese perfume that stung your nostrils.

"Do have a seat. Everything will be ready in just a moment. My goodness, a fancy box of cakes for our pitiful meal of rice and vegetables!"

"Your husband isn't home yet?"

"No. He took the plane for a meeting in Hanoi this morning. They called all the town presidents for an emergency summit. Our own president is convalescing after appendicitis. He's at some vacation spot in the Soviet Union, so my husband went to replace him. This evening it's just you, me, and my daughter, Lien."

She raised her voice: "Kim Lien, come greet your Elder Brother."

The young girl's voice rang out from the kitchen: "Just a moment, I'm cooking the fish."

Just as my father guessed. That's their wild card. They want to seduce me with their cooking.

Hoan was both amused and exasperated by the scene that was about to unfold. He had known Kim Lien since she was a little girl and he found her abrasive and spoiled. Every time she came by the shop, she gave Mrs. Lan the chance to play the virtuous mother who knew how to indulge but also educate her precious daughter. And Kim Lien loved to show her power as an only child; her parents could refuse her nothing. But in recent years, the girl hadn't been seen much around the shop. Mrs. Lan claimed that her daughter had left for Hanoi to learn foreign languages so she could go study in Germany. But now, suddenly, here she was—she had reappeared in the role of the sweet young thing preparing fish for the male guest.

We'll see if the spoiled thing can cook. She certainly has neither beauty nor virtue.

Hoan tried to contain a smirk as Mrs. Lan bustled around, bragging about her luxurious home. Hoan felt embarrassed by such immodesty, and the truth was that no amorous adventure appealed to him as much as his dream of boarding a train headed north. No girl was as seductive as the vast horizons of his imagination. What's more, Kim Lien's cheap Chinese perfume was nauseating.

Mrs. Lan chattered away, interrupting these thoughts. "Even though we live by the sea, I don't like serving fish. It takes too much time. But tonight, we're having steamed sole with mushrooms, a sweet-and-sour fish soup with pineapple and herbs, and tuna marinated with fresh ginger. We'll finish up with a chicken stewed with white lotus seeds."

"Why such a banquet? There are only three of us . . . You shouldn't have . . ."

"No, I like to stay simple. But like it or not, tonight you are my guest of honor."

She laughed, her eyes twinkling. Her thick lips puckered lasciviously as if they were going to purse into a kiss. Hoan looked down. He wasn't used to this kind of smile on the lips of a woman his mother's age. Mrs. Lan set a plate of fruit on the table and rubbed her hands together: "Everything's ready. I'm just going to wash my hands while Lien goes to change. It's too hot in the kitchen and she's broken out in a sweat."

When she had left the room, Hoan picked a comic book off the shelf and flipped through it. His stomach was churning. He had played five sets of volleyball that afternoon, and in his family, by this late hour, everyone had eaten. A humble meal, but always with the kind of dishes he liked. His mother and his sister Nen were both superb cooks. In their capable hands, a simple plate of shrimp sautéed with pepper and chives, or pork marinated in coconut juice, was so delicious that Hoan could eat five heaping bowls of rice. And for dessert, a refreshing bowl of cold *chè*.

What bad luck! Curse that rainstorm. If that whole thing hadn't happened, I'd be stretched out on my bed with a book right now.

He berated himself and felt his stomach cramp while Mrs. Lan and her daughter continued to chatter away in the bathroom. Hoan looked at the clock on the wall. Forty-five minutes had gone by. They weren't just changing clothes; they were torturing his poor stomach so their cooking would taste sublime.

What a nightmare. How can they treat a guest this way?

He hunched over trying to calm his stomach. Sweat poured down his back. He turned the pages of the comic book, but couldn't read a word—he was too frustrated to concentrate. He stayed crouched in this position until his hostesses returned. They both sashayed into the room, the mother wearing a rose-colored silk *ao dai* and the daughter a frilly skirt. Hoan could barely meet their eyes, he was so angry. He felt like turning over the table and walking out, but the well-raised boy in him took control. He forced himself to smile when Mrs. Lan asked him, "My poor guest, you must be starving, no? What can I serve you to drink, Hoan? I have Russian champagne, but there's also some of our own, very fine Vietnamese rice wine."

"No thanks, I don't drink."

"Now, now, you know what they say: A man without alcohol is like a banner without wind. Lien, hand me that glass over there."

She filled the glass with dark red liquid, raising it to the lamp to admire it in the light. "Rice wine must be served in a Czech crystal glass so it shows its colors. Kim Lien, you go get two more Czech glasses."

The girl left the room with a flip of her skirt.

Hoan was almost dizzy with hunger. His nerves were on edge. *I've got to have some soup first to calm my hunger, or they are going to force me to drink and I'll get drunk.*

He waited for the moment that his hostess would begin the meal by serving a bowl of soup. But she just raised her glass, mumbled something unintelligible, and thrust it into Hoan's hand, urging him to drink with them before they started the meal.

"What man would let a glass go empty before a banquet? Bottoms up!"

Hoan lifted the glass to his lips, emptied it, then set it down on the table and served himself a bowl of the fish soup. He gulped the soup down so fast he couldn't even taste or smell it. His hunger began to subside. But with the soup, the wine went straight to his head. Hoan had never tasted so much as a drop of alcohol. At home, his parents sometimes allowed him to eat fermented rice, but only after the meal. This was the first time that Hoan had been forced to submit to this ordeal. His head reeled. He couldn't taste the difference between the various dishes. He ate fast, swallowing everything Mrs. Lan and her daughter put in his bowl, replying mechanically to their questions. He remembered only that he spoke when they spoke to him, that he laughed when they laughed. He felt his body start to sway. Every time Mrs. Lan raised her glass of red wine, his body would began to tip and pitch from side to side. It was as if this red liquid had stirred an otherwise quiet sea into a violent squall. He closed his eyes, oblivious to the waves that washed over his body, lured by the distant chant of a lullaby into a sleep crowded with dreams.

Hoan woke abruptly, but kept his eyes tightly shut because he felt as if his body were afloat on a vast green sea. A sea that called to him, that attracted him with its indescribable sensation of sweetness and peace, with strange waves of light that danced like shards of violet crystal.

Let's drift toward the open sea, this last adventure before the train for the north.

Hoan had already swum very far when he felt a sudden peace wash over him. His body floated over the water. Suddenly, the green gleam and the flashes of red crystal disappeared. Above his head, a moonless, starless night. Pitch black. Absolute calm. His soul, too, was totally serene. He stayed like that, motionless, for what seemed like ages. Then, he sensed dawn approaching. The peaceful horizon glistened in the sun, and he began to swim back to port.

Hoan heard three strokes of the clock fall from the black sky. Either he was dreaming or these sounds had come from the wrecks of ships buried in mud, the echo of their grief and regret rising through the watery depths, carried on the waves.

He turned and shifted to his side.

Something brushed back and forth against his body. Hoan didn't have time to understand where this strange sensation came from when he shivered with pleasure. He lay motionless, attentive, savoring this new, totally unknown pleasure, his skin aflame from the silent, unnameable kisses. Magical, caressing fingers, like those of a mermaid, slowly kindled his most secret organ, and the slumbering male that lay hidden inside his vigorous but virginal body suddenly sprang and pounced. Hoan stretched his muscles like a cat emerging from sleep. After this prelude, he threw himself into lovemaking, as precisely and skillfully as a master lover.

Then Hoan awoke. Not because the mermaid had pushed him back to safe port, but because he heard the voice of the mistress of the house: "Hoan, Hoan, wake up."

Hoan opened his eyes suddenly and saw Mrs. Lan's face leaning over him. He wanted to sit up, but he realized that he was as naked as a worm; only a bath towel shielded his penis from public view. Lying next to him was her daughter, Kim Lien, wearing a transparent nightgown. She had all her makeup on, but their lovemaking had smeared the powder and rouge into a sticky film; she looked like an actress caught in the rain. So, they had slept in a double bed, their heads resting on twin white pillows embroidered with turtledoves, cast as a couple of young lovers on the first night of their honeymoon. Suddenly, Hoan realized what had happened. His heart froze.

"Hoan, wake up," Mrs. Lan repeated. "Your parents are waiting in the living room." Hoan was dumbfounded: His parents had been summoned to take responsibility for his actions. Hoan hadn't begun to repay his debt to these two revered human beings and now he had caused them almost indelible shame.

He glanced over at Mrs. Lan's daughter, who had just shifted in her sleep, yawning without even bothering to cover her mouth with her hand. This fifteen-year-old girl was clearly no stranger to the pleasures of the flesh. Hoan was horrified and disgusted. He looked up and searched for his clothes, but Mrs. Lan was already one step ahead of him: "I've put your clothes in the bathroom. You wash and change first. Then I want both of you to come down to the living room. We need to talk." She turned and left the room.

Hoan tightened the towel around his waist and disappeared into the bathroom off the bedroom. He splashed his face with cold water, struggling to wake up, then washed and scrubbed vigorously, as if straining to rub off his own skin. His head throbbed. He couldn't think of anything besides the fear: His parents were waiting for him in the living room. What would they say? Especially his father, a man who never cursed or acted with vulgarity.

How is he going to face our family, our neighbors? Will he disown me in front of the altar to the ancestors, banish me? . . . Or will he just stare at me in silence?

If that was the case, Hoan would simply have to leave home himself. He couldn't bear the thought of living with the contempt of the man who had brought him into the world.

Fists pounded on the door, followed by the girl's voice: "Darling, are you finished?"

The tone of her voice enraged Hoan. "Who's there? What do you want?" he snapped back. He doused himself with buckets of water, as if it could extinguish his rage. When he stopped, the voice spoke again, defiant: "Hurry up and come to the living room. Your parents are waiting."

Hoan was stunned. *So she's been in on it from the beginning. It wasn't just the mother. Only fifteen, and she's already deceiving people like this.*

Hoan slipped on his trousers, pushed open the door with a single shove, and stormed out. Kim Lien pushed her way inside the bathroom. They didn't even greet each other. The girl stared him down with an arrogant look that seemed to say: *Like it or not, you're going to marry me. Don't even try to escape. There's no way out.*

Hoan glanced at her puny, squat face, her dimpled chin, her thin lips and eyebrows traced with brown pencil. This was the face of Fate. Like a dagger already plunged deep into his hate-filled heart, this face would haunt him for nine years—three thousand two hundred and ninety-five days from the moment they glared at each other at that bathroom door. Fate had bound them in a shared life, but with each passing day it also tightened a knot of hatred so intense that, even after their divorce, it still screamed for vengeance.

The marriage had robbed Hoan of his youth, and from that day he had found it impossible to rid his soul of the murderous hatred that had lived inside of him. It was only a long time after, when he met Mien and their love had overpowered this hatred, that he finally let go of the past with all its sadness and pain. He thought his happiness would last because he had built it on his past suffering. But now, just at the moment when he thought nothing could threaten his future with Mien, this catastrophe had befallen him.

Mien, my darling, what are you thinking? What will you decide?

Another convoy of trucks loomed behind his motorcycle, raising a cloud of dust. Hoan suddenly realized that he had moaned aloud. He stopped his bike and spat out a mouthful of dust. Then he removed his helmet, pulled out his handkerchief, and wiped his nose. As he put his helmet back on he realized that there were only twenty more miles left to Mountain Hamlet. He would be home in less than fifteen minutes. His wife and son were there, his real life was there. Everything else could wait.

When he arrived at the hamlet, Hoan didn't notice the neighbors who had lined up by the side of the road to greet him. He didn't even take the time to say hello. As he sped toward the house, he kicked open the gate and drove his motorcycle all the way to the threshold.

Mien is here. My son is here. Everything is the way it was.

Still seated astride his sputtering bike, Hoan craned his neck to see the inside of the house. Mien was playing with Hanh, but she turned at the sound of the engine.

The same rosy face, the same sweet eyes.

Hoan shut off the engine and stepped off his bike. He slowly lifted off his helmet, hung it on his arm, and climbed the steps to the house. Mien just stood there, staring blankly at him. She didn't laugh as she normally did or ply him with any of her usual questions, the sweet nothings people use to hide their joy, or longing.

Nor did Mien rush to greet him, her silk clothes clinging to her slender, curving, familiar body, every inch of which made him shudder with pleasure. She set down on the table the bowl she had been holding, her hands dropping limply to her sides. Her dark eyes were distraught and teary. The eyes of a condemned person.

Hoan took a few steps toward her. She too stepped forward, and then fell into his arms. They embraced each other and wept.

5

A peaceful night.

So peaceful that even the humming of insects and the fitful warbling of the night birds seemed to deepen the stillness. Silence dripped off the silvery leaves of the orange trees, down the twisting vines at the base of the stone wall. The wind no longer sounded like wind, but more like a furtive sigh of sadness, the kind that eats at the heart of the fearful and the vigilant. The moon gleamed more brightly as night fell; it was no longer a golden light, but a silvery glow that covered the hamlets and these wild, rolling hills. Everything—all shapes and all lines—seemed to merge in this surreal, watery space, this sea of moonlight that flickered, phosphorescent, at the edge of the forest. To the west, the Truong Son Cordillera, like an inky black line, separated the ocean from the sky. And rising from behind these mountains, a dense yellow haze.

It was Hoan who spoke first: "Everyone has turned off their lights."

"We're the only house that leaves the light on," Mien replied.

Then they stayed silent.

It was the first time they had climbed onto the roof terrace together to survey the surrounding countryside, the familiar landscape that they had somehow never found the time to contemplate. Hoan had built them an old-style house with high walls, tall columns, and thick tiles. But above the shed, he had built an expansive terrace more than twenty yards wide, where Mien could dry her laundry and, at night, take her tea. A banister ran around the perimeter of the terrace so Hanh could play and run around safely, and they kept a small table and two stools for neighbors who dropped by for tea or a game of Chinese chess after dinner. Hoan's buddies used to come by to listen to the news on the radio, chatting while they watched the sunset. But whenever the men assembled there, Mien was always off bathing Hanh or tidying the house. So, aside from the times she went up to hang out laundry, she rarely set foot on the terrace.

But that night, Hoan had asked her to join him. "The moon is beautiful. Come, let's sit out on the terrace."

Mien had agreed, without really knowing what he wanted. When Hoan took her hand to lead her up the stairs, she was seized by regret.

I'm going to have to leave this house soon, and I've never even really seen it at night. Like the orange grove that I didn't ever notice until the night Bon came back. I'm going to lose all this, everything that I was just beginning to cherish.

This thought unsteadied her for a moment, and she rested her head on Hoan's shoulder. His large body had always been a refuge for her. She felt his arms reach around and clasp her back. This familiar gesture made her want to cry. He had held her that way when they had first fallen in love, when she had fainted during her pregnancy . . . and once when she had just stepped out of the bathroom, he had caught her in his arms, pulling her back into the steamy room with him, laughing. And how many other times? Hoan hugged her every chance he got.

"Are you cold? What's the matter?"

"Nothing."

"My shirt is soaked with your tears. Give me your handkerchief."

Suddenly, the sudden, shrill hoot of a barn owl broke the silence. Mien hugged Hoan to her. "It's like the pig bird's cry before someone dies."

"Well, if that was true, then we'd be dying all year round. You don't believe that nonsense, do you?" Hoan fell silent for a moment, then continued, "But this time he hooted right on our street. Perhaps, this time, it's really a sign."

"What are you thinking?"

"Of our love. Like a human being, it has a whole destiny of its own, a birth and a death."

He sighed and pulled Mien into his arms, hugging her so tightly she gasped for breath. "Mien, could it be any other way? How am I going to live without you?"

"Every woman would dream of marrying you, Hoan."

"Just as any man would pray to Buddha and the heavens to marry you. Why are we even talking about this?"

"What else is there to talk about now?"

Hoan said nothing.

"Do you think I am happy about this?" Mien said, her voice choking as she pulled away from him. Hoan lowered his head. The scent of the basil blossoms in her hair reached his nostrils. It was a perfume he must have whiffed in a thousand previous lives. Suddenly he felt a terrible longing for this fragrance, as if he had wandered for years in search of it, only to lose it in that instant. He lowered his head farther and sat down on a stool, pulling Mien gently into his lap, nuzzling her hair hungrily. She had jet-black hair, as smooth and as shiny as the finest silk, and when undone it fell all the way to her legs. As a girl, her hair reached all the way to the ground and she had to stand on a ladder to comb it. After her marriage, Auntie Huyen had ordered her to trim it a few feet: "Your maiden days are over. You've got to shorten it or the little rice you do eat will go only to your hair. There won't be anything left for your skin and your flesh."

Mien had once told this story to Hoan, her voice filled with regret. Hoan had laughed. "That's the past. Why remember and suffer? Even now, your hair breaks all the world records. I've never seen such beautiful hair."

Hoan had combed and knotted Mien's hair countless times. He liked to pull it out, extending the thick, glistening locks with his hand. Hoan dug his fingers into her chignon, his head spinning.

It's the last time, the last time.

Hoan undid the chignon, unfurling the thick mane that fell over his hand and Mien's shoulders before it tumbled down her back. Hoan buried his face in it as if to weave each silken strand into his memory. He loved inhaling its clean scent, the sweetness of it spreading through him. The scent of grapefruit and basil flowers blended into one warm but elusive perfume, like a butterfly merely darting past.

"You belong to me!" Hoan suddenly cried, unable to contain himself. His grief seethed and reared in him, the injustice and unfairness of it all tightening in a noose around his heart. He clasped her to him tightly, kissing the downy nape of her neck, a mixture of desire and pain tearing him apart.

"Mien!"

He had clenched his teeth, but the moan had escaped him. He realized he was losing all self-control, that soon he would have to scream, to break something, beat down the gate, or rip up an orange tree. If only he had a weapon that could smash this too-serene sky in two, setting it all ablaze, this too-calm night, these mountains and hills and fields, these plantations and hamlets and sleepy villages, this insidious world, with its tyrannical order, its impassive, unbending rules. And all the powers-that-be who would soon conspire to crush his happiness and ravage his life.

Mien, you are the love of my life. My wife, my beloved, the mother of my son. We cannot be separated so senselessly.

His heart screamed, but no one responded. The only echo came from Mien as she wept against his cheek, calling his name over and over . . .

Later that night, the moon dimmed and turned milky, opalescent, its surface streaked by veins as tangled as the brushstrokes of some drunken young scholar. A doe cried out in the distance—a shrill, distraught call, as if she had been wounded or abandoned by her mate. This plaintive wail echoed through the hills and fields of the hamlet, awakening the couple. Unmoving, their hands clasped, their hair mingled, they listened. Slowly the wailing ceased, leaving a vast silence whose spell was broken only by a sudden cascade of dew onto a banana leaf.

"Are you cold?"

"No."

"It's past midnight."

"Yes."

"It's starting to get cold. Mien, you know I love you."

"I know."

"I love you more than anything in the world."

"It's the same for me."

"How can we accept this separation?"

Mien said nothing.

As Hoan groped to button her shirt, his hand grazed her firm breasts, rekindling his desire for her. He remembered her round, white, rosy breasts, their small nipples. How her skin had glistened like mother-of-pearl the nights they made love. The color and light were preserved in his memory. Now, the thought of them excited him. He began to open the buttons he had closed. He wanted to see her in the moonlight. For months, years, he had contemplated her breasts by firelight, or candlelight. Now he wanted to see them in the glow of the full moon. He freed the last button, brushing Mien's hair back across her thigh. Her breasts stood erect, a strange, sublime whiteness, as if they were sculpted in marble. To him, Mien was like some mountain nymph exiled to earth whose time was now up, so she was preparing to rejoin the depths of the forest. Seeing him so dazed, Mien stroked his chin. "What's the matter?"

"Nothing."

Mien grasped Hoan's face in her hands, just like she did with little

Hanh. She stroked his chin and cheeks, the curl of hair on his fore-head, with all the same small maternal gestures.

"You're still young, you can make a new life. You're a man, the pil-lar of the family, the one who struggles with the world. You'll have more children."

"Why are you so worried about me? I don't need this."

"I'm worried because I love you. In any case, we can't continue to live together."

"That's up to you . . ."

"Stop torturing me. You decide then! I'll do whatever you decide."

Hoan said nothing.

"You decide!" Mien repeated, her voice trembling, challenging but tearful. "Go ahead, you make the decision. I'll obey!"

Hoan slumped forward, his head against her bosom, and broke into sobs. He knew she was right—they could no longer live together.

If he had been drafted into the war, he, too, might have been in-scribed in the book of the dead. He, too, could have lost his way, been forced to live like a wild animal in some jungle pit, and then to return like a common beggar, with only a tattered knapsack to his name. Like every other young man of his generation, Hoan had volunteered for the army. At the time, being a soldier was the only way to prove your dignity. But the recruiting service had refused him, citing a birth de-fect: He had flat feet and could never run or walk as fast as the other soldiers.

Hoan's own guilty conscience forbade him from vying for Mien with an unlucky, ruined, homeless veteran. And aside from the ruth-less judge of his own conscience, there were so many other juries, so many people who would soon step forward and claim the right to judge them.

The cock crowed, signaling the first watch. The moon seemed to shiver and pale. Drops of dew drummed down on the banana leaves. Mien wiped the tears from Hoan's face.

"Let's go downstairs now . . . I'm afraid Hanh is awake."

She stood up and took his hand, guiding him as if he were a child. A lamp set on a high table still flickered in a corner of the room. They both gazed at their home: the armoire decorated with mirrors; the dresser that held all their documents and money, where Mien kept her jewelry; the lacquered box set on top filled with her combs and hair ornaments. And next to all this, across from the table with the lamp, another table set with a vase full of orchids. The windows were hung with lace curtains that Hoan had recently bought.

"Are you tired?" Hoan asked.

"I'm wide awake."

Hoan went into the living room to make tea. A moment later, he came back with two teacups and a plate of sweet green bean cakes.

"I don't care for any," Mien said. "I just brushed my teeth. Those cakes leave a bitter taste in your mouth."

"Take some. You can always brush your teeth again."

Mien looked at Hoan in silence, realizing that soon they would no longer be able to take tea together, that from now on every moment lived together, once gone, would never be repeated, and that in just five days and six nights, she would have to leave him and this house forever.

She got up and went over to sit on their bed. She watched her husband attentively.

The woman who will marry you is a lucky woman. Who will she be? You'll probably go back to the city. There's no shortage of well-dressed, well-groomed women there.

She tried to imagine the face of the woman he would choose. A city woman, with white skin and crimson lips, used to happiness from an early age. Younger than she was, more educated, richer, more elegant. She would share Hoan's bed and go into business with his sister. She would be the one to go along with Hoan on all his trips. It was only natural that Hoan's new life would fall into place like that. Meanwhile, she would be crouched in Bon's cramped, shadowy hovel, sleeping under a mosquito net as limp as a shrimp's shell, filled with dust and dead centipedes, right next to his aging sister, a promiscuous woman who was as filthy as an old street beggar. This humiliating vision only filled Mien with more self-pity, and her nostrils flared.

"What are you thinking about?"

"Nothing."

"Then why are you crying?"

"But I'm not . . ."

Hoan opened the dresser and pulled out a handkerchief to hand to Mien. He put his arm around her, consoling her. "Please don't cry. Have you seen the new clothes?"

"Not yet."

"Here, let me show you." Hoan opened the armoire and removed the nightgowns he had just bought for Mien, spreading them out on the bed.

"Come, try them on."

"No."

"Please? Just to see how they fit?"

They'll be of no use to me in the miserable life I'm going to lead. I'll never need them.

But Mien didn't dare share these thoughts. And Hoan kept insisting, trying to force her to do what he wanted. In the end, Mien got up and tried on the nightgowns, one by one. Standing in front of the mirror, Hoan stroked each panel of silk, carefully examining the lace borders that he had taken such care to choose. While the couple lost themselves in this game, their son woke up suddenly. He sat up and rubbed his eyelids. "Mommy, what are you doing, Mommy?"

Hanh spotted the plate of bean cakes before she had had a chance to reply and was immediately distracted. "I want some cakes!"

Hoan went up to him. "Okay, but will you brush your teeth afterward?"

The little boy hesitated, thought a minute, then shook his head. "No, no, I'll eat some tomorrow." He pulled the covers over him and fell back asleep.

Mien gazed at her son for a long moment, forgetting that Hoan was waiting for her to try on the last nightgown.

"He's such a sweet boy . . . How am I going to manage living so far from him?"

"You can go over to Auntie Huyen's every day. And I'll come see him on Sunday evenings."

"You're not going to take him with you back to the city?"

"No. I know you couldn't bear to live without him."

"You're so good to me."

"I love you."

Hoan looked deeply into her eyes. Mien lowered them, already brimming with tears, and stared at the lace hem of the new nightgown. Then she took it off and tried on the last one.

"They all fit me perfectly. You chose well."

"It's not because I chose well, but because you are so beautiful, so much more beautiful than all the city women."

"Don't say that."

"It's the truth."

"I love them all, especially the green one with the white flowers. But I'll never touch them."

"Why?"

"I'm going to take only a few old clothes with me. I'll put them away in this drawer, where I keep our clothes."

Mien carefully folded the nightgowns one by one, piled them up, and carried them over to the dresser.

"No, leave the old ones. Take the best with you."

Mien turned and looked at Hoan. She spoke slowly: "Everything still bears the scent of you and Hanh. It all belongs to this life that was ours, that we had here under this roof."

"No, but you're the real owner of this home. You know that."

"Once, yes . . . but that was once. Soon I'll belong to another house. We must accept this reality."

Hoan fell silent, slowly realizing what she had said.

So this is how it is, the separation . . . the separation. Still can't imagine it. Each in his or her own corner. And this house a tomb where we bury our memories.

He lit a cigarette, hoping the smoke would help him shake off the chill that had come over him. With his sadness, the tobacco's taste had changed; now it was bitter, abrasive. He flicked the cigarette outside, into the garden, only half smoked. Seeing Mien struggling with all the clothes, he spoke up. "Mien . . . you're not going to find a thing in that heap of clothes. The best thing would be to take the silk I just bought you to the tailors. If you give them two or three times the price, they'll be able to make something for you in time."

"But the colors are so beautiful. None of this fits with the life I am going to lead."

"Why are you punishing yourself?"

"Leave me alone, will you? Just leave me alone!" Mien shouted. She bent down and opened the drawers, pulling out clothes and putting them back like a madwoman. Every time she pulled something out, it felt like she was turning a page of their love story, revealing a memory. Hoan watched as she pulled out a faded old black pants suit that she had stuffed in the back of the dresser years ago, and that she had never touched. It was the loose kind worn only by old peasant women.

"You're not going to wear that?"

"Yes, I'm taking this with me."

"Oh, please, leave it behind. Leave it for me. It's the one I most treasure. I'll give you a hundred other pairs if black is what you want."

Still bent over the drawer, her face down, Mien shook her head.

"Do you remember when you last wore these clothes?" Hoan asked. He knelt down behind her, moving close to her back. "Hey, Ma'aam, could yaa give me a glaass o'waadda?" he drawled, imitating the mountain accent.

Eight years earlier, one sweltering afternoon, as the Laotian winds scoured the surrounding hills, Hoan had been wandering in the region, looking for some land on which to build a plantation for his father. For five straight hours, he had searched in vain without coming across a farm or a stream where he could find a sip of fresh water. Parched with thirst, totally exhausted, he had tried to keep going, but he had trouble finding his way under the pounding sun. Suddenly, he had seen an old woman hoeing at the base of a hill. He guessed that she was harrowing the land, because there were just a few shoots poking up from the ground. From the back, the old woman seemed tall. She wore a black outfit, a straw hat covered with camouflage leaves that made it look tattered, ridiculous.

"Maadame, eh, Maadaame!" Hoan had cried out, affecting the local dialect, as he knew that the locals weren't used to a standard accent.

The old woman had continued her hoeing, seemingly unaware of the presence of another human being in these deserted hills. She must be deaf, Hoan had thought, or perhaps the wind had drowned out his cries. He even wondered whether maybe his thirst had choked his voice. He took a deep breath and shouted again. He tried to climb to the summit of the hill and when he was just a few feet away from the old woman, he shouted right into her ear: "Ma Dame, could you please give me a drink of water?"

The old woman dropped her hoe and shrieked in fright. She bolted like a mountain goat and grabbed the hoe with a gesture that stunned Hoan. As she turned around, under her straw hat, Hoan glimpsed sparkling black pupils and a patch of skin as white as porcelain. Her eyes twinkled and squinted into a smile. She laughed from behind the scarf that hid her face.

"My goodness! You must have been calling to me for some time. I didn't notice a thing."

"Sorry, sorry . . . It's my fault." While Hoan was mumbling these excuses, "Ma Dame" walked briskly toward a stand of bushes.

"I've got some tea under these bushes. Hurry up," she said abruptly.

Hoan followed her, but he no longer felt thirsty, stunned by this strange beauty in the middle of the remote patch of mountain. Curious, he secretly prayed that "Ma Dame" would take off the black scarf that masked her face.

The bushes must have been three yards high, but the canopy of their leaves cast enough shade to shelter several people. The sun had wilted the leaves and their sap had a pleasant smell. The jug of water lay in a bamboo basket wrapped in white reeds, a long, fragrant, strawlike grass that was very resistant and turned as white as bamboo in the sun. The woman raised the jug and poured green tea into an earthenware bowl.

"Drink!"

Hoan knew there wasn't a second bowl in the basket. "After you, Ma Dame."

"Just call me Mien. Don't be so polite. Please, just go ahead and drink." And "Ma Dame" lifted her scarf, spreading it on her knees in the wind. Hoan watched her as he lifted the bowl to his lips, fascinated by this Cinderella of the mountains.

Many years had gone by since. These memories flooded back. And so did the pain imprisoned for so long in Hoan's heart. Unconsciously, he cried out, "Ma Dame, could you please give me some water?"

But he wasn't talking to Mien this time; he was speaking to himself. He wanted to hear the echo again, once more, so he would know it clearly, both the joy and the pain. Just as he had sat by his dying father, so he could hear all his final adieus to this world.

A man has to accept his life, whether it is happy or unhappy, rich or poor, peaceful or turbulent. If God gave man a different stature than animals, it was so he could look forward.

That's what his father had told him, and not just once.

After Mrs. Lan had trapped him, he had been forced to marry Kim Lien.

But Hoan had resolved to struggle against fate. In the middle of the marriage banquet, in front of both families, he announced that he had been entrapped. He had related the facts coldly, calmly, down to the last detail, without concealing his contempt. Like everyone said later, he had muddied the face of the bride and her entire family. Even worse, he had sullied the reputation and the honor of the town's vice president, a man who was more powerful than the president himself thanks to the protection of the provincial Party secretary and his comrades in the Central Committee.

After the ceremony, Hoan went to live by himself in Bao Hamlet, a fishing village nestled on the bank of the Nhat Le River.

But back then his fate had another visage. And that fate was made of flesh and blood, wore certain clothes, answered to a name—even had a residence permit and all the other subsidies and allowances the average human being needed to survive in those days. And now fate was utterly different. No one had trapped him, no one had betrayed him, no one had deliberately tried to hurt him.

How could he oppose this fate? By what means?

He felt powerless.

He suddenly uttered the same cry for the second time: "Ma Dame, could you give me a sip of water?"

Again, he wasn't calling to Mien, but to himself. It was the lament of his own past, the light that had illuminated their life together, that now burst into this room and reflected countless tender images and memories of their happiness.

"Mien, I love you."

"I love you, too."

"Are we really going to be apart?"

"I'll leave everything here. Tomorrow I'll buy a few clothes."

"Mien."

"All I ask is that you not let anyone touch my things. That way, it will be as if you were watching over our love."

She spoke in a monotone, her voice gloomy, like some abandoned cemetery inhabited only by wraiths, where wisps of fog drift along with the wind.

You have already submitted to fate. Your voice is no longer the voice of a conscious, lucid woman, just a chorus of anonymous sounds, some witch's curse on the lips of hungry ghosts.

Hoan watched Mien on her knees in front of a pile of clothes, her gaze filled with pain as she asked him to be the guardian of their memories. No doubt she imagined some other woman would replace her.

But who could ever replace you? And if that person exists, who is she?

He couldn't imagine another woman breathing the same air he had with Mien, making love with him where they had made love, gazing at the moon together through the window slats, shifting in bed with him as the rooster announced each dawn watch. Who else would open this armoire to bring him his clothes? Who else would kneel in front of the dresser as Mien had just done?

Who?

He couldn't imagine her.

Mien folded and put away the last article of clothing in the drawer, then gently closed it. Hoan watched the white nape of her neck lengthen as she bent over, the shimmering reflections on her smooth black hair. He felt close to tears. But he knew he had no right to cry, that it was ridiculous, and unworthy for a man.

My son, do you know who man's worst enemy is? Neither the barbarians nor the foreign invaders. No, it is impropriety. And we are always responsible for our own indecorous actions.

Hoan gritted his teeth and swallowed his tears. He squeezed Mien's shoulders and drew her toward him, gazing deeply into her eyes.

"I promise you, no other woman will ever touch your things."

6

During the last days of their life together, no one came to visit. Not even the neighbors who used to drop by for tea and a game of chess on the terrace. Hoan had always been a good host, he kept fine tea in the house, and cakes and candy on hand for children. No one here went to the big cities as regularly as Hoan did to bring back luxury foods. When he was home, aside from the stormy days, people came to visit him almost every night. This last week, though, everyone had disappeared. Even when he and Mien bumped into friends on the street, people would greet them with a wave of the hand and then turn in another direction. Early every morning, Auntie Huyen would come to get little Hanh and look after him until nightfall, when she brought him back to Mien. Everyone treated the young couple as if they were condemned prisoners waiting for their execution. Hoan understood: This late honeymoon they were being granted was like the last supper.

And yet, even during their precious final moments together, Mien had so much to do that he felt as if his time was being stolen away. He had to take her to buy fabric "suitable for her new lifestyle," as she put it. Mien had ordered three black outfits and two blue suits. She bought a few wool shirts, a padded cotton jacket—the kind the old women wore—all in black. She had tucked away in a drawer all the mirrors and combs and hairpins he had bought her in town. To replace all this, she went to the commune market (where they sold a bit of everything, from gas to salt to fish sauce) and picked up a small buffalo-horn comb and a few cheap hairpins. Then she arranged it all in a tiny, crudely varnished box made of ordinary wood and held together with nails and aluminum strips.

"You have two suitcases. Why don't you take one of those?"

"Please. Just let me be."

Faced with her hardened, stubborn attitude, Hoan didn't dare press the issue. But when her moments of brusqueness and anger had passed, Mien was more tender than ever—not the tenderness of a woman secure in her happiness, but the desperate, anguished tenderness of one who knew she would soon be expelled from paradise. At night, for hours on end, she would tirelessly stroke the curls on his forehead, his ears, the hair on his chest, the beauty mark on his neck just above the first vertebra. Sometimes she would huddle against him for hours, like a lizard nestled in a rock crevice, and when he thought she was asleep she would grab her handkerchief and wipe her eyes. When Hoan touched the pillow, it was always soaked with tears. As the dawn grew, the cries of the birds became more insistent. Then the sky would brighten, the white fog dissipating and the morning light flowering on the leaves of the trees.

"Hoan, will you remember me?"

"I miss you already."

"But you'll forget. Little by little, you'll forget."

"Well, you too, won't you forget?"

"No. Never."

This unanswerable question repeated itself over and over again, with a kind of fury. The sun flitted through the slats of the window, striking them in the face. They both sat up in bed and Hoan rose to close the shutters.

As he drew open the curtains, the pattern of the lace on them stood out clearly in the daylight. He had bought them for his and Mien's peaceful, happy life, not for this sinister honeymoon, this strange time when he prayed that the sun would never rise.

"Where are you going?" Hoan asked.

"I'm just going over to Auntie Huyen's for a moment."

"Why?"

"I'm going to ask her to help me hire a few young men to help me harvest the virgin grass. You stay here, relax, I'll be back in ten minutes."

The "virgin grass," as they called it, was a weed with long, pointy leaves like rice seedlings that grew on the mountain rocks. After it was picked, the grass was dried and packed in a wicker basket to be used for bathing. Then, you threw a handful of the grass into boiling water and the bath was ready in an instant. Virgin grass was used in purification rituals, and its perfume was reserved for those who had chosen celibacy, who renounced the crowds and their distractions for a life apart. This grass was for people who retreated to the mountains, or to thatched huts, or secluded pagodas. And now Mien had decided to gather some for herself. How could she know now whether her life with Bon would be loveless? Had she decided, since her body no longer belonged to her, that she would live the life of a nun with him? Hoan didn't dare ask her these questions because it would probably enrage her, and she would snap back, as she had these last few days, "Leave me alone!"

The following afternoon, a dozen young men came by the house carrying the harvest of virgin grass on their shoulders. They spread out bundles of it in the courtyard and all along the paths in the garden to dry. From the kitchen to the house, all the way to the gate, scattered everywhere underfoot, was this pungent-smelling grass. The house suddenly began to look like a pillow-stuffing factory. Every hour, Mien would walk around turning the grass, and as the sap evaporated in the sun it gave off a smell that was a mixture of grilled cane sugar and medicinal herbs.

"Mien, your hands are covered with sap. Why are you going to all this trouble? Take some soap instead. Everything here belongs to you."

"No."

"Everything under this roof belongs to us. Not just to me. Why are you inventing all these excuses?"

"This is what I want to do."

"Why are you being so stubborn with me? I've never forced you to do anything since the day we met."

"You're not forcing me. I'm forcing myself."

"It makes no sense."

"Everything here in this house belongs to our son. He's the real owner. I'm leaving him everything."

So that's what it was. That was why she was preparing for her departure as if she were going into exile. Hoan watched Mien as she darted around the courtyard, tending to the herbs, and he felt tears brimming in his eyes.

That night would be their last together.

The sun lingered for a long time on the Truong Son mountain range, reluctant to set. When it finally disappeared, blazing red clouds continued to glow, incandescent. The sweltering, oppressive sunset seemed to taunt the unhappy couple. Mien hadn't even bothered to cook rice; had she, neither of them would have had the heart to eat it. Little Hanh had gone to sleep at Auntie Huyen's after his dinner.

"Would you like some chicken porridge?"

"Don't make anything. Come close to me, we don't have much time left."

Hoan took Mien's hand and pulled her toward him on the bed. They lay there motionless, hugging each other.

Outside, the sunset flickered out, and the violet sky turned ashen. There was no moon; even the North Star wasn't visible, as it usually was. As the house sank into shadow, they felt their limbs go weak, their spirits fade. They no longer had the strength to weep, or even to make love. Sadness, as stealthy and as invisible as the beating of a bat's wings, brushed against their faces, stifling them. Mien lay with her head propped on Hoan's arm. The night advanced, drawing them deeper into dream. In the end, exhausted, they both fell into deep sleep.

The rooster crowing at dawn woke them with a start. They realized they had missed dinner and fallen asleep without remembering to put up the mosquito net. A few bugs were still buzzing about, ecstatic at this rare chance to sate themselves. Mien was the first to speak: "Shall I turn on the lamp?"

"Yes, go ahead."

"Are you thirsty?"

"Yes. Is there any boiled water left?"

"I didn't have time to make any last night."

"I'll do it."

"No, you rest for a while. I'll put the water on."

"Okay, but let's go to the kitchen together."

They walked to the kitchen and lit the fire, watching as sparks and flames rose, and the sap of the logs started to spit and crackle. Suddenly, they fell into each other's arms.

"Hoan, do you remember the day we built this kitchen?"

"I remember."

"Do you remember your promise to me?"

"I remember."

Hoan gently stroked his wife's back, baffled as to why she should remind him of that beautiful memory at that moment, when she would have to leave in just a few hours.

He remembered the dazzling flames in their kitchen the previous winter. They had just finished building the house and were preparing a traditional banquet to celebrate. They had begun the preparations several days in advance. Hoan had ordered a nice fatted calf to make grilled veal, which was the first course. Mien was in charge of the second course: steamed chicken with lemon leaves. She had been to the best chicken coops in the hamlet to reserve thirty young hens. The third course, tuna stewed in ginger and pork fat, she had made herself. The villagers in Mountain Hamlet dreamed all year of eating fish. At every ceremony or ritual meal, their chopsticks always darted first toward the fish platter, passing up other meat dishes. Mien had also bought all kinds of herbs and meats to make a few sautéed dishes and two special soups. For dessert, there would be dumplings filled with a sweet paste of beans, coconut, and crushed, grilled black sesame seeds.

The bulk of the cooking was already done; that night all they had left to do was watch the pot with the sticky-rice cakes and wrap the *in* cakes, made with grilled sticky-rice flour, green bean paste, candied squash, and watermelon seeds. These would be the gifts for their guests to take home for their children. Though these were not as crucial as the main banquet dishes, the couple couldn't afford to overlook them.

That night, Hoan had lit the big Manson lamp and hung it in front of the door to the kitchen. The shaft of light it cast was strong enough to light a wedding or a meeting of over a hundred people, and with the blazing flames from the hearth, the kitchen was aglow. Brand new, still smelling of the varnish and the fresh lime of the whitewash on the walls, the kitchen looked more like a living room. The wealthy of Mountain Hamlet liked to build tall, skinny, five-story houses with thick walls and beams made of precious wood and old tiles like those used to build the village meeting house, while leaving space for a miniscule bathroom made of scraps and a kitchen the size of a pigsty. But Hoan had gone to great lengths and expense to build a spacious kitchen and bathrooms made from the best materials. This was Mien's kingdom and he wanted the kitchen to be the most beautiful room in the house. He couldn't bear to see her toil and suffer like the other country women who had to bend over to enter their low kitchens, to squat and hunch over cooking fires, buttocks in the air, their eyes red and blurry from the smoke. And he didn't like the idea of Mien bathing furtively in a makeshift outhouse, or stooped behind a bamboo screen for fear of being spied on by some teenager, or caught unawares by some male visitor searching for a place to relieve himself. Hoan had left the city behind, but he still valued domestic comfort. He had wanted Mien to enjoy all that she deserved.

. . .

Haunted by the lure of the siren of a train departing for the north, Hoan had scarcely paid attention to material realities in his youth. He was happy with his fate and he dreamed only of advancing his career. But that fate had been shattered in a flash of lightning; his forced marriage to Mrs. Lan's daughter had set him on another path. After he went off to Bao Village, he first lived off net fishing, then went into the lumber business. Then came the war, and he left the city with his parents to live at the foot of the Truong Son Cordillera. Before his death, Hoan's father had given him some advice: "My son, the planter's life, though tiring, has its pleasures. If you manage things intelligently, life in the mountains can be very comfortable. Life in the cities can't even compare. Once the French built great plantations, but they were too greedy; they never learned, as we do, to 'know when to stop; know when enough is enough.' They exploited the workers, which inevitably led to their own ruin. As for the State communes, they were just plantations without owners, with headless, incompetent snakes running them. Think about it. One of these days they should allow private plantations so we can avoid famine. You're smart and have some business experience with your mother. And with your determination and self-sufficiency, sooner or later you're bound to succeed."

For Hoan, each word from this frail, sweet man was like an order. Less than six months after his father's death, he left in search of fallow land. And when he met Mien he felt he had truly found his other half. What then is good luck? And what is bad luck? He often thought about this, and whenever he did he found them hard to distinguish. And a career, what was that? Many times, he had sketched out the various scenarios in his mind, to come to only one answer: If he had boarded the train to the north like everyone else, he would have become a student at the Polytechnic College. A talented student would be kept on as a researcher, and then as an associate professor, or even sent abroad to get a master's degree or a doctorate. He would have been given a teaching position and a decent salary, and he would have paid for this success in long years confined within the four walls of a laboratory, the seat of his pants worn threadbare from sitting on library benches and his eyes dependent on reading glasses so thick he would be blind without them. But that kind of man would never have noticed the beauty of the skin of the woman he loved. No, Hoan would never have been able to pay the price for this kind of success. A career like that was a glittering dream, like the mother-of-pearl from an oyster shell; it would have had only decorative value, but it could never replace real life.

Hoan knew that the heavens had blessed him in finding Mien. He was happy with his fate. All he wanted was to fully enjoy this honest, wholesome life and its simple pleasures. He wanted to watch Mien bustle about in their spacious kitchen filled with sparkling clean appliances. He wanted to see her dressed in thin silk in front of the flames of the hearth, where her face was most radiant, her body most lithe, as dazzling as the fire itself. He wanted to host guests around a huge table that he had designed himself. Just as he himself had chosen the kitchen cabinet and the shelves for the pots and pans. He had been happy to see Mien's joy. She had had a miserable, impoverished childhood, but she was not stingy. Like Hoan, she loved to entertain in style, and the festive atmosphere inside their home made their life in Mountain Hamlet no less exciting than if they had lived in the city.

The night that they had tended the pot of sticky rice and wrapped the *in* cakes together seemed like only yesterday to Hoan—the flickering flames, the smells of grilled rice and bean paste, and Mien's whispers and murmurings. When the sputtering of the pot became regular, when it was time to damp the fire, Mien had suddenly asked, "How many children are we going to have?"

"As many as the heavens grant us. Our land is vast. We can extend the plantations as far as we want."

"Why the heavens? We're the ones who decide."

"Yes, we decide, but the heavens have to agree."

"You're not afraid of what people will say?"

"No. I'm from simple stock. I'm no aspiring politician obsessed with power or glory, so I'll have as many children as I want."

"How many do you want?"

"Two boys and two girls. We'll plant a few more strips of land and when we're old we'll live with the youngest."

Hoan looked at Mien. She blushed, lowered her eyes, and bent over the cake mold in silence. They had been married for some time, but she always blushed when he spoke like that to her. He often found her a bit of a shy teenager, and this innocence and modesty only added to her seductiveness. Hoan knew that many women—and not only brazen women like Kim Lien—lacked this eternal virginal quality. He gazed at Mien's rosy, radiant face and gently stroked her cheek with his finger. "And you, how many children do you want? Four, five, six, seven, or a gaggle of twelve?"

Mien, her face turning even deeper red, shook her head violently. "How could I know? Everything depends on you."

Seeing her confusion, a wave of desire overcame Hoan and he embraced her hungrily. Then he made love to her right there on the kitchen floor despite her hesitation and resistance.

Why did Mien remember that now? Because they were in the same space they had been that night and they would have to leave each other in just a few hours? Did she regret that she hadn't had time to bear him another child? In fact, they had put aside money and had agreed to have another child the following year, when Hanh turned six. But that was before this brutal separation had befallen them. Hoan stroked Mien's back.

"I promised you four children around our holiday platter. My promise still holds. And you still owe me three."

Mien fell into his arms and hugged him to her tightly, her bosom heaving against his heart. The crackling of water evaporating on the coals suddenly brought her back to her senses. "The water is boiling. I've got to fill the Thermos." Her face suddenly went blank, distant, unfathomable: "Let's have our tea here. I want to sit here, one last time, in this kitchen."

Hoan went into the house and came back with tea and a few cakes. Mien lit the oil lamp and five candles. She loved the proverb "Live by the light of an oil lamp and die to the sound of trumpets and drums." Behind her back, jealous women might call her extravagant, or vain, but to Hoan, Mien would always seem naturally aristocratic. Her childhood appeared to have left no mark on her face, her demeanor, or her gestures. When they were first married, the war was still raging and their life was terribly hard. But Hoan remembered the way Mien had borne hardship differently from the rest: She never complained or grew irritable, but she didn't bow her head and resign herself to her dark, difficult life either. She could calmly eat an entire bowl of potatoes, savoring it as if it were some royal dish, not just dried potatoes and flea-ridden beans. She used to pick out even the smallest bits of grit from her rice with a deliberate but dignified gesture, looking straight ahead like a crane.

"Would you like some sweet pudding?"

"The bean cakes will be enough. I'm not hungry."

"What tea did you use?"

"Our tea, the one you dried yourself."

Mien walked to the closet and took out a white china plate with a gold border they used to serve tea cakes. She wiped the cup with a cotton cloth, unwrapped the cakes, and arranged them on the plate. Then she carefully rinsed the teapot and prepared the tea.

Hoan waited in silence, his chin resting on his fist.

Oh Mien, how are you going to live in your new dwelling? It's not even a house, just a dark and gloomy room covered with a roof made of dried leaves. Where are you going to find a decent kitchen to prepare meals? They probably don't even have a bathroom or a toilet. You love cleanliness. How will you be able to stand such destitute living conditions?

He contemplated the pristine white napkin in his wife's hand, the way she gracefully folded it and put it away, the gestures she used to open the armoire, to pull aside the skirt of her silk *ao dai* before sitting down facing him. All the beauty and poignancy.

"Have some tea, Hoan, it's ready."

"You have some, too."

"The jasmine scent hasn't been fully released yet."

"It's already very fragrant. Has our jasmine bush flowered lately?"

"You haven't even noticed? The whole neighborhood can smell it!"

"No, it's true, I must not have noticed. After all, there are so many flowers all year round. I can't tell them apart. I wasn't born in the Year of the Dog, so I don't have a very fine sense of smell. Are the cakes good?"

"Very good, but a bit too sweet."

"Yes, they put lots of sugar in them to preserve them. That's why I prefer yours."

Mien said nothing. She always stayed silent when he complimented her. She neither rejected nor thanked him, just lowered her head, shy and happy. She was really his woman, his alone. When they made love, at the summit of pleasure, she also kept silent. Only her breathing grew faster and, sometimes, he saw her lips part ever so slightly.

Inside, the clock struck four o'clock in the morning. The cocks began to crow. The two of them looked at each other. Hoan could see the pain flooding into her eyes.

"I have something to ask of you."

"Yes?"

"Promise me first that you'll agree."

"No, tell me first."

"Mien, please."

"I can't agree without knowing what it is that . . ."

"That's why I'm asking you, Mien. This is the first time I've ever done this since we've been married."

Mien said nothing for a long time, then spoke. "All right, I promise."

Hoan took her wrist in his hand. "This house will always be yours.

Everything we own belongs to you. You can take everything whenever you want to."

Mien pulled her arm away and stood up. "No, I can't do that."

"Well, then you won't honor your promise."

"I'll accept anything else, but this house belongs to our Hanh."

"He's your flesh and blood. But he's too little. If he was at an age where he could understand, he would never allow his own mother to live in such misery and privation. What's more, he's my son. If he was so heartless that he could live happily while his mother was in need, then he wouldn't deserve to be."

Hoan spoke in an uncharacteristically harsh, strained tone. His fine eyebrows rose like blades on his wide forehead. This sudden determination overcame Mien's willfulness and she let her arms fall to her sides. Hoan took her hand, made her sit next to him, and spoke again in a low voice: "I know that you love our son, that you want to sacrifice everything for him. But a human being must know how to give *and* receive. Even if you can't be my wife, you will always be the mother of my son. Hanh just cannot have a starving, shabbily dressed woman for a mother."

Then he stood up. "Wait here a minute. I'll be right back."

He went back inside the house and returned with a brick-sized package wrapped in plastic and bound with elastic bands. "I've put aside some money for you. I want you to make sure you eat properly. A human being is not some pure spirit who can subsist on incense and wind. If this is not enough, you'll find more in the house. Every inch of land and brick here bears a trace of your sweat. We have a substantial estate. I'm going to start a new business in town. Auntie Huyen will take care of Hanh."

He stopped a minute, then added, "You know that I can't stay here . . . I can't . . ."

Mien looked at him. Rage and terror flashed in his eyes.

. . .

At exactly six-thirty that morning, the bell rang at the gate.

"I'm going now," Mien said to Hoan. "You stay here, please don't go out."

"Let me carry your bag."

"No, I can get it."

"Then I'll carry the sack of virgin grass."

"No, it doesn't weigh a thing. It's nothing."

"How are you going to carry all this at the same time?"

"I'll make two trips."

"Why are you doing this to yourself?"

"Because this is the way I want to do it. Please, let me be." She carried the bag of dried grass outside and then returned to give him her set of keys. "Here, keep these."

"No, these are yours. There are already two other sets."

"No, I have no right anymore," Mien said, setting the keys down on the table where they put the oil lamp. Then she picked up the second sack, turned on her heel and left.

Hoan watched her, silhouetted from the back, as she walked out of their bedroom. He slumped back on their bed. The gate creaked. So, there had been no conversation. Mien had returned to that man in silence. Just the rustling of bamboo leaves swept up by the wind, the sound of footsteps— or was that his imagination, the lingering echo of their past happiness?

How am I going to go on living? How? How?

He ran out into the courtyard and raced up the stairs to the rooftop terrace. He could see her; she was walking with him, that man, on the main road. She was walking ahead of him, carrying her own suitcase. He followed her with the sack of grass. Mien looked straight ahead, her head high, her neck and back rigid. She seemed to be walking toward another world. And yet Hoan was certain that this world still belonged to him and his son. The man who shuffled behind her with the sack of grass, did he know this? Would he understand that he was going to live with a woman from a world where he had no place ... or did he believe he could win her back?

7

"Mien . . . please, you sit here, right here."

Bon set the sack of grass down in a corner of the room and wiped the chair with a dirty undershirt. His elderly neighbor, Dot, had given him a pair of chairs, and his friend Xa had repaired the old table his parents had left him by adding two feet and reinforcing the joints. With its ebony surface and new white legs, the table looked comical, like a speckled donkey. Bon had asked Xa if he could have an old earthenware vase that was kicking around in his kitchen. Bon had scrubbed and washed it, filled it with a red galanga flower and a few sprigs of heather, and set it on the table to make the room look brighter. He remembered how the sergeant had once remarked: "You farmers try to impress people with food and clothes. But people need beauty, too."

Bon silently thanked the dead man for his advice. The red galanga flower and the tiny violet blooms of heather made the room a little less cold, a little less miserable.

I'll put fresh flowers here every day. I'll plant a row of flowers in the garden and pick ixora and wild chrysanthemums from the hillside. I'll decorate this room for our new life. I'm still young. There's still time . . .

Bon couldn't help feeling a secret pride: He was the same age as Mien, and that was seven years younger than the other man. Nature had given him almost a decade to win back everything he had lost. It was the only advantage he had.

"Please sit down, Mien. Rest," Bon repeated, more like a host to his guest than a man speaking to his wife. He didn't know why, but every time he started to say "Younger Sister" to Mien, he felt his tongue freeze. A certain shyness, a hint of doubt, stopped him from using these traditional, intimate forms of address. Fourteen years ago, in front of the old flame tree, Mien had lit sticks of incense and sworn to call him "elder brother" after their marriage. The tree that had witnessed this vow was still there, shading the ground with its purple flowers, but Bon had lost his old confidence.

"Mien, I came to get you early so we could avoid people, all their comments."

"Yes."

"Well, it's been fourteen years. We'll have to start all over."

"Yes."

"I know you've been generous for my sake. Back at that place, you led a rich life . . . with . . . everything you needed. But we're still young, we can build our own fortune with our own hands."

Mien kept silent.

Bon continued, "I love you . . . I want . . . I want us to be to-gether . . . like we were back then." But his voice suddenly cracked.

Like we were back then.

Tears spilled from his eyes. Back then all he had was his youth, his strength, his passion for the most beautiful girl in the region. But now she had become a woman, even more radiant, more seductive. Mien said nothing. Nothing except "yes." Bon knew that her replies were hollow, mechanical, just a string of meaningless sounds.

Motionless, seated on her chair, Mien gazed at the room. There was nothing of value. But Bon had put up a wall and sealed up the roof with a bamboo screen to shield the couple from the prying eyes of his sister's family. He had replaced the wooden door and his friend Xa had used an entire bottle of varnish on it. Xa had also lent him enough money to buy a double bed and a wooden box for Mien's things—her mirror, her comb, needles and thread and all the rest of the stuff women had. Bon hoped to eventually frame a photo of them together. A new reed mat was spread on the bed. And at the foot of the bed lay a mosquito net and a flowered bedcover. Bon had put all his love and tenderness and all the money he had managed to set aside during the war into fixing up this room . . . Would she understand?

"I've boiled some water for you."

"I'm not thirsty. When I am, I'll do it myself. Where are Ta and the children?"

"She sent the kids to Old Dot's tonight. She'll be back tomorrow."

"We're sharing the kitchen with her, right?"

"Yes, for the moment we are sharing the old kitchen. Later, when we get rich . . ."

Mien stood up, moved to a corner of the room, and opened the cover of an earthenware jar. "You still keep the rice stored in here?"

"Yes, how did you know?"

"Because it smells like fresh rice, but the jar smells moldy and dusty. Why didn't you wash the jar first?"

"I was in a hurry . . . I forgot . . . ," Bon stammered. He had forgotten how meticulous she was about cleanliness. She couldn't bear the slightest bit of dirt and thought it should be the same for everyone else.

When he first returned to the village, Bon learned that after he left for the front, Mien had returned to live with Auntie Huyen. She couldn't stand Ta and her family, not just because she was promiscuous, but also because everything about her was filthy—her hair, her clothes, her body. Bon looked at Mien, his ears burning red with shame. She stood there, her back toward him, peering into the jar. They used to keep rice there back when they were first married; now, fourteen years later, it was in the same place. During the war, people had hid jars, vases, and all kinds of pottery by burying them underground or in their duck ponds. Then, when peace came, they fished them out again. These earthenware utensils survived for centuries, like the flints and tools of cavemen. For Bon, the rice jar was not just a memento his parents had left behind for him; it had also borne witness to his love story with Mien, and their early days together. No doubt for her it was just another crude, vulgar, filthy object.

Why didn't I wash it before pouring in the rice? I'm hopeless.

He cursed himself in silence as he watched Mien, her eyebrows furrowed above the delicate bridge of her nose. Suddenly, he said: "Leave it, I'll clean it out. There's not much in there anyway, barely eleven pounds of rice."

Mien didn't reply. She pushed the jar into the middle of the room. "Bring me a basket," she said finally. Bon hurried into Ta's room, found a basket filled with children's clothes, and dumped them out. Then he brought it back and handed it to Mien. He watched her hands as she transferred the rice from the jar to the basket, thinking to himself: *There isn't even enough there to live on for a week. When it's gone, what am I going to do? I've spent my last dong. The change I've got left in my pockets is just enough to buy two packs of cigarettes. But I had to buy those bricks to repair our room, the mat, the bedcover, and the mosquito net. They were unavoidable expenses. To please Mien. I'll borrow some money from One-eyed Xa, or from Binh, or Dot, to get a plantation started. This will be enough for now. After, I'll have to see.*

Mien called to him. "Bon, take this jar into the courtyard and let it dry out long enough to get rid of all the weevils. We'll clean it later."

"Yes, of course."

"We've got to winnow this rice. Does Ta have a winnowing basket?"

"Yes . . . At least I think so. Wait here, I'll go and see."

Bon went into the kitchen so Mien could avoid dirtying her hands on Ta's decrepit collection of crockery and cooking utensils. After looking through everything, he still couldn't find a single usable basket. All Ta's utensils were old, broken, or filled with holes. Bon felt as if Mien were staring at him now, her eyes filled with contempt. He knew she wasn't the only one either; the entire village, men and women alike, all disdained his older sister. But only Mien's contempt hurt him, humiliated him. He mumbled something: "Wait, just a minute . . . I'll go borrow one from a neighbor."

When he returned, Bon found Mien conscientiously picking out the grit and the rice husks in the rice. She took the basket from him in silence and began winnowing, patiently, just like any other peasant woman. Bon felt as if he were dreaming. The woman winnowing rice out on the veranda was his wife, the woman who belonged to him, the one he had yearned for so long: She was right here under his roof; her forehead covered with fine down; the rosy nape of her bare neck; her skin so white you would have said it was not a woman's but a fairy's. She stood just a few feet away from the new bed. Tonight, they would sleep together. Yes, tonight he would slake the thirst he had endured for fourteen years.

"The rice is filled with gravel."

Mien's voice startled Bon and he laughed nervously. "I'm a man. That's the best I could get. Next time, you'll be the one in charge."

But where will I find the money for her to buy rice? I can't borrow from Xa forever. He's not very rich and he has three young kids to raise. But aside from him, who can I turn to? The authorities? Their assistance is over. And their charity always came in small change anyway. I can still ask Dot for help. She's kept Ta and her kids going for years. Or Binh. In any case, I'm going to need money to live. We can't get by just on rice and grilled sesame seeds. Even this salt-stewed chicken is enough for only two meals.

Bon shot a glance at the scrawny chicken in the coop out in the garden. Once it was cooked, there wouldn't even be enough to cover one plate. But he would tell Mien to pan fry it with lots of salt to make enough for two meals. He hadn't even bought the chicken; it had come from Xa's wife, who had taken it from her own coop so that Bon could "make a meal to receive the beauty in his palace." If Soan hadn't thought to give him a chicken, Bon would have had to welcome Mien home with just rice and vegetables.

To think that on the day of my return, Mien served me a sumptuous meal.

He remembered the bronze platter heaped with food that Mien had placed under his eyes that evening. He had sat at a table lit by five candles. But that was in another world, one that didn't belong to him. She had agreed to come back, and she would have to adapt to her new life.

You are my woman. You'll live under my roof, in my arms.

The echo of this imperious voice, full of confidence, resonated in him, each word reverberating in his brain, his body, his nerves, and his muscles, until he felt big, powerful, imposing. He paced to and fro past the veranda while Mien was winnowing the rice. He gazed at the Japanese lilacs in the courtyard and began to dream of fields of pepper trees. He had decided not to plant any coffee bushes. He would harrow the land allocated to him and plant it solely with pepper trees, even though this crop demanded far more of an investment.

In any case, I've got to borrow money for the start-up. If I make a mistake, it will be too late to do anything about it.

As she finished the winnowing, Mien looked up and asked, "Is there any more water in the well?"

"Oh, yes. Tons of it."

"Is it clear?"

"It's clear, very clear. Ah . . . I haven't checked yet, but everyone uses it. I've also built a bathroom for you near the well. Would you like to see it?"

"No. I'll bathe after I've finished cooking." Mien dusted herself off and carefully put away the baskets. "Here, you take these back. People use these as often as they use their own hands. We can't impose on the neighbors for much longer."

When he had left, Mien carried the basket of rice into her room. Bon told himself that when he came back he would give her a long kiss, a reward that was his due for all those days of waiting. But when he came back, Mien was already back outside on the veranda, ready to throw herself into a new task.

"Where are the bowls and plates? I'm going to wash them."

Bon was crestfallen. Mien was trying to avoid him; she was inventing all kinds of chores.

*Okay, you are clever. But sooner or later the sun will set, night will fall, and you
won't have any more excuses. You're mine and will remain mine, as heaven and earth
are my witness.*

Reassured, he replied in a bold, dignified voice: "I haven't been able
to buy dishes yet. Let's use sister Ta's for the time being."

"No. Sooner or later we will have to have our own dishes. We can't
keep bothering other people. You go weed the garden. I'm going to the
market."

"It's not necessary. We're family. We can borrow dishes for a few days."

"I don't want to live off loans and debts," Mien retorted icily.

"But I haven't had time to earn the money," Bon replied, his voice
hoarse. "I've invested everything in repairs—the bed, the mat . . . not
to mention . . ."

He almost said "not to mention all the money I owe Xa," but he
stopped himself in time. It was too humiliating; he couldn't lose
face—a man was supposed to provide for his family.

Mien still stood her ground. She glared at Bon and spoke sharply,
enunciating each word: "Just how are we going to rebuild a life together without pots and pans, without wood?"

Each of her words tightened what felt like a noose around Bon's neck.

"Don't worry," he replied hastily. "I've got a friend in the neighboring village who promised to loan me money so I can hire labor to
plant pepper trees. I was just so busy with all the preparations for your
return that I haven't had time to go see him."

Bon felt his neck go damp with sweat. *What am I saying? All I have are
two backers, Dot and Binh. Neither is a sure thing. And if Binh isn't as rich as the
rumor goes, then how am I going to borrow such a sum from him? I'll have to lie constantly. You start with a boast and you end up buried in lies, and maybe even in
fraud. It's a slippery slope.*

The more he thought about it, the more he panicked. Sweat

streamed down his back. He wasn't in the habit of lying, or even boasting. Bon shot his wife a glance, straining to divine her thoughts. Had she believed him? Or had she realized that he was just a shameless liar? Mien was staring into the distance, floating somewhere, off in her own world. This attitude tortured him even more, but it saved him from the cowardly trap he had laid for himself. Bon knew he stood outside this world, this place she had just plunged into. He kept his silence and waited. After a long time, Mien pulled a lock of hair back from her forehead and said, "You go over to Auntie Huyen's and borrow a dozen bowls, the Hai Duong bowls."

Bon realized this was an order. Mien didn't want to have anything to do with Ta or her promiscuity. She hated filth. He glanced at the rotting wooden stand where his sister and her children kept their crockery; it was only about a foot high—any chicken could jump up and defecate on it, any wandering dog or pig could shove their muzzle or snout into it. And the crockery itself was pitiful: cracked earthenware bowls and cheap tin cups, their enamel dented and chipped. This was the sad estate of the poor, picked up here and there and brought home.

Mien is right. She can't eat from these filthy bowls. She's used to a comfortable, dignified life.

The day of their wedding, Mien had also brought her own dishes and bedcover. But at the time, they had been young, in love, and it was during the war. Their imminent separation by the war had blurred the boundaries and distance between them, compressing space and time into the fleeting moment of a first love.

Now it's not the war that separates us; it's life.

Bon didn't dare pursue this further. He knew that if he followed this thought to its logical conclusion, he would find himself in a dangerous place.

"And remember to get some big bowls for soup."

Mien's voice startled him, wrenching him from his thoughts. "Okay, I'll go and borrow some dishes from Auntie Huyen. Do you need anything else?"

Mien gazed over at the hedges: "You could borrow five porcelain Hai Duong plates. She'll be glad to give you whatever you need."

After Bon left, Mien returned to their room, opened her wooden trunk, and took out the wad of bills that Hoan had given her. She carefully undid the plastic packet they were wrapped in. The money was tightly compressed, as hard as a brick. Nothing but big bills. Mien knew that the village men could only dream of earning one of these bills, and even then, only after an exhausting harvest. This was a fortune, not just a bit of money to get by on. Hoan had seen to everything, prepared for everything. Mien remembered her stubborn attitude and his patience and determination. Without him, faced with this situation she would have been lost. He had looked after her better than a husband, a lover, and a father combined. Perhaps, for the rest of her life, she would never stray far from his gentle, protective shadow.

8

For Bon, that day seemed to last a century. After the midday meal, the sun stood still, scorching the earth with a dazzling, seething light, as if it hated the world. The thatch of bamboo leaves on the roof was still thick, but the only window didn't face the wind, so the room was suffocating. Even if it hadn't been, Mien would find some excuse not to lie down next to him on the bed. So Bon kept silent after lunch when she went out to the garden alone and sat at the foot of the guava tree to fan herself. Mien had already dug up all the wild sorrel and weeds, and hoed around the monk's basil he had planted. There was nothing more you could do with this small patch of land dotted with only a few old guava and carambola trees. The trees, which hadn't had any fertilizer for at least ten years, were stumpy, incapable of growing new branches or leaves. And the dirt was hard and dusty, kicked up in piles by the kids who played there. Mien had reminded him of how lush the garden had once been. There used to be a row of lemon trees that yielded tiny but very fragrant fruit, and a stout jackfruit tree. And it had all been completely fenced in by thick hedges covered with spinach vines; all you had to do was reach out and gather some to make a nice soup. Now the garden was barren and withered to the point of desolation.

Sprawled on the bed, Bon sighed heavily. He watched Mien nap-ping, slumped against the stump of the guava tree. Her bamboo fan had fallen from her hand and lay on the ground next to her.

She is making a martyr of herself. Women really are gluttons for hardship; they love problems, complexity, twists and turns. But like it or not, they're just women, incapable of pissing higher than the grass . . .

He squinted and gazed up at the sun. It no longer had a shape; it was just a blazing white inferno against the vault of the sky. They say this ball of fire is heavy, that one day it will explode into a thousand pieces. And that the earth will fall into shadow. Imagining this, he suddenly felt at ease.

When the sunlight has gone, the tile roof and the thatch roof will be equals. In the darkness, Mien will be mine, all mine . . .

He remembered their trysts, long ago, the laughter of the skinny, shy little girl named Mien, the shimmering scarlet of the flame trees against the sky, the infinite joy and giddiness of his youth. He remembered . . . he remembered . . . as sweet memories lulled him to sleep.

Out in the garden, Mien slept, too. But it was a fitful sleep and thoughts raced and collided in her head.

. . . I'm going to have to hire people to help plant. But it's useless to invest our efforts in this garden. The earth simply won't be able to sustain flowers or fruit.

. . . I'll probably have to build a separate house; I just can't live under the same thatch roof with Ta.

. . . But why should I have to take all this on? The money for the crops and house will all have to come from what Hoan gave me.

. . . Do I love Bon to the point of stupidity?

. . . No, I don't. I came back here out of duty, one ordained by some ancient, unwritten law that, though it was never recorded anywhere, never laid down in black and white, has become THE law.

. . . And if I oppose this law, I'll never live in peace. Anywhere. Even if I left this village.

. . . But to live only out of duty is even harder than living a nun's life. Will I be able to stand it?

We get used to everything. I must accept this.

Hanh is still little; I can't leave him alone in this world.

But should I submit to this unjust fate? Did I ever really love Bon? I can't even remember. Once, he held out his hand to me. And then, after a few dates, a hasty marriage right before the war.

I must have loved him, it seems. But why are the memories so dim? One thing is certain, everything was different then. Bon's eyes weren't bleary, his lips weren't pale, his breath didn't reek. He was never handsome, but he was charming. He played the monochord well. I remember listening to him, once, as the village kids crowded around.

She sighed. The sun was too bright and she bent down to pick up the fan that had fallen to the ground to shield her face. Her head still propped against the trunk of the tree, she searched her memory for a melody, some sound that might rekindle this past love. But her memories were a swirling, nebulous cloud of dark and light spots jumbled together. Finally, in a blur, a winding road flanked with thick reeds appeared. A hill covered with pineapple groves. A flaming crown of trees. And then, these images suddenly dissolved, and Mien could see nothing more . . .

A birdcall from the bushes jolted her. She opened her eyes. The sunlight streamed through the slats of her fan, stinging her eyes. Quickly, she closed them again until she had turned in a different direction. But she was completely awake now, and through the door to the room, she could see Bon sprawled on the bed. He must be sleeping, the poor man. He had forced himself not to touch her, to wait; he hadn't dared anything impulsive that might risk offending her. But his gleaming, lustful eyes seemed to stalk Mien's body, follow her every movement, and it both moved and terrified her. She was his wife. Tonight she would not be able to avoid her conjugal duty. But even thinking about it made her shudder.

Oh heavens, please, may the sun never set behind the mountains.

But to the west, the sun was already falling to the horizon at the appointed hour, despite her prayers.

Dinner passed by quickly; that night there would be no moon.

"Let me do the dishes, Mien."

"No."

"When I was a soldier, we always did the dishes. Let me at least clear off the tray. You go take a bath. I've already filled the tub for you."

"No."

"I have a nice, scented soap for you. A bar of real American soap I picked up after we raided a camp." Bon stopped, looked at Mien, then added, "I've saved it for almost nine years now."

The pleading, loving look in his eyes moved Mien. "You shouldn't have gone to such trouble . . . I could have washed with anything, you know."

Avoiding his gaze, she gathered her clothes, and walked away, toward the bathroom. The "bathroom" was just two square yards tiled with leftover bricks and surrounded by a bamboo hedge. The volunteers from the village had built it when they repaired the house. The old tub had been scrubbed and thoroughly cleaned, set in a corner and filled with water. A parachute string strung taut between two branches was hung with laundry. Bon had left the soap in the fork of two branches of the guava tree. Mien took it and examined it. It was Camay. The white wrapping had yellowed and the folds at the corners were torn. At home, Hoan used to buy this kind of soap by the dozen. But Bon had kept this single bar for nine years in his knapsack to bring it back to her. The only present he had to offer after the war. She felt tears in her eyes.

Bon was washing the dishes at the edge of the well; she could hear the swish of water and the clatter of pots and pans. She sat down, numb, listening as he carried the dinner platter and clean dishes into the house, his sandals clacking as he shuffled to and fro across the courtyard. The feeble light of dusk slowly faded. She looked up. The clouds had darkened and the sky looked as if it were a mass of crushed eggshells streaked with color. The sweat on her back had dried. A slight wind carried night smells. Her head empty, she couldn't think clearly; in fact, she stopped thinking, stopped the fretful worrying, the waiting in fear, and her soul felt like little more than an inanimate skin. She plunged her face into the basin of cold water, splashing it over and over again with her hands.

Meanwhile, Bon went back into the room and searched everywhere for a piece of cardboard. He had toiled all day trying to make a small shade to shield the flame from the wind and to dim the light. But there wasn't much wood left and this odd contraption looked like a man in shorts. Ta's kids didn't go to school, so he hadn't been able to find an old notebook or a piece of paper. In the end, he found some old newspapers he had bought on the train still in his knapsack. He took them out, rolled them into a cone, and covered the shade. Finally, he had succeeded in making a bedside lamp for Mien. Now, nothing would stand in the way of their lovemaking.

His work finished, Bon crossed his arms and gazed at the courtyard. Dusk had fallen quickly. The night was already almost as black as Chinese ink. His heart raced, and his breathing felt choked, constricted. He had waited and waited and waited, and now the boat had almost reached port. In a moment, all he would have to do would be to reach out and touch the shore.

Mien suddenly entered the room. She had finished bathing and her body smelled fragrant, seductive. Bon closed his eyes, inhaling deeply. Mien silently moved toward the corner of the room and began to tidy things on the table. She tidied for a long time, so long that Bon lost his patience and got up.

"Do you need to go out?"

"No."

Bon pulled the latch shut. Someone was screaming in his head: *This is my house. No matter how small, it's my territory, and this is my wife. She is mine. Mine, mine, mine . . .* This cry echoed in his brain, as if someone had hurled it against the wall of a cliff. He touched the latch, turned it, pulled it again and again until he heard a loud click. Only then did he regain his calm. He walked over to Mien, who was still busying herself with who knows what, her back turned to the light.

"Mien . . ."

Bon grabbed her back, lifting her into his arms and carrying her to the bed. Her chignon came undone and her ebony hair tumbled out, catching on the back of a chair. "Ouch, you're hurting me!" she cried.

But Bon didn't hear her. He had lost control. He lay her on the bed and feverishly kissed her body all over.

"Mien, I love you . . . I love you . . ." He moaned plaintively as he embraced her.

Mien silently gathered her hair and tied it back into the chignon at the nape of her neck. Her hair was so thick she could barely grasp it, and she had to tie it back tightly. The light illuminated every feature on her rosy face, a face that frightened Bon. Why was she so silent now? Fourteen years ago, she wasn't mute as a log. He remembered her laughing, how she used to pinch his cheek, a gesture that was somehow both coy and flirtatious.

"I love you, Mien, don't you know that? I even missed you when . . ." He almost said "when I was making love with another woman," but he restrained himself in time. He bent over and began to unbutton her blue shirt.

But Mien didn't notice anything. She was oblivious, sprawled on her back, as motionless as a marble statue. Her eyes were neither tightly shut nor entirely open; she left them open just a crack, enough to allow her to stare at a random spot on the ceiling. Bon kissed her stomach, near her navel, right where he remembered she had a beauty mark the size of a sesame seed, a bit to the left.

Screams continued to echo through his head.

I love you . . . and you must love me . . . We'll be together like we once were. When we made love from dusk to dawn. When you slept with your arms coiled around my neck . . . Just like we once were.

The last shout echoed, piercing his heart, exploding like lightning. In its shimmering light, he could see the roads filing past, mile after mile, hill after hill, forest after forest, all the regions he had crossed, all the long nights of longing when he had tossed and turned in his hammock, tortured by lust, all the damp caves where he had shivered through bouts of malaria, his body as useless as a rotting leaf. After all the years of famine and misery, he remembered only the woman he loved, her face, her skin. And now happiness was finally within his reach.

We will love each other enough to bridge the long years apart. We'll love like we used to. We were both seventeen. After lovemaking, I would fall asleep for a half hour and then wake you for more. My vigor seemed infinite.

Mien's pants were thin and cold. Bon gathered the fabric suddenly in a ball in the palm of his hand. This gesture gave him the feeling he possessed her, easily, totally. He squeezed this ball and threw it aside, sliding his hand toward her white underwear.

As white as cotton and softer than cat's fur. Why is everything about her so beautiful?

A dull moaning followed a sigh. His heart felt a sudden fear. Mien's dazzling beauty was like a chasm into which he would plunge, lose himself, never to return.

Another voice rose over his heart's anxious sigh.

I'm still young. I'm still young. I've still got enough vigor. I'll make love to her and she will bear me children, a whole brood of kids just like the old general that the sergeant told me about. Our love will return, will grow with the months and the days, through our children. I must have lots of children, lots of heirs.

This insistent voice made Bon's eyes go misty. All he could see was Mien's white, sweaty body, the gesture she had just made with her arm . . . and he plunged into her.

Waves of pleasure rose and fell onto the shore. He felt as if he would dissolve and disappear into the tide. This sea of love, after fourteen years of absence, seemed both to come back and to surge forth for the first time—passionate, awkward, obsessed. An ocean rose, waves billowed and peaked, tirelessly, continuously, pushing the intoxicated boat farther and farther out . . .

I'm making love to Mien . . . she's mine, flesh inside flesh, skin against skin.

Between two breaths, a moan escaped his lips. He closed his eyes as a turbulent sea spread through his body. He glimpsed his own youthful visage. But suddenly, an arrow, like a blade of air, pierced his spine, slicing through his body as pleasure and dreams surged and then faded in a single thrust. His boat crashed into shore, lay there sprawling like a rotten plank of wood in a tangle of mud and algae.

What has happened to me? I must be too anxious . . . maybe I waited too long.

His reproductive organ had failed him, as if it no longer belonged to his body, no longer obeyed his will. Fear and shame made him break into a cold sweat. He silently slid down below Mien's feet, too scared to look her in the face. He laughed nervously. "Maybe I'm not used to . . . or maybe . . . because I've been away from you too long."

Mien said nothing. Indifferent, she didn't even look at him. It was as if he didn't exist. Bon grabbed his underwear and put it on to hide the piece of sagging flesh that hung from his body. "Maybe later we'll . . . Sleep now, rest up. The night is still long. Later, we'll . . ."

She still said nothing, silently slipping on her pajama pants. Her long hair shimmered and rustled, covering her back as if she were some kind of mountain fairy.

"Mien!" Bon called to her, then fell silent. He knew there wasn't anything more to say now. He pulled on his shirt, lay down, and shyly stroked Mien's mane of hair.

Your hair is so beautiful. The most beautiful hair in the world. I'm going to lift up this mane so I can kiss the nape of your neck, before making love to you. Later, I'll . . .

Before he could finish his thought, he fell into a deep sleep.

It was the slumber of a man shipwrecked, a sleep that slowly dragged him under.

When he awoke, he thought he was still in his hammock and reached out a hand to touch what he believed to be the tree trunk behind his head. But instead he touched the box filled with Mien's things. Then he remembered everything. The oil lamp was still burning behind the makeshift shade. The peony bedspread lay at the foot of the bed. He remembered all the hopes he had when he had bought it with his veteran's bonus, how he had carefully washed and hung it to dry on a branch of the guava tree, thinking, *These peonies will bring back my youth. The warmth of the covers will restore my love.*

The crowing of roosters began to echo in chorus through the hamlets. About a month had passed and he had failed to make love to Mien. He squeezed his thighs and began to slip his hand furtively down his abdomen. But the door was open. Mien had already gone out to the courtyard. She probably wouldn't be back for a while. He felt paralyzed with fear, a new kind of fear that he didn't recognize. Like a thief, he slid his hand to his groin. There was no doubt; he was as wizened as a wilted cabbage. Even if Mien changed her attitude and suddenly began to shower him with kisses, he wouldn't be able to awaken this flaccid, shriveled piece of flesh that hung between his thighs.

He was overcome with the desire to weep, but he gritted his teeth. It would be too cowardly. He was not a coward. He had joined countless battles, even been decorated and cited as a model soldier. The war would have brought him glory if he hadn't been so unlucky. But it was no longer a question of battles won or lost on battlefields, but in bed.

I'm not seventeen anymore. I'm not like I once was.

This silent confession seemed to sprout needles that pierced his gut one by one. Bon sat up and stared at the pattern on the reed mat. He didn't understand the meaning of the Chinese ideograms enclosed in the circle. What did they symbolize about human life that they should be printed on mats for sleeping? To him, it was just another labyrinth. The more he stared, the more his mind went blank and his soul drifted. But just as he began to fall into despair, a name surfaced in his memory: Old Phieu.

He remembered the story about the sixty-year-old who continued to father sons, the potion concocted from wild goat sperm, medicinal herbs, and alcohol brewed with the goat's blood. Suddenly he saw a light at the end of the dark labyrinth.

I'll go see venerable Phieu. I'll master his secrets of virility and lust . . . a new world, a new ground to harrow . . .

Bon felt his testicles once more, then pulled back his hand and stood up. His blood was slowly beginning to warm. He pushed open the door and went out. It was early morning and still chilly out. A bonfire near the well illuminated the courtyard, the roof of the house, and the guava branches. The scent of virgin herbs suffused the air. He stopped suddenly in the middle of the courtyard, stunned: Mien was boiling herbs for a purifying bath; she was washing herself after sleeping with him. As a child, Bon had accompanied his friends to the mountain to gather virgin herbs and to sell them to a Buddhist temple in the provincial capital. The monks used the herbs to make a bath that would cleanse them of all the impurities of earthly existence before entering the temple gates.

She reserved this little cleansing ceremony for me, just me. With him, everything would be different. With that man...

The image of the man's red-striped underwear hanging in Mien's bathroom suddenly flooded back to him in all its clarity. Even clearer, more precise, was all he imagined underneath that underwear. Suddenly, he wanted to kill Mien. Kill the woman who was bathing behind those bamboo hedges.

A stab of a bayonet, from the chest to the back, half an inch above the left breast... or a machete to the neck.

He could almost see her blood spurt in a scarlet stream. This vision of horrific massacre suddenly freed him of the rage that had seethed inside him. Another thought slowly trickled into his brain, like a small rivulet of water in a dry streambed: *She's right. I'm worthless. An impotent being who can't bring her happiness. It's my fault. I've got to find the medicine to restore my vigor. Be patient. Be willing to try anything. It's the only way you'll get your happiness back.*

He stepped softly, not wanting Mien to know that he was awake. Like a thief, he tiptoed toward the entrance to the garden, urinated in a corner, then furtively darted back into their room.

9

Xa was preparing materials for a trip into the forest with a team of woodcutters. He sat scrubbing down a saw, his shorts rolled all the way up to his groin. Slung over his sweaty shoulder was a small, dirty cotton towel. By the time Bon arrived on his doorstep, he was sharpening the teeth of the saw, and the screech of steel against steel was ear-splitting. Bon must have called to him four or five times before Xa stopped his work.

"Wait, I'll open the gate for you!" he finally called, putting the file away in his toolbox. He wiped his chest with the towel and went to open the door. "I told Soan not to lock the gate because I'm here working this morning, and what do you know, bang, she's padlocked it! Women! Can't piss higher than the grass. Can't think of anything except their hair."

"What are you talking about? Shouldn't you lock the door behind you?"

"Yeah, but I've done that about five times already this morning. Just a waste of time! First for my eldest who comes back to get the notebook he forgets to bring to school. Then, when he comes back for money to go on some school outing. And the third and fourth time for neighbors who came to borrow nails and oil. And finally, for Binh."

"Binh? I've been to see him several times now and never find him in. How is he?"

"So-so."

"I hear he's done well for himself."

"Better than I have. But since Tet, he's had a streak of bad luck. His savings were devastated after his father-in-law died suddenly. His wife, Lam, was the only daughter and since they live in her house, he had to pay for the funeral. What's more, Lam is five months' pregnant and has an inflamed spleen. Binh's so worried he's wincing all the time. This morning, he came to borrow money. Since I didn't have any more, I asked Soan to loan him some jewelry so he can pawn it and take Lam to the hospital in town."

Bon shivered. His boat of hope had just sunk. The previous night, he had thought he could borrow a large sum of money from Binh. They hadn't seen each other for a long time, but Bon knew that their friendship was unshakable. They had been classmates for all six years of secondary school—those halcyon days when they were both determined to pass the university entrance examination, to trade in their mountain lives and become city boys. And since they were both gifted students, this dream was within their reach. During those hard, adolescent years, if it hadn't been for Binh, Bon would never have been able to finish his studies. He barely had enough money to buy paper, pencils, and other bare necessities, not to mention food. Everything had come from Binh, a generous soul who helped everyone he could. But they both had had to abandon their dreams of an education at the same moment—the day they joined the army. And in the end, they were separated, sent to two different units.

When Bon came back from the war, Binh had sent word through Xa that he planned to drop by and cook up a feast to celebrate their reunion. Bon thought he had just been busy; he never dreamed that Binh had fallen on hard times.

I always thought I could hang on to the shirttails of my old friend. Who would have guessed he himself was in the middle of a shipwreck?

Even though it was hot, Bon felt a chill run down his spine.

I'm just a lousy dreamer, useless.

One-eyed Xa raised his head, scrutinizing Bon with an inquisitive look.

"Have a seat. What's got you looking so down?"

Bon was startled, but his mind still felt dull, slow. He pulled up a stool and sat down. Xa had dozens of them in all sizes and shapes. Woodsmen and carpenters live on scraps of wood.

"Come sit over here." Xa's voice was gruff, and it felt to Bon as if he were shouting in his ear. "One minute. I've just got to finish washing this big saw."

Before Bon could say a word, Xa stopped and stared at him with his one good eye. This time his stare was prolonged, piercing, searching Bon's face. Bon felt his ears redden. Suddenly, Xa lowered his voice: "So? Did you do it?"

Bon understood, but didn't know how to reply. His face flushed.

Xa continued, insistent, "Could you make love?"

"Sort of."

"What do you mean, sort of? We're friends, that's why I'm taking the liberty of asking. Were you able to get it up?"

"Kind of."

"The needle at three o'clock?"

"Not exactly."

"So then what?"

"Oh, I don't understand anything anymore . . ."

Xa scowled and shouted, "Bullshit! And stop mumbling, will you. Just one look at you and I knew you were having problems." He frowned, stopped washing the big saw, threw the file into his toolbox, and stood up. "Listen, this is serious, my friend, no joking matter. Do you understand?"

Without waiting for Bon's reply, Xa walked toward a corner of the room and pulled a packet of tobacco out of the pocket of his shirt. He grabbed another stool and sat down facing Bon. "Want a smoke?"

"Yeah."

Xa handed Bon the packet, lowered his head, and began to roll a cigarette. "I told you. To live together, a man and a woman have got to love each other."

"I love Mien. Mien and no one else."

"Yes. But what about her? Does she love you? That's the problem. It's got to be reciprocal. And don't be angry with me for saying this, but you'd be better to jerk off in a hole in some tree trunk than to sleep with a woman who doesn't love you."

Xa took several long drags on his cigarette before asking, "Have you met Hoan?"

"Not yet. He's in the city. He only comes back on Sundays, to see his son."

"So you never go over to Auntie Huyen's place?"

"No, not unless Mien sends me for something."

"That's understandable. She doesn't like you, the old sourpuss. But, if you ask me, I think you should meet this Hoan guy at least once."

"Why? It's useless. Everyone has to follow their own destiny."

Xa's forehead was creased with worry. He tossed his cigarette butt into the garden, picked up the packet of tobacco and rolled himself a new cigarette.

"Listen, Bon. The truth is sometimes hard to face, but today try to hear me out. We aren't brothers or relatives, but our friendship is an even stronger bond. That's why I feel responsible for explaining the ins and outs of life. Right now, you're riding the back of a tiger. It's not easy to mount, but it's a thousand times harder to get off. As intelligent as you are, you should understand why Mien abandoned her big house for your cramped room. Only a woman of honor would force herself to do something like that. Any other woman would have left you by now. But there are limits. Mien can't live the rest of her life with you out of duty. Like I say, in bed, you've got to love each other for it to be worth it. You need to know your adversary. Why don't you try to meet Hoan, even just once?"

Bon felt his face burn, his ears ringing. "I'm not going to waste my time trying something so stupid. I'm not going to challenge him to a duel or anything. We're not in the fifteenth or sixteenth century anymore."

"So you are diving into the water, eyes closed, not knowing whether the water is deep or shallow?"

Bon didn't answer. And Xa didn't push him any further. The two men stayed seated, smoking in silence, flicking their cigarette stubs into the garden. The heat grew more and more oppressive. From time to time, Xa wiped his muscled chest and back. Bon didn't look at him. He was envious of those bulging muscles, of Xa's clownish face that always seemed to be laughing, radiant with happiness. From time to time, the birds in the garden sang out, making the sky seem higher, bluer, more transparent. Time passed. How long, Bon didn't know. Finally, Xa sighed and broke the silence: "Listen, Bon, did you know that the province just started a state-run plantation right near here?"

"No, I don't read the papers."

"It's called Dawn Plantation and it's about two hundred miles away. They made it for the women who left for the war. The ones who are now too old to marry and too ashamed to return to their villages, but who have trouble finding work in the cities. The idea is to help these women plant pineapple bushes and pepper trees, just like here. It so happens that a good friend of mine was just named chief of the administrative department. You know, Bon, you could go and live there. It would be much easier to find the funds you need to clear the land the commune gave you. Dawn Plantation is still state-subsidized, and the management cadres have a fixed salary. It's a good fit for you. But the main thing is that you'll have your pick from two hundred single women!"

"You're crazy. My family is here. This is my home . . ."

Xa snickered and shook his head. "Home is only home if you can find a roof over your head. Wherever you find that, that's the place you can call your home. Think a bit. There's no guarantee that Mien is going to love or understand you as well as an older woman would, especially a former volunteer who's longing for a man. Only people who've been through the same experiences can really love each other. Anyone who came back from that war had to pay some form of tribute, leave something of themselves on the altar to the tutelary genies. Take me, for example. All it took was a piece of shrapnel, as tiny as a speck of dust, to strike out one of my eyes. So I've paid my tribute. Now as for you..."

"I lived years in exile, as you know."

Xa shook his head. "That's not enough, my hero boy."

Soan came through the door in a hurry. She was carrying a basket filled with custard apples and guavas. She wasn't beautiful, but she was attractive, and like her husband, her face always seemed to beam with goodness and the glow of contentment.

"Ah, hello bridegroom. So, how did the beauty like returning to her palace?"

Bon didn't even have time to reply when Xa began to scold her. "You really are a difficult woman, you know. I told you not to lock the door, but you still haven't cured yourself of the habit. I've been breaking my back getting up and down to open it."

Soan set down the basket. "You see, Bon? On the battlefield, he's just another trooper, but the minute he gets home, the man begins to act like a general, as arrogant as they come."

She smiled, revealing a crooked tooth in front that gave her an even more radiant look. She gazed at her husband, at once loving and mocking. "I've got to tell you that he screamed like a cow being butchered when I had to dress a pimple on his ass."

"So? That's human flesh suffering, not wood, after all. And if it had happened to you? You would have dissolved into tears and moaning."

Soan picked out a few of the ripest custard apples and guavas and set them on a plate. "Enough, I'm not going to waste my breath arguing with you. Do you recall ever letting anyone have the last word?

Now, Elder Brother Bon, taste one of these guavas. See if it's as sweet as the ones you have in your garden."

Bon bit into a guava. But its sweetness did nothing to soften his heart. The scrawny guava trees in his garden hadn't borne a single fruit. Ta's kids had picked and eaten the guavas as soon as they started to turn yellow. And the ground in his garden was so poor that even the basil didn't grow very well. The galanga bushes never flowered. And the woman he loved was as cold and silent as the mountain mist. Xa was right. A man and a woman have to love each other to live together. All he had to do was to look at Soan to see how much she loved her husband.

Somehow, Xa had always been able to turn his fate around. Once demobilized, all he had to his name were a few old soldiers' fatigues and just enough money to celebrate his reunion with his family with a few trays of rice and vegetables. Xa's parents had died while he was on the front, and his elder brother had taken advantage of Xa's absence to strip the house. So Xa went to live with his uncle, and that was where he gave his homecoming feast. A few days later, he left for the forest with his woodsman's tools and began his Montagnard life. By chance, Xa met Soan one day when she was out gathering firewood. They fell in love exactly as they say—like lightning. Soan wasn't beautiful, but she had grace and charm. Many of the local boys had courted her, even a cousin on Xa's mother's side who wasn't rich, but had a three-story house in town. Each story of the house was only about fifty-two square feet, but that had been enough to set up a wholesale cereal business. The money poured in. This cousin, Khien, was two years older than Xa, and he had an elaborate strategy in place to win over Soan's family. He had come back to the village, after all, on a sparkling new motor scooter, stepped off, and warmly greeted all the elders along his way. He had paid a visit to everyone in Soan's family—the head of the clan and all the branch clan chiefs, both the paternal and maternal sides—and remembered to bring gifts and cakes to set on the altars to their ancestors where he would dutifully light incense and pray. There was lotus tea and the best-quality cakes for the clan head, jasmine tea for the branch clan chief, wool scarves for the neighbors, and persimmon and orange candies for the children—all of it wrapped in brightly colored packages. Compliments and praise virtually echoed through the family grapevine.

"Miss Soan has really found herself a good husband, one worthy of her beauty. She's found a man she can count on."

"Well, of all the young people, there's no one wiser than Khien. He's still young, but he already has our family history memorized. The other day he recited the year, the month, and even the day that one of our ancestors attained the rank of second mandarin on the imperial examinations . . . and who was with him! Well, my hair's already gone white and I don't even know the history of my ancestors that well."

"He has education, money, and he's generous with both his neighbors and his compatriots. Now, that's a perfect husband for our Soan."

It goes without saying that Soan's parents were thrilled. They celebrated in the expectancy of THE biggest wedding the village—and maybe even the region—had ever known.

"Listen, everyone in the village is singing Khien's praises. Such a virtuous man must also be faithful. If you marry him, your whole life will change; you'll lead a life of luxury, totally different from the rest of the people in this hamlet."

Soan shook her head. "No, I'm not marrying anyone. I don't want to get married. I want to stay here, at home, with all of you."

But not a day passed that she didn't sneak out and find Xa. They were consumed by passion. One day, Soan's father surprised them during one of their hillside trysts and he gave his daughter a slap that made her see stars. Then he brought her back to the house and tied her to a post in the stable for an entire night to teach her to obey their family's rules of conduct.

Xa's friends gave him the following advice: "Your adversary is too strong, Xa. You're going to lose face. They'll drag you through the mud. If you're wise, you'll just bow out now."

Xa was confused. He didn't know what to do. He loved Soan, but their love affair seemed hopeless. He was no match for Khien. He was a veteran without anything to his name, without house or garden, nor even a single plantation. The commune had given him a small plot of land in the hills, but he didn't even have the means to fence it in, let alone cultivate it. He figured that he would have to work as a woodcutter for at least two harvest seasons to raise enough cash.

Xa was panicked. Soan appeared, her face red and puffy with mosquito bites, streaming with tears. She told him how she had had to scream until her parents, afraid of their neighbors, finally let her go.

Xa couldn't help asking, "So you don't love him at all?"

"No! No!" she screamed back, glaring at Xa, furious. "You know how deeply I love you and you dare ask me that question? Who do you think I am, some two-faced hussy?"

Terrified, Xa tried to stammer an explanation. "No, no, I'd never dare— It's because—" He couldn't tell Soan what he was really thinking.

"I will never marry that guy! I could never sleep with him, even if he was filthy rich," Soan wailed.

"But what can I do?" Xa asked her. "I love you, but I don't dare oppose your parents. It would be disrespectful, unfilial."

Soan blurted out without the slightest hesitation: "We have to make love right away, yes, right away. . . . If I'm pregnant, my parents can't force me to marry Khien. That bastard has already ordered eighteen wedding banquet platters for our engagement party next month."

At the time, Xa lived with his uncle. The house was big enough but there was no separate room. All the rooms were large, but none were closed off with doors. He couldn't do anything in that space.

Xa sighed. "It's not possible . . . I had planned to make enough money to build a house. The commune has given me the land, but I have to buy wood, bricks to even think about . . ."

Soan exploded with anger: "By time, everything will be ruined. We have to make love tonight, and tomorrow night, and the night after, too. I have to get pregnant."

Xa went home and came back with a hooded jacket that an American soldier had given him, a trophy that he had often used when he went into the forest. They crossed the valley, the hills covered with pineapple bushes, and climbed toward the heights covered with prickly grasses. They sat down, waiting for the sunset, that sacred moment when nightfall would cloak the hamlet in a fog that would shield them from curious, indiscreet looks.

"Well, do you like the taste?" Xa asked.

Bon was startled by his voice and replied hastily, "Yes, it's sweet, very sweet."

"Your garden has to be completely redone. You've got to cut down all the trees, dig up all the roots, and make them into firewood. Then you've got to plow the soil, mix it with fertilizer, and let it rest for a long time before you can even think about planting anything."

"I understand." Bon knew that Xa had also started from nothing. Xa hadn't even had enough money to pay for his wedding. Soan had been the one who had taken care of everything. As soon as she became pregnant, she had herself examined at the commune's local health unit and announced it to the entire family. She told them that they would have to organize a wedding immediately or become the laughingstock of the entire village. If not, Soan threatened to elope with him and they would lose a daughter they had struggled to raise. In the end, she won them over, and the family organized a wedding banquet of more than a hundred platters. Soan gave birth to a son and Xa made a fortune as swiftly as a kite carried by a strong wind. Just as Soan had predicted, Xa became the most devoted son-in-law in the entire village.

Xa repeated his question to Bon. "So, you still want to plant pepper trees?"

"Yes, that's what I'd like to do. I don't know the woodcutter's profession like you."

"Well, you'll need serious funds."

Bon kept silent. Disappointed and ashamed, he felt he could see his shipwrecked boat sink slowly into the muck.

"And you're set on staying here in the hamlet?" Xa asked.

"I'm staying," Bon said, hesitating a few seconds before adding, "I love Mien."

But Bon hadn't the heart to tell the truth about his financial situation, even to Xa, the devoted friend who had so innocently offered his help. Xa kept silent. He picked up a ripe custard apple, broke it in two, and ate it. "Okay," he finally sighed. "Since you're determined. But first you've got to heal yourself. Your breath stinks. Even at this distance, I can't stand it, to say nothing of what a woman . . ."

Xa waited until Soan had disappeared into the kitchen and then continued: "If you want to live a long time with Mien, you're going to have to do something about your breath. As for the rest, we'll deal with that later. I'll take you to the hospital in town. I've got an uncle who practices traditional medicine there. We'll check both sides. When you're ill, you've got to consult healers from all over. I've only got tomorrow. After that, I've got to go pray to the tutelary genies with the other woodsmen before we head for the mountains."

10

There is no moon over the cities; or, rather, one could say that the moon there is shamefaced and pallid, overshadowed by garish, multi-colored lights, a mere corpse floating in a sky clogged with smoke and dust.

But here, on this deserted beach, the moon reigned in all her proud, haughty beauty. The waves, the fishermen's nets spread on the dunes, the boats lined up waiting to embark for the open sea—everything sang an elegy to her incomparable power. Not a cloud in sight. Wind whistled through the reeds and the briny smell of the sea hung in the air. Hoan hungrily smoked cigarette after cigarette, flinging the butts in a pile on a dune in front of him.

A pack and a half . . . Since I've been sitting here, a pack and a half.

He lit another cigarette, took a drag without tasting it, unable to savor the smoke. The water's edge lay only a few yards away. He could see the waves lap and swirl, the pale foam, the folds left in the sand after the tide had receded. He listened to the waves pound the shore, hearing in them the plaintive wail of a lovesick man. And as they receded, in their listless murmur, a sigh of both fulfillment and regret. This was no longer the sea he had known as a boy; it was the sea that spoke to a man forged by life's ordeals, who was no longer happy.

The moon is starting to wane, just like that night back in Mountain Hamlet.

A month had passed since the night he had taken Mien up to their terrace. Hoan didn't know how he had survived the last thirty days. He had gone through the motions like a waxen effigy. Undoubtedly he had kept up appearances, had maintained his dignified, confident air. He had behaved like a mature, well-balanced, serious heir of a respectable family. The strict, moral principles of his father still guided his every act and word. He had coolly analyzed his predicament, reorganized his shop, subcontracted the hiring of new personnel, found suppliers for more promising products, and hired transporters to carry merchandise from Saigon or Da Nang. His family shop was no longer just a general store; it now specialized in home supplies, appliances, wood utensils, and a few expensive decorative objects. Hoan's retooling of business had been extraordinarily successful, as if directed by some good fairy's magic wand. In less than a month, the changes had earned the admiration of all the townspeople.

When he paused between the time he spent doing his accounts, or inventorying the merchandise, Hoan gazed at the street with its bustling waves of life floating by like a river. A few years ago, who would have guessed that this area would be so bustling? Nor would anyone have foreseen that his grandparents' house, confiscated by the State, would suddenly, and discretely, be reinstated to him.

At the time, Hoan was still living in Mountain Hamlet. Chau, Nen, and the family had all gone back to the city. After their mother's death, Chau had taken over as head saleswoman, though still under Mrs. Lan's authority. Chau had to submit to the vengeance of this pretentious, debauched woman after Hoan decided to expose his forced marriage to Kim Lien. One day, a car stopped suddenly in front of their door. Two men got out. One of them looked the shop over and asked, "Is this teacher Huy's place?"

Chau stepped forward: "My father is dead. This house once belonged to my grandparents."

The man looked her over for a long time and then growled, "Is that you, Chau, my niece? How dare you speak to me so coldly. Do you know who I am?"

Terrified, Chau didn't know what to say. The strange visitor motioned his assistant into the house, then he turned back. "I'm your Uncle Huyen, do you understand? I've been gone for more than twenty years. Did your father ever mention me?"

"Yes, my parents often spoke of you."

"That's right. Once we often played cards for money. And how is your mother?"

"She died the year after my father passed on, right after his first death anniversary."

"It couldn't have been otherwise. When two people love each other like that, how can they live in two different worlds?" He chuckled, but his eyes filled with tears. He took out a handkerchief, wiped his face, then turned to the man with him: "I'm going to make an old man out of myself. I cry too often. It's been so long since I've set foot in this house. Almost a lifetime."

He began to cry again. Chau guided him through the shop all the way to the room in back where they had built the altar to her parents. The visitor lit three sticks of incense, planted them in a bowl of rice, and invoked the soul of the dead as mechanically as if he were speaking to the living. After that, he got out his wallet and handed Chau a wad of bills.

"Here, tomorrow you can buy some things for the altar, to honor your parents' memory."

"But Uncle, it's not the right day tomorrow."

"Oh, it doesn't matter. As long as I've prayed, your parents will rise from the tomb."

He pulled his companion's arm. "Let's go!"

On the sidewalk, just as his chauffeur was opening the door for him, he pulled aside the Party official who had come with him and turned toward the shop.

"What became of the house?"

The official was embarrassed and replied, "It was confiscated in 1956 and turned into a department store."

Mr. Huyen rolled his eyes, furious. "Confiscated! Teacher Huy's own house? And you think you'll live in peace with anyone after doing that?"

"It was a casualty of history."

"Well, we've got to make amends. We made history, after all. We're the elders now. Some of us were leftists, rightists, demagogues, extremists, even terrorists . . . We've got to see right from wrong before acting, no? And if there were an unwed mother in the crowd, would you shave her head, smear her with lime, lock her in a basket, and drown her, like they used to do in the old days?"

Worried by Huyen's outburst, the Party official quickly pulled him into the car. "Okay, okay, I understand. I'll tell them to . . ."

The car left in a flash. The next day, at exactly noon, Mr. Huyen returned. The provincial Party secretary, the same party official who had lectured him the previous evening, accompanied him. He gave the order to reinstate the house to its owners, as "benefactors of the Revolution." Mrs. Lan and her employees had to clear out their merchandise from the state warehouses and wait for their new assignments.

It was like a dream. Chau traveled to Mountain Hamlet to tell Hoan the news and to invite him to return to town to live with his family. But Hoan didn't need the money and his heart was committed to life in the mountains. Chau went home, divided up the land into two plots, and built two identical houses with her own savings and the money her mother had left behind. Once the work was completed, she opened two shops and turned over the management of Hoan's shop to their sister Nen. Every month, Chau checked the accounts, putting the profits aside in a safe for her little brother.

When he returned to the city, the two women handed him the keys to the safe. He felt tears spring to his eyes; the seeds his father had sown hadn't been lost. He decided to tear down the wall between the two shops to build the biggest shop in town. He changed the décor and the merchandise. He wanted to create a refined, prosperous life for his two sisters, to keep warm and dignified feelings among the family, according to the moral principles his father had once embodied. As if he were protected by some mysterious force, Hoan met with almost immediate success. The merchandise he chose became the latest fashion, bringing him huge profits. And the fashion continued even after he had changed his merchandise. Those who exhausted themselves trying to keep up with him would wipe their brows and sigh. "Luck is with him. The heavens protect the man."

Hoan himself couldn't fathom how or why he had succeeded so easily. His business plan was unfolding like a winning chess game. To forget his pain, he traveled constantly: from Da Nang to Nha Trang, from Nha Trang to Dalat, from Dalat to Saigon, from Saigon to Da Nang. And in the course of his travels, he noticed that people had different needs now that the war was over, that the trends and fashions changed from one day to the next. He made decisions quickly, after only a few hours of reflection. Every one of his cargoes was sold according to the principle "Attack promptly and then withdraw." His well-honed business formula never failed, and Hoan found he had more and more free time. He planted rosebushes and cacti in his garden, even designed a small, ornamental pond—all to re-create the landscape of his childhood, so he could journey back in his memory and relive the evenings when his mother prayed, while his father, that gentle, elegant man, had stroked his hair, and he, a young man of only eighteen, excelled on the volleyball court.

But nothing eased his suffering. The past is just the past; the only thing it can bring a man is the illusion of strength. But it is not life, and Hoan's had slipped away from him. Sometimes, it was as if he could leave his body to watch himself, this dignified, rich, leisurely man who sat in front of his cup of coffee, gazing out at the street with joyless eyes; this outsider, this businessman who had gotten lucky; this man who was the envy of the entire town, a good catch for any woman of marriageable age. He knew that he drew stares. He had been prey before and he had paid dearly for the experience. He saw himself clearly as he spoke, smiled, greeted people, and shook hands, as he offered a cigarette, and even now as he stepped gallantly aside, yielding the way to an attractive young woman who had deliberately swayed her buttocks in his direction. She strutted on her legs like a movie star, drawing back her lips into a provocative smile. All this reminded him of Mrs. Lan's fateful glass of red wine.

And he realized how pitiful he was.

He was overcome by a misery that he couldn't talk about with anyone, that he couldn't free himself of.

His sisters loved him and doted on him, but they also feared him as they would a landlord, and because they were of a simple nature, they couldn't understand. Once a week, Hoan went back to Mountain Hamlet to oversee the plantations and discuss business with old Lu, the manager he had found in Quang Tri, and to visit Hanh. His boy's good looks were a mixture of their two different beauties, his own and Mien's. Every time Hoan looked at his son, another visage surfaced, another body pressed up against his, the scent of another skin beckoned to him. At these moments, the joy of being reunited with his son yielded to the pain of an absence.

City life rolled on, relentlessly. Sounds, colors, lights. But this continuous anarchic mix was only a fleeting distraction for Hoan. He felt empty. The previous night he had climbed to his rooftop terrace to look back out over the city. He stood motionless for a long time. Solitude was a space even more vast than the celestial dome above his head. He felt scared—as if he were the lone survivor of a catastrophe. He quickly climbed down from the terrace, jumped on his motorcycle, and hastened toward the beach.

The sea lay before him, rescuing him from his panic. As he sat there on the sand, he felt a wave of calm wash over him with the cool, evening breeze. All he had to do was take off his shoes and socks and step forward to feel the water on his feet. The waves would lap and lick at them as they had when he was a boy, more than thirty years ago. Every time his father took him to the beach, Hoan was surprised by the tickle of the sea foam in his hair and on his skin.

And what if I stripped down to plunge into this tide, let it caress and cover me?

He remembered the playful caresses of the waves, and suddenly wanted to relive that happy time. He sat up and began to unbutton his shirt. When he reached the third button, his hand grazed his navel and he stopped. He was no longer a kid, "little Hoan" perched on his father's shoulders for a long walk down the beach. He was no longer the little boy who so loved his dips in the sea, who imagined a whole world beneath the waves, all the secrets of the universe revealed to him each time he rose for air, the vast, salty water an infinite source of joy.

He was too old for all that. He had been married twice. He was thirty-seven years old, separated from his wife and child. He couldn't save himself with childish games, by scampering naked in the waves. For the past twenty years, how much water had flowed down the river to tumble into the sea, how many times had the sea churned this water in her entrails? Hoan lay back down on the sand and lit a cigarette.

His sea was no longer here.

In the distance, a shadow approached. A teenage girl, a basket in her hand. No doubt it was one of the food vendors who worked the beach. The bathers had gone home at sunset; what was she still doing here? Perhaps she hadn't been able to sell all her merchandise, so she stayed to try and sell it off to the few couples who still lingered. And she found Hoan, a lone client.

Hoan had guessed correctly. Her basket in hand, the girl hastened toward him. In no time she reached him, kneeled down, breathless, and took out a flashlight to display her wares.

"Uncle, want to buy a few of my snacks?"

"I don't drink."

"Then have some sweets."

"Well, afterward my father will want me to wash out my mouth with salt water so I don't ruin my teeth. Do you have any salty water on you?"

As he said this, Hoan was reminded of his son, the faces he would make every time he had to do this. The vendor was dumbfounded and gazed at him, stunned. She wondered whether he was serious or teasing her. The glow of the flashlight shifted, illuminating a tiny, elfin face and pretty lips.

She's still so young. She must have left school to earn her living.

"Okay, let's see what you have. I'll buy some for my neighbors."

"Oh, yes, of course, buy some, please," the girl murmured. The flashlight revealed a paltry display of snacks. A pile of rice pancakes with some almost liquefied peanut candy. A bowl of boiled peanuts. A few bruised guavas, no doubt stolen from someone's garden and then resold to these poor children. A few packets of grilled squid. Two mangled packs of cheap cigarettes.

"Do you go to school, little niece?"

"No. I've got to sell stuff. If I went to school, how would we eat?"

"What do your parents do?"

"My mother sells snails at the market and my father is a street vendor. He sells tofu patties."

"Are there many of you in the family?"

"My parents and five kids."

"And nobody goes to school?"

"No."

"Do you want to?"

"No. Once my uncle taught us how to read and write. But the letters just wouldn't stay in my head. My uncle said that our brains were just too dense to learn. Why, there's nothing more fun than selling stuff. You can earn money and walk all over the place."

So that's the way it is now. There's a world of kids now who don't want to study. Not everyone complains, like Mien, about having had to leave school.

"Okay, I'll buy everything you've got. How much do you want for it?"

The little girl's eyes widened. Suddenly, Hoan could see the sly calculations of a city girl. Hoan watched her add up the price of each item in her head, raising the price of one a few dong, getting tangled up in her calculations, pursing her pretty lips. Her eyes danced over her miserable, pitiful little kingdom.

"All together it makes eleven dong, but if you buy the whole thing, I'll give you a one dong discount, so that makes ten dong."

Hoan almost burst out laughing. *What a little fox. She must think I come from another planet. But she's right. No one would be crazy enough to stay on this beach all night.*

"Hey, that's a strange way to count! At most all that is worth about four or five dong. Next time, before you play games, choose someone else."

He got out three five dong bills. "Here, little niece, I'm giving you fifteen dong. Take your stuff and go back home. Hurry, you're going to catch cold."

"Oh, thank you, thank you, from the bottom of my heart."

The girl took the bills from Hoan, bowed, grabbed her basket, and darted off, disappearing as quickly as a squirrel. Hoan followed the little black shadow as she faded into the distance. The line of her pretty red lips reminded him of another pair of lips.

Why am I here?

At that hour, in Mountain Hamlet, he would have been out on their terrace drinking tea and chatting with one of his neighbors. As he talked, he would keep an ear out for the sound of his son chattering away with his mother out in their courtyard. On the days when no one came to visit, the three of them would sit out on the veranda to enjoy the breeze, the air heavy with the fragrance of all the flowers in their garden. And who had created this small paradise but the woman he loved and who loved him in return. He had chosen to set anchor there. Why had he suddenly been tossed into a cold, strange world where everything seemed unreal to him?

Hoan had often asked himself, *Why? After all, I'm a city boy. I was born and raised here. And yet, I always feel as if I'm just passing through.*

This uneasiness seemed to gnaw at him. Every time he met with go-betweens, suppliers, or salespeople, he had the distinct feeling that he was acting, like a puppet in a show. A hand shaken too early or too late, a sigh at the right or wrong moment, a misplaced laugh, was either worth its weight in gold or could cost him his fortune. A lavish meal with fine wines could consolidate his business network, or even undermine an adversary. These were lessons in competition that anyone who wanted to be part of the new competitive society had to know by heart. But Hoan felt as if he would suffocate each time he played the part. He was the kind of man who needed space—vast, clean, open space. In this city, his garden was the only place he could escape to, where he could breathe easily and take off his mask. But this garden was too small, and the scent of roses and cactus flowers only reminded him of another absent perfume. And this absence that had seeped into his skin, and blood, that raged each day more insistent, had suddenly become mingled with lust.

From where he was seated on the beach, Hoan could see more people approaching. They were no longer small shadows but three tall imposing young men. They passed in front of Hoan, chatting noisily, their fishermen's voices rising above even the roar of the waves. He overheard them quarreling about a woman.

"So you like the little one, eh?"

"Leave me alone. It's none of your business, is it?"

"If you like her, then I'll stand back. If not, I'm going for her."

"Well, go ahead."

"Is that a challenge?"

"I'm not challenging anyone."

"Don't provoke me. You've been hanging around her for a month with no success. Me, as soon as I touch a woman, she falls for me. One caress here, one caress there, and up, I've got her in bed."

"Stop bragging. Go on, let's see what you can do."

The third man raised his voice. "Enough! Women aren't scarce here, you know. It's not worth sacrificing our friendship for them. You can switch girlfriends but you can't switch friends, especially when you've known each other as long as we have. You've really got blinders on. I don't find her beautiful at all. Her tits are no bigger than two coconuts and she's got a tiny ass. The poor guy who marries her will have to be underneath for life."

Laughs rang out, staccato. The three men trudged on, spraying water with each step. One of them broke the silence.

"Who's that?" He looked in Hoan's direction.

The second added, "Hey, what are you doing sulking all alone? Come join us."

Hoan kept silent.

The first fisherman continued, "Well, well, I think he looks like a jilted lover. Don't resign yourself to your suffering, my boy. Come have fun. Women are plentiful and they all have the same thing."

A third voice interrupted. "Shut up! Leave him alone, you mad dogs."

They walked right past Hoan, continuing in the direction of the bungalows that were nestled amid the fishing nets, the black shadows of which lined the shore. Their voices were slowly muffled by the wind.

As the night deepened, the wind grew colder and more violent. The sky seemed to widen and gape open, the horizon lost in a dense fog that blurred the sea, the clouds, even the moon. He searched the distance, trying to find something familiar in the sounds and images that filled this vast space: the wail of the lighthouse siren; the *click-clack* of the sails in the night's wind; the anguished cries of lost seagulls; the shadow of boats fishing for squid; the blinking of lamps to attract fish. But the familiar sights and sounds of his childhood had vanished. The sea was as deserted as the town. Hoan was alone.

He revved his motorcycle and started to return to town. A halo of light flashed before his eyes and made his limbs go weak. When the motor had started to hum more softly, he could hear the roar of the waves at his back. The sound followed him. Was it the call of days past or days to come? Or was it only the echo of his suffering heart? He didn't know. He continued to race ahead, pursuing a silent, still formless, and yet irresistible goal.

11

They say that women in the fishing regions are particularly sensual because they eat more fish than rice. They are huge, as tan as the men, with large, muscled arms and legs, as if sculpted from ironwood. They marry at fifteen and by age thirty they have at least ten kids. And they keep having babies. Even grandmothers can be seen in the maternity wards, their daughters and daughters-in-law at their sides. This is particularly common in Bao Village, to the north of the Nhat Le River. Half the village fishes for freshwater fish while the other is out deepsea fishing. And apparently there are few poor people here.

At night, the music blares from the commune loudspeakers while the radios inside the houses are set at full blast. But these fish-eaters have nerves of steel and they sleep like logs, even with thunder rumbling all around.

The city began its sprawl on the other side of the Nhat Le River, so it seemed that the urban way of life was already present in every home, even though it might still reek of fish and seafood. On weekends, the young people in the village would gather at the commune clubhouse to sing, or dance to disco music, their hair slicked back, stinking of perfume. Just like in town, the young women here liked to sing karaoke, strutting up and down a stage, teetering on high heels, clutching their microphones. Some flicked their long hair back like pop singers to reveal their dreamy faces, others lowered their eyes modestly to affect a youthful sweetness. Later, after they left the club, the girls would kick off their high heels and carry them back to the village under their arms. The boys would also take off their shoes and follow, because it was easier to walk barefoot in the sand.

And while the clubhouse lights still lit a corner of the sky, the teenagers gyrating and singing on the dance floor, the real adults gathered in an even more exciting club on the beach, under the reeds, or in the fishnet cabins. Here, the smell wasn't only water, wind, and algae. Nor was it merely the stench of the beached and swollen puffer fish, the burnt smell from fishing boats left baking in the sun, or the pungent scent of lemon rinds cast off by the people who had come to eat blood oysters. No, it was another smell, even stranger, that seemed to thicken the air into glue, and when you inhaled, you were seized by desire. It was the smell of lovers, of couples who groped and fondled each other in the warehouses filled with nets, on the deserted sand dunes, amidst stands of tall, shadowy reeds. Like faithful night watchmen, the waves crashed continuously on the shore, their roar muffling the moans and sighs of the young couples. But the briny smell of the sea could never cloak the penetrating scent of lust that was such a potent lure for the sex-starved who strolled and wandered there.

Misery, oh misery. Why have I come here? I should have turned at the intersection.

Hoan cursed himself, but his feet kept pulling him along the beach and his ears kept straining to hear the exquisite moans and gasps of lovemaking that he recognized only too well over the rush and crash of the waves. These sounds conjured images all his own—Mien's body, the sound of her breathing, the scent of her hair and sweat, and all the small, intimate gestures they alone understood.

Why have I come here? This is madness, stupidity.

But his feet kept moving forward, his eyes seeking out the couples all around him, his ears filtering the sounds, gathering the moans that sprang from bodies aflame with desire, drenched in sweat. This atmosphere charged with lust plunged into his heart like a spear, searing his flesh, blocking his breathing. "Over here . . ."

"Wait for me, just a moment . . ."

A couple had just crept shoulder to shoulder out of a stand of reeds about ten paces in front of Hoan. The wind carried the smell of sweat mixed with the scent of lotus all the way to his nostrils, and he recognized the fragrance of a cheap perfume from the Huong Sen Market. Chau sold that brand. Suddenly, the young woman wrapped her arm around his neck. With her long, shorebird's legs, she was at least a head taller than her lover. The man was broad-shouldered and had a cocky, self-satisfied stride. Suddenly, he turned to her. "Shall we go home?"

"No, let's stay awhile," said the woman, shaking her head of long hair.

"Aren't you worried about getting home to your mother?"

"No."

"Shall we go out on the rocks?"

"Yes, out on the rocks."

"It's really cold there. Let's wait until the moon clouds over. We'll do it again and then go home."

The girl nodded silently. The man began to hum something and kept walking.

Hoan slowed his pace. The sand slipped inside his open sandals. He watched these happy lovers, unbearably envious.

If only you were here, Mien. If only you could have emerged from that cabin. We would take the boat out, leave everything behind, far behind. Go live on some deserted island, like our ancestors.

Hoan shot a glance at the boats teetering on the sand. Which one would carry him and the woman he loved out to the open sea? He remembered all the novels he had read, especially *Robinson Crusoe*. Yes, with the woman he loved, he too could become a kind of Robinson, the happiest man on earth.

And with a swift kick, he sent an empty milk can flying into the air. *Coong . . . coong . . . coong.* The clanging sound made the couple turn around, putting an end to Hoan's reverie. The man glared at him, hands on his hips. Hoan glanced at the milk can; it had rolled right under the woman's legs.

"Sorry," Hoan muttered. "I wasn't paying attention..."

The woman giggled, realizing that it was an accident. "I wonder who left that milk can on the beach?" An empty question, addressed to no one in particular. The man shrugged, put his arm around her waist, and they continued walking.

Where will I go now? Hoan thought, stopping suddenly in his tracks. *After all, I'm not going to follow them out onto the rocks to spy on their lovemaking. When did I become so obsessed?*

He sat down on the sand. When he turned his face to the sea, the salt in the wind seemed to sting his soul.

As he sat there, he remembered a classmate, a burly, bearlike guy who resembled the man who had just emerged from the reeds, and who had helped him find a way out of his doomed marriage to Kim Lien. His friend was the eldest in a rich fishing family from Bao Village and his dream was to continue his father's business and replace his old boat with a new, larger one, equipped for deep-sea fishing. That was the only reason that he had devoted ten years to his studies, which served him no real use. At Hoan's shotgun wedding to Kim Lien, the young fisherman had shown up with twenty pounds of langoustines and jumbo shrimp. When Hoan revealed to the assembled guests that he had been trapped into marriage, his friend was the first to speak out: "There is nothing nobler than honesty. Hoan is the most honest man on Vietnamese soil. Let's applaud him!" He clapped noisily in the direction of the young male guests. "Come on, you young fellows! May we live like our comrade, Hoan. Let's say what we think and live the way we want to live."

Stunned at first, people eventually realized what had happened and they broke into thunderous applause, banging their chopsticks on their bowls and cups. The wedding banquet degenerated into complete pandemonium: The bride's family had to retreat and go home, while Hoan's family finally dared to break their silence, eagerly questioning one another amid the chaos. Finally, someone shouted over the din: "Let's raise our chopsticks and eat!"

That was what broke the ice. Then everyone pounced on the platters heaped with banquet food. And this happy chain of events was all set in motion by this good-hearted young man from Bao Village.

After the wedding, the bride insisted on setting up house in Hoan's family residence, employing a military strategy used during the American War and adapted to circumstances by her mother: "Attack the enemy by holding on to their belts!" As for Hoan, the groom, he went off with his weapons and his bags to Bao Village. There, his friend built him a hut raised on stilts and taught him the art of fishing with square nets. The hut, perched right on the banks of the Nhat Le River, was airy with a cool breeze both day and night. Hoan usually slept there, retreating to his friend's house only in stormy weather. Net fishing was Hoan's only activity aside from reading. Once a week, his sister Nen would bring rice and money to his friend's house. And so the family had provided for Hoan, as they would a student who had failed his exams and was waiting for the next session. Hoan was happy with this life, even though his friend was always leaving on deep-sea fishing trips. When he returned, he would chat with Hoan and then dash off to meet a girlfriend.

Hoan's hut was exceptionally situated, with a spectacular view: Clouds in the sky reflected in the water below. Sun. Waves. Birds in flight. Hoan didn't have to struggle to make a living, or see people he disliked. The villagers were welcoming and took an instant liking to this handsome young man, with his gentle smile and friendly gaze. The young women liked to flirt with him and they would throw all kinds of things into his hut: ripe guavas, grapefruits, cakes, toads, even frogs. Sometimes, while he read, they would creep up behind him and slip a live shrimp or fish down his back. Hoan would pull off his shirt in silence to throw off the creature, revealing his fair, muscular chest.

He was good-natured and could put up with all kinds of tricks. He also knew that the girls in Bao Village were in love with him, but he didn't want to get involved with anyone. He had tasted real bitterness; and besides, he liked his freedom. From time to time, the distant howl of a train siren from Thuan Ly Station would remind him of a dream that had been snuffed out. And he would sit up in bed, gaze out at the white clouds scattered on the horizon to the north, and remember happier days and the call of a future that had vanished into thin air. His suitcase, the piles of clothes, his personal belongings, all fit into a corner in this fisherman's hut. Here, night after night, day in and day out, he watched the river flow. A small, insignificant river in the middle of a vast region, and yet it lay between him and his dreams. So much unhappiness, and all because of a scheme concocted by Mrs. Lan and her daughter to legitimize a fetus that the prematurely sex-crazed girl was carrying. Or had it been his fault? Had he been in search of a siren who could satisfy the lust that had already seethed within him? Yes, he too was guilty; his own body had ensnared him, dragged him into this nasty little drama. And he would often curse it, knowing full well that the longing to meet another siren was already growing inside it. Was it the air here, the sea wind, or the fresh fish that he ate every day that seemed to sharpen his desire? Hoan didn't know.

One dark night, the ladder to the hut began to shake. Hoan thought perhaps his friend had returned unexpectedly from his expedition and had come to pay a visit, so he grumbled, "You told me you wouldn't be back for three more days . . ."

No reply. Just the sound of footsteps mounting rung after rung. If it had been his friend, he would have called noisily from the foot of the ladder. Hoan sat up, stunned; he had barely risen to his elbows when a woman jumped on him.

"Who are you?"

"It's me, Gai."

"You're . . ."

"I come by every morning. I'm from Ha Hamlet."

"Ah . . . ah . . ." Hoan suddenly understood. She was probably one of the women who trudged by at dawn, baskets slung over their shoulders, on their way to buy fish at the dock before crossing the river to resell it. The villagers here in Bao referred to them disparagingly as "those Ha people." Ha Hamlet was just a few miles away from Bao Village. The Ha people there couldn't live from fishing nor could they grow crops from the sandy, impoverished soil there. They survived off small trades that depended on the city markets. A few of their menfolk had become woodsmen or lumberjacks farther upstream. Apparently, no one had ever made a forture. They used to say that there wasn't a single brick house in Ha Hamlet. The richest household had a cement courtyard. That's why the girls from Ha always seemed more timid than those from Bao Village. They liked to tease him but they were never as impudent as those from Bao. Usually, they just walked by his hut, shooting him furtive glances, mumbling something vague but laced with sexual innuendo.

Who is she?

Hoan searched his memory. There had been a plump woman with a garish, flowered blouse. The others were skinny and wore conical hats tied beneath their chins with big silk ribbons. They all looked haggard, in a hurry. And their faces were all masked by their hats, so from his hut they looked like so many walking mushrooms.

Maybe she was the one with the faded green uniform and the freckles?

Hoan suddenly remembered her face. "Are you . . . ?"

"Don't speak too loudly," she pleaded in a whisper.

She put her hand gently on Hoan's chest and untied her hair, which tumbled down, grazing his face.

"Don't be afraid," she murmured again. Still panting, she struggled to catch her breath. "I'm a widow, I have children. I don't want to hurt you, or bother you. I've watched you for some time now . . ."

"I . . . ," Hoan said, then stopped, not knowing what to say. He wanted to sit up, but he didn't dare.

"I'm not going to cause you trouble . . . Believe me. I have a family, but my husband is dead. He drowned in the flood last year. I have to work hard to earn my living, so I don't know leisure like you city people, but I'm only two years older than you . . ." She said it all in a single breath. It was as if she had thought it all over already and then rehearsed it in her broken heart. Hoan was moved. He could smell on her skin the sweaty odor of a hardworking woman. After the market, she had probably come back to Ha Hamlet to bathe her kids and cook for them. Then, she had probably gone to bathe in the river herself before coming here. Han had never been to Ha Hamlet, but he imagined the long, eleven-mile road that she must have walked before finding her way in the darkness to his cabin along the bumpy, rock-strewn dunes.

"I . . . I've known about you for a long time now. I know your story. The people in Bao Village told me all about you. Trust me . . ."

These last words of hers seemed disconnected, tired. Suddenly, she nestled her face against his chest, caressing him with her rugged hands. "Is it too scratchy, am I hurting you?"

She didn't wait for his reply, but caressed him with the back of her hand. Confused, filled with pity for her, Hoan could only manage to stammer, "No, no . . . Don't worry."

"Oh, you are good to me . . . so good to me . . . ," the woman murmured.

And, as if these awkward, simple words couldn't express her gratitude, she kissed his chest. And from that moment, he was aware of nothing but the violent sensations that she awakened in his body. Her hungry lips plunged him into a world of unknown pleasure.

He was totally lucid, hadn't had a drop of alcohol, and yet she had somehow led him, step by step, up the infinite ladder of pleasure.

"Don't move . . . don't move," she murmured in a moment of silence during their lovemaking. She took out a towel from somewhere and wiped the sweat on Hoan's brow and back. "Let me . . . let me . . . ," she murmured again, as they changed position. Her light, patient hand held up his back when he lost balance. All her gestures were tender, considerate, encouraging, generous, as if she were the man, the one who took charge of everything, guiding him in the art of loving.

Hoan didn't know how long their lovemaking had lasted. Breathless with pleasure, he lay there without moving, oblivious to everything around him. She changed back into her clothes. But it was only when he heard the sound of her feet on the ladder that he realized what was happening, and grabbed the hem of her tunic. "You . . . you'll come back, won't you?"

"Yes, I'll be back," she murmured.

The ladder shook, creaking under her feet. A final squeak and then all was silent. Hoan peered out of the hut, trying to follow the woman with his eyes. But there was no moon that night. She disappeared into the darkness.

Tomorrow, I'll get up at dawn. I'll surely recognize her among the fishmongers at Ha Hamlet.

But their tumultuous lovemaking had left him exhausted and he fell into a deep sleep. The next day, when he opened his eyes, the hands on his watch showed twelve past nine. The sun was already shimmering on the surface of the river. People had been up working for hours already. His net, drying in the sun, swayed in the breeze. On the floor, his little sister had set out tea and a package of sticky rice and green bean paste. The sticky rice had gone cold and the tea was barely lukewarm. The road that wound the length of the river in the direction of Ha Hamlet was deserted, baking under a fiery sun. Hoan knew that the woman had already come and gone, that he would have to wait until dusk to see her again, on her way back. But that night, he didn't see her. He carefully searched the faces of the procession of women from Ha Hamlet, but there was nothing that even suggested a link to the woman who had come the previous night. Somehow, he knew instinctively that she would not come by there again. The next morning, Hoan got up very early, went down the ladder, and stood out on the road to Ha so that no face would escape him. This time, he confirmed his premonition, that the woman who had come to him that night would avoid him as long as it was daylight. And to do this, she would have to go a roundabout route, uphill, an extra twenty miles out of her way via a pier they called the Oyster Inn where the Ha women sold fresh oysters and chowder.

Who is she? My mistress in the art of lovemaking . . .

Five nights later, she returned. Just when he had started to doze off while waiting for her. The shaking of the ladder woke him instantly. He sat up and held out a hand to her. The woman entered the cabin, and he immediately asked her, "Why did you go out of your way via the pier? I waited for you for four days without seeing you."

The woman kept silent. Hoan said to her, "Why are you going to so much trouble? I don't want to make your life even more difficult."

"No, no . . . It's not more difficult. I had to go by Oyster Inn to get some stuff to sell," she said hastily. Then, she fumbled in a small bag and took out some cakes wrapped in leaves and handed them to him.

"Here, I made them. For your breakfast tomorrow." It was like a gift you give to a child to distract him from a lie you've just told. The cakes were still warm; she had saved this tenderness for him, after all the cares and worries of her daily struggle to make a living. He wanted to say that he wasn't a child anymore, that he had had a much richer life than she had, that the disinterested sex they had shared was by far the most precious gift for him, that she shouldn't fuss over him that way. But he wasn't a smooth talker. The words seemed to stick in his throat. Finally, he managed to stammer his thanks.

"Don't thank me . . . Don't thank me," she murmured, grasping his hand and placing it on her breast.

He felt her heart beating, her bosom, ravaged by time and child-bearing, rise and fall. Suddenly his heart felt overcome with pain. "Thank you . . . thank you." He repeated these words over and over again, like an idiot, as he clasped her tightly in his arms. This anony-mous woman held out the back of her hand to caress him, fearing that her calloused fingers, torn by fish bones, would hurt his fair, scholar's skin. And again, she transported him.

. . .

More than ten years had passed since then. The image of the woman from Ha Hamlet suddenly rose from the waves of time, kindling rest-less, painful memories. All week long, he had remembered the fishing hut on the edge of the river, the blinding sun, the fish squirming in the bottom of his net, the shaking of the rope ladder, the creaking of the floorboards under his back when they made love.

It was three o'clock. Hoan rose from his bed with a destination in mind. He jumped on his motorcycle and raced toward Bao Village. The village was practically empty at that hour. The fishermen were out at sea. The fish sauce merchants were working in their *nuoc mam* factories and the salespeople were all at the market displaying their goods. Only the women remained behind, tending their houses and their children. The huts of the fishermen were farther and fewer between along the river than they had been during Hoan's stay there. Everyone said that these last few years the freshwater fish were much scarcer than before the war. Hoan climbed to the top of a sand dune to contemplate the place where his own hut had once stood. Two old fishing boats lay beached on the sand. On the deserted path that led to Ha Hamlet, the white sand reflected the dazzling sunlight. In the distance, a row of filaos traced a dark green curve, a frail note of sadness amid the bluster of wind and sun.

Like it once was and yet different. This landscape is like me: as it once was and yet different. The young man in me is dead; the solitary man strains to remember the swaying of a ladder out of his past. It's always the same suffering but it's no longer the same man. Even the taste of happiness has changed. I must go back to see the woman who gave me my first taste of it, so long ago.

The steep road that climbed toward Ha Hamlet was completely sandy and Hoan had to drive his motorcycle slowly. His watch showed ten to four. He would have ample time to make inquiries. A small place like Ha Hamlet couldn't be very populous. Just as he was revving his motor, a young woman came rushing toward him.

"Hoan, my God, big brother! Why don't you stop by since you're here? We talk about you so often at the house. Come in!"

In one hand she carried a bottle of oil, and with the other, she grasped Hoan's arm. Hoan gaped at her, laughing. "Well, how you've grown, and become so pretty. I didn't even recognize you!"

Hoan looked over this young woman with her flushed cheeks, her plump, round neck and copious bosom jiggling under her silk blouse, straining to find the skinny little girl he had been so fond of, the one who wore boys' shorts all year round and her hair tied back in a ponytail with a red elastic band. Seeing his look, she asked him, "So, have I really changed that much?"

Hoan nodded. "If you hadn't called to me, I wouldn't have recognized you."

They arrived at the gate. The girl helped Hoan lift his heavy motorcycle up the stone steps. Hoan stayed over an hour chatting with the mother and her friend, only taking to the road at five o'clock. The sun still shone, but the sand along the shore had lost its sparkling reflections. Hoan arrived at the edge of the hamlet about twenty minutes later. A few dozen huts with thatched roofs stood in the middle of the fields covered with green rice. Ducks waddled in a crescent-shaped irrigation channel that encircled almost half the hamlet. On this salty, marshy land, only stunted, shriveled trees grew. The main street was a mess, a sticky black mixture of mud and sand. Next to the gate to the hamlet stood a dilapidated refreshment stand that looked as if it had been there for centuries; its rotting thatch roof was crumbling under the weight of vines and their enormous purple blooms covered the bamboo hedge. Next to it stood a rickety old bench with only two legs left and two piles of bricks replacing the missing two. On the bench, someone had piled a few bunches of ripe bananas, a few hemp cakes, a pile of sweets wrapped in banana leaves, and red rice patties sprinkled with sesame seeds like those that the woman had given him ten years earlier.

Hoan turned to the old lady who was selling these sweets: "Do you know anyone by the name of Gai in this hamlet?"

"Gai? Why, there are four by that name in this hamlet. Which one?"

"Uh . . . I'm looking for . . ."

Seeing Hoan's confusion, she continued, "Well, the oldest one has grandchildren, and she lives two streets down from me. The second is sixteen and single and she lives near the duck pond. The third was a volunteer during the war and she's thirty, not married. She lives near Duck Hamlet as well. As for the fourth, she's got five kids and lives in Mung Hamlet, right ahead of you, straight past the sugar cane patch over there." She pointed her fan in the direction of the road. As he listened, Hoan eliminated all but the last, the woman who lived in Mung Hamlet. She had probably remarried and had three other children with her second husband.

Ha Hamlet was sparsely inhabited, and you could see from one house to the next. Low fences separated small plots of land planted with sweet potatoes, spinach, and duckweed. Not a single fruit tree in sight. Following the old woman's directions, Hoan passed a garden planted with sugar cane. A few hundred yards farther, he arrived at a school—a dark patch of land, a few huts without walls or doors, separated only by bamboo hedges, equipped with tables and a handful of rickety chairs. The blackboards, still properly hung up, were the only sign that this was a place children came to study. The school was silent, almost deserted. A few kids played with marbles in the courtyard.

"Do any of you kids know where I can find Mrs. Gai's house?" Hoan asked.

All six of them raised their heads and stared at him. They had dirty faces and snuffly noses.

"Please, kids, tell me where Mrs. Gai's house is? The one with five children?"

Five of the kids turned toward the littlest, who had a round face and flat nose. "Uh, Tun, there's a visitor for you?"

The little boy stared at Hoan. His low, rounded forehead furrowed. Seated, his hands planted on the ground, he looked like a puppy. Hoan burst out laughing. "You're Mrs. Gai's boy? Where is your mother?"

"Over there in front of my house," the boy said. "Can't you see? She's the one chopping duckweed." And with that, he darted off, running back toward the schoolyard.

Hoan stood motionless. He stared at the old woman chopping duckweed in the courtyard, her skinny, hunched back under her old, discolored black shirt. How had the passionate woman become this old hunchback chopping duckweed, just a few yards away, right there under his very eyes? Even in ten years, time couldn't possibly change a person this way. The woman was still chopping; having finished one basket, she bent over and grabbed another from the dirt courtyard. With that movement, the towel she had wrapped around her head fell to the ground. As she turned, Hoan noticed a hairpin made out of water buffalo horn stuck in the tiny chignon at the back of her head. His heart froze.

Yes, it's her.

The woman who had slept with him all those nights in the fishing hut had braided her long, thick hair and tied it up in a bun like that. The braids sometimes came undone when they made love, and Hoan used to grope around in the darkness trying to find her hairpin. He remembered how the crude pin had a ball at one end, how it had been so polished that it must have been used by generations of women. Later, he had bought all kinds of hair clips for Mien. But he had never found such a solid, resistant kind as this one. Now he saw it again on the old woman, stuck in a tiny, gray bun that seemed even more pitiful under the weight of the hairpin. He remembered how that bun had once been as plump and round as a grapefruit. He remembered her body, how during their lovemaking it had labored as tirelessly as a machine. Had that silent goddess, that magician of the flesh, truly become this old woman?

A gust of wind made him shiver. He turned back toward the children playing with their marbles. He called to Tun, "Come over here a minute, I need you."

The boy reluctantly got up. Hoan pulled a wad of bills out of his wallet. "Once, your mother sold fish at the market. I borrowed money from her. I didn't have time to return it because the Americans started bombing and I was evacuated. Bring this money back to your mother."

The boy snapped back. "Why didn't you give it to her yourself?"

"I was afraid she wouldn't take it."

The boy wiped his nose with his hand. "Give it to me then." He grabbed the money from Hoan's hand and ran off. Hoan was afraid he didn't know the value of the bills and would run off to buy candy. In poor villages like this one, even teenagers often had never touched paper money in their lives, since their parents earned only a few coins by harvesting vegetables from their own gardens. Hoan secretly followed the boy. "Mother . . . hey! Mother!"

His mother was still chopping duckweed. "What is it?" Hoan recognized her voice, though it had changed slightly.

"Take this money," the boy said, stuffing it in her hand.

The woman cried out, terrified. "Where did you get this? Who did you take this from?"

"I was playing in the schoolyard. A man came and asked about you. He said he owed you this money."

"What man? What did he look like?" Hoan heard her ask, her voice trembling. He knew she had guessed it was him.

"What did he look like?" she repeated.

"He was fair, tall. Big, just like a Frenchman."

The woman tossed the knife into the basket of duckweed and got up. Hoan quickly turned and ran off down the road. In a few seconds, he arrived at the intersection, sprinted down a backstreet, leaped over a few gutters filled with a sticky, black liquid, and crossed the gardens, springing over fences that barely came up to his knees. He pressed on, his head down, and found the sugarcane patch. Only then, when he was far enough from the woman's house, did he stop to breathe, to let his racing heart slow to a normal rhythm.

Why did I flee like a common thief? Ridiculous. I've never behaved like that before. If someone had seen me, if they thought I was up to no good, I would be in big trouble . . .

He returned to the snack stand where he had left his motorcycle, paid the woman, and took off at high speed. On the deserted road, the wind whistled in his ears. He continued to drive like a maniac.

Well, that was a near brush with disaster. Fortunately, no one saw me.

He imagined the scene: a tall, well-dressed man fleeing like a chicken thief, jumping over fences and irrigation channels, dashing down back alleys like an escaped convict.

Why had he suddenly been so afraid? He himself didn't understand. He had wanted to find her, to see her face at least once, to express a few words of gratitude. And at the last minute he had fled.

When he got back to Bao Village, Hoan parked his motorcycle at another refreshment stand and went to sit at the edge of the river. The sunset had faded and the deserted beach was dark; it was a moonless night. Hoan strolled past two broken fishing boats. In the murky darkness his old hut seemed to come back to life with the sound of the woman's footsteps climbing the ladder, the creaking of the floorboards under her weight, the murmur of her voice.

His eyes filled with tears. *No, no . . . I can't . . . I want to preserve the face of the woman I knew ten years ago.*

He couldn't bear sitting by that riverbank any longer, by this place filled with memories that rent his heart. He stood up, got back on his motorcycle, and returned to the city. But when he arrived at the intersection that led to the wharf, the city lights seemed suddenly cold, foreboding, as if the other side of the Nhat Le River was not the place he had been born and raised, but some wild, inhuman continent. Just then, the loudspeakers from the Bao Village clubhouse started up again. The carefree, silly songs and noisy laughter of the young men and women from the fishing villages seemed to beckon to him. As if spellbound, he retraced his steps, walking toward the halo of light. Standing amid the crowd under the stage, he watched the young people radiant with happiness, remembering his own youth, and the woman he had just lost. His regrets flowed clear and icy, and he realized he was losing control. He didn't know who he was anymore.

When the crowd finally set down their microphones and tossed off their shoes to run along the beach, his loneliness deepened.

I've never run along this beach, despite all my long years here . . . Why not today?

And he followed them, furtively, silently.

Now, seated on the sand, he watched the sea, his thighs clenched together to restrain his desire. But it refused to die down. The sea continued to howl, the wind carrying murmurs and gasps, heavy breathing, and cries of pleasure from the young lovers. Suddenly, he turned his head toward a fishing hut a few dozen yards away.

Mien, where are you? Mien, come out of your shadow.

His heart tightened, his eyes staring at the black frame at the front of the hut. He waited for the woman he loved to step out. Time passed. His eyelids grew heavy and he reached out a hand to rub them, realizing this was only a dream.

You're another man's wife. You belong to someone else now . . .

He wrung his hands. This pain was real. As real as the certitude of another man's right of ownership over his wife. He was exhausted, his heart as empty as a gourd, but he felt his penis swell and harden, violent, fierce, insistent. He closed his eyes and let his head fall onto his knees, dreaming of a woman's voice, a voice that he had never heard before, that might rise from behind him, as the heavy hand of a fisherwoman had once settled on his shoulder.

I'm a widow. I don't want to bother you, I don't expect anything from you . . . I've wanted you for so long . . .

12

On autumn mornings, the valley began to bloom with tiny, dark green flowers, as fine as dawn mist. They were probably the most ephemeral of flowers, since their lifespan was only a few hours. Around seven or seven-thirty, as the warmth of the sun dried the grass, these flowers bloomed, living their extraordinary beauty in the space of an instant. They flowered in bunches, in thousands and thousands of green droplets, dancing on the thick, marble-white leaves, glinting with silvery reflections. About ten or ten-thirty, the gracious petals began to wilt and curl inward, and at exactly noon they collapsed and shrank into tiny black dots. No painter had ever captured the delicacy of this flower's odd green hue; no poet had ever been able to describe its frail, surreal beauty. These smooth talkers were too lazy to wander into a place as remote as Mountain Hamlet.

Now Bon was no poet, but that morning, as he watched the valley begin to glow in the clear, emerald-green light, he stopped, transfixed. Here was his home, ground that had been polished by his footsteps. And yet, this was the first time he had really noticed these strange flowers. Had they sprouted during the long years he had been gone, or been carried here by migratory birds? Or had the poverty of his youth deprived him of the time needed to contemplate these landscapes? He couldn't say. Bon let himself fall onto the grass to gaze at the sun slipping over the flowers. He longed to weep, to dissolve, for his limbs to detach and fall from his body. He let himself long for someone to come and stab his heart with a bayonet, to put an end to his pitiful, lonely existence, or perhaps he could be snatched up, carried off like a hen by an eagle, far, far away, to a desert island cut off from the human world, where he would make a new life, alone, among plants and wild animals. This life might be harder, but it would not be as humiliating, as degrading, as the life he lived here, in this place.

The bleating of goats echoed in the distance. From where he sat, Bon wearily grabbed his machete and reached for his rucksack. Then, discouraged, he flung them back down onto the grass. How many hundreds of pounds of virility grass had he gathered with this machete? He had lost track. For days on end he had dutifully swallowed the medication he had made according to Old Phieu's recipe: virility grass steeped with virgin seeds the old man had given him. To find the grass, Bon had followed the trail of the herd of goats through the mountains. And the old man had provided strong alcohol distilled from sticky rice grown in his own fields. Everyone helped him as if he were some kind of handicapped person, and Bon still couldn't accept such humiliation. And yet, it had become a reality. He now knew that his dream of rebuilding his former happiness—the one he had harbored since the day of his return to the village—was only an illusion, just as impossible as conjuring precious stones out of the dawn mist. He began to realize this one morning after a visit with his friend Xa.

Ever since Xa's door had closed behind him, Bon had been disoriented, not knowing where or who to turn to next. In the end, he decided to go to his maternal aunt Dot's house and appeal to her. Dot's house, built of brick with a tile roof, was smaller than the one that Bon's parents had left behind. The walls, whitewashed with lime, hadn't been repainted in decades and were beginning to mold over. All the same, the house seemed airy and solidly built, and Dot had a huge garden. She couldn't work much anymore, but she was clever and knew how to get the young people in the village to help her. As a result, the garden always seemed to be flourishing, regardless of the season, and she reaped the fruit of its bounty. When Bon arrived, she was dozing, her back against a wall. Two of Ta's children were poking at cooked potatoes in a basket. At the sound of footsteps, the old woman opened her eyes. She woke up with a jolt at the sight of her nephew.

"Ah, come in, my nephew."

As happy as if she had just discovered a small fortune, the old woman fumbled around to find a ripe fruit. She made tea and began to tell Bon her endless stories about her grandparents, his parents, the family, and all their common memories . . . the world of the dead. The old woman lived with that world; it belonged to her and she to it. Bon looked at her and realized that there was no hope. He politely got up and prepared to leave.

"Wait, wait a moment, young man, I've got something for you, just for you," she said, and then hurried off into a back room. He could hear her fumbling through her trunks one by one. Finally, she emerged with a packet wrapped in dried banana leaves. She brought it to Bon and slowly unraveled each leaf, as carefully as one would lift off a piece of fine silk covering some fragile object made of crystal.

"Here . . . here is your portion."

Five layers of banana leaves and one layer of parchment paper. Inside, tiny pieces of barley sugar.

"I had to wrap them so they wouldn't melt."

Bon looked at the candy. So this was it, the family legacy, the treasure he had dreamed about. He thanked his aunt, took the packet, and left.

The road back home was cloaked in the languorous shadows of the trees. Peonies bloomed in the gardens and the cries of birds mingled with those, more distant, of the birds down in the valleys. The peaceful world of Mountain Hamlet, the one he had dreamed of for so many years, was right there, in front of him. All he had to do was reach out a hand to pick a peony, or listen closely as tiny birds flitted about the branches of the trees. But he had no desire for any of this. The nostalgia for the past had faded; it belonged to another time, a time when he lay in an army hammock, chewing his ration of dried food, dreaming of this hamlet's gardens and orchards. Back then, as he trudged along the long, dusty expeditions and marches, he had imagined the springs of his birthplace and in his mind they no longer resembled mere brooks and streams but vast rivers surging with memories and hopes.

Now Mountain Hamlet belonged to whoever had money, big houses, and dense plantations of coffee and pepper trees. His native village was now home to those who had invested their fortunes and built their estates there. The hamlet no longer had a place for him, a veteran who had come back empty-handed, with just enough loose change in his pocket to buy a packet of cheap tobacco. He had become a stranger here in his birthplace, on the same ground where they had buried his placenta. He had no other home, and no other hope than Mien. He would cling to her like a drowning man clings to a wooden plank caught in the currents of a tidal wave. Someday she would understand that no one loved and revered her as he did. And certainly no man had suffered as much for her.

Mien was sewing when Bon arrived. She looked up.

"You're back."

"Yes, I'm back."

Bon had hoped for a question. Any question. Where had he been? To do what? How had everything gone? One question, just one question that would allow him to begin a conversation. But Mien lowered her eyes, her head bowed, concentrating on her needle and thread as if nothing else existed. Bon paced about, opening and closing the drawer where he knew he would find nothing more than a plastic box that once, long ago, used to hold mint candies, and which he now used for a tobacco pouch. These awkward gestures seemed to irritate Mien and she looked up.

"Are you hungry already?"

"No, uh, no."

Mien put down her sewing. "Okay, I'll start the meal."

She piled the clothes she was mending on a corner of the bed, her feet searching for her slippers. Bon stared at her, dazed.

I can't seem to talk to her. How am I going to keep on lying? I could say that my friend has just had some bad luck, he's promised me money next year . . . No, no one would make such a promise . . . Lying isn't easy.

Out in the courtyard, Ta's three-year-old girl suddenly screamed. Mien ran out and scooped the child up in her arms, carrying her onto the porch to brush off the ants that had gathered on her dirty bottom. Then Mien dashed back into the house and reappeared with a tiny tin of mentholated balm for rubbing the ant bites.

Mien is so kind. Ta doesn't deserve it. She even takes care of my sister's dirty kid. I have no choice but to tell her the truth, right now . . .

Bon stood by the door, waiting until Mien had finished. When she turned around, he would say something. But he was facing certain humiliation. He remembered the incident on their second day back together, how he had gotten up late that morning. After his failure in bed with Mien, he had fallen into a short, exhausted sleep. But he had spent the rest of the night awake. When Mien came back to bed after her bath, smelling of virgin grass, he was still lying there, silent, motionless, not even daring to sneak a glance at her. Mien stayed as tight-lipped as a grain of paddy rice. She breathed so softly he couldn't tell whether she was asleep or awake. Like a criminal waiting for a verdict, he listened, waiting anxiously for a sigh or a curse, hoping to divine her thoughts. But she didn't give him the slightest clue. The woman who lay beside him was as hard and icy as a statue. Bon's ruminations lasted until dawn, the hour when the neighborhood loudspeakers announced that it was time for calisthenics, when people called loudly to one another to go gather firewood in the forest. It was then that Bon fell into a deep sleep. When he awoke, the sunlight that crept past the curtain had already reached his eyebrows; it was at least nine or nine-thirty. The house was deserted, silent. He rushed out into the yard, but he didn't see Mien weeding or raking dead leaves. Suddenly, he felt his blood run cold.

She's gone back to that man. And with no explanation, not even a good-bye.

He had no time to think further; he didn't lock the door, just took to the road that led to Auntie Huyen's and beyond, to Mien's former house. He didn't know what he would do if he found her or if he didn't find her. He knew only that he would follow her, wherever she went, even to hell if necessary.

Either she comes back or it's going to be a one-way ticket for both of them . . .

Suddenly, Mien was standing right in front of him on the road.

"Bon! Bon!" she shouted, exasperated.

Bon panicked when he saw her eyebrows furrowed in anger.

"Where are you going like that?"

Bon was stunned. Mien's look told him that she had guessed his mad, lugubrious thoughts. All he needed to see was the fury in those sparkling eyes to be convinced of that.

"I . . . I'm going . . ."

"Where are you going like that?" Mien repeated her question in a dull voice, ticking out her words one by one. Each word that fell from her mouth seemed to bounce off the bridge of his nose, dizzying and paralyzing his brain.

"Who are you looking for? Who are you going to bother?"

Bon stuttered something. Suddenly, he seemed to tremble all over.

"I . . . I was looking for you . . . I couldn't stay at home . . . alone . . . I . . ."

Mien smiled contemptuously. "What are you? Some kid who's afraid to stay home alone?"

Bon said nothing, not knowing how to reply. Mien continued, "Please, don't make us the laughingstock of the entire village. If you think I came back to live with you because of your self-destructive tendencies, you're wrong. I've always respected men of honor, never those blinded by despair."

She stopped and turned as a scissors and knife grinder passed by them and continued on his way. Then she lowered her voice. "Let's go home."

She walked ahead and Bon followed, a few paces behind. Mien was holding a fish so fresh it was still wriggling and some cabbages. They walked in silence until they arrived at the house and their bedroom.

"Why didn't you lock the door?" Mien asked.

Bon didn't dare reply. He had been happy to see her back in his kingdom; he was ashamed to realize how thoughtless he had been.

"What if I hadn't had enough money to buy the groceries? Were you thinking of surviving on grilled salt or boiled garden weed? Other people can always pick some spinach or tamarind out of the garden to make soup. But in your garden, the best you could do would be a bit of grass."

Bon knew it was true. In his kingdom, there was nothing to eat. He knew that this was a world that had been reserved for the truly destitute, where hunger went hand in hand with humiliation.

Mien didn't wait for an answer. "And tomorrow, when we've finished this fish and this cabbage? What were you planning to do?"

Bon was terrified by her questions.

Yes, what are we going to do? Yesterday, I ate the chicken that Soan gave me. If Mien didn't have money, I'd be eating grass from the garden.

An irrepressible bitterness overcame him, and the trembling of his body merged with that of his soul. Suddenly he began to weep, soundlessly, silently, oblivious to the tears that spilled from his eyes and ran down his trembling arms and legs.

Don't cry, don't cry. It's shameful. Don't moan, it's cowardly. Don't beg, it's weak . . . How many times have I recited that poem with Binh. Yes, I'm ashamed, yes, I'm cowardly. I have no face left with anyone.

He wept for a long time, so long he didn't even notice when Mien left the room. Having emptied all his shame and rancor, he felt ridiculous. He went to wash his face in the well and then walked back to the kitchen, where Mien was preparing their meal. He knelt behind her back and passed her tiny branches of kindling.

"I'm sorry . . . I didn't want to get to this point . . . But because you have taken pity on me, please don't give up on me . . . I swear to you, from now on I'll never dare have such crazy thoughts, never do anything so rash."

Mien gazed sadly at the flames. "A man shouldn't vow anything lightly. In a difficult situation like this, try to be sensible. Remember to lock the door. If we lose the little money we have left, we really will have to gather weeds from the garden."

A moment later, she got up and went to bring in the dinner platter. They ate without looking at each other.

Bon could hear Ta's two scrawny pigs squealing for food out in the sty, the smell of their muck mingling with the stench of human excrement. Mien said nothing. She just kept spreading the coals of the dwindling fire over the dead leaves with a stick, trying to limit the smoke. But he sensed that she too was trying to repress something, that she was no less miserable. Many days had passed since that one, but Bon couldn't manage to forget his shame when he had spoken those words to Mien. It seemed to him that the flames of the hearth no longer served to merely cook rice, but to sear his heart and flesh.

"Stop whimpering!" Mien snapped. "And I don't want you playing with ants in the courtyard anymore." She set Ta's little girl down on the doorstep, having just finished massaging her bottom with the balm. Then she went back in the house, the tiny round tin of balm in her hand. Bon didn't know why, but when she passed in front of him, he had simply stepped aside to let her by, vaguely contemplating the crown of lilacs out in the garden, as if he were pursuing some distant thoughts. Mien scooped a few cups of rice out of a stone jar for their dinner. Just at that moment, Ta's eldest son appeared with a basket in hand: "Auntie, gimme a few handfuls."

He spoke crudely, his language only rudimentary. He wasn't even six years old, but he already seemed like a skinny twelve- or thirteen-year-old. He stood in the doorframe, his eyes darting about the room, taking in everything. Since Mien didn't answer, he raised his voice: "We got no more rice at home. My mama asked to lend her a few scoops . . ."

Bon felt his face burn. Mien still said nothing. After a few seconds, she leaned over the urn, scooped out a few extra measures, and poured them into the boy's basket. Having gotten what he had come for, the boy turned and left without a word, as if he had every right to rice from his rich aunt, and that it was her duty to give it to him. Ever since Mien had come back here, this had been the routine. Every second or third day, Ta's son came to "borrow" rice—a loan that the borrower and lender knew would never be repaid.

"Gimme a piece of fish, auntie . . ."

"Gimme a piece of pork, that one, there."

"Why does he get two pieces of pork and me only one? Give me the fish head, so I can bring a piece back to my mother . . ."

Once, brazenly standing behind her children, Ta had laughed. "Why, you're so rich. What would you do with it all if you didn't share with family?"

Mien didn't answer. She never let a word past her clenched teeth. If she had complained, or fought with Bon about this—even if she had brutally refused to reply to this shameless begging and borrowing—he would have been less miserable. But Mien kept her silence. Like a stone, like a tree. As if she wasn't of the same species as Bon, as if they didn't share the same language.

One day, taking advantage of Mien's absence, Bon decided to confront Ta. "Don't you have any dignity left? Here I am, without a dong to my name, already totally dependent on her. How dare you hang on to me?"

"You're my younger brother," Ta reminded him coolly. "And you're married to the richest woman in the whole region. I'd have to be dumber than a cow *not* to hang on to you." Bon studied the woman seated facing him, this person who shared the same flesh and blood, who had shared his childhood, the happiest years of his life. He felt shame spread through his soul. Yes, his own sister was the scum of the earth, somewhere in limbo between human and beast. Yet even if he would gladly chop her to bits and curse the dead, he couldn't change things; she was his elder sister, his closest blood relation. It was like the brand seared on the faces of slaves or prisoners in primitive times. He could only curse her. "You pitiful wretch of a woman. If you dare send your kids over to beg for rice at my place again, I'll chase them away," Bon sputtered. And he instantly regretted what he had said. It was inhuman.

"I dare you to close your door. I dare you not to share your rice," Ta shot back unexpectedly.

Bon couldn't find anything more to say. He felt defeated. Ta's "loans of rice" continued as usual. Every time his nephew impudently handed him the basket, Bon felt his face burn. But he couldn't manage to open his mouth to scold or chase the boy away. Nor could he manage to ask for Mien's understanding. He had already begged for too much in his own life. He couldn't repeat the same imprecations every day, like a professional beggar.

I'm just an amateur. I'll never amount to much. Who knows? Maybe I'll have to become a professional.

This is what Bon told himself, his eyes still fixed on the lilacs. These old, spindly lilacs had once been young and flourishing. Back then, he and Binh had hugged each other's shoulders, reciting poetry.

Binh had a truly rich, melodic voice. Bon would accompany him on the flute or the monochord. But both instruments had disappeared after Bon left for the army. When Mien went back to live with Auntie Huyen, no one had thought to keep the instruments for him.

If she loved me like Soan loves Xa, she would have taken them with her.

But Bon banished this thought from his head.

I have only dark thoughts. Probably because I am bored . . . I should start to prepare the land before hiring workers. Surely, Binh . . .

He stopped, realizing that he had started to lie to himself again. The last buoy that he had left, that he had hung on to so as not to drown, was gone now. Binh had also been shipwrecked. Even if he recited the old poems a thousand times, even if he poured a magic potion over the lilacs to rejuvenate them, he could never restore their youth.

"Crying is shameful, moaning is cowardly, and begging is weak."

These words that Binh had once recited to him had suddenly slipped past his lips. Ta's little girl, seated on the doorstep, turned to Bon. "Are you singing, uncle?"

He shook his head. "No, no. Sing something for me, for your uncle."

The little girl started to hum something. It was the kindergarten song the children from Mountain Hamlet all sang. She had learned it from hanging about in the street. Bon went into his bedroom, fumbled in the basket where Mien kept her things, and took out a few candies to give to his niece, just as Mien was bringing in the dinner platter.

They ate in silence, as usual. A meal in the most austere monastery couldn't have been more silent. At the end of the meal, as Mien started to get up, he held her back by the hem of her blouse.

"Sit down, Mien . . . I want to talk to you."

She sat back down and looked at him. A distracted, vague look. Her spirit was elsewhere, far away, outside the space and time they lived in, a stranger to this room covered with leaves.

Mien, dearest, why don't you look at me, just once? Do you remember how it was, under the flame tree, when we kissed for so long? I still remember the blush of your neck, the freckles on your nape and under your hair.

Bon heard himself moan out loud.

But Mien didn't hear him. She was still off in her world apart. Bon clenched his teeth and lowered his head, fearful that she might guess the thoughts that flashed through his mind.

Yes, you are cruel . . . You totally forgot me, you only think about . . .

He felt a wild jealousy lurking somewhere, ready to pounce, but he contained it, chasing away the wild beast. Just then, a mocking voice echoed inside him.

Don't forget your predicament. You're a good-for-nothing, penniless guy with a stinking mouth . . . Xa is right. I've got to cure myself of this damn illness first. But who will pay the bill?

Bon swallowed hard. "You know, Mien . . ."

The words that he had rehearsed along the road from Xa's house suddenly evaporated. He felt his tongue constrict, his ears hum, and his cheeks go by turns hot and icy. He stammered something, mumbling for a long time. So long, in fact, that Mien lost her usual patience. "What is it? Speak!"

"I'm going to town to see a doctor. These past few years, I've had problems with my mouth, my breath . . . Xa promised to take me to the hospital tomorrow." Bon didn't dare look at her while he spoke. She was both listening and not listening to him.

"Do you need money?"

Summoning his courage, he nodded. "Yes, for the medication . . . It's just that my friend, the one who promised to help, has gone to Da Nang to visit his elder brother. When he comes back, I can . . . pay you back."

I've lied for the second time . . . and I'll have to lie again . . . Where is this going to lead me?

He imagined Mien smiling disdainfully, or pursing her lips in an effort to conceal her contempt.

"How much do you need?"

"I . . . I don't really know . . . Not much. Just enough for the medication. Western and traditional. Xa said I'm going to need both."

Mien got the money out of her pocket and handed it to him. Bon stuffed it in his own hastily, like someone who has just stolen for the first time hides the fruit of his plunder. Then he finally dared to look at her. Her eyes were gazing at some distant sky that was nevertheless present for her, even here within these four bare, peeling walls, in his poor, tiny bedroom. She was in a place beyond his orbit, that bore no relation to this space that he had tried to restore and decorate, where he had hoped to resurrect their love. Bon looked at the vase filled with scarlet galanga flowers that he had arranged with some heather from the garden. All these colors: They were so superfluous, so useless . . . just like him. It was true; she was oblivious to him, to his illness, to all the suffering he had endured. Yet Mien was different from those stingy women who calculated everything, who demanded thousands of explanations from their husbands or their children before offering a single coin from their pockets. She had readily given him the money, not like a woman gives to her husband, but as someone would give to a handicapped person in a moment of charity.

He gazed again into her liquid brown eyes, and this time found them cold and icy. Reeling from the humiliation, he hunched his back in pain, retracting his head and shoulders, his gut tortured, threatening to explode if he straightened. He sat where he was for a long time, his nails digging into the wooden edge of the table. His thoughts raced like blinding shards of lightning, pounding and colliding in his head.

I've become an idler. A reject. I live off charity, my hands held out for alms. But with your money, I'm going to recover, get my health back. I'm even going to have the infinite sexual power of my lousy sister. I'll be capable of inseminating tens—no, hundreds—of women. I'll make you bear me a whole brood of kids. Like so many chains for you. Then you'll be my wife forever. A tired, faded woman who won't be able to show off her long hair and rosy skin anymore . . . And one day, you too will be hunched over in pain, like me. You'll have to plead and beg me to keep you while other, younger women pine for me . . . Yes, that day will come.

Bon felt his pain ease slightly. Taking hold of the edge of the table, he lifted his shoulders and back.

Yes, that day will come . . . I'll be waiting for the moment that you gaze at me as obediently as you once did fourteen years ago.

He smiled, satisfied. But Mien never saw this smile, or guessed these calculations. She got up and carried away the empty dinner platter.

.   .   .

The next day at dawn, Xa came by on his Yamaha to take Bon into the city. This childhood friend, this man who had once needed Bon to help him with his schoolwork, had now become his protector, his guardian angel. Xa dropped him off at the gate to the hospital, glanced at his watch, and said, "I'm going to nip over to the market to do a few errands. I'll be back at quarter to eleven. I'll wait for you in front of the Thien Nga Restaurant." He pointed to the restaurant on the other side of the street. A big sign hung out in front: WELCOME TO THE THIEN NGA RESTAURANT.

"Remember the name, Thien Nga, so we don't lose each other. The crowd here can be as thick as a school of fish trapped in a basin."

Xa mounted his old motorcycle and revved the motor. The exhaust pipe spat out a cloud of black smoke and the vehicle sputtered for a while before taking off. Xa disappeared, swallowed up in the crowd. Bon glanced back at the sign in front of the restaurant on the other side of the street. It wasn't easy to make out, because dozens of other restaurants stood side by side along the street. They all had brightly colored signs. And each one seemed to billow with smoke, a cooking fire on the right and a big glass window on the left where the food was displayed. Bon scrutinized the Thien Nga restaurant one last time. The restaurant owner, a woman about thirty years old with a thick neck and fleshy shoulders, was bustling behind the display window. She wore a man's black T-shirt and must have weighed at least one hundred and eighty pounds. Bon felt calmer, sure now of locating this restaurant that Xa had designated for their rendezvous. He checked to see if everything was in order: his identity papers, the letter of introduction from the Party committee, and the money that Mien had given him the previous evening. The sum was five times what he had been given when he was demobilized.

It's that man's money.

He banished the thought and hurried toward the doctor's office at the hospital. A crowd was already lining up out front. They asked him to leave the letter of introduction from the communal Party committee at a booth shaped like a hornet's nest. He then sat down to wait. His turn finally came three hours later. The medical exam was extremely quick. Bon had the distinct impression that the doctor, shirking all professionalism, didn't feel like looking him in the eyes despite the double-thick white mask that protected his nose and mouth. The doctor prescribed a lengthy list of medications. He told Bon that his sickness wasn't dangerous, but that he would need a lot of determination and a lot of money to cure himself. The muscles that controlled his digestion had lost their elasticity and were no longer like those of a healthy man. If he wanted to improve, Bon would have to follow a long, rigorous training program combined with medication and regular medical checkups for one or two years. Bon took the prescriptions, his back drenched in sweat, and hurried out of the doctor's office, forgetting to say good-bye. A benign illness, but one that cost five times as much as a surgical operation or the treatment of terminal tuberculosis? The room seemed to sway and the benches where the other patients were seated tilted at an angle. Bon headed straight for the hospital garden and stood there for a long time, trying to compose himself. He then went to the pharmacy. When he had made his purchases, he left and saw Xa waiting in front of the gate, his black Yamaha parked at his back.

"What happened? I waited a quarter of an hour in front of the restaurant before coming here."

"I waited three hours before the doctor saw me. There were too many people."

"What did they say?"

"That the illness isn't dangerous but that it will take a lot of time and money to cure me."

"The main thing is the money. We've got all the time in the world."

"I'm afraid I'm not going to be able to follow this treatment."

"Who gave you the money? Dot?"

"No, she doesn't have any. It was Mien."

"Mien doesn't have any either. That money came from that guy,

Hoan. In the long term, you can't go on like this." Xa sighed, lost in his own thoughts. After a moment, he clucked his tongue. "Let's just go eat. My stomach has been rumbling for a while now."

They headed toward the Thien Nga Restaurant. Xa ordered two bottles of beer, a plate of boiled pork with fish sauce, a plate of stir-fried beef and cabbage, and two charcoal-grilled dried fish.

"It's on me," Xa announced. "Don't worry. Let's drink. We'll see what we can do later."

The restaurant owner brought a plate of pickled vegetables for them to snack on. "Here, this is on the house," she said, setting it down on the table and coquettishly pointing a tiny, plump finger at the dish. Xa glanced at the huge gold rings that covered her fingers and laughed. "Thank you, boss, thank you, my lovely lady. These pickles are much better than the usual stuff."

The woman chuckled, her hefty bosom rising and falling. When she was out of earshot, back at the storefront, Xa leaned over and whispered in Bon's ear, "She's giving us a five-thousand-dong plate. But she's also adding ten thousand dong to the bill for these beers. There are no honest city people. Did you see the rings on her fingers? Just one of those is worth five quintals of rice. And to think that we farmers wither our balls to earn a single quintal's worth of paddy. Here, people just pick up money they practically steal from you . . . It's impossible to get rich without a business of some kind . . . If I didn't know carpentry or logging, I'd die of hunger." Xa sighed and sipped his beer.

After eating, Xa got up and settled the bill. Then he turned to Bon. "Now I'm going to take you to see about some traditional medicine with my uncle."

Bon obediently mounted the back of his friend's motorcycle, anxiously hoping for a stroke of luck, a miracle, some reincarnated genie who would be capable of curing his shameful illness. Xa's uncle explained that Bon's intestines were governed by the fire element, and he gave him ten measures of medicine to reduce the fire and hence the stench of his breath. Once they had paid for the medication, Bon still had quite a bit of money, which he carefully put away in his shirt pocket, buttoning it meticulously. He would need money, and lots of it. And the only way he could get it would be to hold out his hand to Mien. Each time a man had to ask for money from his wife, he fell farther and farther into a kind of hell. He was just a ghost living off offerings made to the dead, and his life with Mien was now just a forced union between a woman glowing with health and a walking corpse who had stumbled out of the jungle of the past. Bon knew he didn't have a single advantage. The only way to keep their marriage together was to become a powerful male who would inject his semen into Mien's perfect body, thereby forcing her to share his future. Hadn't the Buddha once taught that children were like golden chains? It was absolutely true.

Xa was right to be practical. Hadn't he told Bon, not once but three times: "Even if you've got balls of silver and an emerald dick, you must absolutely cure your mouth of this stench. No woman will be able to bear this smell. But you also have to cure your impotence. And that's going to require a lot of money. For the moment, don't even think about plantations and seed cultures—that's failure guaranteed. Use every single dong you manage to lay your hands on to cure your illness. The money that Mien gives you is not money that she's earned. It's the other husband who gives it to her. Regardless of where it came from, that money, once it falls into Mien's pocket, is hers. And she's your wife. So you can profit from this to heal yourself. It's humiliating, I know, but what else can you do? No one likes to lose face, but sometimes you just have to in order to survive."

These harsh words were like acid thrown in Bon's face. But by the second or third time, the acid had stopped stinging. He realized that a man could get used to anything. Accepting this truth, he decided to follow Xa's advice. Three times a day he dutifully prepared and ingested a bowl of medicinal herbs. After three days of the treatment, he went to see Old Phieu.

"So, got your lust back yet, soldier?" the old man asked, choked with laughter. He winked and pointed his finger at the billy goat of his herd, who stood at the door to the barn at dawn and, like a copulating machine, mounted every female goat who ventured out. Bon was stunned. How could a seventy-year-old man be so bawdy, so lascivious? Back when Bon still lived in the village, Phieu was in his fifties and such behavior was normal, nothing to pique anyone's curiosity. But fourteen years later, the men of his generation had all aged; they weren't interested in sex anymore. Instead of leering at women, they preferred to stay home, their arms hugged around their knees, watching their grandchildren out in the courtyard and trading stories about the old days. This old man was the only one who refused to let go of his virility; he had remained a man of fifty, the age when sexual desire, like burning embers, flares up in one last, frenetic burst before flickering out.

"Well, now isn't that a sight for sore eyes?" said the old man, grinning and stroking his goatee. He, too, looked like a billy goat.

"So, tell us what a soldier of the people feels when he sees such a spectacle? In every species, the male must huff and puff and tire himself out when he mounts the female. Only the billy goat does it as if it were a game, without ever tiring."

The mischievous old man returned to the courtyard and ordered his thirteen-year-old son to take the herd of goats to the hills, and his wife to prepare green tea and honey cakes for Bon. The woman couldn't have been younger than forty, but she looked much younger, with rosy cheeks and firm, well-rounded breasts and buttocks. She dutifully served them tea—a full platter set with a teapot kept warm in a coconut shell and a small plate of warm honey cakes. Then she slung her pickax over her shoulder and left for the fields. Old Phieu had three fields of pepper trees and two big coffee plantations. He was one of the richest landowners in the entire region. His wife and his kids—a brood of almost twenty people—obeyed this patriarch to the letter. No one had ever heard a single quarrel between his wife and her mother-in-law.

When everyone had left, the old man began his lecture: "The lustful man is not necessarily virile. All you have to do is look at the old billy goat to understand. He doesn't have to pull off the female's panties, or stroke her bottom, or massage her breasts like we men do. And yet he's the lord of virility, as if the heavens had made him to be a copulating machine. To be a machine like that, you've got to train your body."

The old man paused, swilled down some green tea, and swallowed a whole honey cake. From the look of bliss on his face, Bon could tell that with each sip of tea the old man smelled the perfume of the surrounding hills, that with each bite of cake he savored the taste of sugarcane and young rice, the delicious aromas that had haunted him all through the long years of war. Bon knew it, though he couldn't smell the tea he was drinking or taste the sweetness of the cake he ate. He, the educated man, capable of imagining the entire gamut of life's pleasures, was unable to experience real life. He silently counted the old man's two rows of straight, white teeth as he munched on the honey cakes. As Bon watched the old man empty another cup of the scalding-hot green tea, he felt both envy and resentment.

Old Phieu finished eating. Sweat dripped down his face, which was flushed from the roots of the hair all the way down his neck. He waited until he had stopped sweating and then grabbed a cotton towel to wipe himself. Every gesture exuded a calm self-confidence. He looked at Bon and set down his towel. "Why are you eating with so little gusto? If you really savor something, even a simple country cake can be more nourishing than a bowl of swallow's nest soup you force yourself to gulp down in some palace. You obviously know nothing about the art of living."

That's right, I know nothing. I began my adult life as a soldier. Now, with the time that remains for me to live, I need other forms of knowledge.

The old man continued. "You're still young. You've got a lot of life ahead of you. Living without knowing the art of living is like trying to make incense without being able to tell a cinnamon tree from the rest. That's why you have to study, soldier."

"Yes."

"As I told you, to live healthfully, you have to train and preserve your body. And we have to do both. Rich people in the cities usually know only how to preserve themselves, but they don't know how to forge themselves anew. In their homes, you'll always find a dozen bottles of various elixirs and brandies with all the best ingredients: rice wine aged with ginseng, cinnamon, seahorses, tropical larks, and snakes. But do they live past eighty? No. But we mountain people usually never leave this world before the age of a hundred. That's because the city folk may preserve their bodies but they don't train them. They drink good wine and fancy food, make love to their women, but they refuse to develop their bodies. The sweat can't escape and it then blocks the circulation of the blood. The muscles are never used, so sooner or later they grow flabby. Now, where would a man like me find the money to fortify himself the way the rich do? I have neither ginseng nor cinnamon, neither seahorses nor sea slugs. I just drink goat's milk, and then the meat, blood, and sperm—and of course the gelatin, which I extract from their bones. Nothing but cheap, local products. But if I'm in great health it's because I practice Tae Kwon Do every day, and work in the fields or weed the garden. How many years younger are you? You look like you're about forty, no? But you wouldn't be able to follow that herd of goats over there up those cliffs in Black Deer Valley. I'm sure of that. Even a lot of twenty-year-old guys would give up halfway. As for me, I could climb to the very last cliff."

The old man stopped talking, served himself a half bowl of tea, and emptied it. Bon looked at his tight, powerful jaw and teeth; he was probably capable of chewing wood if he wanted to.

"It's not because I've got a young woman that I like to brag. But people often dare me to rise to idiotic challenges . . . That's enough, let's talk about you. You're young. You still have time to improve your life. But don't forget that you fought a war for ten long years, that you led an unstable life, totally different from this one. We, too, have been through the bombs and the bullets, but we always lived in the same village, with the same air and vegetation. Far from here, throughout those long years, you must have drunk poisoned water, eaten fetid food. When you were in the jungle, chemicals must have seeped into your body. I'm going to explain the physical exercises and the medicine you will need to purify your body, to chase the pollution out in your urine and in your sweat. Then, I'm going to give you some prescriptions and recipes to strengthen your virility."

From that day on, two times a week, Bon visited the old man to fortify his organs and purify his blood and his spirit. After a month, Bon felt lighter, and his dizzy spells seemed to subside. His urine turned clear. But his sexual prowess had hardly improved, and he confided in Old Phieu.

"Don't be impatient," the old man said. "Our ancestors teach us that haste always leads to failure. Follow my advice."

But three weeks later, Bon was back. "Please, give me a medical prescription to restore my virility. I need to have a child as soon as possible."

The old man shook his head, but in the end he gave in. He gave Bon the recipe for a potion and instructed him in the art of drinking rice wine mixed with goat's blood. He also instructed him to eat special, fortifying foods, showing him how to mix goat sperm with lotus shoots and seeds; how to steam it with garlic, onions, and five spice; how to eat the bulbs of lily pads; and how to grill and eat goat's heart at dawn.

Bon followed Old Phieu's lessons to the letter. He traveled to distant villages to search for lotus seeds and lily-pad bulbs. For days and nights on end, he patiently shelled lotus seeds, removing the shoots with a pin to prepare the sublime dish of goat sperm. He searched for a certain size stone, as large as two bricks, so he could grill the goat liver according to the traditional method. The liver, marinated in juice and spices and then grilled, appealed not only to his famished nieces and nephews, but also to Mien. But he stubbornly refused to share these dishes with anyone, even if it meant that he appeared a selfish glutton. This was not food in the conventional sense, but weaponry that he would use to conquer his lost citadel. Time was precious.

I must have children, at whatever the price.

Aside from the medicine and these fortifying dishes, Bon went to gather virility grass to replace tea, just like women after childbirth drank infusions made of ginger leaves. Every time he forced himself to swallow this stinking drink, he remembered the majestic profile of the billy goat standing outside the barn at dawn, copulating with every she-goat in the herd.

The next day, after he slaughtered a goat, Bon put the blood aside in a coconut shell. He waited until Mien had gone out, then he locked himself in their room and began to experiment with his penis. He mixed the goat's blood with rice wine, positioned himself so he could dip his penis into it, then he massaged it slowly to facilitate the absorption. For the first few seconds, the precious treasure was cool, but then it began to heat up. Bon trembled with hope. The shame that had tortured him vanished when, bent over the most sensitive member of his body, he saw it behave like a strange animal, like a frog wriggling in the sticky, purple blood. He caressed himself more enthusiastically. But now he no longer felt a sweet warmth but a painful, burning sensation. And what burned the most was his urine. He tried to encourage himself. *You've got to bear the pain, keep on going.*

At just that moment, Mien knocked at the door. She had no doubt returned to the house fearing that rain was about to fall. Panicked, Bon grabbed his underpants, wiped himself off and pulled on his trousers. In his haste, he knocked over the coconut shell that he had set on a brick at the foot of the bed. The makeshift basin rolled across the floor, flooding it with the mixture of blood and alcohol. Mien jumped back when she saw this strange, red liquid spreading at her feet.

"What *are* you doing?"

"Ah, ah, nothing . . ." Bon flushed as he offered this ridiculous lie. Mien asked no further questions and went straight out, realizing that it was some medicinal concoction, or some dish that he hoped would restore his health. This hopeless rehabilitation program had already cost her dearly. For a long time now, Bon had gotten in the habit of asking her for money. She gave it to him without a word, not even deigning to question or advise him on how he spent it. Every time he went off with someone to buy a billy goat or a calf so he could prepare his medication or his fortifying dishes, she would stare in silence like a disinterested spectator watching a soccer match whose outcome did not concern her.

"It's finished. You can come in," Bon said, still wiping away the spots of blood. But the blood had leaked into the cracks in the lime: it was impossible to completely eliminate the traces. In the meantime, Bon's precious member had swollen. That night, he didn't dare sleep in his underwear, so he wrapped a large towel around his thighs. Fortunately, it was cold outside, so he immediately pulled the covers over himself before Mien noticed anything. Anyway, she never looked at him. She stayed lying down, her eyes fixed on the mosquito netting, her hands on her forehead, or she turned her back to him. Usually, this humiliation was an insidious form of torture for Bon. But at the moment, it was just his luck. Mien had no idea what had just happened and he was able to keep his secret for two weeks, the time it took his wounded member to shrink to normal size.

Bon's efforts were not entirely in vain. His health improved a bit. He was able to eat an extra bowl of rice per meal, and he could accompany the goats out on to the rocky hillside slopes to gather virility grass. This improvement seemed to excite him, but whenever he was about to make love to Mien, his confidence would evaporate. Their marital bed was unlike any other battlefield he had known. He couldn't raise his fist toward the flag and vow to exterminate the enemy . . . Still, he knew that his determination was fierce, knew that he was lucky enough to be sowing seed on fertile ground, a promised land that any man would dream of. He tried to bolster his faith, thinking of his most beautiful hopes the way a devout follower would recite his prayers morning and night so that these aspirations would flood his body and soul, metamorphosing into a material force . . .

But as soon as he mounted Mien, her motionless body rigid, her absent face turned away from him, her spirit wandering in some remote, inaccessible land—all this took his breath away. He suddenly felt alone, as terrified as a child climbing trees with no one to catch him. And the despair would quickly snuff out the flame of his virility. With each passing day he began to resemble someone swimming against the current. At any moment a sudden gush of water would smash him against the rocks, or push him into the abyss.

Mien stood far, far away, on the opposite shore, her eyes fixed on a horizon that belonged to her alone, at a great distance from Bon. She lived by his side, but she was like a sleepwalker, lost in this world that excluded him. As for his sister and her filthy brood of kids, they lived like wild animals, like weeds, unconscious of their own existence. How could he expect them to understand his suffering?

In the vacillating light of dawn, the bunches of tender green flowers broke his heart. They were at once silky soft and poisonous, crushing all willpower and patience within him. He tossed his sickle and his rucksack down and rolled on the ground in agony. He wanted to scream and shout, to smash the façade of this peaceful sky that hung over the valley. But a herd of goats was grazing on the neighboring hillside. Their keepers were probably nearby and he did not want to be taken for a madman. If he wasn't careful, they would lock him up in a camp for the mentally ill. And there he would truly go insane and die inside the walls of the prison. He resigned himself to pummeling his thighs, hips, and chest. But this physical pain gave him no peace. A vast expanse of nomadic flowers, an emerald sea across the sky dancing with waves, wild yellow and white butterflies, and dragonflies in heat . . . Why couldn't he live their innocent, joyful existence? Why couldn't he transform himself into this strange flower that lived but a few hours, only the fullest, happiest, and proudest? Incapable of restraining himself any longer, he cried out, "Oh sergeant, oh sergeant, I'm so unhappy!"

This cry was partly choked in his throat, for he had not forgotten the presence of the goats and the herdsmen on the opposite hill. He felt his vocal cords tremble under the pressure of the imprisoned sounds.

"Sergeant, oh sergeant . . ."

Bon watched a ladybug with its red shell climb a blade of grass. The bug shimmered as if it had been underwater—or had he merely seen it through tears?

Suddenly, he could see him, the sergeant—he was right there at his side. Overjoyed, Bon got up, but the sergeant raised a hand, gesturing him to wait.

"Stay right where you are; don't tire yourself out."

"Oh sergeant, I'm so miserable."

"I know."

"Sergeant, I miss you."

"I miss you, too."

"Why didn't you come back to see me?"

"I wanted to, but we belong to two different worlds. Who can pass the gates of heaven?"

"I don't want to live anymore."

"Don't say such things."

"I can't . . ."

"I know you're suffering, but . . . whatever happens . . . you must summon the courage to live. You survived all those long years of war. You don't have the right to die."

"But I don't want to live!" Bon screamed.

The sergeant pointed a finger at him. "Quiet!"

He fell silent, gazed at Bon for a few seconds, and then spoke again, his voice filled with reproach. "How can a man be so pitiful? And you cry, on top of it all!"

The sergeant shook his head.

The ladybug glistened in the dew. Time slowed, crawling along in silence with this tiny insect. The sergeant turned his head to survey the field of flowers, then sighed.

"It doesn't matter . . . Go ahead, weep . . . Weep to ease your heart."

13

The boy was sleeping soundly. Now the two women were alone in the spacious house. Autumn was already waning, but the last red peonies of the season were ablaze in a final, passionate burst on the other side of the garden wall. The peaceful, silent atmosphere was disturbed only by the loud cackling of a rooster circling a hen. Hearing these amorous cries, Auntie Huyen and Mien turned. The old woman shook her head as she swung the hammock that held her nephew.

"What a devil! That rooster never stops."

Mien got up without a word, took a pebble, and hurled it at the immodest bird.

"Get out. You're hurting our ears."

The hen was pecking at grains of paddy rice. It let out a throaty cry and fled toward the kitchen. The rooster chased after the hen at breakneck speed, but when it arrived at the wall, it realized that its object of desire had escaped into the kitchen. The space fell back into silence. All one could hear was the creaking of the hammock, the monotonous music that accompanied life in the mountains. Auntie Huyen looked up.

"Did you go out to the fields this morning? How's the ground?"

"Very dry, sterile. The best land was allocated a long time ago."

"Yes, the tardy buffalo must drink murky water... There are so many families with handicapped veterans and soldiers who died for the country. You know the returning, demobilized veterans must be last on the list. And, of course, everyone was thinking Bon was really dead."

"Being really dead would be a solution, now that he doesn't know what to do to make a living, and half dead as he is."

"I know you can't live forever on Hoan's money. It's a question of dignity. No one with any sense of face could ignore it. Does he ever talk about it?"

"He says he has to 'cure' himself first. After that, he claims he's going to redo everything."

"After? When is that?"

"I don't know. For the moment, he's incapable of doing anything. He's tried to harrow the fields twice now, and both times he's fallen ill and taken to bed."

"So what are you planning to live on then?"

"I don't know."

"You can't go on like this, with your eyes shut, my niece. If we overgraze, the mountains will be barren. You've got to have a long-term plan. All the money you've given him for medication, the billy goats—why, it would be enough for someone else to build a house with!"

"I was planning to start a plantation, but I got discouraged. I don't know why."

The two women said nothing for a long time. Suddenly, Mien broke the silence. "That day, why didn't you try to stop me from going back to live with him?"

"How could I have known?"

"You knew it . . . but you said nothing . . . You knew it, but that night when I asked you to stay at the house with me . . ."

The old woman sighed. Mien continued, insistent. "Why did you leave when I needed you to stay?"

Auntie Huyen sighed again. "I was afraid," she finally said. She turned and looked at Mien, her eyes dark and filled with shadows. "You know very well that when Bon came back here it gave everyone a chance to curse us. That day, they all thronged here in a crowd to see Bon, like he was a long lost son or a brother. They told him no one had looked after Ta and the kids in his absence. Even though his family has been in Mountain Hamlet for generations, none of them has ever succeeded. Bon was the first to succeed, the only one who managed to get an education. He had a chance to rise above poverty, to live a prosperous, honorable life. And then he had to leave for the front. When he returned, they all came to gape at the man who had stepped out of his own grave. And they all whispered in my ear, 'I dare you to guess which one Mien will choose. The first husband, out of honor, or the second one, for the money?' And then there were the rumors... 'The virtuous woman always returns to her first love. As for the fallen woman, even if she wanted to, it wouldn't be easy for her to return to Bon. Her Auntie Huyen will force her niece to live with the city businessman because he rakes in the money for her as well as her niece... Ever since that Hoan-Mien husband-wife team has succeeded, that old woman has filled her own coffers. Why, she lives a life of leisure.'"

Mien interrupted her: "So you were afraid that they would call you a selfish woman if you advised me to stay with Hoan?"

Auntie Huyen fell silent. Mien knelt down, lowering her head onto the old woman's knees. Auntie Huyen looked down at the silky black hair of the only niece who had stood by her, who was like a daughter granted to her by fate. This hair was no longer adorned with a sprig of basil or a grapefruit flower. And Mien no longer wore purple or emerald-green clothes. She had put them all away. Now all she wore was black. Unable to contain herself any longer, Auntie Huyen placed a hand on Mien's shoulder.

"I'm guilty vis-à-vis your mother... Guilty... But I didn't dare do otherwise. You see, right from the start, from the first day you brought Bon home, I didn't like him. And when you don't like someone, you can only find fault with him. I was afraid I had been unfair, that I would make a mistake if I advised you not to marry him. I thought you were an adult, capable of making your own decisions. It was wartime. He was the only boy left in the entire village the same age as you. Who else would you marry? After all, you weren't going to marry an old widower or wait until some of the other boys grew up. Adolescence, the spring of a young girl's life, lasts only a brief moment. I resigned myself. Now, everything has changed. You have a son. Use this as a reason to leave Bon."

Mien suddenly looked up, glaring at the old woman, furious. "Oh God, why didn't you tell me? You were more intelligent, more lucid than I was. I was completely overwhelmed, just a child . . . And I was afraid."

Auntie Huyen nodded. "Yes, I knew you were afraid. I was afraid, too. And so was Hoan. Just as terrified as you and I were. We were afraid that people would say we were dishonorable, ingrates who were only chasing money. As for Hoan, he feared they would reproach him not just for having gotten to stay back in the village instead of going to war, but also for having stolen happiness from a veteran who had sacrificed for his country. In the end, everything happened because of a single word: 'fear.' "

"You saw it all so clearly. Why do you only speak out now?"

"No . . . no . . . At the time, I wasn't conscious of it. It was only when you returned to Bon's place that I began to think. Who can pretend to know everything right away? The ancestors were right: When a child has all his teeth, we must stop giving lessons."

She stopped speaking. Stunned, Mien stared out into the garden. Something in her face troubled the old woman; she seemed lost, distant, as hard as granite. Never had this beautiful, familiar face seemed so strange. Auntie Huyen didn't dare say more. Then Mien got up.

"I have to go."

"Where?"

"Back to the house."

"Which one?"

"My house, the one that belongs to us."

Auntie Huyen looked Mien in the eyes and began to understand.

"This morning I went to see Mr. Lu out in the fields. He asked me to come see him, to discuss my case."

"You must be discreet. Try not to start the rumor mill."

"I don't care. They can spy on me all they like!" Mien snapped. Then she picked up her hat, leaned over to kiss her sleeping boy, and hastened toward the gate. Auntie Huyen followed her with her eyes. When Mien had disappeared beyond the gate, the old woman sighed again, rocking the hammock more quickly, as she started to sing a lullaby.

Mien walked briskly down the road that she had avoided the day she had gone back to live with Bon. It was a familiar road and she knew every bamboo hedge, tree, and intersection. Both sides were bordered with tall, green bamboo hedges and the reeds at the base swayed in the wind. Here, the air seemed clearer, the blue of the sky deeper, the clouds more animated. Like her heart, everything here seemed to stir and sway. Hoan wouldn't be there; Mien already knew that. Mr. Lu had told her, that same morning, that Hoan had left to go to buy some goods in Nha Trang. But her heart was racing as if, in an instant, she were going to see Hoan's beaming face appear from behind the door. Instead, she saw an old neighbor approaching.

"Ah, Mrs. Mien, it's been so long."

"Good day, sir."

"Are you out for a walk, or were you paying a visit to your old home?"

"Good day, sir."

"How are you?"

"Fine, thanks."

"Come by and see me if you have a moment, later."

"Yes, good day, sir."

Mien replied mechanically, oblivious to this man who watched her go with a surprised, inquisitive look. A few minutes later, she had arrived at the gate. She glanced at the walls of the enclosure, the two pillars, the handle of the copper bell. These inanimate, unconscious objects seemed to her like beloved, long lost friends. Mien pulled on the cord to the bell and waited carefully to hear the joyful carillon reverberate and then softly fade away. Once, she never even paid attention to it. Now, after having lived in a poor, deserted area, this carillon was a beacon to her, calling up memories of holidays and festivals.

"Hello, Madame, please come in." Mr. Lu had been their employee. He had retained his old way of speaking, the old politesse. Mien was still not used to such manners and so she stammered, "Yes—yes, uncle."

The old man stepped aside for Mien, then meticulously padlocked the gate.

Hoan, darling, why aren't you here?

Mien spoke this reproach silently, though she knew it was meaningless. She surveyed the old house; it looked like an opulent mausoleum whose masters had abandoned it, but that was still swept and polished daily by a faithful housekeeper. The once warm, bustling house now seemed huge, vacant. The clock that ticked out the time was the noisiest object in the empty, silent space.

"Mr. Hoan told me you liked cleanliness. He asked me to sweep the house and the courtyard and to clean the dishes in the pantry every day. Please, come in."

The old man gestured enthusiastically to the kitchen. Here it was, her true dominion. Glistening, neatly stacked pots and pans silently reflected the faces in her memory; the mornings redolent of orange and grapefruit, filled with birdsong and her son's happy babbling; the fragrance of jasmine tea and strong, filtered coffee, of sticky rice bubbling on the hearth and fried rice with egg; the evenings heady with the scent of ripe fruit fallen in the garden, the perfume of flowers faded in the blazing sun, and the delicious aroma of dinner. Mien gazed, lost, at each object, stroking the bottom of a pot, caressing the handle of one of the large porcelain Chinese ladles, remembering with emotion how Hoan had bought these fragile objects in the Ben Thanh Market in Saigon, how he had wrapped them in straw in a wooden crate before shipping them back to her. She opened the cabinet, admiring the bowls and plates made in Japan and Jiangxi. Her special stewing pot—he had brought it back from Da Nang after a friend had given him a recipe for chicken. She sat down at the large oval table, big enough for receiving at least twenty guests, its surface as shiny as a mirror. The chairs, neatly arranged, were smooth and so clean that they held no warmth of human presence. Poor Hoan, he had worked so hard to build this kitchen for her, and now it was useless.

Mr. Lu set the kettle on the fire and slowly lit it. Almost instantly, Mien saw the flames dance under the tiny copper kettle that she had once used to prepare tea.

The man poured water over the tea. It had been a long time since Mien had smelled the scent of jasmine tea. At Bon's, all year round they drank an infusion of leaves they gathered in the forest. Mr. Lu unwrapped a bean cake for her. "Here, please have some."

"Why thank you, uncle."

Mien was touched but not surprised by the old man's considera-tion. This was Hoan's paradise, after all. He had begun to build it from the moment they met on that hillside as the winds blew in from Laos. This paradise had been abandoned when she left with her sack of virgin grass and her black nunlike clothes to follow the foggy road back to Bon's place.

"Please . . . the cakes are fresh . . . Mr. Hoan brings them every week, for all of us."

Unless he was called away on some special business, Hoan came back to the hamlet every Sunday. On Monday morning, when she went, she could see that the closet was stuffed with goodies for little Hanh—a new toy or some new clothes. Sometimes, there were Da Lat roses set in a crystal vase, sometimes even gifts that were clearly for her. Traces of his passage. Everything bore his seal, his face, his shadow. "Madame, Mr. Hoan gave me your set of keys. I didn't go to see you unannounced for fear of arousing suspicions. I've waited a long time. Today is the first day there's been a chance . . . Please take them."

He fished a set of keys out of his pocket and set them down on the table in front of her. This set had a pocketknife and a can opener attached and belonged to Hoan. Mien's set was already in his hands.

"Mr. Hoan wanted me to make sure you wouldn't have to work in the fields. If you were planning to with Mr. Bon, I can hire people to help you. All the old plantations here belong to you now. You can do with them as you see fit."

Mien didn't know what to say. She felt neither sad nor happy, merely lost. The man's voice rose again, clearly. "It is my job to submit accounts to you. If you'll kindly excuse me a moment, please."

He climbed the stairs. A minute later, he came back with several thick school notebooks and set them down in front of Mien. She flipped through them in silence. Suddenly, as if hypnotized, she took out the set of keys and climbed the stairs. She turned toward their bedroom and opened the door as slowly and carefully as an old woman. The room was exactly as it had been when she left, every object still in its place. The window onto the garden had been left wide open. A thick bunch of heather was in full bloom in a vase on the bedside table. The large mirror, the windows—everything shone without a trace of dust. The lacquer box that held her pins, her hair clips, sat atop an armoire with three doors. The bed, immaculate, was fitted with clean sheets. Two white pillows and a special pillow in the shape of a half-moon, which belonged to little Hanh, were set on top of the covers. Everything seemed to be waiting, waiting. Mien opened the armoire. Right before her eyes lay a large wad of bills wrapped in a letter.

Darling Mien . . .

A time will come when you will need this. You must not destroy your health or martyr yourself. It would be senseless, idiotic. You may no longer be my wife, but you will always be Hanh's mother. I can at least look after you as I would a little sister. I can't bear to leave you in poverty. I will remain, as always, by your side.

Hoan

Mien glanced again at Hoan's signature at the bottom of the letter. She sat down at the foot of the bed, their bed, and felt that this was truly her place, her lair. At the same time, she was as fearful as if she had wandered into a strange forest. She probably no longer had the right to sit here, in this peaceful, tidy room, for she was the one who had left Hoan to share another man's bed. Her body now smelled of Bon's sweat and stinking breath, it was covered with his frantic, lustful kisses, marked by couplings that no purifying bath could wash away.

Why? Why? Why have I done this?

Because of President Hien's moralizing lecture? Or the warning that was as if writ large on this powerful man's back as he turned to go?

Or maybe it had been all the ghosts from her past, the ones that still haunted and threatened her? All summer long and now, soon, all autumn long, under Bon's shabby roof, she had searched for an answer. She stared at the web of mosquito netting filled with fallen lemon-tree leaves, where lizards stalked mosquitoes all day long. She searched the twisted, dusty branches of the lilacs that swung in the wind at twilight. She scoured the sad horizon of all the sunless days when the dark shroud of the forest swayed in the distance. She had searched and she had waited, hoping to see a face emerge, be it a genie or a demon, that would give her an answer. But all these spirits and ghosts seemed to have left for the mountains. No one had answered her.

At night, after Bon's pathetic attempts to make love, she had tried to find an answer within herself. But even this seemed impossible. One night, after almost a week of living with him, she had pushed him out of bed before vomiting, unable to stand his fetid breath. Ever since, Bon hadn't dared kiss her on the mouth. He merely pressed his face against her belly, showering her with his pathetic, frantic kisses. Mien felt a mixture of pity and horror. Why had the heavens cursed the two of them, condemned them to this existence? On the first day of their life back together, when Bon had given her the yellow, scented soap he had saved in its torn package, Mien had read the truth in his eyes. It wasn't just a lovesick gaze; it was the pleading look of a dog to its mistress, the look of a man who hung over an abyss, desperately clinging to a loose rock, suspended between life and death. She knew that Bon loved her madly. But it was a still-born love. She tried to conjure up her youth the way you would invoke the presence of a dead soul. The gentle babbling of a brook. Slippery rocks. That row of flame trees along the road that led to the place where they had first met. The fragrant hills dotted with pineapple bushes. The first kiss, not on the lips, but on the ear, and the trace of a bruise that lasted more than a week. But the brook, with each passing day, had grown dry. The crimson flame trees had faded to purple. Their dead flowers littered the ground, lay wilting at the base of the trees, the wind churning them with the rotting leaves and the dust. The dead souls floated, hovered for a few hours, and then disappeared at dawn. The crowing of the cocks at dawn.

Mien . . . Mien . . . I love you.

Bon's refrain, which he had used a thousand times, grew weary, like a candle flickering more dimly with each passing minute. She had given him money to treat himself, to buy his revitalizing foods. She had bought him three new suits and a German fur jacket, which was every mountain man's dream. And she had done this when she knew, in her heart, that she was just repaying his pitiful love with money.

She knew it, and she also knew that any love that she had ever felt for him could never be revived.

Even the pity slowly dried up. Night after night, she watched him straining to sow a single seed in her body, as if she were watching someone climb a tree to gather honey, or a child playing with marbles. Sometimes with indifference, sometimes with repugnance. As soon as he had ejaculated, he would wither like a corpse. And she would get up to go boil water for her bath. The scent of the virgin grass would calm her, and she hoped that this infusion would help her erase all trace of this man that she no longer loved. He shouldn't have come back. When he was just a dead soul sitting on the altar to the ancestors he had been honored, even cherished. Every year, on his death anniversary, she would prepare five sumptuous platters of food and invite all his close friends to honor his memory. In the photo of him as a high school student that Mien set on the altar, just behind the ritual plate of five fruits, he appeared angelic, worthy of respect. And they would speak of him as a pure soul from some distant past, that heroic time when everyone had suffered together through all the ordeals and hardship of the war. He was one of the cloud of angels who had braved storms, who had been terrorized by tigers and wolves, who had endured the ravages of volcanoes, tidal waves, and fatal epidemics. But honoring Bon's memory was just an excuse for people in the village to gather together again, to relive the heroic dream, to open the door to a past full of sound and fury where they could still savor their glory and romanticize the tedium of their daily lives. At those moments, Mien had grown accustomed to thinking of him as a distant shadow, an innocent dream that held a stream as thin as a silver thread, a road lined with flame trees that bloomed like a fresh pair of lips. Everything about him had belonged to this world. Like the backdrops in the theaters in town.

But Bon had come back. The little angel of their dreams had suddenly been transformed into a man of flesh and blood, with dark, sad eyes, cheeks sunken by bouts of chronic malaria, and pale lips that exhaled putrid, hellish-smelling breath. This remote, nebulous phantom was suddenly a man frantic with lust who struggled to impregnate her every night, panting the same refrain, like a grave digger laboring over a tomb. And each of his attempts at lovemaking ended in failure, like a burial gone wrong.

Why, why, why?

Night after night she had washed herself with the infusion of virgin grass, meticulously scrubbing every inch of her body, as if his kisses reeking of carrion could somehow soak into her body and change its color. A person can't force herself to love. Love isn't a burden to bear, or a bowl of bitter medicine. If it were, she would have gladly submitted. But love was love; either you felt it or you didn't, and so she was powerless. With each passing day, her life with Bon slipped outside of her real life, like a plank of driftwood carried farther and farther from the shore.

The sunlight began to pour through the bars of the window. Mien suddenly realized it was time for dinner. She had prepared a gingered beef stew, but she still needed to go by the neighbor's house to buy some cabbage. The cabbage she herself had planted had been literally uprooted by Ta's kids. Mien locked the armoire and put the set of keys away in a drawer. The housekeeper was there waiting for her.

"Madame, do you need anything?"

"No thank you, uncle. I've put the set of keys in the top drawer of the chest over there."

"Mr. Hoan wanted you to keep them."

"No, you're here. I'll come back if I need to."

Mien was about to leave when the bell rang. Her son's voice echoed from the gate to the house: "Mommy, Mommy." She could hear his footsteps; he was running. A few seconds later, he entered the kitchen like a storm. "Mommy . . . you've come home!"

Mien lifted the little boy into her arms and hugged him to her, inhaling the familiar scent of his hair and skin. Suddenly, the house seemed to glow with a familiar light, filled with the fragrances and sounds of the past.

The little boy let out a squeal of delight and jumped back down to the ground. He had been waiting for this moment for so long without being able to say it. Suddenly, the expectancy contained in his young heart found words: "Mommy, come back and live with me here. Don't go back there anymore."

"Yes."

"Mommy, hold me tight."

But before she even had a chance to embrace him, the little boy had jumped back into her arms, smothering her face, nose, cheeks, and lips with kisses. Then he jumped down to the ground and grabbed her by the hand. "Come, I'm taking you to the garden."

Auntie Huyen and the housekeeper watched the child, stunned. Dazed, unable to speak herself, Mien followed him. This was the first time he had taken the initiative to take her on a walk.

"Mommy, when I grow up, I'm going to trap a yellow-beaked robin for you. I'll ask Papa to buy us a parrot that knows how to talk like Mr. Khuong's. We'll put him in a beautiful cage right outside the front door. Every morning I'll feed him millet and water. Little Hon from Mr. Khuong's told me how to feed parrots, you know."

The little boy continued chattering away, without hesitating or stumbling over his words. Then he stopped and looked his mother in the eyes. "Mommy, laugh . . . Why haven't I seen you laugh for such a long time?"

His clear eyes were fixed on hers, serious, expectant. Mien realized suddenly that in the last few months he had matured. The vague, indirect answers she had gotten from Auntie Huyen and Hoan hadn't fooled her. He hadn't been himself that summer and autumn. His little heart had burned with the desire to see his mother come back home, and now, underneath his frail, angelic appearance, he had become a little old man at just five years old. Mien felt the tears spring to her eyes, but she held them back and wriggled free of his grasp.

"Let's not go out . . . Let's go and play in your room."

They stepped back over the threshold. When they reached the main room, the little boy took Mien's hand and pulled her toward the room. "Come, Mommy, come."

He pulled off his sandals and jumped onto the bed, dragging Mien until she fell on it, too. So mother and child found themselves in bed, locked in an embrace.

"Hold me tight, just like Daddy does."

Mien slipped her arm under his neck and asked, "Like that, right?"

"Almost, Mommy."

"What else?"

"I want you to massage my back . . . like that . . . from my bottom up . . . just like Daddy does it."

"Oh, so Daddy does it better than Mommy now?"

Suddenly she felt an odd pang of jealousy. Before the little boy could reply, she asked, "So your Daddy gives you nice hugs, huh?"

"Yes, every Sunday, when he comes back, he takes me here. He lies down on the edge of the bed, with me in the middle."

"And then?"

"He massages my back, scratches my head, and says, 'In a few days, when she has finished the pepper fields, your Mommy's coming home. She's gonna kiss you and sing you lullabies and make you cakes, just like she used to.'"

At the mention of these familiar sweets, the little boy sat bolt upright. "Mommy, you'll make the salty cakes *and* the sweet cakes, won't you?"

"Yes, both of them."

Mien let herself go, and as she did an idea occurred to her. *Why not? Why not? I'll come back here, I'll make cakes for him, bathe him in this bathroom, gather oranges, and trap robins with him in this garden.*

This thought set her brain on fire, and as through the flickering of the flames, she could see the faces of everyone in the village, the restless, swirling crowd of ghosts, the president of the commune and the invisible threat scrawled on his back. A wave of hatred swept over her. She longed to scream, to curse them all. Day after day, all through this unhappy summer and autumn, she had lived locked in a dark room, sewing and patching up clothes that didn't need a single stitch, watching the sky slowly change color above the ramshackle kitchen, chasing chickens that pecked at the garden, toiling to cook two meals over a hearth made of dried grass that stung her eyes with acrid, asphyxiating smoke. And, night after night, she had submitted to Bon's desperate lovemaking, like some kind of human mattress. She had accepted this madness because she was afraid and because she had yielded to the will of dead souls. Was she in fact a coward to have submitted to them so easily?

"Mommy, Mommy . . ."

The insistent call of her little boy brought Mien back to reality. The violent urge to rebel, like a fermentation too long repressed, exploded and galvanized her.

"Very well. Tomorrow, I'll make you those sweet and salty cakes. I'll definitely make them. Tomorrow."

She took the child in her arms and left the room.

Mr. Lu and Auntie Huyen were still drinking tea.

"Could you soak about two pounds of sticky rice for me? You could grind it for me, too. I'm going to be making cakes for Hanh."

"I'll see to it, Madame," Mr. Lu replied.

Auntie Huyen looked at Mien, but didn't dare question her further. She turned to Hanh. "What else have you asked your mother to do now?"

Mien interrupted her. "I'm the one who wanted to do it." She kissed the little boy one last time. "Now, you stay with your Auntie. I've got to be going."

Mien walked toward the street. Little Hanh watched her obediently, not daring to run after her. When she reached the gate, Mien suddenly turned and walked back to them. "Oh, Mr. Lu, I almost forgot. Please soak a pound of green beans for the sweet cakes. With the leftover beans, I'll make a pudding."

Mien's eyes sparkled. Tomorrow, at dawn, she wouldn't just be coming back to make cakes, but to reenter her world.

14

"Cry . . . cry to let go of your pain."

The sergeant whispered softly, gently. Not once during all those long years of war spent together had he yelled at his men, not once had he behaved arrogantly. He had a handsome smile and skin so fair that even the tiny scars of adolescent acne were still visible.

Bon's tears wet his cheeks and trickled down into the roots of his hair. "Sergeant, ohhh sergeant, I feel like crying again."

"Go ahead. Cry some more. It doesn't matter."

"You won't be angry with me?"

"No . . . I know lots of men who cry just like women."

"And you, have you ever cried?"

"No."

"That's not true. You forget the day that malaria almost killed me. I was at death's door. When I woke up the next day, the nurse told me you wept buckets!"

"Ridiculous." The sergeant scoffed and turned away, ashamed.

Satisfied, Bon felt like laughing, even though his tears had barely dried. The tears had washed away the sadness. He wiped them with the sleeve of his shirt and sat up. The fields of flowers, the butterflies and dragonflies, everything seemed to sway and dance in the sunlight.

A ladybug climbed to the tip of a blade of grass and hopped over to his knee.

"Look, sergeant, she's so beautiful."

"Yes, she's magnificent."

"When you were little, did you try to chase crickets underground?"

"No, in the city it's hard to find them. I could only chase cicadas."

"Back in my village, there are so many varieties of crickets and cicadas. But I never had the time to play with them."

"To each his fate. But why not lie down and rest now? You lie down and I'll stay seated. Don't worry about me. I've been lying down for so many years that I'm rotting away."

"How can you rot so fast? It's a very dry corner."

"The ground may be dry, but in time all bones end up rotting. You'll see." He tapped lightly on Bon's shoulder. "You lie down now."

"With your permission, sir."

Bon lay down on the grass again. The vertebrae in his back relaxed. The ground under him was soft, warm, refreshing. The ladybug was still perched on his knee. Green flowers danced all around him. Beauty. His heartbeat slowed to its normal, peaceful rhythm. The pain was gone now.

"Do you miss me, sergeant?"

"Of course. Why else would I have come all the way back here?"

"Remember the days in the *khop* jungle?"

"I do."

"Remember those horrible birds that followed us?"

"Which ones?"

"The vultures. There were four of them, males and females, and they followed us every step of the way for days. Bastards . . . I'll never forget them."

Bon suddenly saw the sky above him rise up, higher and higher, infinite. Images dissolved and blurred. Gone were the dancing butterflies, gone the darting dragonflies, gone the drifting white clouds and the dense, cobalt blue light; nothing was left but a vast space filled with ash, without the slightest wind. And this empty space began to spin, slowly, like a gigantic yet invisible weather vane that the wind of the universe had set in motion. Transfixed, Bon watched the slow, spinning rotation of the vane in the sky, without noticing that it was sucking him toward its center, like iron dust to a magnet.

"Sergeant, help, sergeant!"

Bon tried to scream, but couldn't fully open his mouth. His tongue stayed glued to his palate, and his throat constricted as if he were being choked or strangled. The smoke of the bombs mingled with the dust, invading his lungs. He realized he would die if he didn't manage to spit out the dust and saliva that blocked his throat. He mustered all his strength and spat five or six times in rapid succession, sending stars exploding in his bulging eyes. Dizzy and pale, now, he saw black and yellow fireflies darting through the air. He suddenly closed his eyes and covered them with his hands. When he regained consciousness and was able to pull his hands away, the vast swirl of ashes had disappeared. On the violet horizon facing him hung a bloody, motionless sun. Hill #327 had been bombed to a pulp.

"Sergeant, oh, sergeant!"

As if in response to his cries, three grenades exploded one after the other. A column of dust billowed over the other side of the hill. The shattered, upturned earth was as crumbly as flour. The slightest noise sent the dust swirling again in the air. After the explosion, Bon's cries faded out. "Ser . . . geant . . . ser . . . geant."

The sounds of the grenades were only echoes now, reverberating across the hillsides strewn with corpses and debris, above a churning sea of flames. Billows of smoke rose and curled toward the sky. The sun was tinted a color somewhere between congealed blood and the orange saffron of monks' robes. As if these tortured, twisting curls of smoke were whispered prayers, the rasping, labored breathing of a land intoning a chant of forgiveness, imploring with each hollow, rhythmic beat of the wooden tocsins in the distant pagodas. Bon listened, hoping to hear his sergeant's moans and calls, however feeble. In the village, they had called him Bon, or "bat," because he had the finely tuned ear of a bat. But in this silence all he could detect was the ticking of his watch, the one that a guy he called Bitter Loi had given him shortly before he died of chronic dysentery. Loi had been in his unit and had come from Ninh Binh province.

Here, Bon, you have this; it's worth nothing to me in the next world.

The old Swiss timepiece was still there, in working order, even after it had been buried in innumerable bombings. Bon leaned over the watch, pondering it, and murmured, "Loi, wherever you are, show me the way to the sergeant. He was good to all of us without exception."

The second hand passed forty, fifty, sixty. Soon two minutes would have passed, and not the slightest sound. The swollen, crimson sun dipped behind the hillside until all that was left was a half-circle surrounded by violet clouds. Another grenade exploded, propelling pieces of cloth and something that looked like an arm into the air. Then everything fell back into silence. The forest behind him began to darken. Another few minutes and it would all be swallowed up by the night. Bon panicked; if he didn't find the sergeant quickly, in the next fifteen or thirty minutes, the American planes would come back and spray the corpses with gasoline and set everything aflame. Then, there would be no trace of the men who had lived here.

"Sergeant, oh, sergeant!" Bon shouted, listening to his own quavering echo. Birds flew up, panic-stricken, from the forest behind him and then scattered.

"Sergeant, where are you? Do you hear me? Sergeant? Sergeant? Sergeant! Sergeant!"

He screamed like a madman. "Sergeant!"

One last time. One last scream. A scream choked with tears. An adieu. Bon swallowed his pasty saliva and salty tears. He tightened his belt and felt his water pouch; there were just a few mouthfuls left. He cast a final glance at the guard post before running into the forest. And just at that instant, he heard the sergeant's voice.

"I . . . I'm . . . I'm here . . ."

The voice was clear, but feeble, a thread of sound filtering through a black mass of corpses, of broken beams and pulverized cement. Bon turned and began fumbling through the rubble, pulling and dragging corpses from one another, making no distinction between those that were already cold and those that were still warm. Horrified, he continued to rummage and search, shoving aside bricks and shards of cement. The bombs had mangled and smashed everything—men and objects alike. The sergeant wasn't even in the last layer of corpses; two more bodies lay beneath his. It was a miracle that he had survived under the weight of so many corpses and beams. As soon as Bon had extricated him from the rubble, he hastily slung the man over his shoulder and ran into the dark forest. The sergeant's arms hung limply around Bon's neck, and they grew heavier and heavier. A water tin banged painfully against Bon's throat, but he didn't dare stop and push it aside. Instinctively, he knew that the planes would soon come and transform everything into a sea of flames. The sergeant was much taller and heavier than he was, but Bon was oblivious to that as he ran at breakneck speed toward the bridge that lay just ahead of him. On one side, death, and on the other, life. In the end, Bon managed to escape. He had barely reached the edge of the forest when the planes descended, ripping through the sky with their shrill cries. The red lights under their wings, at the tails of the planes, blinked continuously, like giant, scarlet eyes. Then the planes formed a circle, and the circle slowly closed. Containers of food floated and then fell onto the hillside. A few minutes later, the planes banked and soared back into the sky. A round of bombs rained down on Hill #327. The flames rose, toward the sky, clearly illuminating shreds of clothes that flew up off the ground, half-dancing half-burning, carried by the wind. A few solitary trees stood burning, boiled alive in their own sap.

Bon wiped the sweat from his face and neck. On his shoulders he felt the dead weight of the sergeant's head. He too seemed to stare at the flames, his kind, dreamy gaze slowly slackening, turning dull as it drifted toward another world. "The fire . . . it's burning . . . Then . . . everything will turn to ash," he murmured.

"Sergeant, are you wounded? Please, let me see," Bon pleaded.

The sergeant shook his head. "No, no, it's useless."

"I've got one more bandage left. Let me see . . ."

The sergeant shook his head again. He seemed to smile, a strained, difficult smile through pallid lips. "Don't waste your strength . . . I won't make . . . it . . . The main artery, it's been cut."

Bon screamed, "The main artery? Why didn't you ask the nurse to apply a tourniquet?"

The sergeant didn't reply. His eyes closed. Bon suddenly realized that his question was absurd. How would he have even found a nurse at a time like this? They had only five nurses and three had died right at the beginning of the battle. The two surviving nurses were carrying the wounded back behind the front lines. Had they escaped alive or had they too been crushed under the bombs?

But Bon couldn't give up; he began to search for the wound on the sergeant's body. As long as the man was alive, there was still hope. A piece of shrapnel had severed the sergeant's left thigh. Blood had co-agulated on the pants, leaving the fabric as stiff and rough as a co-conut shell.

"Sergeant, I'm going to cut your pants open with my dagger," Bon cried.

The sergeant shook his head. "No."

"I've lost my dagger . . . I'll use yours," Bon continued.

Bon felt for the sergeant's belt. The sergeant lifted a hand to stop Bon, but his hand fell back again, limp and inert. His eyelashes fluttered a few times and he slowly opened his eyes.

"I can see a red sky. Red. Like the flame trees. Like roses. Just beautiful."

He spoke each word painfully, slowly, as if his tongue grew shorter, stiffer with each breath. But his voice was clear. A stream of light flickered briefly on his face. He smiled. "So that's how it is . . . the end of a life . . . Just as well . . . in the end."

The light flashed through the sergeant's eyes one last time, as if to take in the image of the cruel, blazing inferno that once bore the name 327, this fire that had taken so many lives on both sides. No one would know how many bones had been reduced to ash, swept into the dust, and then carried off by the wind. In this cloud of ash, how many had been lucky enough to taste love's savor? How many innocent, naïve young men like him had never even touched a woman? Even if they had read hundreds of novels and seen dozens of films, boasted and bragged about making love as if they were veritable Don Juans.

... *Life is a game... but it's a game we must play...*

A thin ray of light streaked across the sergeant's eyes. Thoughts bobbed and drifted like clouds, then vanished, leaving behind the sky flaming with crimson flowers. In the distance, majestic tiers of azure sky overflowed with sunlight that poured down. And these blue spaces pulled him into their vortex. The sun stopped spreading along the ground and condensed into shimmering currents that sucked him toward their center, his soul rising, as light as gossamer, floating and hovering like a bee or a butterfly's wing, scattering like pollen, vaporous and ethereal. And these shafts of light rose higher and higher, lighter and lighter, before they twisted into curls of smoke, like sparkling drifts of clouds gathering into a human form, a young man, a stranger who both resembled and did not resemble him, a copy of an infant God.

When the sergeant's soul had reached the distant blue of the horizon, the body Bon still held in his arms changed color. The face, once as white as if it had been sculpted from marble, turned to gray, the eyelashes stiffened, became motionless, and the arms slackened and fell limp.

"Sergeant!" Bon screamed, his voice cracking. He held the sergeant by the shoulders and shook him violently.

"Sergeant! Don't abandon me!"

The sergeant's limp arms began to gesture wildly from Bon's violent shakes. His face was blank, totally dark, distant. There was no sergeant there anymore. He had gone. Forever. Departed for a sky blooming with roses and flame trees.

"Sergeant! Sergeaaaant!

Tears spilled silently from Bon's eyes. If only he knew how to lament, to chant the songs the elders knew by heart, the ones they used to send off departing souls. Perhaps this would have eased his suffering. But he didn't. And so the pain swirled round and round inside of him.

Sergeant, do you remember the day we met? I was just seventeen and already married. You were twenty-three and still a virgin. Your eighteen- and nineteen-year-old troops were all married. We farmers marry young to make sure we have heirs before going onto the battlefield. You city boys were so naïve . . . The very first night, we tossed you into some woman's bed. Just to see how far a city boy's penis could go . . . Two days later, you threw us a banquet with all the sticky rice and sweet pudding we could eat.

Bon wiped his tears and dragged the corpse to the foot of a nearby tree. He leaned his back against the trunk to rest. The sergeant's water tin slapped against Bon's Adam's apple, crippling him with pain. Bon lifted the sergeant's arm off his neck and put the water tin back in place. The arm had already gone cold.

The limbs are the first to go cold. Then the stomach, the chest, and the head. With loving men, the heart is the last to go . . . . That's what they say. Sergeant, you were the most loving person I ever met. Your heart must still be warmer than all the rest . . .

Bon slipped his hand under the sergeant's left breast, and felt a current of warmth slowly spreading.

The flames on Hill #327 slowly subsided, flickering softly. It was no longer a three-yard-high sea of flames but a vast, craggy, undulating expanse sparkling with small bonfires. And between the small blazes lay carpets of still smoldering embers dusted with silver-gray ash. From time to time, the wind lifted them in sprays like fireworks, at night, on Lunar New Year in times of peace and prosperity. Bon leaned over the sergeant's face. But the light that still emanated from the hillside was now too feeble to illuminate it. In another instant, when the fire was extinguished, everything would sink into darkness. There would be no one left with him but the corpse he still held in his arms. This would be his first time alone, without a comrade. Ever since his recruitment until this disastrous battle, he had always lived in a group, surrounded by his friends and fellow soldiers. Now, he was going to taste the bitterness of solitude.

He glanced around. The sky seemed more vast, more mysterious, and the landscape more devastating, more desolate, than any carnage he had ever witnessed. He was terrified. Of what, he didn't know. Spies? Tigers? Wolves? Or ghosts? Perhaps all of them. He still had a rifle and a few bullets. He had lost his dagger, but now he had the sergeant's, which was even newer, thinner, sharper. He could even fight the commandos if he was alert, if he could bear to hide in the darkness of the underbrush. As for the wild animals, after such a fierce battle the place would be teeming with boars, bears, and old tigers who had fled the forest. And the ghosts? Yes . . . he probably feared them, too. There were the horrible, terrifying images that had been engraved in his memory from a very tender age and that had remained even after he had reached the age of reason. Now that he lit incense to his own deceased parents, he knew that the world beyond was peopled only with souls of fog and smoke, and that one day he, too, would join them there amid the shadows. All the same, it was difficult to surmount his fear. For him, the realm of the dead was a distant, remote place that terrorized the living, a world where light didn't emanate from the sun but from phosphorescent skulls that tiny, hairy, dirty demons paraded on the tips of spears made from human femurs. In this terrifying light, all skin was livid, bloodless, all eyes were just sockets, and all lips were the color of dried blood. This was the murky gathering place for all those who had been betrayed, tricked, martyred, for those who had never gotten to taste the sweet, young wine of the new harvest, for those who sacrificed themselves, body and soul, for an entire lifetime without attaining their goals. A place for the young men and women who died in their prime. And these hungry souls, these virgins, liked to torture those who have had the chance to drink life's sweet wine . . . Yes . . . Bon was afraid, this fear still lived in him, inextinguishable. Sometimes, the presence of his comrades helped him forget.

This was still the jungle, but it was so familiar to him. On the nights when they had all slept in hammocks hung from the tree trunks in tight rows, all you had to do was reach out a hand to touch your neighbor, lean your neck out to light a cigarette. Hundreds of hammocks created a warm atmosphere of security. The jungle became a cloak of foliage that shielded them from the mist even though their frantic eyes were always fixed on the sky, tracking the movements of enemy planes. But now the night seemed alien, sinister, to Bon. Bizarre green, hairy, sticky faces. Arms and legs severed from their bodies gesticulating like the tentacles of an octopus. Snakes swung from the branches of trees, their tongues clicking in hollow, dry echoes. In the rustling that agitated the treetops, Bon thought he saw ghosts moving, fierce, icy shadows that judged him, pondering the punishments that he deserved to suffer. They would rip out his tongue, hang him by his feet from the trees, inflict a slow, painful death by the steady pecking of birds. All that would be left of him would be a tuft of hair swinging in the middle of the leafy branches. Bon shuddered.

But as he imagined these scenes, an idea suddenly occurred to him: *If everyone becomes a ghost after death, the one I'm holding in my arms is the person closest to me, the man who has protected me in this world. The sergeant taught me how to put on my boots and pick my teeth, fold my mosquito net and organize my pack, even how to cook. He was the one who always took the blame for me with the lieutenant, who forgave me for losing a document, who gave me half of his own dry rations. In the world beyond, the sergeant will protect me, too, so I have nothing to fear.*

Bon hugged the corpse in his arms. It was his shield, a wall against his invisible but terrifying aggressors. Bon breathed deeply several times and then shouted, "Listen back there! Listen up! The sergeant shoots well with both hands. He can throw a dagger at a target thirty yards away. Watch out!"

The forest rustled noisily. Bon heard his own voice reverberate, triumphant and clear, bouncing off the crowns of the trees. He gazed at the forest surrounding him, saw the pale faces slowly dissolving like smoke, watched as the legs and arms that swung from the branches as if they had been hung there by some crazy torturers fell and disintegrated into dust, leaving no trace. The hateful eyes without lashes or brows that had stared at him from their enormous, deep sockets disappeared as if by some spell. The forest now seemed as peaceful and as reassuring as the nights when he had slept in a hammock in the open air, under the lush foliage.

They've all fled, sergeant. They're afraid of me. I can sleep peacefully now.

Bon touched the sergeant's icy arm, took his dagger, and hung it on his own belt. He slipped his rifle behind his back and buttocks, readying himself to fight the enemy scouts, then he fell fast asleep.

The next morning, the sun filtering through the foliage woke Bon. He was lying on a bed of leaves, his rifle under his buttocks, the sergeant's cadaver on his chest in the position of a man fornicating. Bon slipped his hand under the dead man's shirt, searching for his breast. The body was stiff, icy, and the clothes, damp with mist, gave off a strong, acrid smell of smoke and, even more nauseating, of dried blood. Bon turned the corpse over; he could see each beauty mark, each tiny scratch, even the minuscule wrinkles on the sergeant's face. The face was strange now. Not just because the color of the skin had changed, but because of the impression of absence and distance. Bon touched the tiny beauty spots on the sergeant's cheekbones, stroked the crow's feet at the corners of his eyes. He could never have done this when the sergeant was alive; it would have seemed bizarre, like the overtures of a homosexual or the pandering of a soldier to his superiors. But the sergeant was dead. And Bon was alone in the forest. There was no one to spy on him, or to mock him.

Sergeant, no one has been as kind as you have been . . . but I can't carry you on my back to go search for our unit. In a little while, I'll have to bury you in a corner of this jungle. Forgive me.

Bon stroked the dead man's cheeks, temples, and chin one more time.

If the heavens allow me to live, when peace returns, I'll go to Hanoi to visit your birthplace; I'll bring your journal to your aunt and set your photo on the altar. I'll go to the places where you strolled as a child—the Temple of Literature, West Lake, the Red River. I'll swim toward the islets to gather ears of corn to grill.

Bon saw the pale lips of the dead man tremble slightly, as if to restrain a smile.

Bon could hear the sergeant's laugh clearly. He had always laughed softly, almost noiselessly, with a gentle, comical air about him. Bon clenched his teeth to hold back his tears, stroked the sergeant's stiff eyelashes, and set him on the ground so he could open his satchel. He found a journal and one army-issue autumn-winter uniform.

Before leaving for the assault on Hill #327, the sergeant had suddenly summoned Bon. "You are the most careful man in our platoon. Keep this journal and this uniform safe for me. I'm sure you won't lose them."

Had it been intuition or had the genies already informed him of his fate? Bon shivered as he remembered the sergeant's gaze. A dreamy, vacant look that was no longer human. His eyes shone with an eerie light, as if they were already drifting toward eternity.

Yes, he's finally left this earth, floating in the void somewhere where there are no stones, no jungles, no rifles, no trenches, no order to mount an assault, no battle plan, no contingency plan. No sweat, no urine, no blood.

Bon set aside the sergeant's new uniform and journal and pulled out a piece of nylon they had used as a roof over their hammocks. He spread the piece of plastic sheeting on the ground and lay the body on top of it. He fumbled in the sergeant's pockets and found a pen, a dirty handkerchief, and a half pack of cigarettes. He put everything in a backpack, and closed it tightly. He pulled the sergeant's arms and legs to straighten them, then rolled the body in three layers of sheeting. He was proud to have saved the nylon for this moment, when he needed it, while most of his other comrades had lost theirs, or traded it in for potatoes when they had crossed through the minority villages. Once he had carefully wrapped the body, Bon pulled a spool of parachute thread out of his back pocket and bound the plastic tightly at the head, stomach, and legs. Then he raked aside the rotting leaves with a dagger and started to dig. The ground wasn't very hard and the blade was sharp. Less than half an hour later, he had dug a grave. The sun started to roast the forest. There was no wind, but waves of torrid heat seemed to lap at his back. His sticky sweat tickled him like so many ant bites.

I have to bury him quickly. Corpses rot fast in the sun.

He set the corpse in the ditch, then rose, bowing his head in memory.

There's no music to accompany you, no flowers to pay tribute to you. I should at least fire a round, but I'm afraid of the enemy commandos. Forgive me.

Bon lowered himself to his knees and filled the grave with dirt. A few minutes later a mound took shape, just one hand's width higher than the ground. The dead leaves kept falling, spreading the crimson red of death and the yellow of rot. The *khop* leaves were as large as the palm of one's hand. When they faded, they took on tragic, sinister colors.

Sergeant, the leaves keep falling and falling . . . One day the rain is going to come . . . and the old trees here will fall . . . The forest will change and no one will be able to find a trace of you.

Bon pulled out his dagger and stabbed it into the trunk of one of the trees around the grave. He proceeded to mark each tree with a large "X." He cut furiously, his soul plunged in a sea of smoke, knowing that he would never return to this place. When every trunk of every tree around the grave had been marked, he picked up his knapsack and went off sadly, afraid to look back, to hear the cry from the grave that would sap him of all courage to leave.

He walked for two hours without stopping, tortured by thirst, his tongue stuck to the roof of his palate. He touched his canteen then pulled back his hand, licking the condensation from his lips, and continued walking. He knew he had a little water left and he didn't know when he would find a spring. An hour later, his throat started to swell and he resigned himself to sitting down at the base of a tree and taking a few mouthfuls from the tin. Drop by drop, the water seeped onto his tongue and trickled down his throat. But just as his throat stopped suffering, his stomach, empty for two days, began to unleash its fury. It started with plaintive lamentations that, little by little, turned to violent wrath. Bon cinched his belt tighter at the waist. For the past two days and nights, he had totally lost the sensation of hunger. Now, as all his senses converged toward his stomach, he felt it churn, the gastric juices twisting his gut, convulsing him with pain. Dizzy, Bon pulled his belt a notch tighter and leaned his head against a tree. He closed his eyes and began to search his memory for a fragrance: grilled rice, a portion of dry rations, sweet potato roasted over coals, grilled venison. Wild game! Oh, what a tantalizing smell! Though he had tasted it only once in all his years in the army, he still remembered it perfectly.

During all those years at war, Bon's unit had crossed countless uncharted forests and jungles that had once been teeming with deer, tigers, bears, foxes, and birds. But these animals had all disappeared. Sparse patches of trees were all that was left now, vegetation ripped apart by bombs, defoliated by dioxin. The streams had lost their dreamy, romantic appearance because soldiers had ripped up all the edible grasses and plants from their banks. Most of the time, for fresh food, there was only monkey meat accompanied by rice porridge and a salad made of banana flowers that they sometimes salted with the powdered shrimp sauce they had carried with them from the plains. Once in a while, they would see a stag or a young buck. But here in this devastated landscape, the only hunters were the tigers, and they no longer stalked jungle animals but careless young soldiers.

Just one bite of venison. If only it would fall from the sky. Just one piece the size of a hand, or even as small as two matchboxes.

Saliva filled Bon's mouth. His stomach rumbled as if it were being flooded by a small stream. He shut his eyes tightly and swallowed hard. But the thoughts only came faster, flashing through his mind.

Back in the village, I often used to find wild beehives. Why didn't I ever get lucky like that during the war? Were the bees afraid of the bombs, or did I just never have the time to go look for them? That must be it. Even when the bombs were exploding, flowers continued to bloom and butterflies still flitted about the cliffs. So the bees must still be here, building their hives to make honey. I'll try my luck. For the moment, I've got to sleep to regain my strength. Then I'll go looking for hives.

Bon plunged a hand into his pocket to make sure that his lighter was still there. And it was. The heavens were still on his side. After his nap, he took out one of his oldest undershirts. He would burn it to smoke out a beehive and chase away all the bees. And then he would climb to the top of a tree to grab the hive before the bees came back or a bear attacked him. He imagined quite clearly how he would confront a hungry animal if it tried to grab his loot. He would quickly shoot it right between the eyes. Afterward, it would make a nice barbecue. As starving as he was, bear meat would be just as tasty as venison. This hope eased his hunger a bit. Before he fell asleep, he silently murmured to himself, *How many miles have I come? Seven or eight. No, perhaps just exactly six. If I walk to the east, if I'm lucky enough to cross a narrow jungle, I'll have to walk for another forty or forty-five miles before reaching a sparsely green area. Ah, a sparsely green area. Who taught me that expression? The sergeant. He had read it somewhere in a poem.*

Bon thought he heard the muffled echo of a verse that the sergeant had once recited, somewhere long ago, and he slid from the tree trunk he had propped himself against, falling onto the soft bed of dead *khop* leaves. Sleep dragged him down a shadowy tunnel, a vast, dark, circular hole without sides or a bottom, a ghostly well. He kept falling, falling, falling, not knowing when he would ever hit the watery bottom. He woke suddenly when a dead branch crashed down against his shoulder. Bon lifted his eyes toward the crown of trees, tinted shades of crimson and gold in the sunset, and he realized his plan for finding beehives was doomed. In less than a half an hour, the light would go and the jungle would be shrouded in darkness.

He wasn't hungry anymore, but he was still thirsty. He shook his canteen to see if he could drink one last swig, then decided to tighten the top and repress his thirst. Once his unit had taken three weeks to cross a dry region. The men had had to drink their own urine, and when they came upon a steaming pile of elephant dung, three of his comrades had rushed to plunge their chapped, shriveled faces into it just to soothe their itching skin. Bon would never forget that. He had to save the last few swigs of water for the next day. How many days would it take to get out of this jungle? He didn't know, but he did know that he had to carefully prepare for the following day. He would have to employ a strategy used by soldiers in times of famine and ideological and military reeducation: sleeping instead of eating.

Bon shivered from the cold and quickly fumbled for the sergeant's autumn-winter jacket. He put it on and hung up his hammock. Tonight he would not be able to sleep on the ground because it merely hid another world where wandering souls could rise at any moment to attack him. He walked around the hammock and urinated in a circle to drive away the ghosts. He put his rifle and his knapsack in the bottom of the hammock and lay down on top of them. Night fell. He closed his eyes.

Sleep. Sleep again to regain your strength. Tomorrow, there's no rest. You've got to cover twelve miles without stopping. And you've got to do this for two or three days before there's any hope of meeting someone. No matter, as long as they're on our side. Nothing to eat. Nothing to drink. Sleep is the only way to regain your strength. Just sleep.

These thoughts resonated in his head as clearly and as imperiously as a commandment. He stopped thinking. He waited for sleep. It didn't come. He began to count to a thousand. He started again. A noise suddenly ripped through the air, followed by a stinking odor. Bon opened his eyes. It was pitch black. An eagle must have flown by, leaving a putrid stench in its wake.

Damn bird of misfortune, damn you!

He felt his heart racing as he cursed the bird. Bon felt ashamed of himself.

Why have you become so fearful? You've been through so many battles, carried your comrades' corpses on your back at least seven times before. And now you're afraid of a bird's cry in the night? You idiot. Sleep now.

But a loud, mocking laugh echoed somewhere in the forest, behind Bon's hammock.

"My dear soldier, there's no sleep for you tonight, even if you count to a million. Tonight, you're going to keep watch and chat with me. I've waited for so long here."

My imagination.

Bon closed his eyes and began to count—one two three four five six seven eight nine—but the mocking laughter echoed again, this time right at the foot of the hammock, as sharp as a razor.

"Open your eyes. You're not going to sleep tonight. You can't lie to yourself and you certainly aren't going to avoid me. Open your eyes. I'm here. I'm watching you."

Bon pulled at the edge of the hammock to cover his face. But his hands felt suddenly clamped and painful, as if steel claws had clenched them shut. The ghost leaned over, his icy breath grazing Bon's face. Bon felt his cheekbones go cold and his blood thicken, all against his will. Suddenly, his eyes blinked open like an oyster springs open over the flames.

"That's good . . . open your eyes." The ghost spoke louder. "Now, think where have we met before?"

A transparent face, as green as paddy rice shoots, floated in front of Bon's eyes. A face with a high forehead, and a jeering laugh.

"So, do you remember? We were destined to meet."

"No . . . it's impossible . . . I don't remember," Bon murmured.

The shadow lifted its right hand: There were only four fingers on it, and the joints were pointy and sharply outlined like an X-ray.

"Look at my right hand. It's got only four fingers. The index is missing."

Bon nodded. "Yes, you've got only four fingers, but I don't remember where I've met you."

"Search your memory one more time. We were both very young. The brain is as clear as a white leaf. Many things are easily registered there."

Bon began to get irritated. "Let's stop the guessing game. I don't remember, I just don't remember, full stop."

The ghost laughed. "Hah, hah, such indifference! How can you forget so easily? Remember White Star Hill?"

"Yes, that's where the enemy had an entrenched camp to the southwest of Binh Quoi. My unit exterminated the enemy in a single night. After that battle, we were decorated and received a medal as a heroic unit. They also gave us three cows to butcher for a feast in celebration of our victory."

The ghost chuckled again. He had the loud, ringing laughter of a child, but then it turned bitter, pained. "So, were the dishes tasty at your banquet feast?"

"Well, yes, the cooks made a delicious bean sauce to go with the grilled meat."

"Over the smell of your beef barbecue did you whiff the smell of our burning flesh? My brother, the commander of the fortifications on White Star Hill, and all his comrades were killed by your rockets. And I was the last to receive your gifts. You killed me in a hail of your own submachine-gun fire while I crouched in a hideout between the walls of our warehouses. Remember now? The walls had been washed with yellow lime, and my blood and brains splattered on them, making it look like a painting. Remember how you fell onto a pile of wooden crates? From my hideout, I could easily have killed you with a single shot from my revolver and you wouldn't have been able to gun me down."

The shadow spoke in a monotone, at once cheerful and sad. His green, translucent face suddenly looked up at Bon, the eyes squinting.

"So, comrade, now do you remember me?"

Bon didn't answer. His memory was like a valley buried under too many burning embers, ash, stone, dirt, and dust, scattered by the bombs and shells in the course of the endless battles that followed one after the other in rapid succession, their countless names swirling in his mind. And the tiny paths that joined the large roads, his unit going from east to west and north to south, only to return from the south to the north. How could he remember? The shadow seemed to guess his thoughts.

"Do you remember the small young man dressed in a parachutist's uniform, standing between the two walls of the warehouse on White Star Hill, the one who had big, thick glasses and raised a white shirt of surrender, waving it above his head?"

A scream echoed somewhere in Bon's soul.

"Yes, I remember."

The face of the young man with the thick glasses rose from the depths of Bon's memory, drifting up through countless layers. Yes, he remembered tripping as he hurdled over the wooden crates, running into the building with the broken roof, the supply warehouse in flames. Suddenly he had seen a young man crouching between the walls, waving something white above his head, turning toward Bon, his glasses glinting in the sun. Not stopping to think of anything, Bon had let loose with a rain of submachine-gun fire, still running ahead, following the retreating enemy while his comrades' shouts urged him on.

"That was me," the ghost said gently. "The man in the glasses. I don't wear them anymore. You don't need them in hell."

Bon kept his silence. He realized that the hour of the dead had finally come. This soul was here to settle a score with him. Why had he ignored the white shirt that the man had waved as a flag of surrender? He didn't know anymore. Perhaps he had forgotten military discipline, that theoretical law they had all read once on a slanting page. Perhaps the assault had been so brutal that he couldn't even imagine the enemy's surrendering. Or was it because during the previous battle, more than half of the men in his company had been killed and that the survivors were no longer capable of respecting martial law? It was also possible that in that instant, his brain had been deranged by explosions and rockets and machine guns and submachine guns, by his comrades screaming and shouting at him to mount an assault, by the flames and the smoke and the sight of bodies falling, and by the surreal, terrifying symphony of the battlefield, a music beyond all imagining. No orchestra could rival the way it intoxicated men, plunging them into drunken orgies of hatred and massacre. No. No, he didn't know and he didn't feel the need to justify himself.

Then Bon spoke: "I remember now. But the war was the war. When you were raining bombs on us, when you reduced entire companies to ash and then returned to Saigon to have a cold beer and hug a girl in your arms, did you remember us? Did you smell our blood in the fragrance of your beer? Don't ask me stupid questions. You want to settle scores? Let's do it!"

The green wraith slid toward Bon. "That's right. War is war. My brother, my commander who was posted to White Star Hill, would also have fired on every last Vietcong soldier if he could have . . . But me, I was a deserter, a convict who had come back to visit his family before returning to Saigon." The ghostly shadow brandished his hand with only four fingers in Bon's face.

"Look, I cut this finger off with the hatchet of an old Ede minority tribesman when my unit was based in Dac Lac. I had just been enrolled after having done everything to avoid it. I got five years of forced labor for this crime."

"How could I know that your hand had only four fingers?"

The shadow nodded. "It's true, but I had raised my white shirt over my head. You should have known that I meant to surrender."

"I had learned that, yes, but I didn't remember at that instant. If it had been a white flag, clearly visible, then that would have been another story. But it was a shirt. How was I supposed to interpret that?"

The green shadow smiled sadly. And his laugh was no longer as threatening or as mocking as it had been. "You seem sincere to me. Where are you from?"

"I'm from . . ."

Bon wanted to say that he came from a mountain village nestled at the base of the Truong Son Cordillera, in a deserted, poetic region. But he didn't have time to open his mouth. Another shadow rose from behind the green wraith.

"Shut up . . . The moment has come for you to pay your debt."

This shadow was solidly built, fierce and taller than the pale green shadow by as much as a head. "Assassin, it's time you paid your debt to my brother, a life for a life!"

Bon felt half of his face sting and throb with pain, as if he had just received a punch, or a blow from a staff. He wanted to grab his rifle, but his arms were stiff and icy. He couldn't move. The frail wraith slid toward them.

"Stop, Elder Brother. What's the use now?"

The burly shadow barked at him, "Imbecile! No one should be magnanimous with such a contemptible enemy as these Communists."

"Please . . . He's still so young, and he didn't get to study . . ."

"Enough of your logic. I'm a soldier and I act like a soldier."

From behind the shadow, a whole jostling crowd of shadows appeared.

"Yeah, wring his neck, that assassin."

"Cut out his tongue."

"Stab your bayonet into his heart. But I doubt the peasant has a heart. In that chest, all you'll find is a cow's or a pig's kidney."

The ghost soldiers pounced on Bon, screaming and spitting. They all wore their soldiers' uniforms. Bon could smell the pungent odor of sweat mixed with coagulated blood from their wounds, the dank odor of their hair and clothes, the gum they chewed. The familiar scent of the enemy. The ghosts from the other side of the front were even more terrifying than the statues of demons that Bon had seen in the pagodas. These were not the sculpted statues of legend, but real enemies who remembered what he himself had completely forgotten.

I'm facing them all alone, but I've got a rifle, and whatever happens, they are just wandering souls. Fight!

This thought flashed through his indignant soul. The blood surged in his heart and a wave of heat passed through his body, warming his stiff, freezing arms. He clenched and unclenched his fists until it hurt and he began to feel sensation in his fingers again.

"Fight! Fight!" he cried. He grabbed the rifle at his back and fired three shots in the air. The forest was filled with the rustle of falling leaves. Bon listened as small animals scurried and fled, as birds scattered and flew up into the trees. The shadows disappeared, the jeering crowd as well as the frail wraith.

"Attack! Attack!" Bon shouted again, dizzy with victory and the feeling of having purged himself of his shame. "I'll show you that there's a heart in this chest."

Three more rifle shots resounded. The leaves fell again in heavy drifts all around him. Bon glanced up to the sky. The night was like black velvet, dense and silent, as safe as it had once been long ago.

"There you go!" His voice echoed over and over and replied to him as if the forest genie were imitating him. Relieved, Bon lay back down, one hand on his rifle and the other clenching the side of the hammock to his stomach.

Now I can sleep until dawn. Tomorrow I'll walk forty miles to the east.

But his body felt as if it were on fire. His tense nerves prevented him from closing his eyes. Bon knew that the frail shadow was the most fearsome ghost, for it had disarmed him. He couldn't hate the man anymore. He couldn't even fire on him six times in a row as he had against the ghosts of those other bastards. He fingered the trigger of his rifle, praying that dawn would come quickly, that if ghosts were to return, they would be those of the soldiers from White Star Hill, enemies that he could attack without fear or remorse. He would fire on them, or even piss in their faces, to use a more traditional method.

But dawn was still far off. A half hour later, when his spirit had re-laxed and his muscles had gone slack, as he drifted toward sleep, an icy hand came to rest on his forehead.

"So, you can't sleep?"

Bon opened his eyes to see the green face and his wistful smile.

"I didn't want to hurt you. But I don't understand why you did what you did. You see, I didn't understand my own death, can't make sense of it. I want to talk about it with you."

Bon sat up. He knew that if he remained lying down the intense green light that emanated from this young face would suffocate him. Perhaps it was some noxious vapor that had risen from a lake polluted by mercury, or a flask of poison from some witch doctor they used to exterminate their enemies.

"You seem younger than me. People in the countryside recruit their soldiers very young."

"I told you already," Bon said. "War is war. No one is master of himself when the bullets are whistling past. I don't feel any hatred to-ward you, but heaven and earth lost you somewhere out there on the guard post on White Star Hill. I had to treat you as my enemy."

"I understand," the shadow replied gently, not looking at Bon's face but straight ahead. "Right from the start, I told you: I've been waiting for you for a long time here in this part of the jungle. I want to talk. I have no intention of settling a debt with blood, like some knight-errant. Don't worry. I won't hurt you."

"I'm not afraid. Do as you like."

"Why are you angry? The night is still young. We'll have time to talk to our hearts' content. Are you married?"

"Yes."

Bon groaned silently. *The night is young and I want to sleep, I don't want to struggle with you or talk with you. No one wants to chat with his own victim.*

But the wraith didn't seem to divine these thoughts; it continued in a tolerant, forgiving tone. "The mountain people marry early, don't they? . . . You were married at nineteen?"

"Seventeen."

"My God! So your wife is the same age?"

"Yes, the same as me."

"Is she pretty?"

"She is as beautiful as a fairy. She's not ugly like me."

"You're not ugly. You may not be handsome, but you've got thick eyebrows, dark, sad eyes like the Cham. Does she write you sometimes?"

"The first year, I received letters. But nothing since."

"On your side it must be hard to keep up the lines of communication."

"Yeah, I mean we don't have help from the Americans. We don't have a steady supply of canned meat or dried goods, or milk or cigarettes or medicine like you."

"But as far as weaponry goes, you've got a vast choice."

"Yes, but there are times when it's not enough. . . . Sometimes we have to retreat early because we don't have enough ammunition. Especially B40 and B41 shells."

"But you're getting ammunition from both the USSR and China. How could you have shortages?"

"I don't care where it comes from . . . I don't feel like talking about all this anymore."

Bon was angry now, his heart ached. Why did this conversation feel like some kind of hypnotic trick that had forced him down an impasse? The farther he went, the more strained his breathing became, the more his soul seemed to slacken and come apart like newspaper in a torrential rain. He had to tear himself from this dialogue before he was transformed into a corpse himself.

"That's enough, get out!" he shouted. "I'm not talking to you anymore! Get the hell out of here!"

From all sides, the forest responded in a single, terrifying, diabolical echo. Bon no longer recognized his own voice, just muffled sounds that seemed to rise from a cave or a deep ravine. He grabbed his rifle, loaded it, and aimed it at the shadow.

"Get out, I don't hate you but I don't want to see you anymore. Get out or I'll shoot!"

He heard a feeble laugh. The green face didn't budge.

"Bullets can't hurt dead souls. We appear as we were at the moment of death. Forever. Look, the hole in my forehead is still there." He leaned closer to Bon, pointing a finger at a round, black hole in the middle of his broad forehead. "I'm not going to harm you, but you can't avoid me any longer. We can't deny our actions, and that applies to everyone. Why did you fire on me? I spared your life. I was ready to surrender. I knew that we were the same people, that we shouldn't be killing each other in this horrible civil war."

Bon couldn't stop staring at the hole in the pale forehead. And there had been other bullets fired, aimed even higher, that had smashed this young man's skull, projecting his brains and blood on the lime-yellow walls.

Yes, his eyes were glistening. I remember; they were well-meaning. If I had stepped closer, he would have obediently followed me. I could have locked him up somewhere and then sent him back to the city after the battle was over.

These ruminations left painful furrows in Bon's brain. The frail young man had died because of him. No one had noticed the hand without an index finger when they had cleaned the corpses from the battlefield. Who could have known that he was against the war, that he deserved to live again under the sun? Bon felt as if he were going to suffocate. "I don't know, I don't know . . . I don't remember anything from that moment, and . . ."

His tongue froze and his breathing slowed. He would choke and die if he had to submit to another hour of this shadow's relentless interrogation.

My God, if only the sergeant were here, at my side, I wouldn't have to suffer like this. The sergeant came from the city, he would find arguments to convince this city shadow, he would know how to protect and defend me . . .

I should have carried him on my back. Now here I am all alone and he is, too.

The green shadow still stood facing his rifle, but without the slightest trembling from fear. Bon spoke again, his voice desperate now, imploring, "Go . . . just go . . . go away . . ."

The shadow sighed. The icy wind carried off the sigh. As this vapory breath grazed Bon's face and shoulders, he felt goose pimples cover his body and his spinal column went limp, as if he would soon be paralyzed. He clenched his teeth and pulled the trigger. A burst of gunfire shook the forest. He opened his eyes wide. The shadow had risen suddenly into the air like a balloon, like bird's feathers fluttering and dancing in space. Bon knew that in just an instant, when the smell of gunpowder had dissipated, the forest would fall back into silence, and the shadow would flutter down again like a butterfly, alight in front of him, stare at Bon with empty eyes, and then he would continue his courteous, but terrifying interrogation.

Bon knelt, unbuttoned his pants, took out his penis—the only weapon he had left—and urinated. But he hadn't had much to drink, so there were just a few drops. He sucked in his stomach and pressed his bladder, trying to extract the last few remaining drops. Even if there was only blood left, he wanted that blood to be transformed into a nauseating, fetid urine. But it was all in vain. He zipped up his pants and watched the shadow lazily floating in the deep, dark space of the jungle. His hand was still on his rifle, but he didn't dare fire again. He had to save his ammunition for any enemy scouts that he might encounter. Then he heard the shadow's bitter laughter, saw the thighs floating, those thighs without knees, or legs, or feet, so light that they swung in the air, drew close to his face and then retreated, drifting elsewhere.

Bon was drenched in sweat. Little by little he felt his knees bend, the joints dislocate, clacking against each other like pieces of wood inside his pants. He screamed out in pain. His rifle slowly dropped to his side, and by the time it had finally come to rest on the hammock, Bon stopped feeling the stiffness and cold in his arms. He fell, facedown, headfirst, into the hammock, right on top of his rifle. He felt a hand slide down his back, stroking him, a bony hand that had only four fingers and was missing the index.

The next morning, Bon woke up in a strange position. He was hunched over, his knees gathered under his stomach, his face pressed against the netting of the hammock, his buttocks in the air. His rifle was pinned under his knees, which were bruised violet, and his clothes were drenched in sweat and icy dew. His heart racing, Bon jumped to the ground and untied the hammock. He opened his canteen and allowed himself to drink two long swigs to regain his strength. He screwed the top back on tightly and attached the canteen to his belt. Then he slung his knapsack over his shoulder and walked toward the sergeant's grave.

He walked without turning back, not stopping even to catch his breath. He walked quickly, as if possessed, driven by the desire to survive. The road he had traveled the previous day had been neither long nor steep; it had taken just over two hours to return to the spot in the forest bordering Hill #327. Bon looked for trees marked with an "X." In the middle, the sergeant's grave was buried under a pile of *khop* leaves. Bon still remembered the distance that separated the grave from the surrounding trees. He pushed aside the leaves and, in just a short time, the tiny rectangular-shaped hump of soil emerged. He tossed his backpack aside, pulled out his dagger, and started to dig. The blade went in slowly and when it reached the plastic shroud, the cries of vultures resounded above him. One, two, three, and then four vultures flocked toward him, circling in a tight ring above the trees, their eyes threatening as they followed the movements of the blade in his hand. Bon scooped up two large handfuls of dirt and threw it at them.

"Get out of here, you bastards!"

And just as he cursed them, he was convulsed by a fit of wheezing and coughing. When it was over, Bon realized that he had choked on the stench of the decomposing corpse. The vultures had smelled it even before he had. Death's fellow travelers, they were always there, on

212 | D U O N G   T H U   H U O N G

every battlefield, whether it was in the mountains, the plains, the valleys, even the dunes by the ocean. Bon had seen them for the first time when he had gone to gather wild vegetables with Tan and Kha, two comrades from Nghe Tinh. They were crossing Xieng Mai Mountain when suddenly, over their heads, they heard shrieking cries, like metal grating against metal. Then they saw the vultures, their wings beating the air, inundating it with the nauseating odor of rotting human flesh. It was the first time they had come face to face with Death's messengers and the three of them had stood petrified: these birds must have come from the site of a mass grave.

When they regained their wits, they decided to find the place in the mountains where the vultures had seemed to fly from. This spot was nestled behind a huge rock, screened off by a dense curtain of green vines hung with bunches of tiny, pale red flowers with black stamens and thick, succulent leaves crisscrossed with veins that looked like dark green plastic. If your skin touched these vines it would swell up in a flash, and a few days later it would be completely blistered with putrid, yellow pus. The three of them had all had a taste of that experience, so they carefully made their way around the curtain of vines. The closer they got to their destination, the more suffocating the stench became. Like reinforcements, more flocks of vultures swirled in the air. But these birds didn't resemble their predecessors; they were plump and flew awkwardly under their own weight, slowly beating their wings. Too fat, they couldn't even call out noisily as the first bunch of starving vultures had, so from time to time they let out a short yelp. Even their gazes were duller, more indolent. One by one, they had filed past the soldiers, indifferent, brazen, utterly fearless. The heavy beating of their wings made the whole atmosphere of the place even more terrifying.

Then Bon and his comrades found it: a patch of dirt of several hundred square feet strewn with skeletons in torn uniforms. The rags on the corpses hadn't even had a chance to rot; they had been torn by the pecking of birds. There weren't even any other animals on the site because the stench of the decomposing flesh had become too over-powering. Only the vultures and a few other owl eagles waddled around, bobbing their horrid bald heads. There were no bomb craters here, not even a trace of exploded mines. How had these soldiers died? Their skulls and knapsacks were scattered pell-mell. Bon counted at least thirty skulls. An entire company. What had they died from? His two comrades looked at him, both stricken with doubt. No one could explain it. No one dared speak. Tufts of hair and smashed flesh remained stuck to the skulls. Dragged here and there by animals, there was nothing human left of their appearance. These were their comrades; they shared the same life. Was this a foretaste of their own fate?

Without a word, they went off to gather dry branches and dead leaves. Then they piled them in a heap on top of the few corpses that hadn't been entirely stripped of their flesh. It took them almost four hours to gather enough wood to cremate them. And they didn't have much time because the sun was starting to set over the mountain. Kha lit a wick and threw it on the pyre. Only then did Bon and Tan begin to murmur a prayer in tandem: "Brothers, you who have lived and died as human beings, be our witnesses. We have neither petrol nor gunpowder to burn, and we can't find enough firewood to cremate you properly. May the heavens and the Buddha liberate your souls and reincarnate you quickly so that you may one day live again in peace."

The three of them had stood and prayed for their anonymous companions while the fire spread from the wick to the dry branches. The pyre was soon consumed in flames.

"Let's go!" Kha shouted.

The three of them had turned their backs on the pyre and run. They ran like madmen, as if the genie of the plague was hot on their trail. Heads bowed, they hurtled through underbrush and down mountain slopes, bounding over ditches that they wouldn't have dared to ford in normal times. They returned to their unit's camp with empty hands, but with the image of their unlucky companions seared into their brains, their clothes and skin reeking of rotting flesh, terror sweating from every pore. And when they reached their cabin, they collapsed panting and heaving on the dirt floor, incapable of speech, choked by their own sobs.

Bon remained alone with his memories. He blinked his eyes to erase the horrific vision. After a long time, Bon looked up at the vultures perched in the trees, greedily waiting. The bastards were still there, still the same repulsive creatures, but Tan and Kha were gone, dead. He would have to fight this battle alone.

Let's attack now . . . Let's take the offensive . . .

He again picked up big clumps of dirt and hurled them at the vultures.

"Get out, you bastards, get the fuck out of here!"

The vultures flew up, shrieking, but then they alighted on a branch a few feet above his head after having traced just a few circles in the air.

The sun was already high in the sky, and the torrid heat trickled slowly through the foliage of the trees. Bon kneeled and continued to dig. He had to leave this jungle, to walk toward the east, toward life. He didn't have the right to waver. Too bad for the stench of the corpse and the vultures. No smell could be worse than the solitude and terror that he had felt the previous evening. Now, the sergeant's presence would be enough to scare away all the ghosts, to bring him security. They would go together then toward the east. Yes, his sergeant's victorious ghost would protect him and give him strength. Bon would show his loyalty by bringing the sergeant's body back to the plains.

A quarter of an hour later, Bon finally succeeded in pulling the sergeant's corpse out of the grave. The vultures started to shriek again, circling tighter above his head. The wind from the west blew even harder, carrying the stench and amplifying the obscene, festive cries of the birds.

"Get out! Scram!"

Bon's hoarse cries faded into the distant rustle of the jungle. They had no effect on the vultures, their eyes glinting, their beaks and claws poised, ready to tear into flesh. Bon cut a branch. Armed with this, he stood taller and glared at the threatening birds.

"You sons of bitches! So you think the banquet is served, eh? Here, take this and this and this!"

With each insult, he whipped the air with the stick, forcing the vultures to scatter. Bon stopped, tucked his dagger back into his belt, and took a deep breath. Then he untied the parachute string that he had bound around the corpse's neck and fished another string out of his pocket.

He opened his tent canvas, made two knots in each end, and threaded the string through, linking the two ends so he could sling them over his shoulder. This way, he could easily drag the corpse, while leaving its face in the open air. The wind would carry a bit of the stench, and Bon would feel a bit less lonely. The sergeant's face was black and lugubrious. Bon didn't dare look at it for too long. He hadn't expected the skin to change color so quickly. In his memory, there was just a fair, happy face with curving lips and freckles clustered like tiny islands on his cheekbones.

If only I had a bit of powder and lipstick, he'd be handsome and smiling . . . If only . . .

Bon had met women from the artistic troupe of the military region one day at dawn when they had gone to bathe in the stream. Their pale skin and lips had made a deep impression on him. Under the stage lights, they had seemed to glitter like fairies and their faces danced in his dreams, mingling with the image of Mien's face, his beautiful wife waiting for him back in the village. And that was how Bon first learned of the miracle of makeup. He would have loved to perform a similar miracle on the sergeant's face. Unfortunately, he had nothing on hand with which to do it. If he had been in a place with red clay, he could have used dust in lieu of makeup. If there had been caves nearby with calcium deposits, he could have crushed a bit of white chalk to cover the dead man's face. But he was in a *khop* jungle; there were only leaves and more leaves littering the ground. A *khop* jungle . . . a jungle where it was impossible to do anything . . .

While he reflected, the vultures were approaching him. They seemed to have forgotten their fear, enticed by the odor of their prey.

Bon whipped the air violently with the stick and then knelt over his pack. He remembered that he had some toothpaste left, a tube of Colgate. It had been given to him at Post #72 by a scout whom Bon had accompanied all day long in the jungle. The two of them had gathered vegetables and the scout had washed his hammock and his blanket. Now Bon didn't have powder or red dust or white chalk, but he still had a bit of this marvelously white, scented paste, and perhaps it could give the face some of the freshness it once had. Bon got out the tube of toothpaste, unscrewed the cap, and started to apply it to the dead man's face. He dabbed some on the lips and spread it evenly to cover them entirely. He continued with the cheeks and the forehead. All that was left was the corpse's chin and grayish neck. Bon thought for a few seconds and then decided to cover them too with a thin coat of the paste. He finished by putting a layer on the nose and between the eyebrows, until the tube was completely empty.

Who cares! I'll ask the cooks for some salt to clean my teeth with. It's even better. The main thing is finding my way back . . .

Bon kicked aside the empty tube, pulled on his knapsack, and slung the strings to drag the corpse over his shoulder, as he murmured, "Sergeant, I'm going to take you to find our unit. You, who were once a human being, guide me to the best path out of this jungle."

He gazed one more time into the corpse's white face, then turned his back and began to walk. The corpse seemed to glide easily on the drifts of dead *khop* leaves, unless it was the soul of the beloved deceased one that gave Bon an exceptional strength. He walked without stopping, without resting, forgetting that his stomach had not had even a single grain of rice for three whole days and nights, and that the few gulps of water he had allowed himself to drink had completely evaporated. As he walked, he licked the sweat that dripped down onto his lips; these salty drops, distilled from his own body, seemed to him like water from Buddha's own gourd, the one that had kept him alive for three thousand days without food. He walked at full stretch like that until sundown. Suddenly he felt something jerk the corpse backward. He turned and saw two vultures perched on the legs of the corpse, trying to tear away the canvas that bound it.

"Oh, you bastards! You miserable bastards!"

The vultures had been following him along the entire journey, flitting from one tree to the next, without ever daring to alight. From time to time, Bon would notice them; they were always in groups of four, like demons at his heels, or even guardians to the gates of hell. For just about an hour now, Bon had been exhausted and had stopped turning back. The vultures had taken advantage of this to silently land on the corpse, with no apparent fear or even awareness of the live man who was just a few paces in front of them. Bon stopped and let the halter of string down from his shoulder. Immediately, without so much as a cry, the birds took flight, perching on the branches of a nearby tree. They stared at Bon's face, their eyes threatening, their heads nodding defiantly.

Okay, so now they're attacking as traitors, behind my back. Now we're talking guerrilla warfare. It's going to be hard to fight off these wretches.

Bon pulled out his dagger and cut down several branches, binding them into a small, rounded shell, like the fisherman used to cover their traps. He attached the branches to the corpse. By the time he had finished, it was almost dark out. The wind had died down and the wilted leaves swirled slowly in the fading light. His thirst suddenly became acute, insistent.

I must sleep. Right away. There are only a few mouthfuls of water left in the canteen for tomorrow and maybe the day after. Maybe even days. Today I didn't even do twelve miles. I must sleep. Tonight, no ghost will dare bother me. The night will restore my strength and my faith. Tomorrow, I'll take to the road again.

His eyelids, drooping and heavy, closed almost instantly.

Should I set up the hammock? No need. I'll sleep next to the sergeant. I'll put him against the wind, behind me. Tonight, I have nothing to fear.

He climbed around the branches and lay down facing the wind. He set down his rifle and his knapsack on the dead branches, stretched out an arm, placed his hand on the corpse's head, and fell asleep.

The next morning it was not a ray of light or a broken branch that woke Bon, but the peck of a vulture's beak that made him scream in terror. He sat up and saw blood streaming down his arm.

He suddenly snapped awake, fumbling quickly to open his knapsack and get out his first aid kit. He got out the bottle of disinfectant and poured some on the wound. When it was completely drenched, he wiped the excess with cotton and repeated the process. Finally, he spread a bit of antiseptic cream on the wound and applied a bandage. Then he lifted the branches off the cadaver and threw them to the side. Three vultures flew out in Indian file, letting out their shrill cries. The canvas had been torn right at the corpse's knee. This rip, about sixteen inches long, had become the main opening for the vultures' banquet. They had started their feasting at the wound on the left thigh. And that morning, one of them, intending to attack the skull, had stabbed its beak into Bon's arm.

Poor Elder Brother. How much flesh have they already torn from you? How am I ever going to resist them?

Bon started to feel fear. The birds had slipped under the branches he had used as camouflage, silently ripped the canvas, and eaten into his comrade's flesh—all while he slept. A man weakened by hunger and thirst sleeps almost like a corpse. And the branches were not going to stop these birds of prey. What arms did he have to fight them with? It was useless to scream or shout, since none of what he said scared them anymore. And besides, he didn't have the strength left to scream. He couldn't even brandish a stick to chase them away, since he couldn't return to the west to find one while he was walking eastward. He was starving. Even worse, he was thirsty. Sleep had dulled his thirst, but now that he was awake it seemed to scratch and tear at him. The more the sun and the wind heated up, the thirstier he became. Bon put his hand on his canteen, never letting the vultures out of his sight for an instant. They remained perched on the branches above. Their glassy, beady eyes stared at him, attentively, naturally, without the slightest tremor of doubt or hesitation, as if they knew that they were in a struggle with this human being standing below who was tall but run down, this man that hunger, thirst, and solitude had rendered almost completely vulnerable. Bon shuddered. He knew that from now on the vultures had become the enemy, adversaries that he had never imagined, even in his worst nightmare. He had nothing to fight them with, to defend his companion with, except his own body.

I must drink a bit. Just a sip. Just a tiny sip . . .

This thought broke his stride. He unscrewed the top on the canteen and drank some of the water, drop by drop to savor it.

A sip. I have the right to just one more. But tomorrow. And after tomorrow . . .

Tomorrow! This last sound resonated for a long time inside him, like a doubt, like an uncertain, distant dream. He looked around. Jungle and more jungle. Trees and more trees. In front of him. Behind him. To the left and right. The vast, rippling jungle snared and enclosed him in its labyrinthine nets. This was the most enchanting, spellbinding battlefield, the one from which no one ever escaped. And for the first time in his life as a soldier, in all these years in the countryside, Bon, the mountain dweller, feared it.

Sergeant, you who have lived as a human being, guide me. All I have left is a few swigs of water. How will I ever resist your predators?

Bon prayed in silence. He no longer dared speak aloud; it would just waste his remaining strength. He had to save all the energy that he had left to keep walking. He gazed up at the branches, seeking a way out. If he couldn't protect the corpse with large branches, he could perhaps fashion a cage out of the tiny green branches. He could bind them together with parachute string in a kind of basket or helmet that he would put over the corpse's head to protect its eyes. When the soul departed, the light shed by the eyes would guide it to paradise or the path to reincarnation. The soul of a corpse without a skull or without eyes would wander forever in the shadows, falling easily into the hands of devils. He couldn't let the vultures touch the sergeant's eyes any more than he could allow them to peck at his own heart.

Bon sat down and fished a tiny ball of parachute string out of his pants' pocket. The sergeant and his companions called him Bon the Bazaar, for he always kept all sorts of odds and ends in his pockets. His jumble now proved very useful. He cut the string in pieces and knotted the branches together to form a double-walled cage. The *khop* branches were hard and twisted. It took Bon two hours to make a deformed object that was somewhere between cage and basket. But in the end, he had made what he wanted: a double wall of branches interwoven perpendicularly that would prevent the vultures from pecking. He placed the cumbersome contraption on the corpse's head, binding it tightly to the shoulders with the thickest string and winding it several times under the arms. He dragged the corpse a short way to test it. The small cage swayed but stayed solidly tied to the skull like a chain or armored helmet, the kind used by medieval knights in jousting tournaments. Confident of his invention, Bon glanced back at the vultures, muttering silent curses at them.

You whores. Now you can fly at me. See if I care.

Bon continued his walk toward the east, toward hope, toward life. His feet sank into the dead leaves like a plow in furrows, and they had probably started to swell, since Bon felt they were heavier, slower, more hesitant.

What's happening to me? I'm walking like a drunkard.

He pulled the rope on his shoulder halter tighter and, head bowed, he walked on, heedless of the slopes, oblivious to whether the ground under his feet was flat or bumpy. At times, he would let himself roll down a hill, dragging the cadaver and an avalanche of dead leaves in his wake. He walked like this until he felt the sun starting to burn his neck. He felt his foot trip on a cord, as if an invisible hand were pulling him backward. He turned again to look behind him. The vultures were hanging on to the corpse, and one perched on the torn canvas was pecking at the flesh. Three others had managed to slip under the canvas and their thrashing and poking rippled the surface of the plastic.

Suddenly, Bon stopped looking at them and covered his eyes with his hands. They were shaking uncontrollably, like an old man's. His arms and knees had started to shake too now, as if in unison. He knew that he was at the point of collapse. From hunger. From thirst. From the tension. He sat down and contemplated his limbs as they shook uncontrollably. They seemed to no longer belong to him. Sadness flooded Bon's heart but he felt just two tears wet his lashes. No doubt tiny tears, as they didn't even trickle down his cheeks and barely managed to dampen the swollen pores of his eyelids. His lids closed, heavy, impossible to reopen. The sun beat down on the nape of his neck, a searing heat, like flames from a brick oven back in the village. In his memory, he relived the white smoke floating in a peaceful, distant sky, the clear, star-studded nights, the smell of sticky rice grilled with honey and ginger, the steaming goat thigh that one of the brick makers had once pulled out of his basket. Bon's sleep on the fourth day began with this reverie, a peaceful daydream haunted by the tantalizing aroma of sticky rice, honey-flavored rice and grilled goat washed down with a well-aged rice wine.

When he awoke, the sun was at its zenith. He must have slept for almost twenty-four hours straight. The torrid, steamy air of the *khop* jungle mixed with the stench of the corpse to create a thick, gluey, terrifying atmosphere. The glassy eyes of the vultures gazed at him calmly, patiently, from their perch atop the corpse. They preened their feathers and wiped their beaks, straining their necks to observe him. These were the looks of torturers waiting to execute a condemned man. Bon knew that from now on, he was no longer an adversary to them but a prey-in-waiting; he was just a mass of flesh that had lain motionless for an entire day and night, a potential corpse that would inevitably decompose. Bon was seized by a terrible fury, as if the life remaining in his soul had suddenly spurted forth.

"Bastards!" Bon shrieked, as he bounded toward them.

They flew up and away in a single fluttering, without the slightest cry. Bon's brutal gesture had not scared them, only surprised them. The birds made a few circles in the air and then came to land on a tiny mound of dirt just a few feet from Bon. There, they continued to preen their feathers, as if to mock him.

"Sons of bitches!"

This time, Bon's curses didn't even get past his throat. The sounds stuck at the base of his tongue. His thirst had hardened the skin inside his mouth. He stumbled and staggered toward the mound of dirt and threw himself at the birds. This time, he collapsed, his face against the ground, while the birds moved past him to alight on the corpse.

"*Bastards! Sons of bitches!*"

For the third time, he cursed them. But this time, only in his head. He stood and kept lunging at the vultures. He didn't know why he acted this way, but his rage wouldn't let go of him; he had to catch them and wring their necks with his bare hands.

But he kept missing his target. His head crashed against the corpse's shoe. Now he didn't feel pain so much as shame. His nerves were almost completely numb, but his anguished conscience remained. After a long time, he finally sat up. He, the starving, thirsty, lonely man, had been defeated, utterly vanquished.

No, no, no, no, no . . .

The shouts sprang from his heart. But they were feeble, as quavering as the strains of a monochord wafting through the valley. Bon remained lying down for a long time, his face pressed against the ground in order to breathe, to feel his rage slowly subside.

Oh Tan, Kha, Quy, Thanh, Tran, Tuong, Phien, Tru, where are you? Come to me . . . I don't want to die, I don't want to die. I must get the sergeant out of this jungle.

He pressed himself up on his hands, sat up slowly, and pulled the rope over his shoulder again. His arms no longer shook as they had the previous evening, but he swayed, accomplishing each gesture as if on tiptoe, watching himself carefully like an old man in the grip of a serious illness.

Sergeant, let's forge ahead toward the plain. Toward the plain. We have to escape this place. We will bury you near the plain and when peace returns to the country . . .

These thoughts rose as thin as wisps of smoke. Bon could still make out the glow of the sun at the hill's summit, and beyond it lay the plain, the land near the blue horizon and the waves. He tugged at the corpse and put one foot forward. Another foot. The parachute string dug into his shoulders, but his skin was numb. Forward. Onward, to the plain.

Bon couldn't remember how long he had been walking. He concentrated all his energy, his entire consciousness, on making his feet step one ahead of the other on the ground, on ordering his body not to let go of the rope that linked him to the corpse so that they could keep moving ahead. He had drunk the last mouthful of water and thrown the canteen into the bushes. He didn't desire anything now except sleep. He moved forward even as his eyelids drooped, growing heavier and heavier with sleep. When he couldn't walk another step, he slumped forward like a banana tree and sank into a dreamless sleep, a dark, bottomless cave. The next morning, he woke to the sharp claws of the vultures piercing his chest. Furious, he grabbed his cap to whip them off, but his movements were too slow, too feeble. The vultures had more than enough time to fly off and then alight on the corpse. The cap rolled on the ground. Bon crawled slowly toward it, grabbed it, and put it on his head. Pushing his hands against his knees, he managed to sit up. He hitched himself to the corpse again and started to walk. To the east. Patches of light filtering through the foliage stung his eyes, warming his body. And at that instant he saw it, one of those marvelous rainbows of his childhood, the kind that always appeared after the early summer rains.

Oh Giao, Thinh, Ton, Nguyen, Du, Yem, Minh, Quang, Tao! Where are you now? When will we see each other again? When?

Once again, he hurled these trembling cries alone, inside his head.

These calls summoned up the memory of other dawns, of grasses drenched in dew, of young boys wrestling and tussling in the fields, gripping one another by the shoulders, thumping and punching one another's backs, teasing one another and boasting about who had the biggest balls. The sounds of these distant dawns resonated in him, swaying the bell-shaped orchids, a fairy-tale forest with a babbling brook, where leaves rustled and whispered. Not like here in this *khop* jungle, this dry, sinister pit that echoed with the raucous cries of vultures. The bell-shaped orchid swayed, back and forth, back and forth, endlessly, until the moment when, incapable of walking any farther, he fell, facedown into the rotting leaves, and lost consciousness.

When Bon woke up, it was late afternoon and the vultures were fighting over intestines that they had just pulled and dragged out of the sergeant's belly. The canvas was completely gutted now. The predators let out rasping yelps as they tore the intestines, as if they were not merely content to eat but also wanted to turn this feast into some mocking festival.

Sons of bitches!

But these curses had barely begun to take shape in his head when they scattered like ash. Bon was seized by fury, a rage like a torrent of lava, like a poisonous wave that choked and engulfed him. He dragged himself toward the birds, preparing to whip them with his hat, but he couldn't even lift his arm. He let it drop, limp, staring dumbly at the horrible creatures. Slowly, tears filled his eyes. Two tears rolled down his cheeks. He hadn't had anything to drink for several days. The tears, no doubt, must have been distilled from his blood. He had lost the battle. He was beaten. He put his hands on his thighs. Why had he wasted his few tears on these ignominious birds? If the sergeant were alive, he would have smiled and said, *It's not dignified for a man.*

One scarlet *khop* leaf dropped from its branch and twirled down in front of Bon's eyes before falling on the dirt. This was probably a sign from the sergeant, calling him to order. He had to keep walking.

I've got to walk. I can't admit defeat. Never . . .

Bon slung on his pack, put on his cap, and pulled the rope back over his shoulders. He shuffled along, dragging the corpse, the only thing he carried now, having thrown away his rifle and his canteen. With each step, he called the name of a man who had been enrolled the same day, in his platoon, his company: *Dinh, Nghia, Sinh, Khanh, Hanh, Phat, Thuoc, Tuan, Tan, Doan, Hung, Son, Hung, Chi . . .*

And the *khop* leaves kept falling in front of him, behind him. He felt as if he too would fall and tumble headlong into a lead-colored river, as smooth and motionless as a mirror, that he would fall and fall and fall and fall . . .

I'm going to die . . . Die in this putrid khop jungle. Oh Mama, oh Papa, oh Mien . . .

Horrified, he saw these three beings whom he loved most in the world rise like three shadows from the other side of the lead-colored river that had no bridge, no boat, and no waves. They didn't reply to him, didn't even wave to him, not even the slightest gesture to let him acknowledge his call. They just stood there, like three indifferent, unfeeling statues, their eyes empty.

Oh Mama, Oh Papa, Oh Mien . . . I'm going to die.

Tears fell slowly in his soul, like drops of mist from the valley at dawn. Why do tears resemble mist when a man weeps for himself? He didn't know. This poignant question floated, accompanying him like dandelion fluff as he summoned his last breath of strength to drag himself forward.

The higher the sun rose in the sky, the more Bon panted. Just as his eyelids were about to glue shut, he saw the shadow of a soldier moving through the *khop* leaves. A joyous cry rang out: "Hey, brothers! It's one of our men. He's one of ours!"

Then, the familiar clatter and clanking of ground troops, the crunching of boots on dead leaves, the snapping of branches and a chaotic jumble of voices.

Who is it? He looks like Na, Quoc, Duong, Mai, Nha, Dang, Tuan, Huan, Ha, Thong . . . Brother, it's me. I'm one of you . . . Oh sergeant, we're saved. We've found our comrades. The vultures won't be able to peck your eyes out. Your soul will rise to paradise, there where the dawn is peaceful, where there is birdsong, where boys tussle on the grass near clear, babbling brooks.

After these thoughts, he suddenly remembered the vultures who had stalked and pursued him throughout this journey.

Whores and sons of bitches and bastards all of you!

And this time the curses echoed clearly, if only in his imagination. After all these curses, he felt free, light, happy, and then he lost consciousness.

Twelve days later, Bon woke up in the army headquarters' hospital. Of his battalion of eight hundred and eighty-eight men there were only seven survivors. A company from another battalion had discovered him just as he was losing consciousness, hitched to a corpse that vultures had skinned clean and on which all that remained were the shoulders and a skull. They buried the sergeant at the edge of the *khop* jungle.

Just five hundred yards farther lay the plain.

15

People in the cities get up later than they do in the countryside. At about six-thirty, the shop windows were still padlocked. Only the doors were opened slightly, left lazily ajar so the shopkeepers could sweep the sidewalk outside. The owners, women with their hair still in curlers and their clothes still unbuttoned, yawned as they waited impatiently for the street vendors to pass so they could buy a quick breakfast of dumplings and hot sticky rice, or sandwiches and meat pâtés for their husbands and children. By seven o'clock, all the shops were open, brightly lit, their merchandise impeccably displayed, with customers already milling about. At this hour, the city was a bustling space shimmering with color, vibrant with sound, the dust of the day starting to swirl about. Hoan lived like a sleepwalker in this world. He neither stayed up late nor woke particularly early. He would get up at about seven-thirty, but liked to lie in bed for at least an hour while his sister Nen prepared his bath. Though city people washed themselves with fancy soaps and imported gels, Hoan still bathed with the traditional herbs his mother had used—lemon and grapefruit leaves, basil, lemongrass, or whatever was in season. When boiled, these herbs gave off a perfume that always reminded him of the countryside and wild roses, that made him dream of both purity and naked breasts.

That morning, as he got out of his bath, Hoan found Nen waiting for him.

"What would you like for breakfast?"

"Don't worry about me. I'm not hungry."

"You're strange. You're in the prime of life. How are you going to have energy to work if you don't eat breakfast?"

Hoan could see how concerned his elder sister was, this mother and faithful wife. So he yielded. "Okay. Well, get me a packet of sticky rice with green bean paste."

Reassured, Nen went off to buy the food from one of the street vendors while Hoan began to prepare tea. Every day, the two women—Nen and his other sister, Chau—would bring him three eggs with salt and pepper, with some bread or a handful of sticky rice and coffee, exactly as they had once done for their father, Huy. But they didn't know that all this rich food only heightened his repressed desire. His wife had become another man's wife. The widower of Ha Hamlet slept peacefully in the past. But at night the bat of desire refused to be still, and he found himself alone to confront it.

"Here, the sticky rice is still hot. Have it right away!"

"Thanks."

"By the way, this morning Mrs. Kim Lien came by with her daughter."

"Again? What does she want this time?"

"Money. You forget that you have to give her alimony every month for the child, as the courts decided."

"Oh my God!"

Hoan had forgotten, truly forgotten, because for a long time now his sisters, Nen and Chau, had taken care of it for him. The sum was modest, but this monthly contribution forced him to confront his past, a past that refused to loosen its grip despite his desire to forget.

After the scandalous marriage, Kim Lien had shamelessly set up house, both her baggage and her weaponry, at his father's home, even though Hoan had left for Bao Village. Six months later, Kim Lien gave birth to a daughter with brown skin and frizzy hair, who was clearly no descendant of his.

Hoan's parents waited patiently. The child was born given Hoan's family name Tran. As if to remind Hoan's family of the marriage, the vice president himself—Kim Lien's father—named the little girl: Tran Nguyen Kim Loan. To celebrate the child's first birthday, he organized a feast more opulent than many wedding banquets. Hoan didn't return to his family's house. He retreated in stony silence to his hut in Bao Village, reading and fishing, and waiting night after night for the swaying of a ladder. The vice president had to swallow his humiliation in silence, longing for revenge.

Then the war broke out. After a few reconnaissance flights of American planes and a few skirmishes near the border regions, the city people and the officials from the provincial capital had to study texts on the enemy's machinations, wartime dangers, and the importance of revolutionary vigilance.

One night, while Hoan was airing out his hut, a shout rang out. "Who is up there? Come down immediately!"

Hoan didn't realize what had happened. He descended the ladder slowly. Armed men were waiting for him at the foot of the hut. As soon as he reached the ground, a voice barked, "Who are you?"

The haughty, officious tone irritated him. "I am me," Hoan replied.

"Don't be impertinent when you're speaking to the authorities! What's your name and surname?"

"Tran Quy Hoan."

"Show me your residence papers."

"17 Pham Ngu Lao Street."

"Everyone has to be where he resides. What are you doing here?"

"Fishing."

"We've been watching you for several days now. The fish that you catch, you either eat them or put them back in the water. You're not a real fisherman like the others. Now, tell us the real reason why you came here to Bao Village."

"I don't have a reason."

"We have orders to arrest all suspects, lock them up at the Central Committee Headquarters, and then to turn them over to the city authorities for investigation. You are such a suspect. I hereby arrest you."

Hoan didn't even have time to react. He stood there, dazed and disoriented, as the despotic voice continued to shout at him.

"Tie him up, comrades! Take him to the Central Committee."

Two men bounded out of the mass of black shadows and bent Hoan's arms behind his back. A third man tied his hands together at the wrists with a thick rope.

"Let's go," the haughty voice barked. Hoan felt the barrel of a rifle prod his back. The men marched him along the sand dunes on the beach. He didn't recognize a single face among his captors. Since he had come to Bao Village, he had met only a few people from Binh Hamlet, the riverside community that specialized in net fishing. The men who had arrested him were probably from the militia in the neighboring Cat Village, which also belonged to Bao Ninh Commune. What an embarrassment! He had never imagined that he would one day become a suspect, that he would be arrested, tied up, and treated so brutally. But this was war, war, war . . . He remembered everything that the commune radio and the radio from the town on the other side of the river broadcast nonstop from their jabbering loudspeakers. Heroic, determined, crystal clear, merciless words . . . a literature that promised rifles, knives, blood, and death.

I'm so stupid . . . People must have set up in fishing huts along the river to serve as informers for the enemy planes or to gather information on the local situation, defense infrastructure, or even our troop movements in the region.

While the men dragged him along the road to the cell swarming with bugs where they would lock him up, Hoan kept reproaching himself for having led such a suspiciously idle lifestyle. The black outline of the houses all along the road only heightened his terror. Since the provocation tactics of the American war planes, people no longer had the right to use lights at night. There were only the antiaircraft lamps nestled in their boxes, perforated with holes tinier than fireflies. The buildings at the Central Committee Headquarters were also completely dark. One of the men in the group moved his torch toward a padlock, and another man opened it. A barred iron cell door creaked open. A hand untied the rope around Hoan's wrists and shoved him into the cell.

"You stay here. Tomorrow, you'll be interrogated."

They closed the shutters, tied them tightly with a chain, and clicked the padlock closed. Standing alone in the cell, through the iron bars, Hoan watched the men walk away without a word. He stood there motionless, uncomprehending, as they melted into the night. He had never harmed these people. How could they tie him up, push a rifle barrel into his back, and throw him in a moldy cell? He didn't sleep at all that night, just sat on a pile of wood and torn fish nets in a room that appeared to be both a warehouse and a makeshift cell. Bugs crept out of every corner to attack and harass him. He scratched and swatted at them, their pungent smell merging with the nauseating stench of fishing nets and mold.

When the sun finally rose, Hoan noticed that the cement floor was covered with blood. During the night, he had squashed masses of bugs, but they had also sucked his blood to their hearts' delight. Their bloody traces spread in lines from the pillars of the room. Hoan stood up to examine them. Thousands of bugs had been swarming in the cracks in the pillars. The wind had dried the corpses strewn on the ground, sweeping them to one side like bean shells, mixing them with the sawdust. In the middle of the nets lay a pile of broken bricks, snail shells, and a few boxes. Hoan kicked aside a few empty boxes and a needle fell out. He grabbed the rusty old needle and began to massacre the bugs. First he stabbed holes in the wood, then he got them out one by one and cut them in two with the needle. The corpses that he stuck to the pillar dried in about ten minutes and then fell to the ground. Crack by crack, he continued until he had killed almost all the bugs in the first pillar. When the tiles started to heat up over his head, he realized that it was already midday and yet no one had come to interrogate him as threatened. Hoan threw down the needle and sat down on the ground.

They lied to me, these men who say they represent the authorities, who shouted at me and pushed the barrels of their rifles in my back. Why did I let them tie me up? It was dark and they didn't even read an order to lock me up. I'm an educated man and I just submitted like some illiterate peasant.

He was furious with himself. A cock crowed, announcing the beginning of the afternoon. Famished and exhausted, Hoan couldn't do anything except stretch out in the fishing nets and go to sleep. Yet even in sleep, his heart beat heavily, anxiously, filled with hatred for a nameless enemy.

At about four or four-thirty in the afternoon, the padlocked door squeaked and chains clanked against the iron bars. A young girl with big, round eyes carrying a bamboo basket kicked open the shutters and then entered.

"Here's your meal."

She glanced at Hoan as she opened the basket and lifted out a bowl of fish soup that was still steaming and a plate of rice with a spoon.

"Eat."

"Did the men who locked me up here say anything to you?" Hoan asked.

The young girl shook her head energetically. "I don't know, I don't know anything. Eat. I'll be back soon."

She got up suddenly and left the hut, locking the padlock behind her. Hoan realized that he couldn't hope for anything from this girl. She was perhaps one of the hundreds of young girls in the fishing village who had once secretly admired him or teased him. But in the commune, she was also a militia member whose duty it was to feed a man suspected of being a spy, and she had to obey. He took the plate and ate, his spirit serene again. One piece of fresh fish garnished a soup of broth full of fresh chili peppers. This was a typical frugal meal for the people in Bao Village. Hoan was famished, but he fished pieces of mint and dill out of the sour soup and savored them one by one, sipping the broth slowly and to the very last drop. After he ate, he set the bowl and plate aside and stretched out on the nets to sleep.

He slept until he sensed another presence in the room. He opened his eyes and saw that it was already dark outside the iron bars. It was the young girl with the round face again. She sat motionless in a corner. Hoan stood up. "How long have you been here?"

"A long time. But I didn't dare wake you. I brought you some more soup, so you won't be hungry."

She lit a flashlight and pointed it at a bamboo basket. Hoan could see a green bean soup with garlic-stewed pork, garlic cloves floating in the broth. "Please, eat."

She turned off the flashlight and crouched back. Hoan ate his soup in the darkness. When he had finished, she handed him an aluminum cup filled with something steaming hot. Hoan sniffed it. It was green tea. After he had finished drinking, the young girl silently set the cup back in her basket and went out.

"Thank you, miss," Hoan said as she fumbled with the padlock.

She mumbled something and then disappeared into the night. Hoan stood up and went to a corner to urinate. The makeshift cell was a single room without a toilet or a sink. In one corner, there was a hole dug under the wall, opened onto the outside. The prisoners urinated in this ditch and the urine trickled out into the sand outside. If he had wanted to defecate, he would have had to pile up wood shavings and use them instead of ash, as they once did with chamber pots. Hoan had taken time to examine this not-so-professional jail. He wondered who, before him, had been imprisoned here and why.

The next day, the commune Party Committee began their work sessions in earnest. Hoan could hear them pacing back and forth in the courtyard outside. They were probably fishermen who had come for permits, or school kids who needed a stamp or a political dossier. A few people were dressed like city dwellers. Hoan thought that they would surely interrogate him that morning, that they would then launch an investigation. From Bao Village to town, all you had to do was cross the river in a boat. He would certainly be able to return home that evening. Seated, his knees hugged to his chest, he waited patiently, his mind wandering. Suddenly, the cocks crowed again, announcing the afternoon. Hoan got up and looked out the iron bars: The sandy courtyard was empty. Not a human shadow in sight. The sun was at its zenith. The commune cadres had gone home and had no doubt already finished their lunch.

Those wretches. Do they want to make me scream and trash this cell to demand justice? Or do they just want to humiliate me, to push me to commit some real crime so they can sentence me to prison? Who set this all up and why?

Furious, Hoan searched desperately for the logic behind his arrest, but he could find no answers. His hands behind his back, he paced back and forth in the cramped, airless, filthy room. It was sweltering inside, under this tile roof and no real ceiling. He was hungry. He was angry at himself. He hated the men who had locked him up in this lousy pit. But it was also his own fault. He should have screamed and shouted, let everyone know that he had been kidnapped by men who concealed their faces, who didn't even have a warrant for his arrest.

More than once he had felt like screaming and shouting, but he couldn't manage to open his mouth. He was incapable of imagining himself—he, son of Schoolteacher Huy—heckling a crowd of people to bemoan an injustice, or to beg for their pity or their help. No. He couldn't. Each time he went to the door, turned his face to the iron bars, and got ready to shout, he paused and retraced his steps. In the end, he lay down on the torn nets and waited for the young girl with the firm intention of following her out, of going to find the head of the gang of men who had arrested him the previous evening. But he stayed there until the end of the day, his eyelids heavy, incapable of sleep. The young girl with the round face never came. At about eight or nine o'clock, the padlock creaked again. A man entered. A totally new voice that didn't resemble any of the voices he had heard the night of his arrest.

"So, you're very hungry?"

Hoan didn't reply.

The stranger paid no attention to Hoan's attitude, and continued, "not too far from here, near the dock, there's a really good savory porridge vendor. In front of her stall, there's an antiaircraft lamp. Let's go."

"Why did you arrest me?"

"I didn't arrest you, but I know that you are under arrest."

The man stood facing Hoan. Hoan could see that he had a haircut in the shape of a horseshoe and a square jaw. He was a well-built, stocky man with broad shoulders. Hoan didn't have time to question him further when the man continued, "Let's go into town. Living alone here you're going to raise suspicions."

"About what? What have I done to raise any suspicions?"

"The country is going to war. And the war is going to send a lot of accusations flying. It's not easy to clear yourself of an alleged crime during wartime. Follow my advice. Go back to the city."

Hoan scrutinized the man framed in the vague glow of the window frame.

"Who are you?"

The man sighed. "I was one of your father's students. That should be enough to make you trust me, no? Go, get out of here, the sooner the better."

Hoan didn't say another word. He left the shadowy hut instantly, leaving the man still standing behind him. Outside, everything had merged into a black mass. It was a moonless night. He made his way to the landing dock, found the porridge vendor's stall, ate three bowls, and then returned to his hut by the river. His clothes and personal belongings were still there, untouched. The next morning, he hopped on the first boat to cross the river back to town. He didn't want the people of Bao Village to know he had left. He had come discreetly and he would leave discreetly.

When he arrived at his family's house, he went straight to his room. Kim Lien, seated on the bed, ceremoniously attired, watched him, her eyes glinting. He suddenly understood what had happened. Without a word, he went to the market and bought a hammock and a jute mat. He hung the hammock under the porch at the back of the house, a busy place where people came and went both day and night, where no one could fail to see him, or avoid him on their way to shower or to the outhouse toilets. He used a few pieces of string to hang the mat up and make a roof to shield himself from the dew and fog.

He never left that hammock, day or night, except to go on walks or to go swim in the sea. He read, slept, and contemplated the clouds and trees in the garden. His father didn't say a word, but Hoan knew he approved of his decision. His mother heaved long, sad sighs. She loved and respected her son, and didn't dare contradict him. So she resigned herself to enduring Mrs. Lan's remonstrances and insults about Hoan's failing to live up to his duties as a husband and father. At mealtimes, Nen would prepare a separate platter of food for Hoan, who ate before or after everyone else. He never even looked at Kim Lien or her mother.

In the end, Kim Lien resigned herself to leaving. She went back to her parents' home several times, weeping and begging her parents to allow her to divorce. The vice president and the manager debated the issue for a few months before starting their negotiations. They decided that they would accept divorce if Hoan would provide for little Tran Nguyen Kim until she reached adulthood. What's more, Hoan would have to give Kim Lien a sum equal to five taels of gold as compensation for her honor.

That year was the year the country was preparing to go to war. Kim Lien's child was just one year old. Now, she was already thirteen. The months and years seemed long, interminable even, and yet looking back they seemed to him as brief as the shadow of a passing cloud.

Nen brought Hoan a plate of ripe mandarin oranges, a variety that grew only on very sunny hillsides. "Here, have a few of these, something fresh."

Hoan peeled an orange, silently calculating how much five taels of gold was worth back then. Suddenly, he realized it was absurd to even try. His mother had paled and fainted in a heap at his feet when Mrs. Lan had demanded gold in exchange for Kim Lien's signature at the bottom of the divorce papers. At the time, five taels of gold was a fortune, a sum simply unimaginable for common mortals. In a society where everything was rationed, both needles and thread, where every child had the right to just three and a half ounces of meat per month, you could actually show off by wearing a simple gold band.

Hoan's parents didn't dare even discuss the sum; it was completely out of their reach. Fortunately, although the family was destitute, Kim Lien herself showed them the way out of their predicament. Unable to bear abstinence for very long, she took a lover—the chief of the town's tax department. The man had a wife who was clever and responsible and had borne him three sons in a row. She raised their children and pampered her husband with all her heart. Her jealousy, however, was commensurate with her devotion. No one knew how she did it, but when she learned of her husband's adultery, she managed to mobilize the leaders of the fiscal department—the Party, State, and Communist Youth League heads—to apprehend him and Kim Lien in flagrante delicto. Her trap was perfectly set. All the participants got an eyeful as they spied on the adulterous couple and the woman waited for the climactic moment to scream her revenge. The two offenders both had to sign the police report before they were allowed to put their pants back on. And that wasn't all. When they got out on the street, they found that all the neighbors, who had been tipped off, had flocked to the site of the crime to witness the spectacle ...

Thanks to this scandal, Hoan's family never had to come up with the five taels of gold.

After the war, Kim Lien and her mother returned to town. The shop had been given back to Hoan's family. Mrs. Lan had been named assistant to the director of commercial administration. But her husband died, taking with him both the power and the privilege that she had used to her advantage for years. Because she no longer earned enough to eat, she tried to open a café-bar. Apparently, the business didn't work out so well and mother and daughter could barely make ends meet. Every month, they came by to ask Hoan's sisters for the child support. And each time Hoan had to drive his motorcycle past the Café-Bar Kim Kim, he did so at breakneck speed, staring straight ahead. In his heart of hearts, he wanted to see the two women emerge at the door, just to learn what had become of his enemies. But he never spotted them.

Time went by and his spiteful curiosity waned, but the child support continued. Hoan ate the oranges lazily, one by one, remembering how, in the eyes of the law, little Tran Nguyen Kim bore his name. And as his daughter, she could one day lay claim to her share of his inheritance. But he also knew that the money that he threw around could change that, so he decided to try to see a contact who worked in the courts.

After his breakfast, Hoan went to pay a visit to a man named Cang, a business associate whom he had spent some time with in recent months. He had made an appointment to discuss a common investment they had in a Saigonese company that produced insecticide. Hoan intended to find people who would have influence in the courts after he had finished the deal. On the way to Cang's place, he realized that he had a terrible headache. The pain was so bad that he felt his head would explode into a thousand pieces, his brains spewing everywhere. He was sure it had to do with his abstinence.

Hoan knew that monks had a special powder to ease sexual desire that they drank diluted in an infusion of parsley. He wanted to ask Nen to buy him this antidote, but he didn't dare. The two sisters secretly hoped that he would find a new wife, but they knew he still loved Mien, so they didn't dare speak of it. From time to time, however, Hoan would notice that they would invite young girlfriends of marriageable age to stop by. Like bait, these beautiful women waited, flitting about the shop, chatting with his two sisters, waiting for him to finally forget his wife back in Mountain Hamlet. Hoan pitied them;

he was not going to fall into a trap a second time. Nevertheless, he was still tortured by sexual desire.

One day, a well-meaning friend introduced him to a woman who claimed to have herbal cures and owned the Tradition Restaurant, an odd, somewhat private establishment that opened onto a back alley. To get there, Hoan had to park his motorcycle in the street and then wind his way on foot down the twisting alley with countless old electrical posts. The small, narrow houses were built tightly against each other in a kind of anarchic jumble. Some were made of wood planks and others of brick, but they all had a lush hedge of frangipani outside. The restaurant was at the very end of the alley; it was literally carpeted by flowers and indicated by a wood sign with the word "tradition" painted with tar. The restaurant itself was in one of the low houses covered with tiles. Inside, the unvarnished wood furniture reeked of cigarette smoke and had been polished smooth by sweat. The walls were completely devoid of decoration—there were no paintings or artificial flowers, or even lightbulbs. In brief, not a single detail of modern life had managed to slip into this place.

The owner was a sixty-five-year-old woman, but still very energetic, alert, and clever. Her white hair was pulled back in a chignon fastened to her head with a tortoiseshell hairpin and she wore a traditional black silk pant suit, with a quartz watch at her wrist. Half fairy, half witch. Her restaurant was famous for its sophisticated cuisine as well as its simple but popular dishes such as eel, stewed snails, and fish grilled in banana leaves. But the owner was even more famous for having mastered the art of divination. She reputedly could see your destiny by merely taking your pulse. She could also prescribe aphrodisiac cures and medicines to help kill desire, cure sterility, or induce spontaneous abortions. Not just womanizers but also unlucky husbands who were faithful but impotent, lined up at her door to ask for help. Her late husband had been Chinese, a famous doctor who had transmitted his secret science to his wife.

When Hoan came to consult her, she was playing solitaire in her room. She served him a tiny cup of green tea and said, "We must live in harmony with nature. When the male and female principles are united, the *qi* of life and the blood will circulate freely, the body's organs reinforce one another and develop favorably. But you pull the lock on the door shut, your house becomes dark and airless. Inevitably there will be obstructions, a kind of slow degeneration."

Hoan didn't respond. He had trouble confiding in people, so he merely said, "Thank you, Madame, but I just need the medication."

The old woman gave Hoan a discouraged but curious look, and then she handed him some of her special brown powder. Hoan was to take a teaspoon of the medication three times a day after every meal. And three weeks into the treatment, he indeed no longer felt any desire. But he had become a different man, one who craved sleep and who could lie in bed for almost twelve hours a day. His skin had a greenish pallor. He walked around in a daze. He began to worry when he realized that he no longer felt like thinking or observing the world around him, that he was just half-alive. His sisters panicked and tried to find a doctor, but Hoan had refused help.

Now he understood the old woman's advice. He knew that he would have to choose between two equally unwholesome states. And he chose to live like a man, both lucid and vigorous. He still had to work for his son's future, for his relatives, for the woman he loved.

Lost in these thoughts, Hoan had completely forgotten his invitation to Cang's place for lunch. He massaged his temples before getting on his motorcycle to drive to the businessman's house.

In the course of lunch, he didn't dare drink any wine, and he limited himself to just two bowls of rice with some tofu and soy sauce. Cang burst out laughing. "Why are you eating like a monk, depriving yourself like this? Even a working-class guy like me can't restrain myself. So why the stoic abstinence, my friend?"

Hoan felt unmasked, and he blushed. Cang watched Hoan attentively, as delighted as if he had just laid hands on a vast sum of money.

"My God, you're all red! I didn't expect to see the most powerful businessman in all of central Vietnam blush!"

"Everyone has their Achilles' heel. I can't bring myself to hang out in brothels."

Cang opened his eyes wide and stared at Hoan. "What do you take me for? Some kind of pimp? Before living alone here in this city, I had a wife. And like you I thought I could sleep only with the woman I loved. But life isn't like that."

Hoan said nothing. He sighed. Cang was probably right. His father had raised him to believe that you could only find happiness with the woman you loved. And he had believed that totally. Yet even his first time with Kim Lien had brought him pleasure. He didn't even know who she was; he had slept with her in a kind of trance. And then there were the nights with the woman from Ha Hamlet, in the hut on stilts at the edge of the Nhat Le River. There, too, he had climbed the summits of pleasure, even if it wasn't the kind of perfect happiness that he had shared with Mien. Maybe a man has to find an outlet to free himself from the demands of the flesh, just like a traveler crossing an arid mountain must quench his thirst in the first pool of water that he comes across. He suddenly thought of Mien. She had to sleep with a man she no longer loved. These carnal relations were outside of love, outside of the norms that his father had taught him.

Cang, who didn't let his eyes off Hoan, continued, "Your situation is different from mine. Your wife isn't some kind of hussy. Fate forced her to leave you. You can continue to love her, to miss her, even while looking for another woman on whom to dump the garbage you have piled up in your body."

Hoan knew that the oldest profession in the world was still active in their city. No doubt this profession was a great service to unhappy men like him or even those too poor, or too disfigured, to find a woman to love them. Nevertheless, it was humiliating and pitiful to have to go seek comfort in a brothel.

As if he had guessed Hoan's reluctance, Cang spoke up. "Come on, all merchandise has to be tested. Come with me tonight. You'll see that it's not worth all this hesitation. Life is simple. You buy merchandise at a fair price. As the elders have said since time immemorial: You consume and you pay."

Cang glanced at his watch. He had another meeting in just an hour and a half. Obsessed with money, a virtual business-making machine, he could work all the time, regardless of whether the deal was interesting or not. Hoan knew that this strategy rarely yielded the best results and that those who dealt in everything from *nuoc mam* to wicks for oil lamps might toil like water buffalo, but they never seemed capable of building a real fortune.

To think that this peasant who will haggle over the size of a bottle of fish sauce, who counts every onion, is mentoring me. There are really countless games of chess in life. Those who win at one are fated to lose at another...

Hoan finally said good-bye and went on his way. When he got back to the house, he hastened to his room, slept until about three o'clock, and then hopped on his motorcycle to go take a dip in the ocean. When he came home, he found Cang chatting with his sister Chau in front of the shop counter.

"I hope you didn't snack at the beach," said Cang with a complicitous wink. "I hear they sell an excellent langoustine specialty there."

Hoan glared at Cang, but didn't dare say anything in front of his sister, who was oblivious to Cang's lewd insinuations.

"All right, Cang, let's go," Hoan said, shaking his head. Then he turned back to Chau and said simply, "I won't be eating dinner at home tonight."

The two men hopped on their motorcycles, revved their motors, and were off.

"Where are we going?" Hoan asked.

"To a Chinese restaurant."

"Which one?"

"The big one on Tran Phu Street."

Cang fell silent for a while and then spoke. "Before tasting the pleasures of the flesh, we'd better have some Chinese food. It's a lesson I learned from the real Chinese in Cholon."

They stopped in front of the restaurant. Before they went in, Cang turned to Hoan. "You pay for the meal. I pay for the pleasure afterward. That way, we'll be even."

"I'll pay for both. Don't you worry."

Cang laughed shamelessly. "Well, for once it's my lucky day."

He turned toward the kitchen and called out, "Bring the menu, please!"

The waiters replied noisily from the kitchen in a special tone of voice that one encountered only in Chinese restaurants. Almost like a staged line, a formulaic echo from behind the curtain. Despite the reply of a chorus of five or six voices, they still had to wait twenty minutes before a big, stocky guy emerged and handed them a thick menu. "What would you like as an aperitif?"

"Some fortifying spirits, and the best you have!" Cang said with a chuckle.

Cang ordered pigeon stewed with eight treasures and a steamed carp stuffed with pork and mushrooms. For Hoan, he ordered a soup of fish stomach and imperial stewed chicken, a variety of black hen that weighed only about eleven or fourteen ounces and that the kings, lords, and other members of the royal family used to have stewed with special herbs to fortify their virility. So when the waiter went scurrying off, Cang asked, "Have you ever tasted this alcohol used by Emperor Minh Mang?"

"No."

"It's a kind of liqueur invented in the time of Minh Mang. He drank it and he conceived one hundred eighteen children. He is so famous that they gave him the motto 'Six couplings a night for five sons.'"

Hoan knew a little bit of Sino-Vietnamese. Shocked, he asked, "Does that mean that in a single night you have to make love to six women and conceive five children? Are you sure you got that right?"

"I don't know any Chinese, but I'm a real veteran at this. I've tried it many times. Now you try. Tonight, you'll see how it works."

Cang winked and guffawed, sure of himself as he opened the bottle and served it. Hoan pondered the liquid, which was the color of ripe plums, skeptical but excited.

He emptied his first glass, served himself another, then a third, and a fourth. He felt exalted and spoke and laughed more, and louder. Sneaking a discreet glance at the smoky mirror that hung from the wall, he saw, much to his horror, another man, totally different from the one he knew, and who now looked at him defiantly. How could this strange alcohol and these imperial dishes induce such exaltation? Suddenly, in this restaurant where the air was pungent with the aroma of spicy, sautéed food and the stench of cigarette smoke, above the din and clamor of conversation, Hoan heard strains of music he loved. He began to whistle along.

Would this new purple brew link him to another life? Or merely another way of experiencing life? It didn't matter.

"Shall we go?" Cang asked, his mischievous eyes dancing, his face ruddy from the alcohol.

Hoan called the waiter over with a wave of his hand and settled the bill. They left and went by Cang's house, where they parked their motorcycles. Then they began to walk. Hoan didn't remember how many streets, intersections, and turns they passed. He followed Cang, thinking of nothing, murmuring an old song, and from time to time, smiling to himself. They finally arrived at a small street bordered with low, stunted almond trees. Cang moved toward a stall where they sold cigarettes. "Do you have any available?"

"They are always available, but they've had to disperse for a while."

Cang nodded. "That's fine."

The man asked, "Is it for a quick fix or the whole night?"

"For the night."

"You alone or the two of you?"

"The two of us."

"Separately or in a group?"

"Separately."

"I see."

"And the fees?"

"Same as last time."

"Good, let's go."

"One moment. At this hour, there's a new cop patrolling this street. Wait half an hour until they change the guard."

"Okay, we'll wait. We'll go to the toad bar as always."

"Fine. Thu Cuc is still in the same place."

Cang took Hoan by the arm. They moved toward a kind of street-side tea stall that was known by the locals as a "toad bar" because it had to "hop" locations rather frequently. The illegal street vendor would move from place to place with his goods and his teapots, right under the eyes of the police. These so-called toad bars survived remarkably well—sometimes thanks to bank notes surreptitiously slipped into the pockets of the police and sometimes by just waiting for the enforcers to grow weary of enforcing. Vendors would disappear and then reappear on the sidewalk with their bamboo baskets, surrounded by a few low wooden stools for their clientele. Typically, on top of the bamboo basket was a flat basket containing a few packets of dried grilled squid; some chewy peanut candy or pasty sweets; a few filthy, cracked teacups for the tea; and a few glasses for alcohol. The teapot was kept warm in a basket and the alcohol hidden beneath it. The two men approached a stall where a gas lamp was burning. The vendor, a forty-something woman with a sallow face, was squatting beside a tea basket and an odd assortment of low stools.

"The tea is totally cold, isn't it?" Cang asked her.

The woman looked around nervously and didn't reply. Cang pulled Hoan over to a stool. "You're big and stocky, so this stool is going to be a bit uncomfortable. But you'll have to make do. Are you thirsty?"

"No."

Cang turned to the vendor: "We're not having anything. Here, this is for the seats."

He slipped a bill into her hand. The woman took the bill and stuffed it in her blouse pocket, indifferent. The vendors at these toad bars were usually talkative and would try to strike up a conversation with their clients, but this woman was almost mute. Her distracted, haughty air disturbed Hoan. After she slipped their money in her pocket, she took out a piece of grilled squid and ripped it into shreds, chewing it slowly, the way a kid eats a piece of candy. Noticing Hoan's silence, Cang held out a cigarette. "Since it's your first time, well, I've got to explain a thing or two. The girls like to talk in slang. It's more fun than just common street talk. Like, if you want to have a woman once, you say you'd like to 'shoot one off.' If you want her for the whole night, you can do it two, three, or four times, or even seven or eight times like his majesty Minh Mang. In that case, you have to say you want 'the long voyage.'"

At that moment, the vendor swatted Cang's arm with her fan. "Psst! They're calling you." Hoan was stunned by her gesture. It had something familiar about it, even obscene. But Cang turned, without registering any surprise, toward the cigarette vendor's stall at the end of the street. Someone was swinging the oil lamp in the window back and forth in rapid succession. Cang jumped to his feet. "Let's go."

The cigarette vendor paced back and forth nervously in front of his stall. "Our cop has arrived, so go ahead, quickly now."

"Who's our guide tonight?" Cang asked.

The man replied with a nod of his chin, "Her." Then he turned to the tea vendor and said, "Third alleyway, you remember, Thu Cuc?"

Hoan looked at this faded woman with such a pretty name. The glow of the street lamps was so murky that he couldn't distinguish much except a sunken face under a scarf with garish colors, knotted in the style of the Cham. The woman walked ahead as Cang pulled Hoan behind him. They went down an alley and turned past some small, low houses that were half-city half-country, pieced together with scraps of things that one found in trash bins. The houses crossed and piled up against one another, pell-mell, just like the lives of these people who after the war had come from all over and landed here with nothing. Their homes resembled a line of motley snail shells nesting one on top of the other. In just a few years, right after the war, life had flourished here at an incredible speed, and then stagnated. Hoan, Cang, and Thu Cuc ducked between clotheslines hung with rags, crossed twisting courtyards built in odd shapes, tripped over rubbish heaps, and then climbed a crude, ugly staircase made out of unsanded, unpolished wood. Hoan had never set foot in a slum. He didn't even think such a horrible area could exist in his native city. In fact, before the war, this neighborhood hadn't existed; it was the result of shattered lives, a patchwork built by people set adrift by years of bombings.

"Ask her to go more slowly," Hoan said to Cang.

He didn't want to say that he wasn't used to these twisting, dirty, dimly lit back alleys. Cang shouted ahead: "Thu Cuc, wait for us!"

But she kept walking quickly as if she hadn't heard, or was pretending not to hear. Cang had to run after her and Hoan after him. Finally, they stopped in front of a large wooden door. Thu Cuc gave a few violent kicks to the door and then rang the bell. There was a faint tinkling sound from the other side of the wall. The door opened. Then she turned suddenly and disappeared as quickly as an alley cat. Beyond the open door hung a red curtain illuminated by a hazy yellow light. The sight of it stopped Hoan in his tracks. Cang took Hoan by the arm and pulled him forward. "You want to learn how to swim, you're going to have to jump in the water. You're no kid anymore."

The two men entered a rectangular room with yellowed walls. The heavy red curtain hung in the middle, strung horizontally from wall to wall. On the floor, in the middle of the room, was a lamp with a bare bulb, no shade.

Hoan stared at the dark red drapes stained with makeup, lipstick, grease, oil, sweat, and other substances, impossible to identify. Cang explained, "Behind this curtain the room is divided into two separate chambers, but we will have the pleasure of hearing each other. Let's say we'll be able to taste the same dish twice. I choose the right-hand side for you. As a beginner, it's easier."

He grabbed Hoan's hand and pulled him toward the right wall, lifted the red curtain, and shoved him in. Then he lifted another part of the curtain and disappeared from sight. Hoan could hear his footsteps in the other chamber as a woman's voice cooed, "It's been a long time!"

Just then, a pair of female hands clasped Hoan's shoulders from behind, then slid up his neck, chin, and cheeks before stopping to tickle his earlobes.

"First time for you, Elder Brother?"

Her voice was deeper, more gravelly, than the woman's in the neighboring chamber. Hoan didn't reply. Stiff, unmoving, he didn't know what to say. Her hands started to stroke him, her nails scratching his ears ever so lightly, twisting inside them. She spoke again, more clearly and more seductively: "Don't be frightened...Don't be afraid."

Hoan shivered. He felt a woman's body pressed against his back, the heat passing through her blouse to his own skin. Moving up from his buttocks, she mounted his back and spread her legs over his thighs. He remained standing, silent. He could smell the odor of hospital disinfectant mixed with powder, makeup, lipstick, and soap. He didn't understand why there would be the smell of disinfectant here in this brothel, and something about it worried him. But the woman spoke again: "Come to bed. Why are you just standing there like that?"

This time he felt warm breath on his ear. He wondered whether he should reply or just turn in silence and pull her onto the bed that stood a footstep away, under a dark, flowery cover. Slowly, she pulled Hoan's shirt out from his pants and slipped her hand inside and up the length of his spine. A strange sensation made him dizzy. These nails had nothing to do with him, they didn't belong to him, couldn't be compared to the skin, lips, and eyes of the woman he loved, and yet they held a sweetness that he had never tasted before. Hoan stopped thinking, his eyelids fluttering and closing as if to savor this sensation.

The woman lifted her own shirt and pressed her face against his back, staying motionless for an instant so he could savor the gesture and then, while he was still dazed, she licked his spine with her tongue. Hoan's breathing stopped, his body stiffened, totally concentrated, expectant, waiting for the sensations kindled on the skin of his back. A cat's fur . . . the softness of green grass . . . the downy hair on Mien's cheeks . . . the expert lips of the widow of Ha Hamlet . . . the warm rain on one of the first summer days falling drop by drop on his eyelashes . . . these memories and images threaded through his mind. His gaze suddenly darkened. Tonight he felt as if he could make love to . . . no, rape, rape hundreds, thousands, tens of thousands of women. He turned and grabbed the woman behind his back. When he lifted her and set her down on the flowered bedcover he noticed that it was gray with use.

Hoan didn't remember what he did, or what he said that night. But he knew with certitude that he made love like an automaton, like a machine. He hadn't slept a wink between their couplings, just groped around in the dark for a cigarette. He knew neither the name nor the face of the woman who lay naked and panting on the bed.

About six-fifteen in the morning, the siren howled to wake up the town. Hoan stood up, got dressed, and went to the window. The sea appeared beneath his eyes. The sun had just risen to the tops of the waves, and the eastern horizon was aflame with rosy, fresh, radiant light. A bracing wind slapped his face. He felt alive again and his head was light, clear, as if all the black clouds gathered there had burst, as if the first day of the rainy season had swept away all the dust and rubbish that clogged the gutters. He inhaled deeply of the morning air, remembering the happy moments he had lived in Mountain Hamlet, the fresh, clear dawns when he strolled under the pepper trees and coffee bushes lush with dew, his spirit free and clear, his soul as light as a kite borne by the wind.

Sadness suddenly overcame him and he chased away these memories, feeling as if they were offensive, disrespectful to Mien. He turned and looked back at the woman sprawled on the bed. She was sound asleep, her head pressed against a yellowed pillow stained with a trace of saliva, her frizzy hair almost covering her gaunt little face. *She is so skinny . . . How can she do this work every day, every month? Her face is pitiful.*

He moved closer so he could see it clearly, the face of this woman who had just spent the night with him. A metallic noise suddenly rang out. Hoan realized that he had just tripped on an aluminum basin. A liquid began to spread on the floor. Urine? The smell of it confirmed that it was.

"My God, you woke me up," said the woman as she sat up and yawned widely, her eyes still shut. "I forgot to warn you. Not to spill the basin when you got up."

Her mouth was still smeared with lipstick. She yawned again, not even bothering to cover her mouth with her hand. Hoan shuddered. From pity or disgust? He didn't know. The woman's skinny, pointy collarbones showed clearly, as she wore an open-necked blouse that fell off her shoulders. Hoan could see the nipples on her nearly flat breasts. Tiny, pale black tips of flesh surrounded by frizzy hairs. The prostitute finally managed to open her sleepy eyes and she looked at him and smiled. "Sit down."

Her eyes, awkwardly made up, sat in the middle of a square face with no cheekbones; a tiny, pointy, childlike chin; and earlobes so flat that they seemed to almost stick to her jaw. Hoan sat down, noticing the tiny crisscrossed crow's feet at the corners of her eyes.

"Have you . . . have you done this long?"

"Three years. But three years in this line of work are like thirty years of normal life. Nobody lasts very long." She scratched her back. "If I had a client as rough as you every night I'd be ready for the grave in another three years."

Hoan was suddenly seized by pity. "I . . . I'm sorry . . ."

But the woman just laughed and shook her hair. She threw the covers off her stomach and groped with her feet for her slippers; then she pulled the basin over to her, lowered her panties, and urinated noisily.

Hoan was horrified, but he sat back down on the filthy bed; it was cluttered with two flattened pillows and two ripped covers, and in the corner a balled-up towel she had used to mop up everything he had ejaculated.

Countless men have passed this way. She's got a right to behave like this. In her situation, it would be impossible to maintain even basic civilities.

Still, the trickle of her urine into the basin sickened him. He thought of the moment when he would leave this place to meet his clients, when he would have to go home and face his family.

"Well, were you satisfied?" It was Cang. He had come up stealthily behind Hoan's back and placed a hand on his shoulder.

Hoan stood up again. "How do I pay?"

Cang shook his head. "Not here. To the owner. The cigarette vendor we met last night. You can give a few coins to your lover, just enough to calm her hunger, as they say."

The woman had finished urinating and got up, looking at Hoan with eager eyes, the way a dog waits for his master to feed him. Cang whispered into Hoan's ear, "Two small bills, not one more."

Hoan grumbled. A gust of wind blew into the room, whipping up the pungent odor of urine. He glanced around the room, remembering that he had urinated several times during the night in some dark corner. Now, he saw the corner behind the jar of water that the girl had shown him to. A large earthenware pot was there too. At the foot of it was a hole that led outside to sewers. Teetering on the edge of the pot was a white plastic scoop. Next to it was a cotton towel. On the peeling wall, streaks of water were covered with a gray-green and white mold. The room next door must be just as miserable and degenerate as this one—with the same pot in the corner, the same yellowed towel, the same filthy scoop, the same outhouse hole in the ground where, night after night, clients sprayed their urine. The sight of all this squalor was sickening. Discreetly, he slipped a few large bills into the prostitute's hand and said to Cang, "Let's go."

When they arrived in front of the door, the prostitute moved ahead of them. "Thank you, Elder Brother . . . You'll come back, won't you?"

Hoan didn't reply. Seeing the stunned look on the woman's face, he realized that the tip was far too generous. Cang guessed what had happened and he turned to the woman and said, "That's enough now. We'll be back."

As they were going down the stairs, Cang turned to Hoan and said harshly, "None of this stupid generosity. Every business has its rules of the game, its laws."

Hoan didn't comment. But when they got out to the alleyway, he said, "I've got things to do this morning."

"Me too," Cang replied immediately.

Their heads lowered, they both walked quickly. They arrived in front of the stall piled high with cigarettes. The owner was waiting for them. He still had the same huge, puffy face with folds of flesh piled on his thick bull's neck; his eyes were still bulging, indifferent.

"Why are you back so late?"

Cang replied, "Exhaustion. Impossible to get up."

The enormous face looked as cold as ice. "Fifteen percent more for the costs."

"What?"

"According to our rules, you have to leave before the dawn siren. At this hour, it's time for the cops, so we evacuate the girls. Overtime means the clients have to pay for the risks they incur for us."

"Fine, fine, okay," Cang grumbled.

Hoan got up and paid the owner of the café. "I've got to be going."

Cang nodded. "Me too."

And the two men went their separate ways. Hoan returned home, washing himself once again, and then headed for the ocean on his motorcycle. He sat for a long time on the shore, his spirit light, free. He listened in silence to the waves, contemplating the tide as it put on its shimmering green coat under the morning sunlight. A crab fumbled in the sand with its claws. Suddenly, he sighed, remembering the skinny prostitute, her mournful eyes, like some papier-mâché dog.

Even though Cang had said that they were just paying for used merchandise, even though Hoan had given a generous tip, pity for this human life continued to haunt him. He still remembered the woman's flat chest, her misshapen breasts, her face smeared with makeup.

Poor woman. What does her face look like after she's washed away the makeup? Whatever happens, I've got to thank her, poor woman . . . Yes, whatever happens, I'm indebted to her.

16

With the return of the hunting season, the mountains to the east took on the hypnotic colors of a nightmare. The lush, watery green of the forest was suddenly studded with dazzling red flowers and the darting wings of butterflies. Just one look could transfix you, make you gasp for breath. On the rocky ledges, huge ferns sprang up, bursting with sap, swaying in the wind and unfurling in the mist to reveal intense crimson blossoms. The sky was by turns a clear blue or as white as flour, clouded by a thick, misty rain. The horizon seemed to flicker and blink like eyes opening and shutting, crisscrossed from time to time by long, thin wisps of cloud as pearly and as shimmery as silk. And suddenly, while the rain continued to fall, the hunting horns called to the men of Mountain Hamlet and from regions all around, kindling in their veins a sensual yearning, the memory of an ancestral pleasure that echoed in the strains of this ancient music, that set their blood boiling as it beckoned them to take to the open road, to taste adventure. The men would get out rifles they had stashed in secret corners of their homes, unroll them from oil-drenched towels that had protected them from rust. They chose a warm, sunny day to polish and oil the weapons in their courtyards, counting the spare bullets and buying new ammunition.

Then one day, they would go into the forest. There, they would find first-class provisions, the legendary, enchanting savor that they could taste only once a year—if they were lucky, that is, and the tutelary genie had blessed the barrels of their rifles. But they could be unlucky, too, and those who failed could be bloodied, their bodies torn and crushed, their faces mangled by the swat of a bear's paw, by a tiger's scratches, or by a wild boar's charge—especially by the kind of animal that seemed to guess the trajectory of bullets, or dodge traps and kill its enemies with its paws, from behind.

The women watched the lush, riotous green mountains where the hunting horns called to their husbands, but didn't dare intervene. They knew the extraordinary power and attraction of this terrifying green, this horn that trilled, at once peaceful and insistent. They knew that their arguments, even their tears, wouldn't be able to overcome the mysterious lure of the hunt. They resigned themselves to watching as their menfolk went off into the forest.

At the very start of the season, One-eyed Xa and a few demobilized soldiers had come to invite Bon to join their hunting association. He didn't have a rifle? Well, they would give him one. He didn't have enough money to buy bullets? They would lend him some. Bon had never been in a hunting group before? They would make the introductions, initiate him. In sum, they were set on drafting all the veterans into this sacred arena, this theater for expressing the feelings that bonded them to all who had been through the ordeal of war. Bon declined every offer. He didn't want to go into the forest, or to hunt.

As Bon sat in the courtyard, contemplating the horizon to the east, listening to the horns, he felt his soul detach from his body and drift aimlessly. His efforts to conceive a child with Mien seemed more and more hopeless. She had publicly returned to her former home. Every morning she would take her son back there, tend to her garden and her plantations, and discuss work plans with the old manager until dinnertime, when she would finally come back to his place. He had spied on her many times, but he had never run into the ex-husband. Yet with each passing day the time Mien was gone seemed more and more like a prison sentence; he couldn't do anything, not even gather virility grass or cook fortifying dishes for himself. He busied himself doing this and that, but mainly he followed her down the twisting alleys, popping in to see an acquaintance here and there on the pretense of wanting to borrow a comic book or a handful of fragrant herbs. He knew he was pitiful, cowardly, but he couldn't stop himself, couldn't suppress his jealousy or erase the memory of her ex-husband's luxurious underpants two sizes bigger than his own. He couldn't avoid the secret, painful comparisons. He thought of the huge house that man had built, where Bon had spent his first night back in the village, tossing and turning all night on a fancy wooden bed inlaid with mother-of-pearl, where he had gazed at his own wife the way you would gaze at an aristocratic but distant mistress. And at that moment, he thought he had lost her forever. But she had come back to his shadowy cabin to share his bed. He had thought he was the luckiest man on earth, a beggar who had not just been given sticky rice, but red holiday sticky rice flavored with rose-apple juice. The heavens had given him a golden opportunity and he would be able, at last, to swim to his shore of happiness.

In war the most stubborn man wins, and the same goes for life.

He repeated the sergeant's words every morning and evening like a mantra. Like a devout follower recites his prayers, he repeated them hundreds of times on the familiar paths that led to the rocky cliffs where the virility herb grew. He murmured them in his humiliated heart every time he held out his hand to take money from Mien. He repeated them through clenched teeth like some fateful vow each time he failed to make love to her, or while he watched her bathe, desperately splashing herself with water steeped in virgin grass. But this refrain had started to disintegrate, like bits of algae drifting on the surface of the water. One day, Mien looked him in the eyes and announced, "Starting tomorrow, I'm going to take little Hanh back home. My son needs a place to run around. He's had enough of Auntie Huyen's tiny courtyard."

Bon stood stunned, motionless, as if someone had just dealt him a blow to the back of the neck. It was a long time before he finally spoke. "Mien, don't do that . . . What will people say?"

"They can say what they want. It's none of their business. I want my son to be happy. His father lives in town and comes back to Mountain Hamlet only on Sundays. On Sunday, I'll stay here."

After a moment, she added, "Here, there's nothing to make money on. To live, you've got to work. Back there, I've got plantations, orchards, all kinds of resources. Mr. Lu is going to help me cultivate them."

Bon felt as if he were choking. His land still lay fallow. He had tried to dig it twice by hand, but each time he had fallen ill and had had to stay in bed for an entire week.

When Xa heard about Mien's decision, he came by to visit with a dozen eggs on one of the days that she had left to take care of her son.

"Do you think you can dig like you were still eighteen?" Xa said. "You dreamer! Do you know how Mien's husband Hoan built up his plantations? First they dug and labored like everyone else. Then he harrowed three pepper-tree fields and a field of coffee bushes with the help of the people in Mountain Hamlet and the two neighboring villages. At the time, the merchandise was extremely rare—they were rationing underwear, washing soap, but he managed to lay his hands on bags of clothes, scarce foodstuffs, all kinds of cigarettes, nothing but quality products that only high-ranking officers could afford. The people of the hamlet weren't the only ones who clamored to work for him; everybody was lining up. They won on every level, both in reputation and in terms of the consumer products. So that's how he managed to plow and plant even faster than the workers on the State plantations. When it was peacetime again, the shortages weren't so severe. Hoan started to hire workers and pay them decent wages. He was one of the first to buy a small plow, real pumps, and generators. Have you ever visited his plantations?"

"No . . . I haven't had the time." Bon had, in fact, secretly lurked around his rival's pepper and coffee plantations.

Xa let out a long, discouraged sigh. "Even if you put your head in the sand like an ostrich, you'll always be his inferior. Don't be angry with me. An honest man must have the courage to face the truth. How can you possibly compete with him?"

"I'm not trying to compete with anyone. I live my life, work my own field," Bon snapped, furious.

Xa put his hand in his basket, took out the eggs, and placed them gently on a plate for Bon. Fresh, rosy eggs that his hard working, clever, generous wife had gathered from the hens' nests in a hut behind the pigsty. Soan had a lucky hand; Xa and his son could eat as many eggs as they liked all year-round. Bon began to think . . .

Why doesn't Mien raise chickens? Our garden is big and while I may be weak, I've still got enough strength to build a chicken coop.

He cut short his thoughts, realizing that Mien would never raise anything in his house. She had tried to plant a few rows of cabbage, but they didn't have time to grow. Ta's brats had ripped them out almost instantly. He realized that Xa was right, but he didn't dare acknowledge it. In the end, he said, "I'm waiting to get my strength back . . ."

Xa shook his head. "When are you going to get your strength back? Besides, you can't live indefinitely off Mien's money. I told you that the money comes from that man."

"What a strange argument! If you fell ill, wouldn't you seek help from your wife? Or are you telling me you would go and beg in the street?"

Xa stood abruptly and threw up his arms. His good eye was flashing with anger and he shouted in Bon's face, "You can't compare yourself to me! If I fell ill, my wife would bring me food and water, boil fragrant herbs for my bath, scrub my back and wash my hair. If I ever, God forbid, became paralyzed, she would bring me a chamber pot and empty my excrement . . . and I would take care of her in the same way, as would any honorable man who has a conscience . . . But you cannot compare yourself to me . . ."

Xa let his arms fall and sat back down on his stool. He had restrained himself, held back his final words, words that would have struck Bon too cruelly. They both remained silent for a long time. Finally, Xa spoke up. "I'm going home."

"Yes, good-bye," Bon said in a mournful voice. When he reached the courtyard, Xa turned back. "Hey, Bon . . ."

"What?"

"We've been friends since we went skinny-dipping together, but we are also both veterans, do you understand?"

Filled with remorse, Bon replied softly, "I know you're the person who cares most about me in this world."

"That's right, and since you know the bottom of my heart, I'll say it again. You can have another life, another happiness . . . I believe that. It's within your reach."

"Oh, you still want to talk about that farm with those two hundred women volunteers, the old maids, is that it?"

"Yes. My friend, the head of the organization department, has just been made director. He can find you a nice, cushy job there."

"Thanks, but I'm not interested."

"You're determined to stay here?"

"Yes."

"Have you thought carefully?"

"I love Mien. I want to have a child with her. Our child will carry a mingling of our blood and that way Mien will never be able to leave me again."

Xa looked at him, horror-struck. He wanted to say something but instead he turned and left. This time, he didn't turn back.

The second time Bon fell ill while plowing his land, Xa didn't pay him a visit. He sent his eldest son to give Bon a hen. But he didn't ask for

Bon's news. Then the hunting season came. Xa suddenly reappeared with the other veterans to invite him to join their group. Xa hadn't changed—he was still as mischievous and impulsive. He had a twinkle in his eye, and he waved his arms around enthusiastically like a kid. Bon declined again, but as he watched Xa and his friends go, when he heard their laughter and happy conversation, he felt his limbs go slack, saw the horizon shatter into tiny pieces and his soul detach from his body, floating in the uncertain space.

Sometimes, the mooing of cows or the bellowing of sheep going back to the stable broke into Bon's daydream. And at those times, he thought about his conversation with Xa.

Xa is right, no doubt. I can't compare myself to him. Their marriage is totally different from mine.

He continued to struggle to make love to Mien. He seemed each day to become more lost, more enraged, more supplicatory, just as Mien became more indifferent and more icy. At night, they left the light on and after each failed coupling, he couldn't stop himself from furtively examining Mien's face. Each time, she was gazing elsewhere, her eyes dull with resignation, enduring the horror that she no longer tried to mask. After a few seconds, whether it was midnight or almost dawn, she would get up, go boil water with virgin herbs, and then wash herself out in the garden. One night, Ta waited for the moment when Bon went to urinate and blocked his passage. "So, she washes like that, like a duck, every night then?" Ta said, staring at him, her eyes like two glowing coals.

"My wife washes when she wants, and it's none of your business," Bon replied brutally.

"I'm your elder sister."

"Go to sleep."

"Our parents are dead, and I'm all you've got left. I don't want people to look down on you."

"Then start by asking your kids to stop borrowing rice and holding out their bowls to beg for food!"

Suddenly, he was gripped by a violent anger exploding inside him. It was all he could do to keep from punching this woman he had to call Elder Sister. "Get out, go back to your room! Get your face out of my sight and may I never see it again!" he said, hammering out each of his words.

"You imbecile," she hissed. "You're just fighting with someone who wishes you well." And then she turned and hastened back to her room. Bon stood motionless. He knew that Mien had heard everything, but she continued to wash. He listened to the sound of the water rushing continuously over her body, slowly, peacefully. This swishing was as painful to him as if sizzling hot oil had been poured on his face and skin.

Oh Father, oh Mother! Why do I have to bear such humiliation?

A cry rang out inside him. He felt the urge to die, to kill, to put an end to this existence. But he stayed riveted in front of the door. Under the cold night sky, the flames next to the well cast a murky glow over the body of the woman who washed there. He didn't know why he still loved her madly, desperately.

I've chosen this path, staked my life on this hand of poker. The elders taught us: Once you've taken to the road, never look back, because the mad dog shall bite whoever retraces his steps.

Suppose that Xa was right, that he would be able to go to the state-owned plantation to choose a wife from more than two hundred women too old to find love. Bon wasn't sure he would be happier in that situation than he was during the years he had lived in Kheo Village with Thoong. During the time he had wandered from his platoon, lost in the jungle, making a life with blows of his machete, when he was just a step away from death, this deaf and dumb Laotian had taken him under her wing, protected him, loved him deeply, passionately, with humility. And yet, he had made love to her with condescension, and cold contempt, just as Mien did with him. He now tasted the bitter fruit that the young Laotian must have tasted then. And so life goes, ironic, mocking, for those whose fate strangles in ruthless, unrequited love. He remembered Thoong's face, the color of her skirt, her blouse, the years that he had left on the other side of the border, beyond the jungle.

He had gotten lost in the course of a secret campaign. The non-commissioned officers and the soldiers barely understood what their goal was, through the various training sessions and hasty political classes that were short but extremely tense. By day, everyone slept, in combat uniform, fully armed, camouflage leaves on their hats and pants. As soon as the night blurred their faces, the units took to the road without trumpets or drums, without any precise orders. Pass-words were whispered between different platoons as if they feared that the jungle trees were an enemy radar network on the lookout for information. They groped their way ahead in the night, each follow-ing the other thanks to the sound of their breathing or footsteps, or the odor of their sweat, or sometimes even thanks to the phosphores-cent glow of mushrooms or rotting leaves.

One night, a bombing scattered the troops. Bon was thrown and knocked unconscious by a bomb and when he came to there wasn't the shadow of a soldier anywhere around him. The sun had risen and Bon realized that he had been lying precariously, cradled by a bush that hung over a chasm. Above his head, vines hung over a sheer, almost vertical wall of rock. About twenty yards below, he saw the rush and burble of a stream. Thanks to a miracle of the genie or the demon of the jungle, he had fallen on this bush that had saved his life. The vines that hung above him were very thin; they wouldn't bear the weight of even a small monkey, let alone his weight. The path they had taken the previous night had probably been reduced to dust. How many had died and how many had been spared, had had the luck to survive?

Bon was going to shout to call his comrades but he thought that his cries might be heard by enemy scouts or commandos rather than his own men. He resigned himself to silence, searching for a way to save himself. There was no way out above. All he could do was grip the shards of rocks and crawl little by little to the bottom of the precipice and then walk upstream. The rock wall was steep and sheer, but tiny thorn bushes grew here and there in the crevices. Bon grabbed hold of them and let himself slide slowly toward the bottom. It took him more than an hour to reach the base of the chasm. The water there was shallow but icy. He walked against the current, up the streambed. Five days later, when he had eaten the last of his dry rations, he reached a shallow part of the chasm, which was bordered by cliffs that he could cross. When he arrived at the edge, he walked toward the east, hoping to shortcut the road along the border where the liaison agents were guiding troop movements. For the next three weeks he lived on wild potatoes and spring water.

Finally, he arrived at a Laotian mountain village lost in the peaks. This wild country was very beautiful. After days and days of plodding through the jungle, he could finally stand straight, look at the horizon, and breathe the pure air of this valley that was inundated with warm light. Here, you could see grass of a tender green hue that was rare in Vietnam. The war hadn't touched this land. Bon remembered how he had remained for a long time in that valley, half dreamy, half lucid. He was hungry and thirsty, but his soul had grown calm. After a long time, he took to the road again, crossed the valley, and entered a village. A silent afternoon. Even the dogs were too tired to bark. In the houses on stilts everyone was fast asleep. Only the cocks crowed. Bon crossed groves of sugarcane and gardens filled with pumpkins, and walked all the way to a ladder that led to the first cabin. Standing under a row of papaya trees bent under the weight of ripe fruit, he called for a long time without receiving a response. When he had almost lost hope and decided to go over to the second cabin, he heard a rustling behind his back. He turned and saw the round, distraught eyes of a woman. She had walked out of a grove of sugarcane, a machete in one hand and a bunch of sugar in the other.

"Hello, Miss."

The young woman nodded several times, still staring at Bon with her large, frantic eyes. Bon was thirsty. He couldn't help looking hungrily at the sugarcane. The woman understood instantly. She pointed her index finger at Bon's mouth and swallowed several times. Bon realized that she was mute and nodded, pointing at his own throat. The Laotian woman gestured to the ladder with her hand and invited him to follow her up; then she quickly mounted the ladder, dragging her sugarcane behind her. Bon followed. The fetid odor of her dress hit him suddenly, but the unpleasant sensation didn't last. He finally set foot on the floor of the family hut. Once the shadow of the thatch roof was over his head, the cool, silent, peaceful air enveloped his exhausted body, soothing his anxious soul. Like the other houses on stilts in the village, this one was immense and totally empty aside from linen carpets embroidered in bold, dazzling colors. Two children were sleeping soundly, arms and legs splayed, totally unconscious of the presence of this famished, thirsty traveler. The woman picked up a bowl, filled it with water from an earthenware pot near the hearth, and handed it to him. Bon emptied the bowl in one gulp; he didn't even have time to recognize the flavor or scent of the drink. She served him a second bowl and started to cut the sugarcane into pieces. When this was finished, she put them all in a bowl and set it in front of him. She sat down beside him in the familiar pose of mountain women, peeled a piece of sugarcane, and ate it, as if to show him how. Bon didn't say anything as he ate three pieces. In the vast silence of the hut, all you could hear was the ripping of sugarcane peel and the sucking sounds made by the two people eating it. A wordless music, and a rather vulgar one. But Bon felt like he was being reborn, restored to life. He sighed.

A few minutes later, he felt weak with hunger. He realized that he had drunk two bowls of a special old tea, a variety of wild tea that grew in abundance to the west of the Truong Son Cordillera. It had no taste, but it did wake him up and, worse, it sharpened his appetite. The relentless hunger of the last three weeks suddenly cried out in him. Bon tried to suck in his stomach. Again, the woman immediately understood. She stood up and got out a sticky rice pot down from a shelf. Scraping the bottom of the pot, she managed to fill a bowl and gave it to Bon. Then she handed him a small bowl filled with black sesame seeds that had been ground together with lemongrass. He ate the bowl of sticky rice; it was more delicious than anything he had ever eaten. The Laotian woman stayed seated in front of him, her hands demurely set on her thighs, her dress, embroidered with exotic motifs, spread around her on the wood floor. Bon examined the motifs and found them strangely beautiful. This woman had saved him from the chasm, from the depths of the jungle, from fear, hunger, thirst, and loneliness—all the enemies that had hunted and besieged him for nearly a month.

I'm alive. I didn't find my unit, but I escaped the enemy scouts and the jaws of the tigers. This woman is my guardian angel.

He felt filled with gratitude toward her and turned to her and said, "Thank you, Miss."

The woman seemed to feel, even if she did not hear, what he wanted to say. She lowered her eyes, blushed in modesty, and then ran off to one of the rooms. She reappeared carrying a plate of candied ginger. Bon nibbled on the pungent candies. He felt his body quickly warm up. When he had finished eating, the sweat trickled down his neck and back. The woman gave him a large towel to wipe his face and neck and handed him a pillow. Bon lay down, sated, and fell into a deep sleep. He slept until the next morning. A magical, fairy-tale sleep free of nightmares and fear, free of the constant vigilance, on the lookout for the enemy or wild animals.

When he woke up, the cabin was filled with people. They were seated around the hearth, staring at him, their eyes filled with cheerful, curious expectation. Especially a thirty-some-year-old man; Bon guessed he must be the mute woman's brother because he shared her profile and features. But he was more handsome, more refined, with eyelids that slanted upward on his forehead, his gaze piercing and glittering like that of a medium. His wife was seated by his side; she was small and plump as a doll with a fresh, rosy glow in her cheeks. Even though she had two children by her side, she seemed extremely young. Facing this couple and their two sons was a very old couple. They must have been almost a hundred years old, but they still seemed very lucid and alert, and they both wore beautiful clothes.

The brother of the mute woman rose first and moved toward Bon, holding out his hand in a gesture of friendship. A friendship that needed no justification. Bon held out his hand in reply and they shook. This was the only common language they had. After this formality, everyone sighed with joy as if some kind of oath had just been made. The mute woman was particularly happy. She was seated behind her sister-in-law, her legs folded beneath her. Her new dress, draped and flowing, was lavishly embroidered.

A man who seemed to be her elder brother took Bon by the hand and brought him over to meet the old couple. Through his gestures and the look on his face, Bon realized that these two were the village elders, those who had the highest authority in the clan and who could replace even deceased parents in their duties and responsibilities. The old woman spoke up first, and then her husband. They spoke slowly and solemnly in a language that Bon didn't understand. But he guessed the meaning and the rustic simplicity of their words. He kept silent, making a sign that he accepted their words even though he didn't know what they were asking and what he was accepting. After finishing his speech, the old man waved to the mute woman to come to Bon. He took the woman's hand and put it in Bon's. Bon let it happen. He seemed completely overwhelmed by the sequence of events, like a puppet hanging from a fateful thread. His life was adrift; how could he even begin to understand his own needs? He squeezed the hand of this unknown Laotian woman, a gesture that would thereby link him to her. Though he sensed this, he didn't hesitate, was no longer thinking of anything. At that moment, the woman's hand was the bridge that linked him to life. On the other side of the bridge, there were the night, the jungle, the flames that had consumed Hill #327—a vast, crowded, stifling expanse of trees, corpses, and vultures.

Days went by. Gradually, Bon became the central character in this family. The atmosphere in Kheo Village was oddly tranquil. From the deafening, dizzying bombardments along the Truong Son Cordillera, sometimes you could hear vague, surreal echoes, sounds as distant as if heard backstage, from behind a curtain. The sky above the village was pure, cloudless, without a speck of dust, and the crowing of roosters was the only music by which you could measure time. Thoong's elder brother built a hut on stilts for her not far from his own. He carried large, round trunks and with his friends sanded, drilled, and crafted the wood and assembled the beams for the hut. This man had no doubt promised his deceased parents that he would represent them in protecting his mute sister. While he built the hut, Bon lived in another brother's place where he was encouraged to rest and nourish himself to regain his strength. And he even began to practice conversing with his future wife in sign language. He knew that he would have to live with her for a long time, even for life. He had neither map nor compass, vehicle nor horse, and he didn't have the courage to travel through this difficult region to find the road back to his country. After so many ordeals, peace and security were all he dreamed of in life. Every day, Thoong would boil water with fragrant herbs for his bath and prepared sticky rice and steamed chicken for his meals. She kept a huge jar of candied ginger for him to eat with his morning tea, and cakes fried in the honey gathered by the Laotian montagnards for his dessert.

In the chill of the night inside Thoong's brother's hut the sap of logs sputtered, making the indoor space feel cozy and safe. Bon let himself go in this sleepy atmosphere, drifting in the current of this lazy, tranquil existence. Now that his health was back, the blood boiled again in his veins. Every night, he made love to Thoong, a real flesh-and-blood woman whom he didn't love but whom he carried to the heights of pleasure, compensating for months and years of abstinence.

The elder brother finally gathered all the necessary materials for the new hut. The entire village helped raise it for the new couple, a stranger lost in the jungle and a poor, mute woman who had waited thirty years for happiness. In five days, the hut was finished. On the sixth day, the head of the clan and his wife married them. The ceremony was simple. There was neither incense nor firecrackers, and no ceremonial garb to accompany the bride to her new husband's house. The two elders simply made their prayers to the tutelary genies in the open air, imploring their protection, and a long and solid happiness for the couple. The villagers formed a circle around them as witnesses to these prayers. After they had finished praying, the elders bound the wrists of the newlyweds with string. Five or seven old women chanted while young girls threw rice and a bouquet of flowers on the bride's dress. And that was how the ceremony was concluded. The villagers sat down then for the wedding feast—sticky rice, grilled meat, and cakes that were wrapped in banana leaves and steamed in huge vats the size of a grown man. The feast lasted all day. When the sun had set behind the mountains, everyone went home. Two wagons drawn by water buffalo carried a chest full of clothes for the bride, a new mattress, a pot of salt, and plowing tools back to the couple's house. And then the two newlyweds were left alone.

That night, as the creaking of the wagons faded down the road, as the veil of night descended on the vast hut as he found himself face-to-face with his Laotian wife, Bon began to feel fear. They had made him master of this house, the husband of this deaf-mute woman. He would live here forever, in this land that, two weeks earlier, seemed to him a paradise and now seemed to hold only sadness and boredom. This isolated cabin had become a cage that imprisoned him in the company of the deaf-mute woman. No more smiling, pretty children, no more wife like a doll, no more meals together with countless guests who, even without a common language, were bonded to him by generosity. Now there was only him and her, her and him, in almost total destitution. A couple. A couple. A life so remote could work only if they loved each other passionately. But Bon didn't love her, couldn't love her. Danger had left front stage. Sexual frustration had abated.

She was no longer his guardian angel. She was his benefactress and he had to pay her his debt of gratitude. Bon stole a glance at her. A flame illuminated her crude face, throwing her asymmetrical, broken features into sharp relief. What a strange coincidence! On such faces, all the heavens had to do was slip with the knife by one millimeter to transform a goddess into an ugly woman. And though the elder brother's features were noble and seductive, those same traits on his sister's face seemed bleak and repulsive. The ornately embroidered dresses could no longer save her. The shimmering bracelets around her wrists could no longer make him forget her huge horselike teeth. She couldn't offer him anything except for a soulful look and her body to sate his lust. That was it, the sum total of the conjugal life that lay before him.

But he reproached himself for his thanklessness and leaned toward Thoong, putting his hand on her thigh. Moved, she interpreted this gesture as a call to love and she got up and pulled him into the bedroom. That night, he made love like a farmer struggling behind his water buffalo at the height of summer. When Thoong fell asleep, he went to sit by her side at the hearth. The cabin seemed to him as vast as a cemetery in a strange land. Mien's face started to flit amid the flames. He suddenly felt shame and regret. He regretted having greedily chewed those three pieces of sugarcane, having gulped down the bowl of sticky rice like a beggar, and having held out his hand for the elders to lay on Thoong's. He had contracted an eternal debt in a moment of desperation.

During the first week in his new house, one night, he suddenly saw the moon just at the moment it rose between the middle of two high peaked mountains whose flanks stretched to the sky like lark's wings. He immediately recognized in it the face of his beautiful wife who was waiting for him back in the village. Mien was his love and inspiration now, his most sacred force and the most powerful link to his former life. He had to go back home. He couldn't allow himself to lose her. But life had dragged him along in spite of his dreams. Every morning, he went out to the fields with Thoong. It was the corn season and they were going to harvest and set aside the sparse ears to eat, while they hung the others in the attic to dry and use as seed. Thoong's elder brother had given her half of his herd of cows, a fortune that Bon would never have even dreamed of in Mountain Hamlet. Here, he learned how to milk cows and cook their milk into cakes shaped like pieces of sugarcane. At first, he couldn't bear the smell, but in the end, he became almost addicted to these cakes. Above all, he loved the burned pieces in the bottom of the pan, which gave off a tantalizing aroma. Eating these cakes while sipping piping hot tea in the foggy, chill dawn was heavenly. Life in the mountains was as peaceful as the surface of a lake on a windless day. Bon realized that he had changed.

In this time of war, having a peaceful life is enough. I have to learn to accept my fate.

Often, at night, seated in front of the fire, holding his knees between his arms, he would listen to the distant echo of bombs on the Truong Son Cordillera, remembering the years of misery, as a soldier, how just months ago he had dragged the sergeant's corpse through the *khop* jungle, struggling with ghosts and vultures, devastated by the bombing that had wiped out his unit. Day after day, he had fumbled through the dirt in search of edible roots to grill. Night after night, terrified, he had slept in a hammock suspended by parachute string from the branches of the trees, amid the shuddering sleep of wild animals. These memories helped him him accept his present life. The hut on stilts was clean and spacious. Bags of pumpkins and sugarcane hung in neat rows under the stock of salted meat, milk cakes, and dried bamboo shoots. The ears of corn set aside for seed hung gold and glowing by the chimney. Near them rattan baskets were filled with fragrant herbs for his bath. For the space of a dreamy moment he felt fulfilled.

But as the days went by, these moments were rarer and rarer. During the weeks of drizzling rain, the cabin sank into the damp silence of the fog. Sunless days and moonless nights. The fire on the hearth they kept burning couldn't rid Bon's heart of the interminable chill, the sadness and anxiety. He was irritable for no reason. At mealtimes,

as he chewed balls of sticky rice with salt flavored with lemongrass—
or pork so salty it would take the skin off one's tongue—he would
suddenly long for white rice, the sweet-and-sour savor of bamboo
shoots stewed with fresh water shrimp sauce and chilies. Or the spicy
soup he used to eat, panting for breath. He remembered the taste of
fish cooked with galanga root. He remembered the lush greenness of
cabbage fields in his village, the thick carpet of yellow flowers in
spring. He remembered old songs to which he had forgotten the lyrics
but that nevertheless haunted his memory like errant wisps of cloud
and smoke. He remembered the purple glow of twilight back in
Mountain Hamlet, the marvelous pastel colors that dusted people's
faces. Here too he could see the same sky, the same land, the same
mountains, the same forests. But why hadn't he seen this miraculous
glow here in Kheo Village?

Each time his memory tortured him, his life in the hut seemed suddenly dull and unbearable and the sticky rice with salt hard to swallow.
Thoong's face ceased to be a woman's face. Now it was just an inert
object, a wall, a stone. This sensation hounded him through too many
nights. His deaf-mute wife continued to jump on him, poking and
sniffing him like one would a wild boar, trying all kinds of manipula-
tion. But he felt no desire, and the fear of being an ingrate no longer
helped spur him to do his conjugal duty. Either he stayed stretched
out, as stiff as a log, or he pushed his wife away roughly and turned to
the wall, pretending to sleep. Thoong would weep softly. Sometimes,
seized with pity, he would turn over to console her. But that happened
more and more rarely. He couldn't stand it anymore. He had come to
loathe her damp skin and flesh, whose color reminded him of a boa
constrictor, or a snake, or an iguana. Thoong's large, square, mannish
face with its wide, jutting jaw and horsy teeth disgusted him. Miserable, he realized that the source of his pain was nostalgia for Mien—
her white, glowing skin and her shiny black hair, her fresh, full red lips.
She was his palace that neither time nor separation could ruin. Yes, it
was Mien. Behind the smells and the aromas, behind the fields of cab-

bage and the yellow flowers, behind the marvelous clouds and distant melodies was a woman he thought of constantly, his first wife, who was waiting for him back in the village.

And the nights passed, torturously. And the days passed, anxiously. And time passed. And the rain and the sun. And life went by. And he would go to the fields with his Laotian wife to sow corn and to harvest the rice. He would go to the forest with his brother-in-law to gather honey, hunt game, and trap monkeys. He would take part in all the festivals of Kheo Village, speak with the villagers in the few words of the language he had learned. And in the darkness of night, when the vapors of alcohol had suffused his soul, when this fierce, harsh sadness broke his heart, he continued to drink until his body was on fire, until his brain swayed and spun. And then he would climb on Thoong's belly and copulate without kisses or caresses.

Months and years went by. The moon continued to rise between the mountain peaks, beckoning to him. At the beginning of each new lunar cycle, like a man possessed, he would go and sit on the landing from the time the moon rose until the cock crowed for the first wake. On those nights, Thoong was left in solitude. Little by little, she saw a rival in this silvery disk that shed its light on the mountains and fields surrounding the village. She would drink alone and go to bed early. Like a bear hibernates to flee the ordeal of winter, she slept to flee the full moon, and to wait for the dark nights, the lucky moments when her foreign husband, reeking of alcohol, would share the pleasures of the flesh with her, stuttering words in a language that she could neither hear nor understand. As she silently bore her fate, accepting Bon's sudden fits of anger, she began to dream of having a child. More than once, she would put his hand on her belly and sign to him that she was waiting for the day when it would swell like a giant red pumpkin.

Poor woman . . . Did I leave her my seed when I left?

In reality, his departure had been more of an escape. One day, Bon suddenly encountered a unit with ties to his former army unit that was going into combat. He couldn't hide his joy and he prepared immediately to leave. But without his realizing it, Thoong learned of it. She alerted her elder brother's family and the entire village. She cried, she shouted, she knelt down in front of him, her face to the ground. With every sign in her language, she expressed her love, her pleading. She clung to him constantly and watched him day in and day out, sleeping only when someone from her family or one of the villagers stood watch in her place. Her brother's family was totally devastated; everyone neglected their work, cooking and eating quickly to take turns keeping watch over Bon. They were guarding a happiness that they themselves had helped to build. Nevertheless, Bon managed to flee. On a very dark, moonless night, he managed to escape while Thoong went to urinate in the garden. She probably thought he was fast asleep, but he was walking behind her, as lightly and as silently as a cat—and when she crouched down, he slipped outside their cabin. He walked all night, the next morning, and the morning after that, afraid to stop, vigilant, his ears stalking the faintest noise at his heels. The heavens helped him find his way back.

But now Bon remembered that journey with bitterness. Yes, if he hadn't left Kheo Village that day, he could have continued to live a life as peaceful as a lake without wind. His Laotian wife, in love with him, would have continued to prepare fragrant baths for him, begging him to make love to her. He was her prince.

When Bon finally found the temporary camp of his unit, they were already gone, having left for Cambodia three weeks earlier. There was no other choice but to follow them. A hazardous, ghostly pursuit, a folly more insane than all others. Who knows how far a unit can go in three weeks, how many times they might have changed course? And aside from a cigarette lighter, a knife in his pocket, and two changes of clothes, Bon had nothing to defend himself with. During the day, the heat was oppressive, and at night the cold was hard to bear. The jungle lay in wait for him with its lush green foliage, a nightmarish, poisonous green that terrified him. Nothing guaranteed his survival. He could die of hunger or thirst; he could be killed by the Khmer, or fall prey to wild animals or vultures. But the clear moon shone in the purple sky, like a silent, magical call that kept him from turning back. Standing at the edge of the forest, he spat on the ground, swearing to do everything he could to find his unit and return to his country. Once again, he threw himself into the jungle. He walked for three months straight, in the manner of the montagnards, searching for food daily, and finding his way as he went.

In the end, this crazy journey was crowned with success. He found his heroic unit. They still bore the same insignia, but the soldiers and the officers had all changed. They helped him to find army headquarters so he could undertake the necessary bureaucratic formalities and the investigation needed to establish his identity as a lost soldier. He had to go through countless procedures, waiting and trekking from place to place, languishing in front of offices, wearing out the seat of his pants in the corridors. And during this entire time, he lived off the meager rations allotted to lost soldiers, without a single dong to buy even a cigarette. In the end, he had returned to Mountain Hamlet and been reunited with the moon of his hopes.

If only I had been content with my peaceful, easy life in Kheo Village, I would still be admired by a loving woman. I might even have had a child. If only . . .

Bon thought bitterly of all this, knowing that there would never be an if.

Businesspeople often like to keep their relationships ambiguous. Apparently, in this profession where the goal is making money, it's hard for sincere feelings to survive. Hoan had known this for a long time. And yet, sometimes, Cang would do something that would move him. One morning they went together to a restaurant run by an old Cantonese man that served steamed dumplings and soup. The place was the most famous eating spot in town, renowned for its soup's clear, rich broth made with beef bones and seafood. The broth was extremely spicy and the noodles cooked to perfection. Once you'd tasted them, all other dumpling soups seemed like dishes for starving travelers or for vulgar people. Hoan had ordered two large bowls of dumpling soup and a plate of crunchy *cha quay,* a fried doughnut made with a fine flour and fried until golden brown. A bowl of *hui tiu* soup without a plate of *cha quay* was an imperfect dish.

The waiter brought the soup on a tray.

"So, are you inviting me this time or am I inviting you?" Cang asked.

"I am."

"You're really generous. Spending money like you do should have ruined you, but the heavens protect you. Huh, the heavens. Old bastard, I say. Every time I go by a pagoda, I light some incense and say five or seven prayers. And yet I've been spinning like a magic lantern for all these years and I still never get rich."

Hoan burst out laughing. "Because the heavens and Buddha have eyes. You've barely finished praying to them and then you start insulting them. No heavens, Buddha, or genie would pardon you."

Then it was Cang's turn to burst out laughing.

After they had finished their meal, Hoan paid the bill. They left the restaurant and walked across the street toward a café. When they entered, another customer was on the way out, lifting a curtain that hung in the door frame; as he left, he almost bumped into Hoan. It was the cigarette vendor, the pimp they had met the other night. The man recognized Hoan, too. But neither of the men greeted each other, as they passed each other near the door.

"Two black coffees, very hot, please," Cang said, rubbing his hands. Then he leaned back in his seat, crossed his legs, and looked out at the street. Curious, Hoan glanced at him, wondering what he was thinking about. Cang had a hard face, as if it had been carved with stabs of a knife out of wood, beady eyes riveted on his prey out there somewhere, his lips pursed and as crisscrossed with wrinkles as those of an old man, and a long nose with nostrils separated by a high bridge.

Hoan spoke up. "What are you thinking about?"

Cang turned and raised his eyebrows in surprise. "And you, what are you thinking about? Businesspeople like us think about business, about profits and losses. What else is there?"

Hoan sighed. "You're right. But right now I'm thinking about something that has nothing to do with business."

Now it was Cang's turn to be curious. He turned to face Hoan, scrutinizing him. "What are you afraid of?"

"When I saw the pimp just now, I remembered the night when we had to flee and hide in that fish sauce warehouse with the rats darting between our legs. Frankly, I'm still horrified by it."

Cang burst out laughing. "Well, well, aren't you the good boy from the good family."

He leaned over and sipped his coffee noisily like an old woman sips tea. Hoan lifted his cup to his lips too, but he was still preoccupied, uneasy.

One week earlier, Cang had invited Hoan to go back to the brothel. For a long time now, they had returned to the sordid little room on the outskirts of town. Hoan on the right and Cang to the left, separated by a red curtain. Each time, Cang took them there and Hoan paid the bill. One night, they had barely begun when a bell began to clang in the stairwell. The prostitute who lay under Hoan sat up immediately. Even though she was tiny, she pushed Hoan off and threw him back on the bed. "The cops, the cops . . ." she screamed.

At exactly the same instant, from the other side of the curtain, Cang yelled, "Get your pants on. We've got about three minutes to get out of here."

Hoan thrashed about, fumbling for clothes. The prostitute helped him and found them tangled in a pile under the bed. "Here's your shirt, put that on first . . . Here, here are your pants. Quickly, quickly . . ."

She got herself dressed quickly, even as she passed Hoan his clothes. Cang ran out just as Hoan was buttoning his shirt.

"Follow me!" Cang yelled to him, and Hoan clung to him like a shadow. They ran down the bumpy, dimly lit staircase, the cheap wooden stairs creaking as they went. When they reached the last step, Cang waved to him as he whispered, "Over here."

Then he disappeared behind a wall to the left. Hoan bounded after Cang as they crossed a tiny courtyard and then slipped under the staircase of the neighboring house, which was even darker than that of the brothel. Dusty spiderwebs stuck to their faces, and cockroaches rustled and flew about, bumping against their foreheads. They ran down twisting back alleys until Cang finally stopped, breathless, at a low shack with a door coated with black tar. He fumbled for the latch, opening the door with one hand and pushing Hoan inside with the other. The room was pitch-black and Hoan couldn't see a thing, but the pungent smell of rotting fish stung his nostrils. He realized where they were. Cang pulled the latch and crawled over to Hoan.

"Don't worry. You'll get used to it."

Hoan's heart beat violently. He felt himself floating, falling, as if he were walking on a rope taut over a chasm. Why had he suddenly acted like a robber, or some kind of assassin being hunted down? He was terrified, but behind the terror was another, even more powerful fear.

My God, if my father was still alive to see me like this, what would he say? He probably never imagined that I, his only son, could let myself sink so low.

Rats scuttled between the sacks of fish piled up all around, jumping on the men's shoulders, ferreting between their thighs. The harsh stench of the rotting fish made Hoan feel nauseous and light-headed. As if he could read Hoan's mind, Cang whispered in his ear, "Hang on . . . In just a half hour everything will be all right."

Cang groped his way toward the door and pressed his ear against it. Hoan stayed exactly where he was, his eyes tightly shut, enduring his pain and a fear that he could confide to no one. His father was dead, but his soul still haunted this world. No doubt he was watching Hoan in this humiliating moment and sighing bitterly.

"Delicious!" Cang sighed as he lifted the cup of coffee to his lips, savoring it in an exaggerated, grotesque way. Hoan kept silent and continued to smoke.

Cang probably never had a father like mine. He's free to do whatever he likes. He came from the mud and now he's fairly rich in the eyes of his family.

Hoan couldn't believe that Cang was entirely without shame or remorse. "Hey, I've got a question for you, Cang."

"What's that?"

"The other night, when we were standing in that warehouse, what did you feel?"

"Nothing at all. I was just on the lookout, trying to get out of the mess. Eating fish sauce is okay, but no one wants to be marinated in it and have to bear that odor."

"Have you had to flee the cops like that often?"

"Sure. Many times. That warehouse is safe. The cops would never guess."

"So it doesn't bother you that we were hiding out like robbers or bandits, or even assassins?"

"I've never stolen or killed anyone. I ran because prostitution is against the law and my penis mocks the law. In fact, it stands up and screams on a regular basis. So I don't waste time thinking like you."

"But what if they had caught us and locked us up with all the scum?"

"If you think about everything, you won't do *anything*. In my life, I devote my energy to doing deals, to calculating profits and losses, to evaluating my chances of success in this business, that's all."

Cang lit a cigarette, turned, and scrutinized Hoan. "You're suffering, aren't you? And I always thought a man like you who was successful in business, blessed by the heavens, had to be happy. I guess not. It must be hard to have to think every time you get laid by a whore."

Cang looked both surprised and concerned. For the first time, Hoan thought perhaps Cang wasn't solely consumed by making money. But a minute later, he flipped his cigarette into an ashtray and said to Hoan, "Okay, I'm going. You pay for the coffee too, big business honcho of the six provinces of central Vietnam!" Cang snickered. A steely light flashed again in his eyes, his pupils dilating suddenly like a shutter. And then his face closed, changing back into an impassive, hardened mask.

Hoan watched Cang's back as he lifted the bamboo curtain and disappeared. Smoke rose from the cigarette butt he had left in the ashtray, the only trace of the man who had stood by his side in a fish sauce warehouse, who had held out his hand in the darkness of the back alleys, the courtyards, the twisting streets of a distant suburb. Hoan shivered, disoriented. The wisps that rose from the ashtray were just smoke. The man who had looked at him with warmth and compassion for half a second was just an ally of circumstance. All Hoan had to do was turn his back and Cang would probably push him over a cliff. But not before he had grabbed his money and stuffed it in his own pockets. Hoan had always known this, but he didn't want to admit it, didn't want to believe that here in the city he was in fact alone and helpless. He lived in a world that he mistrusted. Yes, he lived here like a clever fish darting through the mud and weeds even as he dreamed of the open stream. He was a businessman who still had the heart of a high school boy and the aspirations of a poet manqué.

The city doesn't belong to me. Here I'm either someone's prey or someone's enemy. Aside from Chau and Nen, I don't have any close friends. I can't trust anyone.

He kept smoking, exhaling and blowing smoke in round circles, or squeezing his lips to make it ripple like the grain in wood. He strained to find a shape or a feature, something that would shed light on life's darker side, that would guide him down the labyrinthine alleys of human relationships. Ever since he had taken over the family business, he had tried to strike up friendships with his associates, but each time he had fallen into a trap. If it wasn't some kind of illegal or dishonest competition to buy or sell, or some vicious power struggle, it was the slander of rumors and gossip. And each time, thanks to either his luck or his intuition, Hoan had managed at the last minute to escape. He was slowly realizing that what had helped him put his foot to the brake, the instinct that had transformed defeat into victory, was none other than the proud soul of his father. This slight, but determined, imperious man continued to guide and protect him. It was as if the soul of the schoolteacher couldn't resign itself to returning to Nirvana in order to love and empathize with its only son. The bitter lessons of life accumulated in Hoan's memory, giving him a second nature, a form of intelligence grounded solely in intuition, the capacity to assess situations as quickly and easily as a stork's wing passes through air as if everything had been arranged for by either a genie or a demon. This second nature made him almost unbeatable in the world of business, where the arrows aimed at him by his competitors rolled off his back, or landed elsewhere. Tall, neatly and extravagantly dressed, he looked like a papa's boy, or even a womanizer. But this seductive gentle façade belied his perspicacity and his prudence. Every soft chuckle, every courteous word, could end in a brutal and definitive decision that could make even the most experienced rivals break out in a cold sweat. But when he did deal one of his competitors a fatal blow, executing some strategy that would lead to his ruin, Hoan's heart would moan silently and painfully: *Do men really have to massacre each other this way?*

Hoan was gripped with doubt. He lived and acted like an experienced merchant, but he aspired to another life. The unfinished journey north still beckoned. Each time a train whistled on the quays, his soul was tortured by regret. Was this just the inevitable, restless character of a child who had been adored, who had grown up in a peaceful, secure home where love had woven an eternal, mysterious mist that life's harsh, corrosive sunlight could never pierce? Hoan didn't know. But he knew that the tender, pensive soul in him still questioned everything, never missed the opportunity to check all the variables in the equation. And the latest variable was a skinny, sad-eyed prostitute.

Despite Cang's admonitions, the tips Hoan had given her the first time and every time thereafter had been ten times the norm. He always felt he had a debt toward this frail, worn-down woman. And by giving her a large sum of money, he somehow dispelled his anxiety. It had become a habit. The prostitute was no longer surprised as she had been the first time. Sometimes she even tried to get more money out of him. For the space of an instant, Hoan would feel suspicious, but he didn't dare admit it to Cang. One night much like all the others, they were waiting out in the alley for the cigarette vendor, drinking tea at the little stall run by the woman with the pretty name, Thu Cuc. She still wore the same flowery scarf on her head, still gazed at the grimy oil lamp. This time, the pimp didn't make them wait long. They hadn't even finished their cup of tea when the lamp started to swing three times in the window.

"Let's go," Cang said.

They got up. The woman suddenly let out a raucous laugh. She shot them a piercing look and said, "The donkey who hurries always falls into the ditch. Like some grilled squid?"

This was the first time she had invited them to eat. Cang was flustered and looked at the woman and then back at Hoan. Not knowing what to think, Hoan kept silent. After a moment, Cang smiled nervously and handed the woman a small bill. "We're leaving."

The woman said nothing, but she didn't put away her goods to accompany them as she usually did. When they arrived at the cigarette vendor's stand, Cang and Hoan saw that she was still seated behind her tea stall, as stiff and motionless as a statue. The tiny flame of the oil lamp made the street seem even darker.

"Today, we're going earlier than usual," the cigarette vendor announced. "The cops have changed their schedule."

"But it's still the same place?" Cang asked.

The man nodded. "Yes. It's not necessary to move elsewhere yet. Go ahead. You know the way, don't you?"

Hoan followed Cang down dark, twisting alleys that no longer intimidated him. The pleasures that awaited him had made him clever, thick-skinned. Cang didn't need to hold out his hand anymore on the ramshackle stairs, in the murky, sinister light. The dirty room and its filthy curtain didn't disgust Hoan anymore. Nor did he feel shame about hearing the sounds of copulating on the other side of the curtain. He had grown accustomed to this situation and sometimes that alarmed him. That night, they had agreed with the pimp to "go on the long journey." The first sexual encounters took place at about nine o'clock. Afterward, Cang spoke up: "Shall we have a drink? I've got her a bottle of 'six couplings a night for five sons' and a few packets of dried beef."

"Whatever you like."

"Get dressed. I'm on my way over."

Five minutes later, Cang brought over the bottle of alcohol and the dried, grilled beef. They sat on the bed, drinking. Rolled up in the thin cover, the prostitute huddled in a corner of the bed, her head entirely covered. It was impossible to know whether she was asleep or awake. They drank and chatted for a little over an hour, then Cang said, "Would you like to sleep for a while?"

"No."

"You're right. We've got time to catch up tomorrow. It's past ten-thirty now. The church bells are going to ring soon."

He put the packets of half-eaten beef back into his pocket and picked up the bottle of spirits. "Hey."

"What?"

"Do you often listen to the sound of bells?"

"Yes."

Cang kept silent for a few minutes, then sighed. "I'm not Christian. But every time I hear those bells ringing, I think of my mother." He left and went back to the room on the other side of the curtain.

Hoan had never heard Cang talk this way. He was surprised. But his disquiet vanished as his lust pulled him toward another arena. He shook the prostitute to waken her. But unlike her usual, submissive haste, she grumbled for a long time, half asleep, almost as if she wanted to deliberately provoke and excite him by refusing to satisfy his desire. Hoan's body was taut, feverish, excited. He felt as if he would go crazy, but he tried to hold back, not wanting to act brutally with this skinny woman half his size. This situation lasted until the church bells began to chime. The prostitute suddenly grabbed Hoan's hand and craned her neck to hear the bells. It was the first time she had ever done that. Had she heard Cang talking about his memories? Had it awakened some sad memory of her own buried under the ash of time? Hoan wondered as the woman strained her livid neck rippled with veins toward the bells, her heavy-lidded eyes suddenly frozen. When the bells stopped, she pulled herself up and, with a snakelike movement, encircled Hoan's neck with her arms and pulled his head down toward her. As if the chiming of the bells was a mysterious command, a sign that her client was near climax, that the moment had come for her to play the part, to exercise her profession in all its perfection.

A few minutes later, as Hoan had lost all awareness of everything except the ebb and flow of his own pleasure, the door swung open abruptly, slamming against the wall. The noise echoed in Hoan's ears, but he was swirling in a vortex of pleasure, like a white mouse in a laboratory cage scurries around a wheel, propelled by his own momentum, incapable of stopping. The prostitute's hands clutched more firmly, as if she were binding him to her, and he didn't even know what the fracas at the door could mean. A bright shaft of light suddenly fell right on her face. She shut her eyes.

"Stay lying down, all of you!" a voice shouted.

The prostitute let out a little cry: "Oh my God!"

The man's voice repeated icily, "Stay lying down or I'll shoot!"

Hoan couldn't see the man, but he guessed that he was standing at the foot of the bed, a revolver in one hand and the pole that suspended the mosquito netting in the other. The light fell on the bed, right where he and the prostitute lay naked.

"Stay lying down, I said! The first one who tries to flee, I'll shoot!" the man repeated. This time, Hoan recognized something strained, not entirely natural about the thundering voice behind him. He realized that he had fallen into a trap, but he felt no fear. The only thing he noticed was the rapidity with which his penis had fallen, slack and cold, from the body of the woman.

The ringleader of this blackmail suddenly spoke up again. "Stay where you are. The first one who moves, I kill him."

This time Hoan knew the ringleader was a fake. In his business, he had often met adventurers, mercenaries, hired killers, the kind of people who could command at the drop of a hat. He knew how they behaved, the way they talked. No one would talk this way, so theatrically: Stay right where you are. Hoan almost burst out laughing, but he held back. Filled with contempt, he was surprised, even impressed, by the strange calm that had come over him. Out of curiosity, he glanced at the woman who lay beneath him. Her eyelids were half open. A flash of light gleamed in her murky pupils, which were neither black nor brown. No, there wasn't a trace of fear there.

So it's a little show. And she's an accomplice. How much money did I bring in my wallet? Lots and lots. No, in fact, before I left I gave three quarters of it to Chau to pay for the merchandise. The cargo from Da Nang that arrives tonight. What luck . . .

Hoan remembered that as he had left that morning his sister Chau had run out to him, her hair still wet from her shower, to remind him that they were going to deliver a cargo from Da Nang that very night. He had apologized for forgetting and handed her his wallet.

Yes, she took the money and then handed me back the wallet.

The man behind him was dressed in civilian clothes, but the way he carried himself gave him away as a cop—a man used to wearing a uniform who had just taken care to put away his badge and his stripes. There was almost no doubt that he was a young boy off the farm who had just finished police school and then been transferred here. He was one of those young men who had been in the city just long enough to appreciate its comforts, the type who walked the streets, their eyes glued to the shop windows, unable to hide their envy. His highest aspiration, his wildest dream, was probably to buy a motor scooter, or to marry a city girl—which would be his ticket to the legal right to live here in the big city. And living here would then open doors to other pleasures, like eating a *pho* or a nice, steaming plate of sticky rice before going to work in an office instead of pushing a plow drawn by an old water buffalo through the rice fields, while gnawing at a potato or an ear of corn just as his father and grandfather had done for centuries.

Not really knowing why, Hoan felt a pang of sadness for the young man. "All my money is in my wallet, in my pants' pocket under the bed," he said calmly. "Take it all, and be quick about it because if your colleagues surprise us, it's all over."

The man was dumbfounded. Hoan's calm voice and cards-on-the-table attitude had made him suspicious.

Hoan spoke again. "I know who you are. Don't waste time. Just take the money and go. But leave me my papers and the photos."

The man shoved the barrel of his revolver into Hoan's back. "Don't move. If you turn your head, I'm gonna shoot."

"Okay, okay. Just hurry up," Hoan grumbled. Underneath him, the woman twisted, restless. The man pulled back his revolver, fumbling in the clothes at the foot of the bed. Hoan heard him toss the clothes in a corner, pull the leather wallet out of the pants, and rustle the money as he counted it.

"Stay lying down. Don't move. Don't get up for fifteen minutes!" he warned as he left the room.

"That's too long, fifteen minutes!" Hoan shouted. Then he got up and got dressed while the prostitute pulled the covers up under her chin.

"My God! I've got goose pimples. And you were so calm the whole time, as if it were nothing. You men are really terrifying!"

Hoan looked at her cynical face, her thin lips smeared with makeup. He felt filled with contempt. He turned away in silence, walked down the staircase and out of the alleys into the familiar streets.

The next day, Cang came early to take him out. Their destination was a tea shop called the Red Rose, which was popular with successful businessmen and famous for its green tea served piping hot with honey. Hoan had a craving for this typically Chinese drink favored by a people legendary for their business acumen. Like the majority of Chinese establishments, the tea shop was narrow with two rows of ten tables crammed into no more than seventy square feet. Here, you drank tea seated on round stools, back-to-back with other customers, so tightly packed in that you could feel the sweat from the back of the person behind you. An unavoidable intimacy. A huge ceiling fan spun and whistled above the boiling teapots. Drinking tea at the Red Rose was like inhaling a vapor of herbs to cure a cold. As you drank you could feel your heart warm, as sweat popped out of every pore of your body. The shop was filled with a noise as deafening as any street market, and clients lined up, waiting for a seat. The waiters ran from one end of the room to the other, as experienced as circus acrobats, darting here and there with small aluminum trays precariously set with tiny charcoal burners and pots of boiling water. The slightest false move and red-hot embers would tumble onto the shoulders and necks of the customers.

Hoan and Cang had to wait for fifteen minutes for a table. When they were seated, Cang finally spoke up. "The Chinese are really clever, don't you think?"

Hoan nodded.

"There are five tea shops in this town. Every one spacious, nicely decorated, with good music. But they're all practically empty. The only one that's packed from dawn to dusk is this one and it's run by an old Chinese guy. Everyone says he's got some magic potion. Something like an aphrodisiac. Wherever he goes he attracts people like a magnet attracts filings."

"When it comes to business, I don't believe in magic potions."

"So do you think the heavens protect the Chinese businessmen?"

"No, they have real talents. First, because they have the experience. The Chinese have been involved in commerce since antiquity. They knew even back then how to build boats that could cross the seas, they knew the value of money—while the rest of us, we Vietnamese, were praising the virtues of honest poverty and the purity of the soul and were disdaining those who made a fortune through commerce and not through farming or by working as some imperial bureaucrat. We made bad choices from the very beginning. So we're paying the price."

"And so you decided to go into business to correct our national errors?" Cang chuckled.

"No. I got into business by accident," Hoan sighed. "Once I lived very well off an entirely different profession."

Cang raised his eyebrows and looked at him. "Oh?" he said in voice dripping with sarcasm and doubt. "And which one was that?"

The waiter set the tiny burner, a teapot, and two cups in front of them. Hoan poured tea into the open-mouthed clay cup set on a large earthenware saucer as rough as a toad's skin. As the tea flowed, a fine, golden foam spread on the surface, overflowing onto the saucer. The fragrance of the tea mingled with the smell of the charcoal embers gave off a delicate, musky perfume that evoked both the bustling city streets where people fought over their prey and the distant mountains and rolling, deserted hills. Hoan lifted the cup to his lips. As he sipped he understood why this tea attracted all the fashionable people. City people hungered after everything they didn't already possess; they made no distinction between themselves and the narrow world in which they lived.

Here, they are as good as chained to a space where they struggle to survive and sell their souls for the sake of their passions. Whether a four-story house, a thirty-square-foot room rented by the month, or a wooden plank the size of one's back, it's a space made of flesh and blood that they can't do without. They have to hug up to this city to feel alive. At night, their souls take flight like domesticated pigeons, flitting through the sky before heading back to the roost. A city dweller can't bear too much open space. He likes his tea at the Red Rose, the aggressive, bustling life of the streets. The scent of this tea, its light, warm fragrance helps him make a few circles in the air, while still casting an eye back at the roost. A sensation of security, total security. And security is what a man needs first.

Hoan drank a few more sips, listening to the noisy conversations all around him. A hot, fat, greasy back pressed against his. One minute later, a woman's thigh grazed his left thigh. Her flesh was already flabby but apparently still filled with desire, and so her rubbing seemed to seek satisfaction. So that was it, life in the city. That was it, the tea at the Red Rose, a brew for those who lived chained to the shops, where the money came and went, where the numbers shuffled and rustled like mah-jongg pieces on a game table. So that was all there was to it, this life that he lived here, and which he was now ready to leave behind.

"What's the matter? Drink before it gets cold," Cang said.

But Hoan didn't hear him. Cang repeated himself, drumming the table with his fingers. "Drink or the tea is going to go cold."

Hoan looked up at Cang. At the Red Rose, you had to drink your tea steaming hot to make you sweat. Cang had played by the rules and his shirt was drenched and clung to his skin.

He inhaled a few long breaths, panting, sated. "Your whole body feels lighter. A real pleasure!"

"Like some more?" Hoan asked.

Cang hesitated. "Hmm . . . that's enough." But then he changed his mind. "Okay, order another pot for me." He pursed his lips in a smile. "This is nothing compared to the sum they extorted from us last night." Hoan signaled to the waiter to bring another pot, and then asked Cang, "Where were you when it happened?"

"I ran as soon as the owner opened the door."

"You mean the cigarette vendor himself opened the door?"

"Of course, who else would have done it?"

"I knew it was a trap, but he could have at least hid his face."

"He ran out and down the stairs right after he opened it. One of these days, if you ever ask him, he'll say he was forced to do it, that they put a gun to his head."

"And the cop?"

"They knew each other, obviously. The cop regularly shares the money with the pig-faced guy. But why did they trap us like that? Real businessmen are interested in regular, long-term profits. Not money extorted in a single blow."

Cang was glaring at Hoan, and he suddenly remembered his admonishments concerning the tip for the prostitute. Cang's chapped lips, as wrinkled as an old man's, suddenly opened into a contemptuous grin. "Nobody wipes their ass with gold coins. If you got burned, well, you deserved it."

Hoan said nothing. He moved aside so the waiter could set another boiling-hot pot of tea and burner on their table. As if he were repeating another ceremony, the man lifted the teapot high and poured out the water, making the surface foam and bubble. And somehow, Hoan suddenly saw in this yellow foam his gardens and plantations back in Mountain Hamlet, the bamboo hedges glistening with dew, the trees bending in the wind. He saw the woman he loved behind waves of familiar mist, the mist that used to roll and unfurl into the valleys where he had lived. He remembered the moist, cool air at dusk that beckoned to him. Hoan raised his cup, staring at the foam for a long time, waiting for the bubbles to vanish, one by one, before he lifted it to his lips. Cang continued to sip greedily, spying on him out of the corner of his eye. But he didn't ask any more questions. He knew that Hoan was elsewhere. It was already eight-thirty when they emptied the second teapot. Their breakfast had lasted more than two hours. Cang let out a long sigh. "I lost a deal this morning all because you dragged me along on this little tea party."

Hoan clucked his tongue and said, "Too bad . . . One has to have a little pleasure now and then. Life is short. It goes by quickly."

Hoan observed Cang for a moment. *He counts time in seconds like he counts coins in his register. But who knows, perhaps he is happier than I am.*

A young street vendor selling cakes and fried doughnuts wound his way to their table. Cang chose a few round cakes and shook them to check the filling of sweet bean paste with coconut inside.

"Why don't you take some? Or is this popular cake unworthy of a prince of your standing?" Cang chuckled, and his laughter, charged with jealousy, had a malicious edge. Hoan felt like telling him that he too had known poverty, even if he had never been as poor as Cang; life was tasteless for everyone in a society where you got your rations of meat and rice. But Hoan knew that it was useless. Cang was one of those men who didn't listen to or trust anyone. He couldn't imagine that there was anyone in the world who didn't seek money or comfort, or admire the city life just as he did.

Why, each day, am I getting more and more entangled with Cang? This man will never be a friend, in the real sense of the word.

Hoan watched Cang take a piece of newspaper out of his pocket, tear off a piece, and use it to wipe his mouth. He remembered having paid him a visit at home one day and seeing a pile of two or three dozen neatly folded handkerchiefs. Hoan had asked him if he was going to add them to the merchandise in his business, and Cang had replied that he didn't usually use handkerchiefs but that he was going to have to practice, the same way he had with ties. Cang had learned the first lesson but not the second. Seeing him crush the newspaper to wipe his mouth like that, it was likely that those handkerchiefs were still neatly folded in some closet.

Cang finished wiping his mouth and looked up. "Exactly how much money did you lose the other day?"

"I don't know."

"You don't know how much money you had in your own wallet? And you live off your business? Are you joking?"

"No, I'm not joking. Before I left I gave my wallet to my sister to settle the bill for a shipment. I don't know how much money she left in there. Probably enough to buy five or six gold bars."

"Five or six bars?" Cang shrieked, lunging across the table, his eyes bulging and his voice suddenly hoarse.

"So, you aren't mistaken? Was it five or six?" Cang asked again, his voice shrill and his temples pulsing.

"No, I made no mistake. My sister took about three quarters of what was in my wallet," Hoan said.

Cang paled and said in a choked voice, "Do you know how much my little sister had to sell herself for?"

Hoan didn't know what to say. Cang's face was contorted. He lowered his eyes and pulled his hand away from the table. Then he sat back down, staring into space, where the cigarette smoke mingled with the steam rising from the tea, where the waiters darted about like bats in broad daylight. Lowering his voice, he murmured, as if speaking only to himself, "She was a pretty girl. Just sixteen. Still a virgin. I remember the date of her birthday and the day she had to submit to this infamy to get the money to buy medicine for my father. They gave her less than a tael of gold. The client was a water buffalo salesman as old as my father."

Hoan lit a cigarette, waiting until Cang's anger had subsided. He knew that these fits of rage were part of Cang's personality, his very flesh and blood. He could hide his rage or express it, but he would never rid himself of it. Cang served himself more tea. His face was pale. He gulped down two cups, then set the cup on the table and laughed softly. "Hoan, I'm going to take you whoring."

Hoan stared at him, stunned. "At this hour? Where?"

Cang was still grinning. His face suddenly went blank, lost all tension, and looked as it did ordinarily, completely devoid of feeling. "Why, with whores, day whores. Today I'm changing the menu. To compensate, shall we say, for what we left unfinished last night. How's your health?"

"So-so. But I'm not in the mood."

"Don't worry. We're going to take a back route. No one will see us."

"It's not because I'm being stingy, it's just that, in broad daylight like this . . ."

"Are you ashamed? We're not fifteen anymore."

"But . . ."

"Please, this time it's for me. The other times you were the one who needed it. Now it's me. Please accept, it's only fair."

His voice was low, his gaze insistent. Hoan had no choice. He called the waiter and settled the bill. They left the tea shop at about ten o'clock. Once out on the sidewalk, Cang hailed two cyclos. He haggled over the price of the trip like an old-timer, then finally signaled to Hoan to get in the second cyclo while he climbed in the first one so he could lead the way. It was early autumn, but there was still sun. The cyclo driver rolled open the canopy of his vehicle. Hoan felt like a sick man leaving a hospital. He was ashamed, but he didn't dare ask the driver to roll back the canopy because Cang had his down as well. With its garishly colored roof, the cyclo looked like an advertising vehicle for a theater. Hoan resigned himself to staying seated, praying that he wouldn't bump into anyone he knew. When they arrived in the suburbs, Hoan recognized the ugly, haphazard buildings, the narrow streets and dusty courtyards piled with broken and discarded objects and piles of rubbish. They stopped in front of a small café.

"Here we are. You go in ahead," Cang said, as he paid the cyclo drivers. Hoan walked briskly, almost running into the café. He sat down on a chair and called out as he was in the habit of doing whenever he went to an unknown bar.

"What do we have to drink here?"

"Here we have the same drinks they have everywhere."

This reply startled Hoan. He looked up and toward the bar, recognizing the faded face that had sat behind the outdoor tea stall on the nights he used to wait with Cang to go see the prostitutes. The woman always covered her head with a flowered scarf, even when it wasn't cold. In the light of day, her sallow cheeks were covered with wrinkles.

"Oh!" Hoan exclaimed, surprised.

The woman lowered her head and laughed. "What's so surprising?"

There was something unspeakably sad about her hoarse, rasping voice on this sunny morning. Hoan didn't dare look her in the eyes, fearing that the wrinkles on her face were a source of embarrassment to her. The bar was tiny and cluttered. Dusty paintings hung from the stucco walls. A bouquet of plastic flowers, blackened by cigarette smoke, stood on the bar. A few bottles of lemonade were in the window. An old song was playing on the tape recorder.

What spot of dust swirls in me, that on this morning my body stirs like this?

The singer's voice crackled because the tape was old, or because the machine was old, or because songs, like seasons, fade as time goes by. The eyes of the woman with the brown spots on her face watched him like the chipped glassy eyes of a statue on some dilapidated roadside mausoleum.

She asked him, "So, what do you want to drink?"

"Give me a glass of fresh lemonade."

"A woman's drink," she commented.

Hoan didn't reply. The woman turned her back and went to prepare the drink behind the bar. A spoon clanged against a glass. Just then, Cang entered: "Don't waste your time. We're here only for a few minutes."

Then Cang turned to the woman. "You'll guide us, Thu Cuc?"

She turned her faded face to him. "During the day?"

Cang nodded.

"It wasn't enough for you?"

"No," he said coldly. But then, after a moment, he asked, "Back at the old place, why didn't you warn us?"

"I did. Too bad for you, you were too preoccupied to understand," the woman retorted as she set the lemonade in front of Hoan.

Cang looked at her for a long time, then let out a cry. "Ah, now I remember. But at that moment, I never imagined that . . ."

The woman laughed, her mouth drawn open in a wide grin. "Well, you'll have to learn." She pranced theatrically around the room, reciting a popular verse:

> Who could imagine that in this world
> Even the most experienced man has something left to learn?

Cang cut her off. "That's enough of your mocking. You take us there. And call the hunchbacked guy to watch the shop."

Neither vexed nor obliging, the woman left the café in silence and crossed the street. Swinging her bony shoulders, she walked stiffly down an alley crowded with a welter of jagged tin rooftops. Cang was preoccupied and edgy, and he watched her through squinted eyes. "Last night, she asked if we wanted to 'eat grilled squid.' It was her way of tipping us off, alerting us to the danger. I can't believe I forgot."

" 'Eating squid' is the danger signal?" Hoan asked.

Cang swiped the air with his hand, exasperated. "You didn't even know that? They say, 'black as squid ink.' It means you risk getting the clap, or that the pimps are going to rough you up. I knew it. I just wasn't paying attention. In fact, Thu Cuc was looking out for us."

"What a name. Well, she certainly doesn't look like an 'autumn daisy.' How did she get such a refined name?"

"You've got her all wrong. She's from a good family. But her life took a bad turn. A lucky guy like you can't understand the ups and downs of fate."

Hoan fell silent. Cang was probably right. No, he hadn't been through as much as others. He had never known hunger or prison. He had never thrown himself into any of the great causes or struggles in life.

Cang continued, "Thu Cuc may not be pretty, but in her youth she was gracious and refined. But how many of us do the heavens really favor? God and Buddha don't have enough love to distribute to all of us; they give it to an elite, but most of us live outside of grace."

Cang turned toward the door. "It's Thu Cuc. She's back with the hunchback. Let's go."

Hoan got up. This woman's story had piqued his curiosity. He carefully observed her as she walked slowly toward them, trying to discern the traces of her mysterious past. The scarf she wore over her head had a geometric pattern bordered by large flowers. At her neck, she wore a thin, silver necklace. That was all. Simple, original. Hoan didn't notice anything else. She wore the ordinary clothes of a forty-year-old woman. Following her was a tiny, dark-skinned old man, a real hunchback, like Victor Hugo's Quasimodo, but with a gaunt face and goatee and thin, slitty Mongolian eyes. The old man shuffled forward with rapid steps, maintaining a distance of about two strides between himself and the woman.

When the hunchback entered the café, Cang took Hoan's arm and pulled him along behind Thu Cuc. They followed her down the same street for almost two hundred yards, then turned down a narrow street crisscrossed by countless side alleys and dead ends. Hoan began to feel apprehensive; if they left him there, he would never find the exit and even in broad daylight he would almost certainly fall prey to some bandits or hired killers.

I'm an imbecile. And yet no one forced me to come here.

Cang marched ahead. As if he had divined Hoan's thoughts, he turned around and said, "Don't be afraid. I know the path well, both the way there and the way back." He laughed, baring his teeth in a wide guffaw, and added, "I might even know it better than the robbers!"

They walked for almost half an hour. Finally, Hoan saw the familiar staircase, the one assembled out of rough wooden boards that had creaked noisily under his feet.

Thu Cuc stopped at the foot of the stairs. "May I leave you two now?"

"If you like," Cang replied but he called her back after just a few steps. "Thu Cuc, we're going to settle our debt with this bunch of thugs. If you want to see, you stay."

She smiled and nodded. "Oh, that's why . . . Okay, I'll wait and see." Then she slipped behind the staircase and disappeared into a back room. They heard the door creak and the sound of shoes. Cang took Hoan's hand and pulled him toward the staircase. "Come on, follow me."

Hoan shuddered when they reached the top of the stairs. For the first time, he saw the brothel in the light of day, in all its tawdriness and filth. Cang was deep in thought as they walked in silence toward the door. But when he lifted his hand to knock, he seemed to wake from his brief meditation.

"Who's there?" a woman's voice asked.

Cang didn't reply. He knocked even more violently, until the door started to shake.

"Wait just a minute!" the voice shrieked.

You could hear wooden slippers scurrying across the floor. The door opened, and the prostitute who usually spent the night with Cang appeared. She was tall, with an angular, inscrutable face and eyes that slanted upward. With her long black hair, she seemed stronger than the other girls and she looked up at Cang without the slightest hint of anger.

"So, free today?"

"Yes. And if I wasn't, I would have made the time. Is La Hong here?"

"Yeah, but she's asleep."

"Okay. You go back to bed. I'll have work for you in a minute."

"I can wait," she said coyly. Her sweet voice seemed somehow incongruous with her large, stocky frame. Hoan asked Cang, "Why do you call her Hong? She told me she goes by Thanh Hue."

"Today Thanh Hue, tomorrow Bich Hong, and after that it's Kim Chi, and after that it'll be Ngoc Diep. Can you ever know a whore's real name? But forget about it. Come on in."

Cang yanked back the curtain and pulled Hoan into the room to the right. There, the so-called Thanh Hue, the woman with the puppy-dog eyes and the sharp tongue who bore the name of the purest of flowers, was asleep, her pale face caked with makeup. Her gaping mouth revealed a few crooked teeth. A few stray curls of hair lay on a dirty pillow streaked with saliva. The wrinkled sheet hadn't been changed for a long time and a few towels were rolled up at the foot of the bed.

Countless times I've slept in this bed, with this dirty, ugly woman, my flesh in her flesh, and even worse . . .

Hoan shuddered. He felt overcome by shame, his face and neck burning. But Cang didn't give him time to question his conscience. He lunged across the bed, grabbed the sleeping prostitute by the neck, and shook her. "Open your eyes! Open them, you dirty whore!"

The woman twisted his hand, grumbling. "What is it? What is it? What's all this noise?" Then she slumped back on the bed, incapable of resisting sleep.

Cang shouted, "Open your eyes! Are you really asleep or is this another show? Whatever it is, I'm waking you up!"

He slapped her hard, five or six times, from left to right and then from right to left, flipping her face back and forth like a pancake. Hoan was stunned. He had never imagined Cang could act so brutally.

Clack! Clack!

The last two slaps resounded like the exclamation points on brief, grammatically correct sentences. The woman's face turned purple. But pain and shock kept her from crying out, or from defending herself, and she fell back on the bed like a wilted cabbage leaf. When he stopped, she finally opened her eyes. Holding her face in her hands, she moaned, "My God, I'm hurt . . . I'm hurt . . . Mama!"

"Ah, so you too call your mother? So you feel pain, too?"

Cang's fingers had left their imprint on the woman's face, in swollen, red streaks across her sunken cheeks. Her chin jutted out pointy and hard like the prow of a boat beneath a pair of tiny ears hung with fake pearl earrings. Hoan could see the veins in her neck throbbing. He wanted to tell Cang to stop, but he realized that it was impossible. He resigned himself to watching this show on this wretched stage where he had played both witness and, possibly, the role of instigator.

Cang was still holding the woman's neck in his hands. He pulled her face up to his and demanded, "What percentage of those six gold bars went to you and your boss? Tell me or I'll smash your face in. Your boss won't dare defend you. As for the cop, he got his ass out of here in a hurry. Now he's put his uniform and his badge back on for his day job as a security policeman. Like they say, a 'people's policeman.' Oh you can scream all you want between these four walls, honey, but it's useless."

The prostitute stayed as mute as a grain of paddy rice. Hoan knew that Cang was right. She wouldn't dare call for help. Those who lived in this underworld had to obey its laws. They pillaged in the shadows and so were pillaged and chased in shadow. They could win or lose, survive or die, but they couldn't call for help. In this murky underworld, among these wild animals, no SOS was possible. Here was a place teeming with human beings and yet at the same time emptier and lonelier than if you were in the desert. Here, love was superfluous. And yet Hoan felt pity for this woman who had trapped him, who had coldly betrayed his generosity. Her whole body writhed in Cang's iron grip, and she wrenched and twisted, trying to free a bunch of her hair that he was pulling behind her, winding it tighter and tighter.

"Answer me! Answer me! How much did those dogs give you?" Cang shouted.

"Aie . . . aie . . . ," she moaned, as if it were her only defense, the only way she could get out of this. But Hoan felt no anger toward her.

There's no question that she trapped me. But it's the way people up against a wall survive. It's not the same as Mrs. Lan's trap.

He remembered the color of the red wine in the crystal glass from Czechoslovakia, the mother and daughter mincing about in their skirts.

No, I don't feel any hatred toward this unhappy soul. I lost money, but no one wounded my honor. That's what is really worth fighting for. I can't stand here and watch this senseless show of force.

He finally spoke up. "Hey, Cang, I've got things to do."

Cang stood up and glared at him. "No! How can you waste your generosity on this little bitch? Six months ago, she trapped another client and robbed him too with the help of the pimps. This time, I'm going to beat her up to teach her a lesson."

"I'm busy. I've got to go home," Hoan repeated coldly.

Cang just snickered. "You can't. It's almost noon and everyone knows you in this town. As for the back route, Thu Cuc and I are the only ones who know it. You actually want to venture out alone in this labyrinth?"

Hoan said nothing. He knew he couldn't do it. He was known in this town as a rich man. Bandits and robbers, hungry street people—everyone would be waiting for the right moment.

Seeing Hoan's silence, Cang lowered his voice. "Okay, we'll go in just a minute. I'm going to wind this game up quickly."

He called out, "Thu Cuc! Thu Cuc!"

"I'm here!" she replied immediately, her head still veiled with a flowered scarf. "Oh . . . oh"—a shrill cry, as cutting as a razor blade, hurt Hoan's ears. He watched as the prostitute who was twisting in Cang's hands sat up, let out a kind of feline yelp, and pounced on the woman who had just arrived, plunging her nails into her face. Thu Cuc let out a cry and stepped back, trying to dodge her attacker. But the prostitute ripped off the veil, revealing a bald head. Thu Cuc screamed when she realized that her head had been exposed to everyone's view. Instantly, her fear was transformed into rage, and her face turned the color of lime, the brown moles and age spots on her cheeks standing out like black beans. Her sad, dull eyes suddenly flashed and glinted like those of a tigress.

"Hong! You bitch! . . ." She spat out these words one by one. In her eyes, Hoan could see a tide of hatred that had been held back for too long, for months and years.

"Hong, you bitch, now you're going to see who I really am!" Thu Cuc hissed, slowly articulating each word as her lips pursed ever so slightly into a smile. Her cheeks bled from the scratches, but she was oblivious, and she pounced, pinning her adversary to the bed, strangling Hong's neck between her large, bony hands with their sharp, yellowed nails.

Cang gaped in disbelief. All that was left in his hand was a slight tuft of her hair. The two women continued to claw at each other, these two wretched lives, filled with neither husband nor child, one bald woman and the other missing a few tufts of hair that still lay in the hands of her aggressor. When the moment of shock had passed, Cang exploded in anger, throwing the clump of hair down on the floor. "Oh, you whore!"

His teeth clenched, he pulled Hong's head backward by the hair. Thu Cuc immediately pummeled his face with her fists. "Stop!" Hoan bellowed. He didn't realize he could shout so loudly. "Stop! I don't want a murder here. If you don't stop, I'll call the police, and I don't care what happens!"

He had never screamed so loudly in his life. He who had been taught since childhood that only vulgar people made scenes like this in front of others. But his screaming had yielded immediate results. Cang said to Thu Cuc, "Okay, let her go."

Thu Cuc dealt a final blow to the prostitute's bloodied face. Blood trickled down from her torn lips and smashed nose. Thu Cuc picked up her scarf and covered her head, turning toward the wall. Then she left. She disappeared instantly behind the curtain.

"Let's go home," Cang said to Hoan.

He turned toward the prostitute, who lay as limp and motionless as a corpse on the floor.

"Remember this lesson, you dog. It's not so easy to rob people."

Cang wiped his bloodied hand on his thigh and across to the opposite side of the curtain. "I'm going. We'll see you another time."

The woman replied, "Okay, I'll be expecting you."

The two men went down the stairs, their footsteps echoing in the silence. In this neighborhood, street sounds faded into the deserted space as the residents scattered in all directions. This was the army of the city's slaves, the ones who fumbled through the garbage cans and sewers, who lived off selling chicken and duck feathers, or scrap paper and metal, old irons or stoves, or any of the detritus of urban life. By day, the old people, the handicapped, or the mentally ill either lay hidden, or came out to warm their backs in the sun that fell on their doorstep. Old women with skin as wrinkled as boa constrictors scattered a few grains of rice to their chicken coops. Hoan knew that at night their children and grandchildren would sell these same chickens at the Doan Market, a place that opened at dusk to serve the poor and a handful of thieves and poets who might suddenly be inspired by nightfall. This wretched, forlorn suburb spread its wares under Hoan's eyes. He had been here many times, but this was the first time he had seen it in the light of day. Suddenly, he felt sad. Brooding thoughts collided in his brain like dark clouds in a winter sky.

"Say . . ." He had been speaking to Cang, but he realized suddenly that he was alone in the cyclo that was taking him back to his house. Cang was seated in the one in front of him. Hoan felt sickened, didn't want to see the face of this man who had beaten a woman right in front of him. And yet something compelled him to see Cang again.

"Please, are you paying or is the other man?" the cyclo driver had stopped to ask Hoan. He realized that the man had driven right back to Thu Cuc's shop. The hunchback was standing in front of the door, scrutinizing him with his beady eyes. Hoan paid the cyclo driver, got out, and went into the shop. Cang was seated there, smoking nervously.

"What'll you have?" the hunchback asked.

"Two lotus teas. Ah, no, we just had tea at the Red Rose. Two hot coffees, and give us the best. If it's cheap I'm going to dump it in the street," Cang said, half-joking, half-threatening.

"How many types of coffee do you have in this shop?" Hoan asked.

"At least five, isn't that right, hunchback?"

"That's right. Five types."

Cang spoke up again. "First, you've got the diluted extract of old shoes that they serve up to dockers, workers, cyclo drivers, security cops, and farm laborers, even to the village kids. The second category—they call it short-sleeved coffee—starts to smell like the real thing; they sell it to college kids, street vendors, and market people, even to the florists and fruit sellers. The third category, the average stuff, you can find anywhere in town. It starts to get strong, and they call it students' coffee. The fourth, the real authentic brew, is the coffee from Buon Me Thuot. Aromatic, rich, dense, they make it in the filters and serve it in real porcelain cups that they've warmed in boiling water. It costs two times students' coffee. That's the papa's boy coffee, and it's reserved for rich folk, for students from wealthy families. The fifth category is the real summit, and I just ordered some for you to celebrate with. It's also from Buon Me Thuot, but it requires a meticulous preparation, with very precise doses of chicken fat, butter, salt, a set grinding time, a certain temperature for the flame, and just the right fermentation before they dry the beans. It's like alchemy—everything about it is like a secret art. What's more, you've got to brew it like the French did during the colonial period, when their chefs knew how to do it and transmitted the art."

Cang spoke passionately, licking the saliva off his lips in anticipation.

Hoan chuckled. "So you're a real connoisseur! I'm from this country and I'd never heard of any of this."

Cang laughed softly, pleased with himself. "The heavens give everyone a different talent. I may not be an ace at business like you, but I was endowed with a terrific memory. I remember everything that's happened to me since the age of three as if it were yesterday."

The owner brought over two cups of steaming coffee, the aroma wafting around the room.

"It's so fragrant! Incredible," Hoan exclaimed.

Cang laughed again. "Yes, incredible that in this rotten shack in some godforsaken suburb you would find such a luxurious drink, eh? Here's to your health."

He lifted his cup, inhaled deeply, and then asked the owner, "Did Thu Cuc come back here a while ago?"

The owner shook his head. "No, she went straight home."

"That bitch Hong pounced on her without giving me time to react." Cang fumed. "I had intended to rape Hong until she was paralyzed from the waist down, but this friend of mine here had to go."

"Just leave her there, someone else will do the rest," the hunchback said.

"You're not afraid of that bastard, the cigarette vendor?"

"No, he's got lots of debts with me. What's more, he just found a few more stray cows. That's why he's getting ready to get rid of that Hong whore."

"Have you seen the stray cows?"

Cang swigged a mouthful of coffee and let out a sigh of satisfaction. Hoan had almost emptied his cup. The coffee was truly delicious. If only he could learn to brew coffee this way to prepare and drink it at dawn in Mountain Hamlet.

"So, wouldn't you class this coffee as one of the best in the city?" Cang abruptly asked him. Startled, Hoan nodded in agreement.

"The best, the best . . . But why don't they advertise it? Why don't they indicate the price of each category to their clients?"

Cang nearly choked with laughter. "Because socialism does not allow one cup of coffee to cost five or ten times more than another. Our society is founded on equality and justice, as you know."

Cang set down his cup and pursed his lips. His smile faded into his familiar, blank face. "Oh, I think the State has its reasons," Hoan said cautiously.

Cang turned and stared him straight in the eye. "Oh you do, do you? You really believe there's justice in this world? I stopped believing in it once I learned how to read. Justice, well, I establish it with my own hands when I can. You just saw that. My little sister, so beautiful, so pure, sells her virginity to a water buffalo salesman for less than a tael of gold, while a run-down old whore gets a fat wad of bills from you every time she spreads her legs? And that's not all. She laid a trap with that cop and her pimp to rob you. That's justice? No way. So I do justice to her filthy face. And there's more . . . A woman like Thu Cuc, the wife of this hunchback here, was she born to work in this pit? No. Fate beat her down, forced her to wade around in this muck. Thu Cuc had made it to university, finished her last year in law. She's from Nha Trang. She landed here after Liberation. She's no illiterate like me."

Cang's brow furrowed more deeply as he spoke, a black vein pulsing in the middle of his forehead. Hoan was stupefied. Here was Cang, an ignorant man who had pulled himself out of the mud, admiring and identifying with an upper-class woman who had been trampled by life, and yet this same man had just used his own hands to brutally beat another working-class woman who had pulled herself out of the same mud as he? And the only logic that allowed him to justify meting out his brand of personal justice was the difference between the two sums of money for which these two women had sold themselves. Hoan no longer understood the logic of life here in the city, this life that he had shared with Cang but that he now yearned to extricate himself from permanently. This existence that he had to face day after day, and yet never ceased wanting to flee. An existence in which the blank face of Cang the businessman merged with the heavy-lidded eyes of the whore Hong, with Thu Cuc's bald head, with a thin, sad pair of lips smeared with scarlet lipstick, with restaurant tables piled with food, with an aluminum basin filled with urine in a whore-house, with a public sewer reserved for their male clients. This was the true face of life here, the life he had come to live and accept—vulgar, extravagant, wretched.

Hoan lifted the cup of coffee to his lips and drained it. The dense, aromatic brew reminded him of coffee bushes in full bloom, of the atmosphere at harvest time back in Mountain Hamlet, of his workers chatting as they strolled down the rows of trees in their orchard, of the vast blue sky and the wind and the birds, and the trilling of flutes the young goatherds played reverberating through the rolling hills. He remembered everything. He saw Mien walking down the furrows of their plantations, carrying a bamboo basket that held a warm sweet bean pudding for their workers in one hand and a large pot of green tea in the other. She was smiling her enchanting smile, her face rosy, a few beads of sweat on her lips. Her large, dark eyes twinkled mischievously, playfully catching his through a weave of leaves and branches, as expectant and as modest as a virgin's. Now he knew it; he could never live a real life here, in this city where no one loved anyone, where everyone prostituted themselves to have money in their pockets. Despite his success, despite his ambition, he would never be happy here. Only one person could breathe life into this being they called happiness, and that was Mien. Mien and only Mien was the pillar of his life. She was the one woman who had given him confidence and joy in life. He wasn't like Cang, this man with the callous, blank face seated across from him. Cang was the real hero of their time—he loved money and was happy to earn it. That was enough for him. But Hoan was a more fragile animal, thirsty for love. And the one person who could give that to him was the woman who had abandoned him one foggy morning, dragging a bag of virgin grass behind her. And then the ebb and flow of life had carried him here, washed him up on this shore littered with garbage and scum.

"What's the matter?" Cang asked, scrutinizing Hoan.

Hoan blinked. "A mosquito, a mosquito flew into my eye."

Cang said nothing, suspicious, but he didn't question him further. After a long time, he asked, "Shall we go home?"

Hoan nodded. "Let's go."

Cang got out his wallet. "This is on me."

Hoan waved his hand dismissively. "No, let me . . ."

Cang protested vigorously. "No, this time, it's on me."

Cang turned toward the owner and yelled back, "Don't forget my order. Two of those stray cows from the seaside. Choose firm flesh, but not too dark. As appetizing as the shape may be, dark skin dampens my desire."

18

During the hunting season, field work was always neglected. Old folks and young men and women alike sat around chatting and drinking tea, nervously waiting for news of their offspring and the hunt. Women paced to and fro, waiting anxiously for their husbands. Even the children stopped their games and huddled together to wait for news of their fathers and elder brothers. Each time a group of hunters returned, they would scamper out to watch the homecoming, then scatter to spread the news. All ears were peeled for the sound of the hunting horns announcing the hunters' return. Just like on festival days, the atmosphere was both jittery and exuberant. Only a rare few had enough willpower to go tend the fields. The entire village lived in silence, anxious and expectant.

One morning, Xa's eldest son arrived at Bon's house, shouting, "Uncle Bon, oh, Uncle Bon, my father is inviting you to drink some wine. Uncle Bon! Oh, Uncle Bon!"

Bon was dozing. The boy pounded on his door. "Uncle Bon, open up, quickly!"

Bon pulled the latch. The boy forced his way into the room, panting and gasping for breath as he spoke. "Come see, Uncle . . . There's lots of it. Two bears, three roebuck, and a wild sow that weighs almost four hundred pounds. My father was the one who killed it, and he's inviting you to taste some of the barbecue."

"Are they dividing up the meat?"

"Yes."

"Where? At the chief's house?"

"No, at the home of the head of the hunting guild." The young man sneered, as if he didn't understand how Bon could ask such a stupid question. Bon suddenly remembered that during hunting season the titles and offices of ordinary life suddenly became secondary. The real power went to the most experienced hunter, who knew how to rally his buddies into his guild and guide them along the best game trails, who knew to choose the best moment to begin an expedition.

"You go back to your house. I'll be over in a minute," Bon said to the boy.

These words were all the permission the boy needed to run off. Bon guessed that the operation of dividing the meat would take several hours. According to tradition, the hunter who shot the game had the right to only one thigh, or one quarter of the prey. The remaining three quarters were then further divided into two—one for his companions in the guild, and the other for the rest of the families in the village. During hunting season, every family got some of the game. And the other members of the hunting guild, even if they hadn't killed an animal for years, got the same portion of meat as the others. In another hour at most, Bon reckoned that the village would thunder with the sound of pestles pounding in mortars and cleavers hacking the meat into pieces on wooden boards, while the villagers called to each other across the bamboo hedges. The air would be redolent with the aroma of sizzling hot grilled meat sautéed with onions and garlic.

I should have a medicinal infusion. There will be time enough to join them.

Bon went into the kitchen to prepare a pot of virility grass. Another bowl of fortifying medicine sat on a table inside the house. Old Phieu himself had given him the recipe. A short time after Bon had taken this treatment, his health had improved. Old Phieu had advised him to keep eating wild boar gelatin. This product was effective in treating kidney infections and back problems, weak nerves, night sweats, overheating of the soles of the feet and the palms of the hands, constipation, dry skin and dry hair. According to Old Phieu, Bon had lost both male and female energy, and his spleen and lungs were weak, so he had to change the remedies progressively to balance the yin and yang and regenerate the vital *qi*. The remedy that he had prescribed for Bon wasn't very sophisticated, but it was quite laborious. Bon had to find enough goat fat and bones, honey from white bees, fresh ginger and fresh Chinese foxglove roots. He could afford all these ingredients thanks to the money that Mien had given him. Every morning, Bon would dilute the gelatin in a half cup of boiling water and drink it instead of tea. As the medicine seeped through his body, the sweat would dampen his shirt and he would feel as strong as an eighteen-year-old again, capable of overcoming all resistance, able to impregnate Mien that very night. But this pleasant feeling and this fervor would last only about a half hour. When the sweat chilled on his back, the pain would return, sadness and despair pushing him once again to the edge of the water, where he would bob, ready to drown at any moment. Little by little, Bon realized that he didn't know what to do anymore. He kept taking the medicine, still hoping to recover, still eagerly soliciting all kinds of advice. But at the same time there was a sad, anxious man who seemed to watch all these efforts with a sneer, a man who knew that all this was in vain.

"Uncle Bon, oh Uncle Bon!"

Xa's son came back, screaming in front of the door, his voice exasperated now: "Uncle Bon, my father is waiting for you back at the house."

"Yes, I'm coming, right away."

Bon hadn't expected them to finish up the division of the meat so rapidly. He went back to his room, swallowed the bowl of goat gelatin and left to go and drink with Xa. This would be one less lonely afternoon, because he usually ate alone. Ever since Mien had taken her son back to her former house, they ate only one meal together in the evening. Every morning, Mien would get up before him and make a pot of sticky rice before leaving for Auntie Huyen's place. At noon, he would make another pot of rice and have vegetable soup with it, or squash. Or he would make a rice porridge with goat's blood according to a recipe from Old Phieu. It was only at night that he still enjoyed his status as husband to the woman who sat across from him at table. And it was only at night that his room became a home, even if he didn't dare think of his home as a cozy nest; rather it was a place where one spouse's coldness was the reply to the one's warmth.

I can still have a good afternoon . . . Xa is a true friend.

He continued to reflect on this, savoring it like a child savors a piece of cake. Still lulled by this feeling of happiness, he crossed the threshold to his friend's house.

Xa was waiting, seated in front of the large, low bed, a bottle of medicinal spirits in front of him, his chopsticks perched on the edge of his bowl. Right next to him, on top of a large bronze platter set in the middle of the bed, a tiny charcoal brazier sputtered softly. Next to him, a large bowl made of dried eel skin was filled with marinated meat. Bon knew that this was the flesh of the wild sow that Xa had killed. After this exploit, Xa would definitely be promoted to the status of guild elder. Hunting deer, buck, monkey, roebuck, or fox . . . that was the business of amateur hunters. But as soon as a man had killed a horse bear, or a wild boar, or a tiger, he would be promoted and could take his seat on the superior mat among the clan of elders. He became a hunter emeritus, just as a martial arts student skips from the white belt to the black belt without going through the blue or the brown. If the wild sow that Xa had killed had weighed only a hundred sixty pounds, he wouldn't have achieved this fame; he would have needed several more hunting seasons before he could even hope to gain access to the superior mat. But because the animal weighed almost four hundred pounds, Xa had leapt to the top of the hierarchy. His face beamed with joy. When he caught sight of Bon at his gate, he called out to his wife: "Hey, mother of my son, hey." Soan didn't even have time to respond before he shouted again: "Our guest has arrived, where are you?"

Soan replied loudly two or three times in succession. As she ran back into the kitchen, she greeted Bon. "Please come on in, Xa has been waiting for you!"

Bon entered the room and Soan followed behind, her cheeks as glowing as ripe peaches. "Please, now you and Xa just go ahead and eat by yourselves. You've got lots to talk about and it'll be more fun that way. Allow me to eat in the kitchen with the kids. We'll also be more relaxed on our own."

Soan smiled, then vanished into the kitchen, which suddenly boomed with laughter and giggling. Bon winced in pain. Even if he had stayed in Kheo Village, even if he had had kids with Thoong, he would never have heard such a laugh from her. A laugh that crackled and sputtered like corn grilled in a pan, shimmering like sea foam, as dazzling as a hot summer's sun. A laugh that gave a man a zest for life. Could he still have children? And would it be with Mien, a woman who enchanted him and yet who had undermined all his efforts, transforming their lovemaking into a kind of battle? Could he heal the wounds that tore at his body to plant the seed of life in hers? And if they did manage to have kids, would Mien ever laugh like that, a laugh bursting with happiness? And happiness . . . was this it, then? No, he would never have what Xa had. This shore lay too far beyond the river of his own life.

"Let's drink!" Xa said, his voice booming as he opened a bottle of medicinal spirits. "Today, it's okay to get drunk. How many of these do you think you can empty with me?"

Bon pondered the two deep earthenware cups. He didn't know what to say. Xa kept talking. "It's excellent stuff, an authentic cure."

"How's that?"

Xa chuckled. "They call it that because this drink solves all a man's problems in bed. With this stuff, a guy can spurt it out for hours and hours, get the woman pregnant just like that. I could force my wife to bear me twelve kids, six boys and six girls—if I could feed an entire platoon, that is! Did Old Phieu ever have you try any of this?"

"Not yet. For the moment, I'm taking goat gelatin and rice porridge with some fortifying ingredients."

"This drink is too strong for you. You've got to wait a bit. But today, you can taste it and there's no danger. You'll appreciate the food more that way."

Xa carefully selected strips of the marinated meat with his chopsticks and placed them on the charcoal brazier. Just a few minutes later, the smell of the sizzling meat and coals began to grow stronger and stronger until you could no longer distinguish the smell of the cooked meat from the garlic, onions, green pepper, burnt chilies, and mint. Xa kept turning the meat on the grill to cook it evenly, and when it was still rare but crisp and brown at the edges, he lifted the pieces into their bowls.

"Let's eat! When we have finished this batch, we'll take a rest and then put more on the grill. We've got the whole day to feast."

They raised their cups in a toast, and then began to eat. The barbecue was delicious. For Bon, it was the first time he had ever had such fine grilled game. They stayed silent for a long time, Xa reveling in both the food and his recent hunting exploits. Fame had come quickly to him. Most of the other hunters in the guild had remained amateurs for twenty, even thirty, years and would remain anonymous in a crowd that scurried behind the sound of the hunting horns. Xa's face beamed with joy and for a brief instant this joy passed to Bon.

Yes, well, I too can have this kind of happiness if I really want to. I'm not bad with a rifle. But what's the point of it all? The sticky, nauseating green of the jungle killed all those desires in me. Elder hunter, amateur hunter, it's all the same. One day, Mien will die, and Xa too. It's all meaningless.

The thoughts flitted through his mind like butterflies. The medicinal spirits intoxicated him and made him dizzy. And yet he continued to drink. Xa kept serving him more, too, as they finished the first course. Xa prepared more barbecue. Again, the aroma of the grilling meat mixed with that of the coals . . . and then faded in the distance . . . far away. When he was young, Bon lived in poverty; he had never known the joys of a real home, never tasted such sumptuous dishes. Nor did he know how to cook like Xa. Fate had been ruthless, never given him a lucky break until the day Mien's friends had pushed her into a stream, until the moment he held out his hand to her. Could he actually leave her to search for another? It was possible. More than two hundred lonely women were waiting for him on a state plantation. He too could become king for a woman who had given her youth to the country, just like he had been for Thoong back in Kheo Village.

No, it was too late. He didn't have the strength to try his luck again. The silver moon that shone over the mountains in Kheo Village had sapped his soul. He had followed her with all the strength he had left, but this quest had drained his sweat and blood. Now he was just an empty shell with dry, wizened, ashen skin, and a heart as bloodless as an old dried-out calabash gourd.

"Tasty, isn't it?" Xa asked.

Bon nodded. "Yes, very good."

"Why do you look so lost? Are a few drops of alcohol enough to get you drunk? What a wimp!" Xa teased, then cocked his head in the direction of the courtyard. "Hey there, mother of my son! Bring us some green bean pudding."

"Coming up!"

And in a wink of an eye, Soan appeared carrying a tiny tray set with a bowl of steaming sticky rice pudding.

"Did Bon get drunk so fast?" she asked, setting a bowl in front of him.

"Have some of this rice pudding and you'll feel better in a few minutes."

Then she went back to the kitchen. Bon lifted the bowl to his lips. *I want a wife like Soan, like Soan . . . I could fall in love with her right away, even today . . . I'll tell Xa that, very frankly . . .*

Bon swallowed his pudding. Sweat poured from his body and down the nape of his neck. He wiped his face, feeling his intoxication subsiding, his mind clearer. Then a chill ran up his spine: He had just committed a felony. He had desired his friend's wife. While he swallowed the steaming hot pudding, he had looked lustfully at Soan's back and rippling buttocks. The desire had surfaced at the moment she set the pudding in front of him.

I'm just a miserable wretch . . . Xa is the most generous of men to me.

Bon glanced furtively at Xa, who continued to drink as he savored the grilled meat, smacking his lips hungrily. You could tell just by looking at him that he was capable of devouring an entire bowl of marinated meat and slugging back a whole bottle of wine without getting drunk. Bon knew that Xa had no idea what had just gone through his mind, but he let out a deep sigh.

"Well, I've eaten my fill. I'll be going now." Bon got up, intending to leave right away. But Xa shouted at him, "Are you crazy? Relax. Have some more to drink. Why, it's been months since you've been here."

"You're so busy, I don't dare disturb you."

Xa rolled his eyes and shook his head, visibly angry. "Oh, spare me your city people's hypocrisy. I've got a few questions to ask you. Sit down."

His voice was as imperious as his friendship and his candor. Bon sat back down. Xa's good eye turned to scrutinize Bon. "I hear Mien has taken the boy back home. Did she say anything about this decision?"

"The kid needs a place to play. Back there he's got a big courtyard and a big garden where he can ride around on his tricycle. And Mien wants to tend to her plantations, look after business."

"And you're accepting this?" Xa shook his head. "Of course you have to accept it. She could have refused to come back to you from the start. But I think she still has some feeling for you. More precisely, she has agreed to sacrifice herself to compensate you for all the sacrifices you made for this country. But there's a limit to what a woman can sacrifice. I knew this would happen!"

Bon got up. "I suppose you're going to start talking about those two hundred lonely women volunteers, right? No, I've had enough."

Xa frowned and grumbled, "You don't need to make a scene. Even if you wanted to go now, I know you wouldn't dare." Xa's forehead creased with worry.

Bon lowered his head, unable to bear Xa's fury.

"Why do you go to such lengths to save face? And why with me?" Xa moaned. The longer he spoke, the more brutal and exasperated his voice became, the deeper the furrows on his brow. For the first time, Bon noticed a few gray hairs at his temples.

Yes, I'm an ingrate. Xa really loves me. He's got to earn his living to provide for his wife and kids, to repair and keep the house together. He's got a hundred and one things to do and yet he still finds time to worry about me.

Pushing his bowl aside, Xa continued, "You must know that I would take your side if you had to face another man as your rival. We've made the same sacrifices, shared the same losses. I know what you are going through, and I only wish you well. Can't you understand?"

"I do. I know you care about me more than anyone else in this world. But you can't understand me."

"Perhaps," Xa replied, his voice softening. "Because if I were . . ." Then he stopped, sighed and opened another bottle of wine.

Bon looked at him, intrigued. "You were saying . . . that if you were . . ."

"If I were you . . . if I found my wife had married another man, I'd have . . ."

Bon finished his phrase: "You would have left . . . Like most other men. Dignified men who put their honor before everything else. But I don't need it. I need happiness. I want to sleep with the woman I love, have kids with her. I'm not a faithful, virtuous husband. I slept with other women during the war. But I know that you only really touch happiness when you make love with the woman you love."

"So, are you happy?"

"I love Mien, she's my wife. I can sleep with her whenever I want to," Bon said gruffly. But in his mind he went through all his failed attempts at lovemaking.

I've got to go home, go home . . .

He repeated this over and over to himself, fearful that one more cup of wine would make his pain overflow, and that his already withered heart would break.

"I'm going home."

Xa didn't reply, he just sighed. His face looked heavy suddenly. As if he had forgotten what they had talked about, as if he too were pursuing some daydream. After a moment of silence, Xa suddenly lifted his head.

"She still isn't pregnant?"

Bon shook his head.

"How much longer does Old Phieu say you have to wait?"

"He didn't say anything specific on that topic. He just tells me to persevere."

Xa pursed his lips in a smile. "A man isn't made to wait. Time isn't some bottomless wallet. I doubt you have much time left and that's why you're turning to desperate solutions."

Bon fell silent. Xa was right. He didn't have any more time. His married life with Mien was slipping down a slope fast. Xa watched him, then continued, "I heard about a remedy, and perhaps you can try it. You take a strong coffee and add a few pinches of salt, about a half hour before making love. You can go for an hour before the cannon melts in the heat. When the sex is more intense, you've got a greater probability of getting the woman pregnant."

"Thanks, I'll see," Bon said indifferently. In reality, he had paid careful attention to Xa's every word.

The two men said their good-byes. Unlike usual, Xa accompanied Bon all the way to the front gate. He didn't say a word. Bon, too, kept his silence.

That afternoon, Bon slept for a long time. When he woke up, he went over to Old Phieu's place and asked him for a bit of ground coffee. The people of Mountain Hamlet plant coffee but they rarely drink it. They prefer young tea or *voi* from their own gardens. It's both cheaper and more practical. Only wealthy families liked this drink that was so complicated to prepare. And Old Phieu was one of them. This sensual, proud old man used to often proclaim: "A man must know pleasure as well as pain. It would be idiotic not to enjoy products that you create with your own hands."

His family applied this principle of his to the letter. When they felt like goat, they would slaughter the tastiest one in their herd. And every day they would gather the freshest eggs in their roost for themselves and sell the rest. Folks from all around the region used to observe the old man's family with envious, admiring eyes. When Bon arrived at his place, Old Phieu had just gotten out of the bathtub and was sipping his tea, a cotton towel still wrapped around his waist.

As soon as he saw Bon coming down the street, the old man called to him enthusiastically: "Come in, come in! The tea this season is very green, it would be a shame not to try some."

He poured Bon a cup of piping hot tea. Bon lifted the cup and emptied it before he dared speak. "I've heard that you drink coffee every day. Could you give me a few spoonfuls?"

The old man looked at him. "You want to try the coffee and salt remedy, is that it?"

Bon didn't say a word. He couldn't hide anything from this old warlock.

"I'm no stranger to this method," Old Phieu said. "It does yield quick results, but it can be dangerous in the long run. It's a two-edged sword. Think carefully before using it."

"I know. But I need to have a child. I need a child immediately."

Bon's voice was suddenly quavering as if he were going to cry. Old Phieu turned his head toward the garden, looking up at the trees, as if waiting for Bon's emotion to pass. Then he got up, opened a closet, and took out a small mill and a glass jar filled with grilled coffee beans. He set these down on the table and slowly filled the mill with a teaspoon. The aroma filled the room. The brown color of the finely ground coffee shimmered with bronze reflections.

"It's really fragrant!" Bon exclaimed.

"I grilled it with capon fat," the old man confided, as he poured the coffee onto a piece of parchment paper. He folded it carefully into a packet and handed it to Bon.

"Here."

"Thank you, Uncle." Bon got up, hoping to go home immediately. But the old man held him back.

"Wait, I've got a filter for you. You weren't thinking of boiling it, were you?"

Bon stiffened. *Oh no, I'm even more of a peasant than the old man.*

Old Phieu returned, handed him a filter, and said, "Don't fill it more than half or the water won't drip properly. And don't forget that the water has to be boiling hot."

Bon thanked the old man and went home.

This will be my weapon, my last chance to win back my happiness. My future depends on this aphrodisiac!

As he walked, he slipped his hand in his pants' pocket to touch the packet of coffee. Luckily, at that hour the streets were deserted, because if anyone had seen him laughing to himself like that, they would have taken him for a madman.

That night, precisely half an hour after dinner, Bon boiled water for the coffee. When she smelled the aroma, Mien glanced at him and looked surprised, but didn't say anything. She gathered clothes that hung drying and folded them.

"Would you like some coffee, Mien?"

"No," she said, shaking her head.

"I thought you used to drink it . . . back there, no?"

Bon looked Mien in the eyes, trying to divine the memories and thoughts that his question might have stirred in her. He knew that in Mien's fancy kitchen there were rows of jars filled with first-rate coffee beans just like the kind Old Phieu had given him. But Mien didn't reply, she just folded the clothes in silence, this silence that she had shrouded herself in from the day she had come back to live with him. After a long time, seeing that Bon was still patiently waiting for a reply, Mien spoke up, her voice indifferent: "Back there, I used to. But not at night. No one drinks coffee at night."

She went to put the pile of clothes away in the trunk. Bon followed her with his eyes, his heart racing.

Yes, no one drinks coffee at night like me. Me, the unhappy fool, the guy who loves you like some kind of slave, or beggar. But tonight you'll see who I really am.

After this secret proclamation, Bon heard a victorious peal of laughter. And then his own laughter mingling with that of another man, who stood watching from a distance. Strange how they both burst into a sudden, crazy fit of laughter, their two laughs striking at the same instant in a macabre echo, like the laughter of ghosts rising from the bottom of a well.

After she had put away the clothes, Mien came back to the bed, hung the mosquito net, and lay down on her side, her hands on her forehead. Bon looked furtively in her direction and started to sip the dense, aromatic, bitter, salty, almost-black coffee. He drank, savoring neither the aroma nor the flavor, concentrating solely on the sensation of the burning liquid flowing toward his stomach. There, it would transmit to his blood vessels its aphrodisiac substance, a diabolical excitement that would inflame his body, make him strong and virile, as fierce as a wrestler.

"Let's leave the light on tonight, okay Mien?"

Her hands still lay motionless on her forehead. Bon looked at his wife. The skin on her neck glowed an almost orange hue, as the lamp next to her was covered with orange tissue paper. Bon loved that color. His thoughts swirled, obsessive.

She probably thinks I'm deranged or that, having nothing to say, I'm just rambling. Tonight I am going to kiss that neck, those lips . . . I . . .

Like the light, this joyous thought exalted him. For a long time, he hadn't dared kiss her. The stench of his mouth hadn't really improved much and fear prevented him from crossing that invisible barrier... But tonight, this marvelous night... she would allow him everything. The salty coffee started to work its magic. Bon felt his body slowly warming. A bit of sweat pearled at the nape of his neck. His stomach started to churn. And from somewhere deeper in his body, a flame; first it merely flickered, like a wick in the middle of a pile of logs, and then it began to rage like the bonfires of his youth.

"Mien, come back to me."

Bon mumbled, a vague smile flitting on his lips. The light spread on Mien's clear white skin that shimmered with rose and orange reflections. Her breasts, with their tiny, soft nipples rising like hills— like the hills of a spring long past, when for the first time, he had felt his penis rise hard and erect, when he had slipped his hand into his wet pants, realizing he had become a man. That spring had been full of youth and joy and rolling green hills covered with grass and trees, with a misty rain whitening space, from hill to hill and valley to valley. And he had rolled down those damp hills, crossed those valleys, rubbed against those trees drenched in drew.

"Careful, you're going to snuff out the lamp," Mien said to Bon as he passed in front of it to climb into the bed.

Bon laughed. "Don't worry, it won't go out. Tonight, it won't go out."

And as he said this he bent over the lamp and revived the flame. The room grew brighter with the flare of light, and Mien turned to him, fearful, but didn't say a word. She closed her eyes and crossed her hands over her forehead. The light illuminated her cheek, the curve of her chin, the nape of her neck. Suddenly, he clasped Mien's hand and pulled her toward him.

"Mien, I love you..."

She didn't have time to react as Bon repeated himself three or four times.

"I love you, I love you, I love you..."

His voice grew hoarser, more and more aggressive. Frightened, Mien cried out, "No, no."

She pulled back her arm and tried to sit up. But Bon pulled her arm down, his fingers clenched like tentacles around it.

"Take your hands off your forehead . . . I've had enough of that."

His fingers, steely, clenched even tighter. Suddenly, his face white, he shouted, "That's enough! Do you understand?"

Mien gasped, her face dazed with fear. In a flash, the latch that had held back the door where Bon's demons had been locked up broke open. Bon jumped on Mien, twisting her arms back. When he saw that she couldn't resist him, he tore the buttons off her blouse with a violence that he had never shown her before.

"I should have done this a long time ago. I've been too patient, too submissive. I've suffered this donkey's life for too long."

Mien wanted to resist; she knew that Bon didn't have the right to manhandle her like this, but the rage on his pale, contorted face terrified her. She was afraid he would scream and commit some unspeakable act, so she resigned herself, letting Bon rip off her clothes and paw her like a sadistic child tortures his own doll.

Mien was speechless with fear. She wanted to beg him to stop shouting. No respectable man would shout when he made love to his wife; the slightest noise resonated in the night, echoing in the curious ears of the neighbors. Now he was kneeling at her feet, gazing fanatically up at her legs and her naked body, crouched like a tiger contemplating his prey. A vague smile flitted across his purple lips, a quivering grimace halfway between laughter and tears. Mien didn't dare look at him, and she shut her eyes as Bon continued to cry out: "I love you, I love you, I love, you're mine. You must be mine . . ."

Every time he repeated it, the flame within him soared higher and in this wild inferno, he saw the sea of flames on Hill #327 as it exploded under a rain of fire bombs, thousands of crimson walls rising up to the dark night sky, burning everything, boiling the sap in the trees, scattering flaming pieces of uniforms that danced in the air like thousands of bats trained by a sorcerer's invisible hand. The fire spattered everything with a shower of shells, ash and the dust of crushed bones. Like an enormous shooting star, the flames glided toward the Truong Son Cordillera, over the green jungle that stretched endlessly before them, consuming millions of lives. Bon saw himself walk out of this fire, a tattered, wizened wraith, floating like ash. He was no longer a man, just a ghostly mirage.

No. No. No. No. NO!

Someone shouted. And the shouting seemed to shake even the surrounding mountains and forests. Bon plunged his face into the flesh of the woman he loved.

"I love you, I love you, I love you . . . You have to belong to me, give me children, be my wife for the rest of this life . . ."

He tore off his own clothes, feverishly kissing and biting her. He felt his blood boil and he laughed maniacally, joyfully, when he saw his penis now stood erect, as hard as an iron pole.

I am your husband, Mien. Forever. And we'll have lots of kids. . . .

He murmured to Mien in his heart, a heart that softened as he stabbed his only weapon, his last chance at life, into the body of the woman he loved.

19

It was cold the day Mien learned that she was pregnant. Dew had frozen on the grass, and the tips of the orange and grapefruit trees stood motionless in the fog, their thick, compact foliage chiseled as if from marble. As usual, Mien had taken little Hanh back to her old home for his daily reading lesson. She had made lunch in her old kitchen, which was still sparkling clean. As Mr. Lu started to eat his own lunch of pickled cabbage, Mien suddenly felt herself salivate. Hunger seemed to claw at her stomach; she was as famished as if she had just come out of a long convalescence. But she had barely swallowed a few mouthfuls when she gagged. Incapable of holding back, she ran to the bathroom and vomited up everything she had just eaten. And at that instant, she felt terribly cold, colder than she had ever felt in her entire life.

"Light the hearth for me, if you will," she said to Mr. Lu.

There was always an abundant supply of charcoal in the kitchen for grilling meat or heat on really cold days. The small stove was easy enough to move. Mr. Lu set down his bowl, got up, and went to light the fire. A few minutes later, the flame had spread to the charcoal. With expert gestures, he revived it with a few puffs of a bellows, and he placed the small stove at Mien's feet, before turning to Hanh.

"Come with me, I'll take you to trap birds in the garden. Let's leave your mother in peace."

Hanh stood motionless, dumbfounded. He couldn't believe what the old man was saying. The garden had once been his private kingdom, the place where he played all summer and autumn, climbing the trees to gather fruit, digging in the ground to trap crickets, and building huts. But he had been banished from this kingdom at the very beginning of winter, when his mother herself had declared it off limits. Mr. Lu had immediately followed her bidding, and had locked the gate with a large padlock, stuffing the key into his pocket. Ever since, Hanh was allowed to play only inside the house, in the main building. So this familiar space would open again? Was he really going to be allowed to flow back into this beloved space? Mr. Lu repeated, "Come now, you didn't hear me?"

Hanh didn't dare believe it. He looked at his mother. Mien felt a second wave of nausea churning in her gut, but she saw the perplexed, doubtful look in her son's eyes and she leaned toward him. "Yes, yes, go ahead my son. Today, I'm allowing you to go out in the garden."

The boy leapt with joy, running toward Mr. Lu. The two of them walked out into the courtyard and disappeared quickly into the garden. Mien ran to the toilet to vomit. This time, she just retched and heaved, coming up with only a yellowish liquid. Her face, arms, and legs felt icy, and her forehead and neck were drenched in sweat. She went back to the kitchen and sat down next to the hearth. She watched the coals. A thought rose in her mind, as clear and sharp as the line that separated the mountains from the sky after the summer storms.

I'm pregnant with Bon's child.

She knew that it had happened on that crazy night Bon had turned up the lamp, when he had pawed and bit her like some kind of wild animal devouring his prey. That night she had been as terrified of Bon as she would have been of a madman or a ghost; she had closed her eyes to avoid seeing his pale face, his features contorted by pain and hatred. She had somehow guessed the source of Bon's hatred, but she didn't understand how sexual potency could have flared up so suddenly. Yes, that was the night she had gotten pregnant. But was this seed of life inside her the fruit of pleasure or terror?

The morning after, Mien saw Bon sprawled on the bed like a limp rag, his face and lips purple. She had gone to get Hanh at Auntie Huyen's, taken him back to the old house, and then returned to find Bon still sound asleep. He slept until four-thirty in the afternoon before staggering out into the garden. He sat there a long time, vomiting and sighing. When he went back into the room, he couldn't even sit up straight anymore. His eyes were yellow.

"What's the matter?" Mien asked.

"Nothing," he replied angrily and slumped back on the bed. "I've got a backache."

That night for dinner, he asked for rice porridge. And the same the following morning. For more than a month afterward, he wandered around the house looking dazed, resigned, a look that revealed that he was finished, that he couldn't be a man anymore after that crazy night when the volcano had spat out its last fires.

Mien was haunted by the stench of Bon's breath, and she relived it all, saw how pitiful he was, panting as he made love, like a man swimming against the current, struggling to revive a past that reeked of corpses. She consoled herself, tried to give her life some goal, some objective that would restore her serenity.

I'll consider myself a widow. I'll devote the rest of my time to raising Hanh. I'm already luckier than most other women. At least I've known real happiness. And now, I don't have to break my back to survive.

Her life had been sundered, irrevocably divided into two parts. Vis-à-vis the past, she still had an unpaid debt that needed to be settled; she would continue to feed Bon, to selflessly care for him, this ghost, this hand that had reached out to her one day in her distant past. And aside from this duty, her future would be devoted to her son, her flesh and blood, who was all the love and hope that remained in her life.

But now another life had risen inside her. Another living being that she had not expected and who had no place in her mother's heart. Suddenly, the world that Mien had organized in her head began to crumble. In this world, all the places were taken already. Where would she put this child yet to be born? This child was also hers, her blood, would grow up nourished on her milk, suckled from the same breast as Hanh, and he would call Hanh big brother, and her "Mama, Mama Mien."

He doesn't deserve it. He can't possibly call Hanh big brother.

This child, the seed of a puny man with fetid breath. This child, the heir to a family of poor, lazy, miserable wretches living off the charity of others, a cousin to people who dragged themselves around like wild animals, the nephew of a shameless hussy like Ta . . .

But why should he deserve contempt? He too is my child. I'll carry him in my belly for nine months and ten days just like I did for Hanh, like all women do for their children. And he too will babble his first words: Mama . . . And he too will look at me with innocent eyes . . .

"Mama!"

She suddenly heard a distant call. Her heart twisted in pain. She imagined the child's features. Would it be a boy or a girl? Would it look like her or Bon, or even worse, like Bon's sister? If that was the case, she would have to separate him from Ta and her family right away. She would have to send him to study in town. Hoan had left her a fortune. With Mr. Lu's help, she would save her child with this money.

A third wave of nausea came over Mien. She warmed her hands over the coals and then went to vomit in the bathroom.

Oh, my child, are you a boy or a girl, will you bring happiness or misfortune? Why do you torture me this way right from the start?

As she kept vomiting, she saw white and yellow stars exploding in front of her eyes. At the same time, she kept imagining the features of the child that was growing in her belly, a tiny face whose uncertain features flickered in the mist. A frail yet piercing gaze. And her heart twisted again as if stabbed by tiny needles.

Oh my child, girl or boy, handsome or ugly, I'll raise you, I'll raise you with all my heart.

She started to feel remorse for having despised and looked down on this seed of life in her belly. She thought of all the women raped by foreign soldiers, who had given birth in pain and shame, sacrificing their own lives to raise children who had been scorned and rejected by their fellow villagers.

"Should I call a doctor?" Mr. Lu asked.

"No, no."

"Let me make you some rice porridge."

"No, it's not necessary. I don't need it."

All the same, the old man went off in silence to prepare some sticky rice for a porridge. He walked back and forth with a light step, his thin, severe, almost skeletal frame held straight and tall. His sunken eyes glistened with a sad, mysterious light, a gleam that was somehow at once close and distant.

He must already know. He acts a bit like a father to me.

"Have some chicken rice porridge, okay?"

"As you like."

The old man went to get a chicken out of the coop.

Thank goodness Hoan found me such a devoted man.

One day, not long ago, Mien had made tiny, sticky-rice-flour dumplings filled with shrimp. Auntie Huyen and little Hanh, and especially Mr. Lu, loved this dish. During the course of the meal, Mr. Lu, normally so taciturn, began to speak: "I'm from Quang Tri, but I have loved this Hue specialty since I was a child. My mother was an excellent cook. In other kitchens, they knew only how to boil the shrimp and season it with salt and pepper, or to grill the crabs and eat them with potatoes. At our house, we had all kinds of crab specialties: crab porridge with oyster sauce, silkworm soup with crab fat and chopped meat, and especially rice pancakes with grilled crabs, and of course the dumplings."

While he was recalling these memories, his eyes seemed to mist over.

"And is anyone left back there?"

"No one," he replied, his eyes dry now.

"There were eighteen of us in the family. Half were killed by shells from the Saigonese soldiers, and the other half were killed by the rockets of the liberating troops. Nine dead for each camp. Perfect equality. I used all my savings to build eighteen graves. The day I meet my maker, I'll have just enough to buy two cups of tea."

He recounted all this in a serious, dignified manner. He added that the heavens had nevertheless been merciful to him by having him meet Hoan, who had hired him and promised to take care of him for life.

"Do you want to go back to your village?" Mien asked.

"No," he replied, his voice gentle but firm.

"And the incense for the altar to the ancestors?"

"I had eighteen tombstones built with the money that I had saved for almost twenty years as a plantation manager. I have nothing to be ashamed of now. The day I die, the villagers will light a few sticks on those tombs. Where I come from, every family was decimated. Whether they were Vietcong or Republican soldiers, in the end, they all ended up as village ghosts, buried in the same village cemetery. Whoever pays their respects to their loved ones always lights a few sticks of incense on the tombs of other families."

"Is it a big cemetery?"

"Yes. Entirely covered with sand. When those black crows swoop down on it, it's a sight that'll make you shudder."

The eighteen tombs in that sandy cemetery were no doubt the essence, the pith and marrow, of his life. But the past was the past, and he didn't want to turn back to look at it one last time. Since he had arrived in Mountain Hamlet, he had never spoken of it. Just as Mien had decided to devote the rest of her life to her son, he would devote the rest of his to their plantation.

Mr. Lu served Mien a ladle of rice porridge. "You take care of yourself, look after your health. I'll look after the little boy."

Mien said nothing, silently observing him.

There's something odd about this man. It's hard to know how to behave. When I treat him as a father, he maintains the polite reserve of an employee. And yet, when I keep silent, he watches me, from his corner, as my own father once did.

Just then, Mr. Lu came back from the courtyard. "Your little man is absorbed in his games. Let's let him play to his heart's content."

"I'm afraid it's too cold."

"Children scamper around, it keeps them warm. Don't worry about his catching cold. Oh, I almost forgot. Have you seen how the pepper starks has shriveled up?"

"Yes, I noticed."

"We should sell it off right away, even cheaply."

"Do whatever you think is necessary. You know the business better than I do. Hoan was the one who handled all that."

"Yes. Still, I have to ask your opinion."

"It's not necessary to complicate matters."

"That's the way the boss wanted it. The other day, he inspected various products in our warehouse."

"My husband . . . Did Hoan say something?"

"He said that next season he's going to change the seed variety. He also asked me to look after your health."

Mien felt a bitter taste flood her mouth.

I'm still living under his protection, but I have to share Bon's bed. Now I even carry a seed of life that comes from his sperm. Soon, Bon's child will live off the money that Hoan has left me, money that should have belonged to Hanh alone.

She remembered the morning when she had left to live with Bon, convinced that she should submit to her former husband, to never again have any contact with Hoan aside from their shared responsibilities to their son. But life had taken them down winding streets. Now, everything was just as it had been before. She continued to live in her former house with her son, she continued to spend the money kept in the three-paneled armoire, totally under Hoan's protection, even if he himself was absent.

That virgin grass was totally worthless.

The fragrance of the mountain herb had only helped her escape Bon's horrible breath, but it had not helped her resist the carnal desire of a man who had come out of nowhere, obsessed with impregnating her. Again, thanks to Hoan's money, Bon had attained his objective.

No, no, I don't have the right to enjoy this life. It's too humiliating. I should give everything back to my son, Hanh. He is the only one who deserves to spend Hoan's money, he's his son after all.

"What's the matter, Madame? Try to finish the bowl of porridge," Mr. Lu insisted.

Mien realized that she had unconsciously set down her spoon some time ago. Outside, the wind blew the dead leaves in small eddies. She stared outside, saw her life like an endless scattering of leaves in an anarchic wind. She couldn't seem to decide anything. And henceforth, all her decisions were useless anyway. She knew that she could never bring herself to leave this house to lead an independent life with Bon. Nor could she abandon him to his fate in the shack with the thatched roof to live here with her own son. She was cornered, incapable of escaping her destiny.

Mr. Lu served her another bowl of hot porridge. Mien lowered her head and ate the bowl, spoonful by spoonful. The old man's attentions made her ill at ease. He had replaced Hoan here, and in so doing, Hoan, in a strange way, continued to be present for her. The real man of her life. The true love of her life. She leaned even lower over the hot bowl so the steam would rise over her face, attempting to hide her thoughts. She could still see Hoan here in their spacious kitchen that he had designed. She could smell his skin, see the sweat beading on his large, strong chest after their lovemaking in summertime. She could smell his fresh, clean breath. Every detail of their life together.

It's as if this is all a dream and yesterday reality.

"Madame, do you feel better now?" Mr. Lu asked.

"Yes, much better."

"You go and rest now. I'll call the little man for lunch."

Mien went upstairs, obeying the old man like an automaton. But when she lay down, she was suddenly blinded by a dizzy spell. She saw the poles of the mosquito netting spin and felt her arms freeze as if she had plunged them in icy water. Terrified, she felt the anger explode in her soul.

I'll get an abortion. I'm not going to keep a child I don't want. Providing for Bon is enough to settle my debt. I can't come back here carrying another man's fetus in my belly. This house belongs to Hoan, and everything in it should belong to him, too . . .

Mien recalled all the women who had gotten pregnant out of wedlock and who had secretly gone to the commune health center. Ordinarily, they would arrive with a satchel of belongings at dusk, a time when the outlines of faces were blurred, and stay twenty-four hours, leaving the following night. Sometimes they would hemorrhage, their blood flowing onto the ground. The next morning the blood would coagulate and darken. Their faces livid, green, gray, these unhappy women would walk with their heads bowed, not daring to look at anyone. Both coming and going, they would shuffle by as furtively as thieves, skimming past the hedges and running across the barren hills behind the medical center.

I don't need to go there secretly. I'll go in broad daylight, and I'll say I need an abortion because I don't have the money to give birth. This child has a father, but one who's incapable of providing for even his own needs. No one will dare gossip. If the authorities get involved, I'll ask the president of the commune to sign a paper guaranteeing me subsidies needed to raise the child until he reaches the age of eighteen.

But no president would agree to sign such a document, and Mien knew it. She also knew that by aborting she would put an end to her sexual relationship with Bon, one that she had wanted to destroy even before it had begun again, since the first step she took away from her home the day she had followed Bon back to his. She wanted and needed to destroy this new life. But she didn't have the heart to destroy Bon's. He was unhappy, had lost so much. And he would always be the man who had once held out his hand to her.

I may still feel for Bon, but I can't keep this fetus. I don't care what the neighbors say. No one has the heart to destroy an entire family.

Bon has no children. But he wants them more than any man I know.

But why do I have to endure all this? Why should I be the sacrifice for his dream? I don't love him anymore. I'm not Bon's slave.

I must destroy this life. I never wanted it.

This fierce, determined thought freed Mien's spirit. She would wait a few weeks to allow the fetus to take shape, and then go to the medical center for a curettage. Or, the following week, she would go to a hospital in town. There, they would use a more modern method of abortion, by aspiration.

I'll go into town with Mr. Lu. We'll leave Hanh with Auntie Huyen. It's simple. It'll all be over in a few days. On the way back, I'll buy a few packets of traditional medicine to restore my health.

She closed her eyes, her heart lighter, and began to doze off. At that moment out in the garden, the wind began to swirl and howl. In this sad rustling, she heard a small voice, a feeble call. A vague echo. And it seemed to come from somewhere both close and far, from some distant horizon, from somewhere out at sea. A baby's wail. A fragile, yet shapeless, nascent life that called out to her.

Where is it coming from? How can he speak even before being of this world?

She listened attentively. This time, the vague call resonated, clearly articulating each word: "Mama, Mama..."

Interspersed with these sounds, Mien heard violent gusts of wind, as she watched the murky horizon reel before her eyes.

"Mama, Mama..."

The call echoed again. She imagined a tiny face with blurred features emerging from layers of fog. The face turned toward her with a pained, desperate look.

This too is my child. This too is a human life demanding its place on this earth. I must allow him, at least once, to see the light of day.

Her heart screamed in silence. Mien felt her skin and flesh tear in the embrace of this single cry. She sat up suddenly in bed, her face drenched in sweat and tears.

20

After spending three and a half months flat on his back in bed, early one warm spring morning, Bon finally paid a visit to Xa. He found his friend bent over, buttocks in the air, kneading a large pot of sticky rice dough. Soan, seated in the kitchen, was stirring a pan of filling. The aroma of chopped onions, meat, and mushrooms filled the air.

"Have you finished? The dough is already very thick."

"I've finished, almost . . . Knead it a bit more, it'll make it even more tender."

"You really are demanding! Night and day, it's always more, more . . ."

"Oh, will you please be quiet, you old curmudgeon? If someone came by and saw you like that, with your butt in the air, now that would be a pretty sight."

"I know, I know, I may not be as handsome as the other guys around here, but admit that as a husband I do excel. And if you have doubts, just go and spy on a few couples in this commune. See if any of them hammer in the nail like I do, eh?"

"You devil! Stop shouting. If the neighbors hear you, they're going to die laughing."

Both Xa and Soan were laughing hysterically. Bon leaned against the hibiscus hedge for a long time, until they had finished their conversation. The two of them were unaware of his presence.

What an odd couple! I wonder if they make as much noise when they make love?

"Hey, my arms are killing me from kneading this dough."

"My filling is ready, too."

Xa carried the bowl into the kitchen and their noisy conversation continued.

"Mmm, these mushrooms I gathered are really fragrant," Xa boasted.

"As if you were the only one capable of finding fragrant mushrooms. You brag like a cat does about the length of his tail."

"Okay, other people's mushrooms are just as fragrant as mine. But as for what I serve Missus in bed, I challenge you to find anyone with my endurance. In that area, I can rival a whole platoon of heroic American troops. You doubt it? Then lend me one of your girlfriends for a few nights and she'll get back to you with her comments."

At this point, Bon heard Xa let out a bloodcurdling scream and begin to moan, "Oh my God, what a dog you are! You almost took a piece of my flesh out! Look at these teeth marks! You lioness! I was just talking. Words, but no action at all, and then you go and unleash this barbaric jealousy!"

Soan began to speak, her voice shrill: "Ah, ah . . . you may be happy just to talk, and I am happy to merely bite your shoulder. You dare spring into action and I'll rip off your engine with my own teeth."

Bon coughed and cried out across the courtyard, "Is Xa at home?"

Xa ran out from the kitchen, still rubbing his shoulder. "Ah, Bon, it's you. It's been a long time. Come in! You've got good timing when it comes to food."

Soan ran out and glared reproachfully at her husband. "Goodness, you are so vulgar. Well, at least it's just Elder Brother Bon. Anyone else would throw salt at our door."

Xa laughed. "We're old troopers. We don't know how to talk elegantly." Then he turned to his wife and ordered her, in a theatrical but imperious voice, "Go turn down the fire or the stuffing is going to be ruined."

Soan ran back into the kitchen, but not before swatting her husband's bottom. Xa shook his head. "That's what it's like, a wife and kids. That's where all this democracy leads. To the crudest anarchy. You see, once upon a time, the elders were dignified, majestic, powerful. They knew how to keep women and children in their place. A woman was never a man's equal; she had equal rights with him only from sundown to sunrise. Women today have all forgotten the hierarchy and the social order. So women start to quibble and argue with us as if they thought men spent all their time making love."

Xa started to cackle. "You devil!" Soan screeched, from her corner.

But after she had shouted, she too doubled over laughing, her head folded over her knees. Xa said to Bon, "Come on into the house."

When they reached the threshold, Xa turned back toward the kitchen and said to his wife, "Hey, Miss, that's quite enough of that brazen laughter. You boil some water for tea before making those cakes."

The two men sat down. Only then did Xa look Bon right in the eye.

"Feel better? How many bowls of rice do you eat at each meal?"

"One and a bit more."

"That's not enough! A man has to eat at least three full bowls to survive."

"I still don't have much appetite."

"Is Mien okay?"

"Yes."

"Soan tells me she's been feeling nauseous."

"I don't know."

"Yes, because you yourself have been very sick, and you've spent your days looking after your own health. You wouldn't know about a woman's suffering, would you?"

"Mien knows how to take care of herself. As for me, it's the first time."

Xa squinted at Bon as if this reply had angered him. But after a second, he sighed, got up, and walked toward a calendar that hung on the wall. He pulled off a page, crumpled it up into a ball, and tossed it into an earthenware bowl. Then he began to rummage here and there around the room for something. Finally, he picked up a new pack of Dien Bien cigarettes and a half-opened pack of Le Nhats and put them in his shirt pocket. He tossed the two packets on the table.

"Want a smoke?"

"No."

Xa lowered his head and inhaled a few drags of his cigarette, flooding the room with heavy, dense smoke that swirled around, almost masking his rugged face. This was the face of a real man, someone who knew what he had, could have, and what he had to do to get it.

Xa is happy with what he has and he knows how to protect it. Me, no. I don't have anything and I don't know how to get what I want. The heavens are truly unjust. At the outset, Xa wasn't even my equal. His family wasn't rich, he wasn't a good student at school, and he wasn't even handsome. Now, he has everything a man could want while I have nothing, aside from a tiny seed of life in Mien's belly. And I've staked the rest of my lousy life on it.

Bon suddenly heaved a deep sigh, remembering the bitter argument that had led him to seek Xa's advice. He had realized then that the seed he had sown was no sure thing, that it could be destroyed at any moment by the very woman who carried it.

"Why are you sighing?" Xa asked suddenly, his face still in a cloud of smoke. From the tone of his voice, Bon could tell that Xa knew everything.

Who told him?

Soan came running in from the kitchen, a pot of hot water in her hand. Xa snuffed out his cigarette, took the pot, and poured it into a Thermos. Then he walked slowly out toward the garden. A few minutes later, he returned holding a sprig of jasmine. "Here, here's a way to perfume the tea without all the fuss. It's not as fragrant as the traditional method, but it's practical."

He rinsed out the teapot, then put in some tea and some hot water.

After just a few minutes, when the tea began to give off its fragrance, Xa put the jasmine flowers in, walked to the door, and sputtered an order: "Make those cakes now ... We're starting to have ants in our stomachs."

Soan's voice echoed out of the kitchen. "It's done, no need to remind me. What a man! Like a hungry devil all the time. You haven't finished digesting one meal and you're already ordering the next ..."

Soan's voice trailed off, as if she were speaking to herself. But the kitchen and the courtyard were deserted. And in this silent, peaceful space, the young woman's grumbling echoed clearly. Xa cocked an ear in her direction, strained his neck, and asked, "Oh, so you're trying to save on rice, eh? Go ahead, say it, do you want me to eat with gusto and work efficiently or do you prefer I stagger about like an opium addict in withdrawal who can't even finish a half bowl of rice?"

Soan kept silent.

Satisfied with his retort, Xa turned to Bon.

"You see? Women, the more they gossip, the more terrifying they are. One threat is enough. Now you see she's mute as a grain of paddy rice."

As Xa spoke, a mischievous grin on his face, Bon kept watching him. And envying him.

I'll never have the power he has. He's king in this kingdom. I'm just a banal head of a family. I'm a parasite, even under the roof my own ancestors left me.

He knew that his sister, Ta, was happy to live under his roof. She couldn't find any other shelter. Without the two rooms left by her parents, Ta and her children would surely have become beggars who lived off charity or worked for hire as day labor, and then slept under the Party Committee's awning at night. But he couldn't resign himself to living like those vulgar savages. He knew he lived as a parasite, that he clung to his tiny room, so he could still feel he had a bit of sovereignty. But he knew this feeling was a sham, a way of deluding himself, like the salads city people made with a few threads of meat mixed with minced banana trunk or green papaya. His sovereignty was as rickety as an old board; he could lose it at any moment. He imagined Mien one morning leaving for her former home, abandoning him without a word of explanation or a good-bye. At that moment, his shack would become what it had always been: a dark hole, an airless pit, a grave equipped with a roof and a door.

"Drink up. The water's boiling. It gets fragrant mighty quickly," Xa said. He raised a steaming cup and took tiny sips. "Ah, it's so good! How do you like my tea?"

Bon drank a scalding mouthful. "Delicious."

Xa emptied his cup and set it on the table.

"Bon, now tell me everything. I know you wouldn't have come if you weren't upset about something."

"How did you know?"

Xa opened his good eye and stared at him as if he were a Martian. "You think the villagers don't know what goes on at your house?"

Bon said nothing. Xa continued, "You can't hide anything. Just like it was between us once, when we were soldiers. Everyone knows what the score is, which guy likes to chat up the women, which guy pees in his pants, who's got scabies . . . the only difference here is that they either spit in your face or turn their heads away in pity, pretending they haven't seen a thing."

Bon felt his face and ears and the nape of his neck burn. His body recoiled, suddenly, unconsciously. Xa's words, like the slap of some ferocious gale, had ripped aside the curtain in front of his door and engulfed his tiny room, smashing the furniture, as wind whipped his face and stung his eyes.

Xa, my friend, you're cruel. Every one of your words is like a knife, stabbing my gut.

Xa continued to give Bon a piercing look.

"You've got to accept reality, have the courage to face it. Do you think there's only one kind of courage, the one you feel when faced with enemy fire? A soldier's courage is easy to honor; it's nothing compared to the courage of a man who has no target at which to aim his gun, no enemies or no objectives, no campaign at all in which he can fight and win. The courage of a man who has nothing at all."

Bon dimly understood what Xa was trying to say, but these ideas humiliated him. He looked up and snickered. "This is too literary, too intellectual for me."

Xa stared him right in the eyes. "I don't give a damn about literature. I'm just telling you the truth. And the truth is that . . ."

He drummed the table with his fingers, his eyes glistening, his cheeks red. "The truth is that you know everything. You understand everything, but you pretend not to . . . Don't try to fool me."

Xa poured himself some more tea. "What's the use of fooling me? I just want to help you. I don't have any political agenda. The only power we've got left is the right to vote once every five years for a deputy to the National Assembly. For me, this power isn't worth a bucket of manure. I don't aspire to become a deputy and I don't need to flatter you to get another vote."

Xa fell silent. This time, he didn't serve himself any more tea, but picked up the packet of Dien Bien cigarettes, ripped it open, and pulled out a cigarette, even though there was already a half-opened packet right on the table.

Suddenly, a gust of wind blew through the house. A late spring wind that whispered of the coming summer, the last green refrain of the hunt, and the first sign of the coming dry season when torrid sun and wind from Laos would scour the surrounding hills and mountains. Xa opened a few buttons on his shirt, poured himself more tea, and continued chain-smoking.

Bon gazed out through the stands of trees in his friend's garden, listening to the intermittent sounds from the village road. He felt his muscles stiffen, the vertebrae in his backbone dislocating from the neck to the spine, everything falling into a pile.

Why did I come? What can he do except lecture me? He's probably going to tell me to go to that plantation with the two hundred women. What an imbecile I am. I should have stayed home . . .

But Bon knew he was lying to himself. He couldn't stay home. Not in that space, not with Mien's hateful eyes, not with their recent fighting, and the drama that had just begun between them. All this haunted him.

It had happened on a happy morning. Bon had just felt the pain in his back softening, finally regained his serenity. Whatever happened, he would still be the father of the child in the belly of the woman whom he loved and, when the baby came into the world, it would be the golden chain that bound her to him for the rest of her life.

That morning Mien had been sick again, and she had stayed at home in bed. Bon got up before she did and made sticky rice with black beans, a dish she loved. He prepared the platter and added grilled sesame seeds crushed with salt and a plate of fine sugar and brought it in to her. This gesture must have moved Mien, because she looked at him more tenderly than usual. "Just set it on the table. I'll eat it later, after I wash up."

Then she went back to sleep. Bon felt a certain satisfaction seeing Mien prostrate in bed; she wouldn't be able to take her son back to the old house anymore, or to lose herself in a world that excluded him. In this feeble state, she seemed closer, almost as if she still belonged to him.

I'm a bastard. Every other man would want his wife to feel good during pregnancy. I'm the only one who feels joy at seeing her this way.

And so he cursed himself. But every time these feelings of remorse threatened to overcome him, he dismissed them, choosing instead to savor his immoral joy. He set the platter on the table and drew nearer to the bed, pressing his face against her stomach as if he could whiff the smell of the future and enter into contact with his child, his heir and guardian angel. But every time he moved to caress her, to lay his hand on her stomach, she would turn over angrily, refusing to let him near her. But now, for the first time, she yielded.

Our ancestors always said, Sooner or later, straw by fire will catch fire. Sooner or later, her love will come back to me . . .

He relished this thought, and as he pressed his face against her stomach he remembered the road lined with flame trees, the scarlet flowers that had once seemed to set the sky on fire. At that moment, Auntie Huyen came in with little Hanh.

"Where is Mien? The boy wants to visit his mother. He refuses to eat breakfast."

Mien sat up and pushed Bon aside brusquely. "My God, why did you bring him here?"

But her eyes shone. She opened her arms and hugged her little boy to her. Standing stiffly to the side, Bon watched this scene, how the boy's face seemed to blur and merge with his mother's, how happy they looked.

She doesn't even give me one hundredth of that love. She's saved it all for this boy.

The joy in his heart flickered out. He thought of the child still to be born. His child would share his fate. Like Bon, he would never enjoy the same love as this handsome, fair-skinned, smartly dressed city boy. This boy belonged to another man, the one who wore expensive underwear, the burly guy who had stolen Mien's heart.

"Hello, sir," Hanh said, folding his arms across his chest and bowing slightly in a polite greeting.

Bon said nothing and stalked off, walking down to the road. He felt his cheeks burn and he turned toward the mountains, waiting for the wind to cool his jealousy, to soothe his tortured soul. He stood there for a long time, a very long time, but he kept his ears open, straining to hear the conversation between Mien and her aunt, imagining the affection that she was showering on the other man's boy. He closed his eyes; he couldn't bear to imagine it. As he stood there at the edge of the road, he saw himself as a pelican reveling in his own death. But this sea bird that supposedly tore out her guts to feed her children was a female, and he, a male, would only be sacrificing himself in vain, immolating himself for a love that had died long ago. His love was just a corpse that even the worms and insects had abandoned. All that was left of it were broken bones buried under the mud, reduced to dust, or fragments that no one could see. He was the only one still searching for them, still wading through the mud to try to pull them out, to reconstruct an illusory silhouette in his imagination. What should he do? Leave? With his sick body, without a dong to his name? He was incapable of earning his daily pittance. How could he possibly build a future? He remembered the beautiful words to the war songs he had confided to the wind, to all his fitful, intermittent dreams as he swung in his hammock, as he lay on his back in the sun at the edge of a stream, lazily watching the clouds flit through the blue sky.

If only my parents were still alive. If only they had been rich. If only my comrades had more money than this man. If only they could fill my hands with thick wads of bills. If only the heavens could give me the infinite strength of the mountain and the river genies, to be able to impregnate thousands of women, fairies, and she-devils.

These marvelous, mysterious legends he had once read as a schoolboy had now come back to haunt him. And then he heard Mien scream, a horrific, blood-curdling scream such as he had never heard from her before. At first he thought it was her aunt, but when he listened closely, he knew it was her.

"Hanh! What did I tell you? Who gave you permission to play with these kids?"

Bon ran into the house to find Mien spanking her son furiously, her eyes shining with anger. "I told you to stay in this room! I told you not to go out into the courtyard! How dare you disobey me? Why were you playing with these brats, these vermin?"

Auntie Huyen scurried in with a bowl of well water and began frantically splashing the boy's face: "Open your eyes! Open your eyes so we can rinse them! Hanh, listen to me, listen to your Auntie!"

The boy didn't hear anything, just held his face in his hands. Auntie Huyen finally had to grab Hanh's hands and pull them aside while his mother opened the boy's red and swollen eyes to rinse out the tiny grains of red chili that had stuck to his eyeballs and lashes. Just a few feet away, right outside the door, Ta's children maliciously watched the scene. One kid had his dirty hands in his mouth. Another was giggling.

Bon realized immediately that his nephews had just played a cruel trick on the boy: They had thrown chili powder in his eyes. He didn't feel any anger toward the filthy brats; in fact, he was even filled with a secret satisfaction. He knew that their game was mean, but he couldn't help enjoying it.

As he walked toward her, Mien stood up. "See what your nephews, these vermin and insects in your family, have done to my son!"

"If you call them vermin and insects, they'll behave like them. What are you complaining about?" Bon replied.

At first, Mien was stunned. But she knew that his nonchalance masked a vicious hatred. She glared at him and lunged forward as if to scratch his face, her whole body shaking. But she restrained herself in time. She clenched her fists to resist the urge to punch Ta's kids, to tear them apart. She just stood there, trembling, furious. Then, suddenly, her flushed cheeks turned ashen. And she smiled. A smile that Bon knew was for him, a smile filled with contempt. She looked at Ta's kids, then spat out her words, hurling them at him one by one like stones she would throw into a pool of water. "You vermin! You pack of wolves! Your mother gave birth to you like pups that she knew only how to feed but not raise. Never come back here! Don't you dare come back here with your baskets and your bowls begging me for rice and food. You little monsters, you beasts!"

She turned to Bon and glared at him, her lips parting into another smile as sharp as a razor to the neck. "You think I'm particularly attached to your precious heir? The only one you have? Well, you're going to get it back, because I'm going to expel it right now!"

Only Auntie Huyen realized what Mien was about to do, and she quickly set the bowl of water down on the table. But Mien had already lunged forward, and was banging her stomach violently against the door, trying to push out the fetus. The old woman screamed, "No! Keep the child, Mien! Keep the child!"

It was only then that Bon realized what was happening. He sprang forward and pulled Mien toward him, making her fall backward. But she knocked him aside and hurled herself again at the door. By that time, Hanh had opened his eyes and began screaming, too.

"Mama, Mama!" he shouted through his tears.

It was the boy who grabbed Mien's legs between his arms, and he was the one who finally stopped her. Mien knelt down and pressed her face against his. And when these two faces joined, Bon knew that nothing could compare to this love, that no one could take this boy's place. He also knew that Mien had stopped for the boy, because her life was still needed, for him alone. Old Auntie Huyen stepped forward and confronted him: "How dare you behave like this? You should have disciplined your nephews! Don't you see what's happening? You groan and moan like an old man. It's only because she's virtuous and generous that my niece endures this situation. She's neither your wife nor your nanny. If you really wanted to show your valor and contribute to this country, you'd do better to check yourself into one of those camps for invalid war veterans!"

The old woman's face was stony. She shook her finger threateningly at him with each word, as if her anger, repressed for too long inside her, had chosen this moment to explode. Bon was petrified. For the first time, he realized that his private life had been on display. People had just turned their heads, pretended not to see anything out of pity for him.

He felt his spine crumbling. Ever since Mien had gotten pregnant, he had pinned his hopes on the fetus, believing that his fate had changed, that the future was now his. But he had rejoiced too soon.

That night, he got down on his knees with Mien and begged her not to abort. He wept like a child who had just been whipped, wept all the tears he had pent up for all the long months and years. Seated, Mien gazed at the lamp, without a tear, without a word. It seemed to him that she considered him not as an unhappy husband, plunged in despair, but as an inanimate object without consciousness or sensibility. Like a lamp, or a table, or a chair, or even a pot of rice. He begged her for a long time, then he went out into the courtyard, looked up at

the pitch-black sky, and prayed to the all powerful, invoking the names
of beloved, wandering souls he knew perfectly well were powerless to
help. He called to the souls of his parents, miserable beings who had
known only famine and poverty, who had left him only a paltry legacy
of shame and their propensity for dreaming.

A dry snapping sound made Bon jump, shattering his daydream.
Xa had just lit another cigarette and tossed his lighter on the table.

"So, are you listening to me?" Xa asked again.

"I always listen to you."

Bon didn't look Xa in the eyes, just stared at a bright red mark on
his neck.

The flaming red mark on Xa's neck reminded him of his own arms
and thighs back then, how they too had been burnished red by the sun.
He wasn't any taller than the others, but he too had once had muscles as
hard as *lim* wood. Every day he used to be able to carry two heavy loads
of firewood on a bamboo pole slung over his shoulder, running from the
forest all the way back to the village. And that made him remember his
wedding night, the rosy light of the oil lamp he had lit, despite his sister's
fulminating, to please Mien. How many times had he made love that
night? Impossible to remember. Who can count the times a virgin makes
love? Especially when it is in haste, with the desperate, frantic lust of a
young man who knew that the next morning he would have to leave for
the war. That morning, when he woke to see the wings of the moths and
butterflies scattered and white, like the corpses of dragonflies fished out
of a lake.

Seeing Bon's silence, Xa continued, "You knew that the people of
this village support the veterans. There's not a single family here that
hasn't lost someone on the front! And a guy who returns from the battlefield is like family. But all privileges have their limits . . ."

Xa's voice was grave and respectful now, no longer haranguing. And
this voice brought Bon back to the present. He suddenly felt as if he
were going to faint. As he touched his neck, he felt as if his bones
would come unhinged, that he would collapse on the floor in a pile of

bones, bruised skin and flesh, exactly like the sergeant, torn to pieces by the vultures.

"Do you think the villagers are going to always take your side?"

"No, I don't," Bon said.

"But you act as if you do. You're emptying someone else's pockets. Put yourself in Mien's place for a minute, and see . . ."

"But I'm not Mien. I can't."

Xa frowned and his voice suddenly hardened, in fury and exasperation.

"And that's why you'll ruin everything. Why you're going to end up with empty hands."

Bon shivered.

Empty hands . . . If Mien aborts, I'll have lost everything in a single hand of poker. What will I do then?

Xa continued, "Did you know that every time I bump into Mien I have to avoid her gaze? Ever since I gave you that horrible recipe for coffee with salt . . ."

"Why? I don't understand."

"You don't understand, or you're just pretending?"

Bon didn't reply.

Xa swallowed a grumbling thought in his throat. He glared at his friend, his face pained. He had eyes that saw and yet looked at nothing.

"Listen, Bon," Xa finally said, exasperated. "I really don't know what kind of man you are anymore."

Bon sighed. "I don't either."

Xa shook his head. "You reject all proposals to change your life. You cling to a woman who doesn't love you and you persist in trying to have a child with her. And then, when you finally achieve your goal and get her pregnant, you destroy your work with your own hands."

Bon's hands started to shake. The trembling began to spread to his legs, climbing the length of his spine to his face, setting off a chain reaction through his entire body, his veins throbbing violently, his heart racing.

Mien could get an abortion.

As long as this idea had been only in Bon's head, it had been just a hypothesis that had worried him. But when Xa himself alluded to it, the possibility seemed suddenly like a flesh-and-blood demon ready to stride forward, hammer in hand, to crush the fortress he had built.

Bon stared out the door, into the void, his eyes stalking this imaginary demon of the future. He didn't see his one-eyed friend gazing compassionately at him, still anxious to protect him. Xa kept his silence for a long time. While Bon sat lost in thought, Xa noticed his friend's purple lips twitching, how the muscles of his cheeks and jaw and the veins in his neck all seemed to tremble in cadence. This was a cadaverous face, vacillating between the world of the living and hell.

Poor man. There are only three parts remaining to his soul. He's sold the seven others to hell. Whether I recite Buddha's sutras for him, or stoke his lust, it's all the same. I'll just waste my breath explaining life to him. He won't retain any of it. And if this continues, he'll end up in a psychiatric hospital.

Xa was troubled, confused. And he was never confused. In his life, everything was clear; there was no place for doubt, nothing was fuzzy or ambiguous. He had worked, studied, gone to war, married, had kids. He had built his own estate, and then tried to help others, lending a hand whenever he could. The people of the hamlet, the villagers, and all his relatives on both sides respected him. In life, Xa always solved problems simply and clearly the way one would fold and wrap up a *banh chung* for Tet. And that's why he was troubled. He didn't know what to do for this friend seated facing him, this former comrade-in-arms all throughout the war, a man whom he had always considered weak and who needed his help. All his sincere devotion, his resourcefulness, seemed useless. Bon no longer lived in the same world that he did. He seemed to belong to another sphere, saw things that Xa didn't see, had ideas that Xa couldn't grasp, acted according to a logic that Xa couldn't comprehend. And if this was the way it was, then all his advice, all his arguments, were absurd. They now stood on opposite banks of a river, one holding out a hand that the other could no longer grasp. Xa looked again intently into his friend's eyes. He could see two currents of trembling light intermingled there: one short, frail, flickering beam that guided Bon in the real world and another, more ghostly current that illuminated a long, dusty road, a path shrouded in fog, lit here and there by shards of stars and the phosphorescence of fireflies that had died millions of years ago. This road, covered by the same grasses and reeds that blanketed the mountains all around, was a path taken by evil fox spirits and ghosts of legend that Xa had read about as a schoolboy. Xa couldn't imagine anything like Bon's mental state except in those fairy tales and ghost stories, or in the legends about genies and demons that all the mountain people told. He was even more troubled thinking about this spirit world. He emptied another cup of tea, got up, and paced around in the room. But the savory smell of the dumplings began to waft out of the kitchen, and he was suddenly as happy as a man who finds a boat on a flood day. He darted over to the threshold and called out: "Are the dumplings ready? Bring them in quickly then!"

"In just a minute!" Soan shouted back. "I'm on my way!"

When she arrived, Xa took the platter of steaming hot dumplings from his wife's hands. There were twelve of them, each exactly the size of a goose egg.

He carried the platter into the house as Soan went back to the kitchen. In a flash, she came back carrying bowls, a dish of sauce, and clean chopsticks.

"Come, let's feast!" Xa spoke loudly, hoping to shake Bon from his brooding and bring him back to reality. The aroma of the hot dumplings and the pungent smell of the *nuoc mam* seasoned with chili pepper, lemon, and garlic, filled the air. These flavors soothed Xa's worries, bolstered his faith in his world, in this vast, comfortable house that he had built with his own hands, in this paved courtyard and its walls covered with flowering vines that he had designed and created, these hedges of peonies and roses that he had taken from his father-in-law's garden and then planted in his own. He was proud of his kitchen covered with tiles shaped like fish scales, which he had also built with his own hands. And the woman bustling around the kitchen making another batch of dumplings was incontestably his wife; she had borne him sons, made love with him every night. His entire kingdom was within reach of his eyes, ears, and nose. And it was this reality, right there in front of him, that gave Xa his extraordinary strength and determination.

"Eat, Bon. A man's got to eat to live, to do what he wants to do, and what he has to do."

He picked up a pair of chopsticks and set them in front of Bon.

Then he poured Bon some wine before filling his own cup. He grabbed a dumpling and dipped it in the fish sauce, eager to taste this traditional delicacy. Smells of new rice, fresh mushrooms, crunchy wood ear, lemongrass, chilies, and garlic mingled, whetting his appetite.

"Delicious, isn't it? Let me pour you a bit more sauce. To really savor this dish, you've got to drown it in sauce. Would you like more chili pepper?"

"That's fine."

"Have another dumpling. You've got to try to eat more."

After a long and painful effort, Bon managed to eat three dumplings, or the equivalent of two heaping bowls of rice. A man in good health could eat four or five of these "goose egg" dumplings. And yet Xa had gulped down the remaining nine. The platter was now empty except for the bowl of sauce. Sated, Xa smacked and licked his chops like a cat.

He's so happy! The heavens have granted him every pleasure in life. In bed and at the dinner table.

Bon stood up. "I'm going home now."

He had forgotten that he had come for advice. But he just felt humiliated, unable to control himself when faced with the happiness of others. As for Xa, he was plagued by anxiety and confusion, alien feelings for a hardened realist like himself. He had forgotten his duty to protect his friend. But Xa had never been the type to acknowledge his own powerlessness. So when Bon rose to bid him good-bye, he just held out his hand. "You travel safely now . . . I'll come by and see you sometime when I've got a minute."

For the first time, the two childhood friends shook hands, a formality reserved for new acquaintances. Here they were, acting like professional diplomats. When Bon had disappeared down the road, Xa stood there, disoriented, his arms slack at his side.

Why did I shake his hand? This is crazy.

In the end, he had to admit that he and Bon now hailed from different worlds, that they thought as differently as two people from different countries, with different languages.

When you can't understand each other, you shake hands. Like a pantomime. How sad.

Xa rarely thought about sadness. He had a hard time with such thoughts.

"Where are you, mother of my son?" he called suddenly.

Soan came running. "What's the matter?"

"Did you finish those dumplings?"

"Not yet. But I can finish them later."

"Then sit down here with me for a while."

Puzzled, Soan looked at her husband and sat down at his side, her hands still dusted with flour. "What were you and Bon just talking about?"

"Nothing."

"Liar. Why hide it from me?"

"I don't understand . . . I can't talk with him anymore."

"I meant to talk to you about this. You know, Bon's face looks strange to me."

Xa sighed. "It's going to be tough to save him." Then he turned away and stared out at the garden. "Tell me, Soan, if you were in Mien's place, what would you do?"

"Me?" said Soan. "I'd never have gone back to Bon. No, never. Sister Mien doesn't love him anymore. She loves Hoan. And the whole village knows it. Including you."

"So why did you help Bon find Mien?" Xa asked.

Soan opened her eyes wide and looked at her husband. "Why, for you! I did it for you! It was my duty. After all, Bon is your friend, and I'm your wife. You idiot! You didn't realize that?"

Xa kept silent.

So she deferred to me. Once again, injustice triumphs over justice, feelings outweigh reason. Now I've got my wife proclaiming in no uncertain terms that she would never sacrifice herself as Mien has. And she's right. To live together, you've got to love.

He remembered their love story. He remembered the young girl who had pulled him down on the grassy hillside, her passionate arms encircling his neck, her tear-drenched face pressed against his, her soft, sweet body offered to him . . . Yes, love is all that, and nothing else can compare.

But if I were in Bon's shoes, would I have the strength to turn away, to leave it all for another land and forget, to wait for a new woman? Yes. In Bon's place, I'd leave Mountain Hamlet and go to the state plantation.

But he remembered his trysts with Soan, and his throat tightened. Even when Soan's entire family had stood against them, not once had he been able to break things off, or to say good-bye as all his friends had urged him to.

He remembered Bon's face, his dull sleepwalker's eyes, his lost smile, the glazed look of a man whose body was of this world but whose soul was already drifting toward the next. Suddenly, he shivered, realizing that the heavens could have just as easily sentenced him to play Bon's tragic role, to love a woman who had no affection for him.

"Sweetheart, come closer to me."

Soan lifted an eyebrow and stared at her husband. "What?"

"Come closer."

Soan walked around the table and pulled up a chair next to him, but he pushed it aside and slapped his thigh. "Here."

She blushed. "Oh please, stop it, you clown . . . Only Westerners do that kind of thing."

"Westerner or no Westerner, everyone is made of flesh and blood. Every man has his stick and every woman her hole."

"What if our eldest sees us when he gets back from school, now that'll be embarrassing!" Soan fidgeted but eventually came around and sat on his lap.

Xa hugged Soan close. She was his lover, his wife, the mother of his children, the human being who had brought him this life filled with happiness.

"We're husband and wife. Someday, the boy is going to have his own wife to take in his arms."

Soan turned toward him and put her arm around his neck, sighing: "Don't be angry with me if I say this . . . You can pity Bon, but it's Mien who's suffering the most. I'm a woman, so I know."

"I know," Xa murmured. "Do you think it makes me happy to help Bon?"

He took Soan's hand. She squeezed his in reply. They said nothing, each immersed in their own thoughts, yet each feeling their shared happiness. A happiness that was real, and yet that they knew was a game of chance in which the outcome depended entirely on fate. When the die was cast, they had just been lucky enough to roll the right number.

The couple stayed seated, silent, transfixed, until their eldest son returned from school and walked slowly across the courtyard. Seeing his father and mother holding each other, an image that he had seen only in Western films, the boy's jaw dropped. He stopped, embarrassed for a moment, when he saw his parents weren't moving. But then he remembered the dumplings waiting for him and ran into the kitchen.

21

In Mountain Hamlet every family's business was brought before the family clubs. Regardless of who they were, or whether they liked it or not, anyone in the public eye was described, analyzed, dissected, judged, and finally subjected to a verdict. The family clubs were in fact the oldest courts in the village. Mountain Hamlet was in reality a large village that had retained its original name; within it were Upper Hamlet, Lower Hamlet, and Middle Hamlet. And each of these hamlets had a public meeting place; here, reunions were held, and people came to chat and listen to the radio when things were calm, or to argue over gains and losses, or to condemn such and such a person each time something odd happened in the village. The family clubs played an important role in the spiritual life of the villagers. No one knew when they had been formed, but they usually met at the home of one of the village elders, usually of a hospitable, wealthy family, where neighbors could gather without fearing hostile looks or stones ostensibly thrown at cats and dogs but aimed at intruders.

At these gatherings, the host and hostess always provided something to eat for the visitors. At the elder's house in Lower Hamlet, there were peanuts and grilled corn. At the elder's house in Upper Hamlet, there was sugarcane grilled over the fire or scented with grapefruit flower. At Old Phieu's house, in Middle Hamlet, they liked to serve candied manioc and sticky rice with honey. Though no one ever officially agreed on a calendar of events, by tacit agreement they always gathered once every five or six days, depending on whether the weather was cold or warm, dry or rainy. In good weather, after dinner, the master of ceremonies would light a huge storm lamp out on his veranda: This was the signal that announced the meeting had begun. But for the last two months, since Mien had returned to her former husband's house, everything had been chaos. People were so eager to talk that they didn't want to wait for the club host to light a storm lamp; in fact, they were so brazen that they came with their own lamps, often while the host family was still eating. They would swarm onto the veranda or into the courtyard, searching for a stool, or trying to borrow a reed mat to sit on. The women went right into the host's kitchen to serve themselves boiling water, as the men pulled tea out of their pockets, their conversations already buzzing like a smashed hornet's nest. No one respected the usual rituals, or bothered to make small talk; everyone just plunged right into the scandalous matter that was causing such a stir in the region: the bizarre, complicated love triangle between a woman and her two husbands. If it had been just another love story, people wouldn't have been so agitated. But this love story was inextricably linked to an event that was of critical importance to them: the construction of a new primary school for children from all the surrounding remote areas. For generations, the children in Mountain Hamlet had had only one kindergarten classroom, located behind their crumbling *dinh*, or village rituals and meeting house. The *dinh* had been half-destroyed by the anti-French resistance, and after the war, the Village Party Committee had demolished the remaining half and built their headquarters there. This building adjoining the *dinh* still stood there like a cripple, hunched over and filthy, with its ravaged, peeling walls without windows or doors, exposed to the elements.

Inside the building, a few benches and an old blackboard had been the only path to learning for the children of Mountain Hamlet. As soon as they could read the alphabet, the older children were sent to attend the primary school in the neighboring village, which was smaller but closer to the district road. It wasn't surprising that so many children never finished their studies; a six-and-a-half-mile walk was hard for them, especially in summer, when they had to cross a stream along the way. And in the winter months there was wind and rain as well. So when the Commune Committee announced that they had gratefully accepted a donation from citizen Tran Quy Hoan to build not just a primary school big enough for twelve classrooms, an administrative building, a gym, and a cultural center, the villagers were ecstatic. To them, this news, while written in black and white, was like a fairy tale come true, still more of a daydream than a reality. People half-believed, and half-doubted, and they could talk of nothing else from morning to night.

But just two weeks after the announcement came that spring, two construction teams of more than ten workers each showed up. The first was assigned to build the school on the land where the old *dinh* had been located, behind the Committee headquarters. The second team was to build a house for Tran Quy Hoan near Little Stream, and along with it a new plantation that was three times the businessman's existing estate. The location of the land alone must have cost him his entire income from the last two harvests.

The size of Hoan's personal estate didn't really bother anyone, even if his wealth did make the face of every inhabitant in the district burn with jealousy. But the primary school raised a thorny problem. No one could imagine that any man in his right mind would build such a project with money from his own pocket, even if he did sit on a mountain of gold. In the eyes of the people in Mountain Hamlet, Hoan was either a madman, or a clever, manipulative businessman who was setting a huge trap for some colossal prey, or some competitor that they couldn't quite imagine.

For these mountain villagers who still had no electricity, the noise from the 140-horsepower generators Hoan was using for the construction seemed like an earthquake or a hail storm they only saw once in a decade. The enormous construction site, harshly lit, was an attraction in itself and drew crowds of young people from all over the region. Every day, the people of the village stood by the roadside, jostling and shoving one another to get a glimpse as convoys of trucks carrying the building materials rumbled past. There were shiny tiles in fancy colors that they had never seen, toilet bowls made of a pristine white porcelain that was even whiter than their crockery, and enormous flowered curtains for the gymnastics room and the cultural center. Everything dazzled them and made their stomachs churn with both excitement and envy. Questions came pouring forth in the public meetings held by the family clubs. The hosts didn't dare refuse; they too were swept up in the tumult, seized by both curiosity and apprehension. So now the family clubs in Mountain Hamlet gathered almost every night, and the atmosphere was different from that of the commemorative ceremonies, or of Tet celebrations, or of other celebrations. Suddenly there was an unusual bustle about these gatherings, just as an unusual need and an odd fervor suddenly animated the ordinarily monotonous lives of these mountain people.

On one such evening, at the home of Old Phieu, conversation sputtered and crackled like corn in a pan. The sun had barely set when people hurriedly finished their dinners and popped toothpicks in their mouths, before grabbing their lamps to go off to the meetings. In front of Phieu's house, more than a dozen lamps were lined up, as if for some ritual. That afternoon, Phieu had asked his daughter-in-law to prepare grilled sticky rice with honey. The grilled rice was served in heaping baskets, and the preserved, candied manioc was set out on high-edged antique plates. More than a dozen Thermoses were also lined up outside so that the visitors could brew their own tea. After everything was prepared, including boiling water and clean cups, the family withdrew to a corner of the house to eat. The courtyard already echoed with the gurgling of water pipes, and the discussion began with the questions pertaining to the seemingly crazy generosity of this mysterious businessman from the city.

"In this world, no one throws a whole basket of his own gold into the river. The fellow must have some hidden agenda. City people are very clever. Money just multiplies in their pockets, so you can bet that whatever goes out has to pull in a profit. How could a bunch of countryfolk like us guess his intentions?"

"Maybe there's gold in the ground under Little Stream?"

"That's it! I've suspected that for a long time. That Hoan must be sure of pulling tons of it into his pockets to risk putting even a few gold bars toward building a school for this hamlet."

"Wait a minute, if there's gold under Little Stream, then there must also be gold under Great Stream, and on Uncle Thoi's plantation, and even in my own land . . . No, you're dreaming. I've visited a lot of the gold-bearing regions. Their topography looks nothing like ours. Our ancestors weren't destined to amass a fortune; they resigned themselves to tilling the earth and gathering grass to eat."

"So, you mean that Hoan spent a fortune just for fame and glory? Nowadays, people like that don't exist anymore."

"Oh? I don't know about that. But I can guarantee that there's no gold in Little Stream or Great Stream. And I speak from experience. I've rummaged and sifted those streambeds. Remember my nephew from Thanh province? Once, we pretended to go hunting hare and armadillo, but we were really panning for gold. We had dreamed about it and acted long before he did. When you're hungry, you've got to be ready to get down on your hands and knees. Poor people like to dream and chase after luck . . ."

"Me neither, I don't believe our land holds gold. And, even if it did, that Hoan wouldn't have the right to mine it. He paid property taxes to farm the land and not to exploit the mines. If he found gold in his basement, the State would take his land away overnight. People can smell money and gold right away. And the government's nose is sharper than ours . . ."

"So you think that Hoan came back here only for his wife?"

"For the moment, I see no other motive. The other day, I saw him taking his son over to Bon's place."

"What did he look like?"

"A bit thinner, but even whiter skin than before. His eyes were sad."

"Chhhhhah! Hasn't he always had those dreamy, clairvoyant's eyes?"

"I don't know him that well, though I used to go for tea on his terrace with Mr. Chi and Mr. Trac. But he really is a sadder man than he was before."

"Well, he's a man, not a piece of wood. He's got things to be sad about. He and Mien were happy together. And they say they were hand-in-hand on the pillow. What's more, their boy is handsome as an angel. Even the city kids would run and hide their sandals to avoid being compared to him."

"Was Bon there, that day?"

"Yes."

"How did he handle the confrontation with Hoan?"

"How would I know? I'm not so pushy that I barge right into people's homes."

"Hah! Manners! Me, I would have gone inside. We're neighbors, people from the same village, the same hamlet, no? Why hesitate?"

"Your words stink! Same village, same hamlet . . . Tell me, has any of your neighbors ever run into your house as you're pulling down your lady's pants?"

"Now, now, now . . . let's not argue over this nonsense. Let me ask a question. That morning, you didn't speak to Hoan, did you?"

"Oh, yes I did . . . But we just exchanged pleasantries. How would I dare interfere in his private life? What's more, he just said a few words, bid me good-bye, and went on his way. We were already far down the road, a good distance from Bon's place, when I saw Bon come out of the kitchen, with a teapot in his hand. He stood frozen in the middle of the courtyard like a statue. So I guess they had never actually seen each other before. This must have been the first time the two husbands met face-to-face."

"And then?"

"And then nothing. I got out of there. I wasn't going to stay and spy on them. If he turned around, what would I have done? Pretend I was a palm sheath or something?"

"My wife heard Mrs. Huyen's neighbors say that Hoan was very humble, very polite. He even inquired about Bon's health before inviting him to go live at his home."

"With Mien?"

"The guy is crazy, that's for sure."

"Crazy, my balls! He's the best businessman in town. He pretends to be interested in Bon's health and his work, but that's just for show. Everybody knows Bon's an invalid, incapable of earning a single dong. He gets his money by clinging to his wife's skirt. The city people are all bastards. They excel in the art of humiliating the poor."

"Even if Hoan were the king of the bastards, he's provided for both Mien and Bon for all these months. If you're such a virtuous man, have you ever given so much as half a bowl of rice to someone in your entire life?"

"Even with my nose stuck in the mud, I still can't buy enough rice and fish to feed my wife and kids. What do you want me to do? Gather my shit to give to charity?"

"Well then, don't go insulting people without any proof. When this guy builds this fancy school, aren't you planning to send your kids?"

"Come, come, put your pride aside. If your sharp tongue itches you, go lick the pineapple bushes behind the garden."

"Let me ask you a question. That day . . . what did Bon say to Hoan's offer?"

"He refused, of course. Even in a hovel, a man is at home. Who could bear the shame of having to set up camp under your rival's roof?"

"They never fought. How can you call them rivals?"

"They love the same woman. If they're not rivals then what would you call them?"

"And what did Mien say to that Hoan guy?"

"Apparently she threw her arms around him and burst into tears."

"Good God! Embracing the second husband in front of the first?

Women today really are brazen. Once, a man could have five wives and seven concubines. But in this day and age, bigamy is a crime. The bee that wants to go for the honey has to do it secretly or the authorities and the villagers will never leave him in peace. So Mien dared to kiss two men at the same time in broad daylight?"

The man spoke in a rasping, vindictive voice, half-earthy, half-metallic, like two sticks of bamboo grating against each other. He smacked his lips. With a wave of his hand, he turned his pointy chin made even longer with a goatee toward the women and young girls who were seated on two mats spread in front of the kitchen.

"So ladies and misses, would you like to have and hold two husbands at the same time? Speak frankly so we know what you think."

The women of Mountain Hamlet had just begun to venture out to the family clubs. They weren't as free to participate as their husbands were because they always had a brood of kids or grandkids in tow. If they did attend, they sat huddled in some dark corner, busying themselves with some mending or sewing, or stroking the children as they fell asleep. Usually these women knew to keep their ears open and their mouths shut. But that night, Phieu's two daughters-in-law had brought two sacks of peanuts with them. More than a dozen women and children bustled about, husking noisily. When they heard the question from the man with the goatee, they just grumbled. All you could hear was the rustling and crackling of crushed peanut shells.

After a few seconds, one thundering young male voice spoke up, breaking through the hush: "Come on, let the ladies shell their peanuts in peace. They're not looking for trouble like us men. Whatever your opinions may be, I have to say that in this world it's hard to find a man as exemplary as Hoan—unless he intended to lure Bon to his house to poison him, or to secretly assassinate him."

"Who would be stupid enough to try that? He'd rot in prison."

"Who knows where love leads? Like the ancestors taught us: He who loves madly loses his head."

"Hoan is rich. The house doesn't mean much to him. It's because he loves Mien, so he doesn't want to see her living in some sordid shack."

"Perfect. Even if he does have a mountain of gold, why would he offer to house under the roof he built with his own hands a man who is sleeping with his wife?"

"Doesn't he feel jealous?"

"Go ask him. How would I know?"

"The heart of the *va* fruit is like that of the sycamore. What kind of man is he if he isn't jealous?"

"That would surprise me. Why doesn't he marry another woman? There are tons of fair-skinned young beauties in town, all like fairies reincarnated. Mien might be beautiful, but she's still a childbearing trout. If I were rich and handsome like Hoan, I'd remarry a virgin, a seventeen- or eighteen-year-old with glowing skin and sweet-smelling young flesh. There's nothing like a virgin. A new vagina is worth a dozen familiar vaginas."

The men all guffawed loudly. When the laughter died down, a woman's voice, raucous and icy as spring water in December, spoke up out of the shadows.

"What a lovely speech! Well from now on, don't come sticking it up this familiar vagina. You ungrateful bastards! You've got neither brains nor brawn. Why, you couldn't even find enough money to pay for your own water pipe tobacco without shaking your wives' skirts! You can't even see how ridiculous you are and yet you're bragging like this!"

The men were absolutely silent. No one coughed or even dared clear his throat. The silence was so total they could hear the mosquitoes humming. The women stopped shelling peanuts. Without anyone saying a word, they all listened, waiting. After a few seconds of this terrifying silence, the woman with the hoarse voice continued: "Open your ears, boys. Listen up so you hear me clearly this time. Night after night you all come here to discuss Mien's business because you're jealous. In this village, who can claim to have pockets as full as Hoan's?

Who is anywhere near as handsome? Who can say he has treated his wife as well? Now, suddenly Hoan donates a pile of money to build a school for your kids. And you're secretly thrilled, but you keep your mouths shut tight, like a bunch of toads. Did anyone dare step forward publicly to praise or thank him? No, because praising him would mean lowering yourself, humiliating yourself, right? But now, if he was like Bon, sick and gaunt, if he had fathered a stillborn monster because of Agent Orange, you would be bursting with joy, unfurling like banners and flags in the wind. You would offer your condolences, your compassion, while secretely congratulating yourselves and whispering, *Poor Bon, you're not as good as me.* From time immemorial, you men have said that we women are petty and envious. But in reality, you're far more envious. It's just that you hide it so well, in so many different ways. Me, I don't beat around the bush. I'm envious of Mien. But I don't hate her; that doesn't do me any good. Who wouldn't envy someone as lucky as her? But when the heavens deny us beauty, we resign ourselves to marrying men without talent or generosity, crippled chickens forced to scramble for their pittance around the millstone—"

Old Phieu stepped in at this point, speaking up to reestablish harmony: "Now, now, I beg you. Let's not transform this joking into an argument. Let's change the subject. It's not right to interfere with other people's lives. I know both Hoan and Bon and I'm fond of both of them. These two men are going through something very personal that we cannot understand. Let them live their lives."

No one replied. Silence again. Then a tall, corpulent woman rose and walked out into the street. There was no doubt that she was the one who had just declared war on those who wore beards and mustaches, who had insulted her husband by calling him a crippled chicken forced to eke out his existence by pecking around a millstone. They couldn't see her features, just her abundant hair, her imposing bearing. A few other women got up and followed, one carrying a child on her back, another hugging a grandchild in her arms. The women who stayed continued to shell peanuts. Among the men, the conversation picked up again, though intermittently and scattered. Some talked of fieldwork, some of seed varieties, others of the cost of fertilizer and insecticide . . . The water pipes started to gurgle and curls of pungent white smoke began to waft and float and then dissolve into the air. Someone yawned and called out, "Oh, what a night, the sky is littered with stars, as if it were sprinkled with sesame seeds . . . What time is it?"

"Light a torch so we can see. Seven twenty-five."

"It's still early."

"They say Mien's child was born without a head. Do you think that's the truth or a vicious rumor?"

The conversation again turned toward the beautiful woman and her two husbands because time is too long, and nights in mountains were too dull, because life here trickled by like a lonely stream, without a single footbridge, or boat, or even a ripple of a wave. In this colorless existence, no one could pass up such a rare chance to use his brain cells, or to revive this ancient tribunal, this invisible yet enduring courtroom where anyone could don the judge's wig and robe.

While the family clubs in Mountain Hamlet bustled with activity, one of the central characters in their drama spent his days smoking cigarettes in a small room. The heavens had given Hoan the right to choose and to manage men. Mr. Lu had only recently become part of Hoan's entourage, but he had quickly become his most faithful and devoted servant. Hoan could delegate virtually any business to Mr. Lu, matters both big and small, without a moment's hesitation. With his blessing, the old man had signed all the papers, hired all the workers, calculated all the costs, and managed all the work at both construction sites. Hoan's presence was required only at the ceremony to inaugurate the digging of the foundations on the banks of Little Stream. According to tradition, he had to stand in person in front of the platter of offerings to the earth spirits, to pray to them to allow him to enter, and to protect him in his life to come. He returned to the city that same evening so he could take the plane to Bao Loc the following morning. He intended to sell his shares in one of his businesses to get his capital back. Managing the shop in town and cultivating the land in Little Stream took all of his time, and as far as business was concerned, he knew that the heavens always smiled on him. But he wanted to live his life again, after all these days and months of silence. And to live his life—the real one—he needed one woman, Mien, and only Mien.

Why? Why? Why? Why only that face, that silhouette, that skin, that flesh? Could I love another woman?

He had asked himself this question so many times. Each time, he was incapable of finding an answer. His sisters knew that he had gone back to Mountain Hamlet several times, that he had invested huge sums in building a plantation and a school. But these projects were part of a secret plan to return to his old life with Mien. Both women were worried, but neither dared speak to him to advise him against it. Hoan knew this, but he himself didn't understand why he had suddenly made this decision. One morning, he had woken up in bed and turned on the radio to listen to the news. Suddenly he heard an old melody, strains of music that he had once listened to for days on end while waiting for the train to the north. And the melody broke his heart. He stayed there, lying down, even though it was already after eight o'clock, smoking as if he had gone mad. The more he smoked, the more he felt his limbs go limp, his mind wander. One minute he felt like crying. The next, he wanted to smash his room to bits, to see the walls come crashing down, to see it all crumble—this shop with people buying and selling, this familiar street, this sickening town. He imagined himself as a blacksmith wielding some blunt object that would reduce the whole world to dust, and first of all this room with its tiny copper bell.

"Hoan! It's almost nine o'clock!" Nen shouted from the other side of the door.

He felt like shouting back, but he contained his rage.

"I'm tired, Elder Sister," he sighed. Suddenly, the tears began to flow. From the corners of his eyes, they rolled down his temples, then trickled through the roots of his hair, slowly cooling.

He stayed there, his back stuck to the bed. His tears continued to flow. There was timid knocking on the door again. This time it was a man's voice.

"Sir, are you sick?"

It was Mr. Lu. Suddenly Hoan's heart let out a silent, terrifying scream.

You're the one, Mien. It's you who's torturing my aching heart. You're the one who keeps me from living the peaceful life of other men. You're my hell, my torture, you are . . .

The scream kept echoing. And she came back to him, as if she were right there by his side, in flesh and blood: the scent of her hair, her smell, the curve of her eyebrows, the way her eyes twinkled under those thick, inky lashes, and behind her as far as the eye could see their lush green fields, the sun-drenched, windswept hills where Hanh like to play, babbling away. His entire past life flooded back to him, swirling and turning, intoxicating him, taking his breath away.

I have to go back. Real life is back there. With you. You alone. Nothing else matters, nothing . . .

He felt suddenly lighter and he raised himself up on his elbows.

"Sir, sir, could you let me in? If you are too tired, I can go back to Mountain Hamlet." Hoan fumbled hastily for a handkerchief to wipe his tears.

"Yes, yes, I'm coming right away."

He groped for his sandals, as his heart continued to roar.

Go back home, go back, go back . . .

He dashed into the bathroom while Mr. Lu still sat outside patiently drinking tea. He splashed his face and hair with cold water, felt his skin and flesh tingle.

Go back, go back, go back . . . I'll go back to Mountain Hamlet, I'll reclaim my life, the life that belongs to me. Nothing can stop me . . .

While his skin and his flesh were still tingling, exalted, his mind, sharp and lucid now, formulated questions: *Why today? Why only now did I dare? Why have I tortured myself with pointless worry and jealousy? I'm the one who is in the right. I've got the law on my side . . .*

As he dried his hair, Hoan remembered the dark days he had lived when he learned that Mien was pregnant with Bon's child. It wasn't Mr. Lu who had told him, but his sisters. The two women had been secretly happy to announce the news. They had hoped that it would put an end to Hoan's love for his ex-wife, that he would give them a new sister-in-law who would keep him in town and help their business flourish. Hoan knew that they harbored these hopes, and he couldn't help resenting them for it. How could his own family be so cruel, so thrilled by such horrific news? It had hit him like a thunderbolt, for he was sure that Mien loved only him and him alone. Returning to her first husband was like a kind of suicide, a self-immolation in the tradition of self-sacrifice of a woman born in a country shattered by endless wars, where human lives were as fragile as dragonfly wings, where the men draw their strength from the fidelity and resignation of their wives.

The image of Mien staggering through the misty dawn flashed again and again in his mind like a film projected over and over. His beloved wife had left with a sack of virgin grass over her shoulder and sad eyes condemned to keep a secret. Each of her footsteps engraved another stone in the path that led to hell. This vision had not blurred with time; instead, day, after day, it was engraved more deeply in his memory. Day after day, it tortured him. Day after day, his anger grew more explosive.

Why should I submit to this? Why should I live here, as if I were in exile? Why?

This pain had given meaning to his life. But now Mien was pregnant with another man's child.

Hoan had locked himself in his room, neglecting all his work. Cang had come by many times to invite him to go out on the town, but he had refused. He felt his nerves and muscles go slack, his body fatigued, his mind preoccupied.

Bon and Mien must have been able to revive their old passion. The flames of memory probably helped them find each other again, just as they were in their youth. And now, they're making up for lost time.

He shut his eyes, but he continued to see Mien's rounded belly. When she was pregnant with Hanh, he had been ecstatic. As her due date approached, Mien's body swelled and her face and legs puffed up. But he had only found her even more beautiful, even more seductive. Now, he imagined her hair falling loose on her shoulders, and those shoulders embraced, kissed, and caressed by another man.

We always cherish our first love, like the beauty that is revealed at the dawn of life . . . In which book did I read that sappy phrase? I never had a first love. Or, to be precise, Mien was my first love. Well, Mien, I love you and you love another man. In the end, life's just a farce where the cat chases endlessly after the mouse. Why then did you love me?

He realized that this question was idiotic. We love because we love. He knew that. But even after all this suffering, he still couldn't find a way out. Humiliated, he realized that he was jealous, that he hated this man, a man whose face he had never even seen, a young, dark-skinned, puny little guy, according to the description he had been given. He was jealous of a weakling.

But this weakling has an invincible weapon: the compassion he seems to elicit from the villagers' hearts.

Why couldn't he be an ordinary man, poor, impotent . . . deserving of compassion from the woman he loved? And this is how Hoan had spent the spring up to the moment Mr. Lu had appeared. "Sir, unforeseen events bring me here to ask your advice. I just brought Madame back from the hospital."

Hoan lit a cigarette and lowered his head to avoid the man's gaze. He inhaled a few long puffs of smoke and then asked quietly, icily, "Everything went well?"

The old man looked at him quizzically: "What do you mean, sir?"

"You took care of her, as I asked you to?"

"Yes."

"Good." Hoan nodded. The manager must have seen something strange flash across his face because he looked down, embarrassed. Hoan got up, paced around the room a bit, then wheeled around suddenly. "Is it a boy or a girl?"

Mr. Lu looked up, stunned. Flustered, he blinked to compose himself. "So you don't know what's happened, sir?"

"What do you mean?" Hoan felt his heart skip a beat, as if something terrible were about to happen, something unexpected. He sat down on a chair and looked intently at his manager.

Mr. Lu lowered his head. "Madame didn't give birth to a child, sir."

"What are you saying?"

"Mr. Bon can't father a normal child. And, then, Madame herself attempted to destroy the fetus."

"She aborted?" Hoan was almost shouting now.

"No. Madame threw herself against the door to Mr. Bon's room several times. It was a stillborn."

Dazed by Mr. Lu's words, Hoan lit another cigarette, trying to appear calm, even cold, while his heart raced.

So you don't love him, you don't love him, you don't love him . . . You wanted to erase every trace of him. So your life with him was hell. So your heart still belongs to me. That's enough for now . . .

He emptied his teacup and asked, "Why didn't you tell me sooner?" Mr. Lu stayed speechless for a moment, then lowered his voice.

"It's difficult for me to tell you this directly. But I've told Madame Chau everything, all the details. . . . Sir, your wife is not well. I wanted to bring her back to the house, but she refused."

"Why? You must make her see that it's her house, that she has the right to use it as she sees fit."

"I've told her that many times. But she always refuses. She says she doesn't want to sully your former home together, that she wants to keep it pure for young master Hanh."

Oh God! Sully my home? So it was your sacred land, the altar to love that nothing impure could touch . . . That's why you imprisoned yourself in the most miserable hovel in the region.

My poor wife, you wanted to preserve the purity of a mausoleum, but our bodies are already sullied . . .

This thought suddenly filled him with bitterness. Through the smoke, he saw a room hidden by a red curtain, a pot with a damp washcloth, and a dented aluminum pan under the bed. He remembered the prostitute's pale, thin face and pointy chin, her puppy-dog eyes, her painted, chipped nails clinging to his arm. Could Mien imagine what he had done? Surely not. A simple, innocent woman, her spirit filled with religious values, would never imagine this. She must have thought he was searching for a new love, a new marriage prospect. With her idealistic faith in him, she must have believed that he had remained an elegant, courageous, noble man, and not some guy who ran, stumbling and panting down back alleys fetid with sewage, across courtyards strewn with stinking garbage, scrambling up a rotting staircase to hide in a hideous suburban warehouse.

In that moment, his past seemed to glide past his eyes like images from a film, like a current emptying into the mouth of a river. And in this flux, emotions crisscrossed, mixed, interwined and displaced one another. The course of time blurred, the threads broke, then rejoined and tightened, inextricable. Hoan could still smell the dank, moldy stench of the brothel while remembering the fragrance of flowers from their garden in Mountain Hamlet, the perfume of the hyacinths and the yellow magnolias . . . and all this began to call and beckon to him. And he suddenly saw himself alone on a beach, pale, exhausted, hunched over in a tiny tea shop, walking down the roads in Mountain Hamlet, across the courtyard strewn with rotting leaves, in the middle of his coffee fields covered with ripe beans. He remembered the tapering, yellow flames that licked the pan in their warm, fragrant kitchen when Mien cooked her favorite dishes, and he wondered if it was the fire or her laughter that had dispelled the icy winter fog.

He had tried to shield and protect her from all life's vicissitudes. During their final days together, they had gone over the difficulties that Mien would face. Despite the pain of separation, despite the passion, they had remained lucid enough to put aside money for her. And Hoan had been clever enough to persuade her to accept it. But now he realized that the money had eased Mien's material deprivation, but not her unhappiness. And he hadn't foreseen his own suffering, or imagined the pain of separation or repressed sexual desire, or the horrible loneliness a man feels when he is expelled from the land he loves, his mooring in life . . . No, he had never imagined . . . the reality was even more miserable than he could ever have predicted.

How did this happen? Did we allow it to happen?

In a flash, the pain and anger rose in him, illuminating the course his life had taken over time, revealing another face that was both stupid and cowardly, a stubborn patience, the resignation of a water buffalo behind the plow.

He reached for an ashtray and snuffed out his cigarette with a brutal, imperious gesture. Mr. Lu looked up but kept his silence.

And in this silence, Hoan began to outline a plan of action. And as he did, it was as if all the preparations and calculations had already been inscribed in some secret corner of his brain. All he had to do now was put them on paper.

"Do you remember the hill by Little Stream?" he asked Mr. Lu.

"Yes, it's about four and a half miles from the third pepper plantation."

"We surveyed that land together, didn't we?"

"Yes, you said that the land by Little Stream was suited to the Malaysian pepper trees."

"And what else?"

"Well, on the other side of the stream, we could level the land, and plant a few groves of coffee bushes. We'd have to terrace the land, and create a difference in height of about thirty-five inches. Between the groves, we could build a pumping station."

"And what else?"

"About four hundred and fifty yards from the dike, there's a fairly deep depression in the land. We could make that into an open well or a reservoir. You had thought that the water there was sufficient to irrigate the trees even during the dry season."

"What else?"

"The base of the hill is hollowed out and protected from the wind, very practical to use as a shelter for livestock or as a barn to stock dried grasses."

"Thank you. You have an excellent memory."

"I don't deserve such praise."

"I've decided to create a plantation by Little Stream."

"I'm at your service, sir."

"You will draw up a detailed proposal."

"When do you need it?"

"The sooner the better."

"I'll do my best."

"Another thing. Design a project to build a primary school for the village on the site of the old *dinh* in Mountain Hamlet. And I'd like this project to be launched simultaneously with the plantation project. It will be a much-needed gift to the villagers. Later, perhaps, my own son will study there. Even if he doesn't go there, the village kids need a place to study. Can you handle all this?"

"Don't worry, sir."

"Okay, then you return immediately to Mountain Hamlet. I want to get things under way as soon as possible."

"I know," Mr. Lu said, and took his leave.

Did the old man read my mind, or is he just following orders?

Hoan would never know. But he did know that he had just launched the plan that would ensure his return to Mountain Hamlet. He had never made such a sudden decision in his entire life—except for the one he made the day he met Mien on that hill back where the pepper trees still grew.

22

Mien woke at about six o'clock in the morning. The clock chimed slowly, ticking out each chime. From where she lay on the bed, Mien counted them one by one. The cheery, tinkling music surprised her, and she sat up in bed.

I'm home. These sounds have been familiar to me for so long now.

Yet she got up and went over to contemplate the finely sculpted Swiss clock on the wall, as if she didn't believe that it was still there, or that the house had been repainted, or the kitchen and bathroom re-decorated. The clock was an antique that Hoan had purchased in Nha Trang, a faraway, seaside town he loved to tell her about, and where they apparently sold all kinds of clocks. Mien didn't know anything about clocks or Nha Trang. But for her, everything Hoan said was the purest truth. And this crystalline music warmed her heart and soul. Like the house, the garden, the kitchen—the clock was no mere object, it was part of her life. Ever since Hoan had come for her at Bon's place and brought her back here, everything seemed new, surprising. When she used to bring Hanh here every day from Bon's place, she had felt as if she were coming out of a cave and returning to earth. Every morn-ing, when she walked toward the gate and pulled the bell, as she pushed open the heavy wood panels, she felt a childish joy, and she would walk down the little path to the courtyard like someone who was walking toward paradise on earth. Even though she no longer lived there, she would still carefully pull up the weeds that had started to grow between the stones and meticulously clip the groves of orchids. Sometimes she would linger for hours, gazing at these frail bunches of flowers drenched in dew. She would even rake up the dead leaves and gather the overripe oranges that littered the ground. Everything in this house seemed to intoxicate her, to have a soul that had been waiting just for her. And each time she told herself, *It's all part of me—everything here, in this garden, on this land, under this roof.*

The first night Mien returned to her former home with Hoan, she had asked Auntie Huyen to stay and sleep at the house. The boy slept between the two women. He was in heaven and fell asleep instantly. But Mien, still exhausted by the birth, couldn't sleep. She looked out the window at the garden, noticing that the curtains had just been washed. For so long she had dreamed of coming back here, of sleeping in this bed, of being able to gaze again at the rustling grove of orange trees that swayed just beyond the silent frame of her window.

A candle still smoldered in the copper candelabra on the table. The old three-paneled closet was still there. And facing it, the large mirror where she had modeled the nightgowns that Hoan had bought for her. He had kept the room intact, preserved it exactly as it had been when she lived there with him. The same furniture, not one article more or less. Each object was in its place, hadn't been moved an inch. She had wanted it this way. Hoan too. And Mr. Lu had faithfully executed their wishes.

Like it once was . . . exactly as it once was . . . But it will never be like it was . . . I'm not the woman I once was.

"Try to sleep, my child," Auntie Huyen murmured, stirring beside her.

"I don't know how I'm going to live, Auntie."

"Only the heavens or Buddha know that. We mortals have to be content to live and let live. I'm afraid we are going to become the laughingstock of this village."

"I'm not. Whoever insults me should listen to himself!"

The old woman sighed again. After a long silence, she spoke again. "From time immemorial, the elders have always taught us: Open your hands if you want to reap rain from the heavens; no one can escape the judgment of men. Even so, we continue to fear public opinion. Every time I remember the day that Bon came back from the war, the curses of the women of Mountain Hamlet send a shiver up my spine."

"That's past, Auntie. If any of those women dare insinuate anything now, I'll throw it right back in her face."

Auntie Huyen looked at her niece, astonished. This new resolve took her by surprise. But for the first time, she realized that Mien had changed, and this change both surprised her and inspired her respect.

The night hummed with the plaintive chant of insects. A few hours passed. In the distant hamlets, as a carillon of roosters announced the dawn, the chimes sounded again in the living room. The scent of jasmine tea suddenly wafted through the air; Mr. Lu had woken up and was preparing tea. Auntie Huyen sat up in bed. "Try to sleep, my child. As for me, I'm going to get a cup of tea."

The old woman walked into the living room, her sandals noisily clapping. Mien heard Mr. Lu open the glass door to the armoire. He was probably getting out a large teapot.

She felt as if, instead of lying in her bed, she lay in a boat with neither sail nor helm. Little Hanh rolled over. Mien pulled back slightly and closed her eyes. Suddenly, she realized that she had hidden her forehead with her hands. She pulled them off and let one hand fall on her son's thigh, gently resting the other on her own hip.

Why?

This nebulous question came back like the lapping of waves on the shore of a faraway lake, the lake of her childhood, back in the village where she was born. She drifted into a half sleep, but woke a few minutes later, when she realized that her hands had moved, almost involuntarily, back to her forehead. Her body was rigid, as stiff as a corpse.

I understand. Finally, I understand.

An idea as sharp as the blade of a knife flashed through her mind. She sat bolt upright. Her shared life with Bon hadn't lasted long, but long enough to leave its mark in this chilling habit she had of covering her forehead with her hands. For too long now she had become accustomed to this gesture of rejection. There had been times when she had had to yield to his advances, but she had always resisted first, protecting herself this way. It was only now that she realized how out of tune with everything she was. Here, when her hand dropped to her side, she no longer encountered the mat spread on wooden boards, but a sheet that covered a thick, soft mattress. Her shoulder and her ribs on one side had been constantly tense and stiff because they had been in contact with Bon. Her muscles, always vigilant, on the alert, couldn't relax. Many times, she had slept on her side one minute, only to change position the next, feeling as if she would suffocate from fear and anxiety. But it wasn't just the shameful, horrific trauma of the birth or their pitiful attempts at coupling that prevented her from becoming her old self, the woman she once was. Even the smallest habits of daily life had pushed her toward other shores.

The roosters crowed again, signaling the second wake and then the third. Auntie Huyen continued to sip tea and chat with Mr. Lu. Mien watched the burning candle, her sleeping son, the objects in the room...this lost kingdom now regained. But the mistress of this kingdom was unable to regain her former peace and happiness.

Three weeks had passed since the night of her return. Almost a month. But Mien was still unable to rid herself of the lost sensation that haunted her. She tried, and eventually managed to resist, the habit of keeping her right hand on her forehead while sleeping. She was still haunted by a nebulous anxiety as dense as fog, impossible to grasp, let alone dispel. Sometimes, on mornings like this one, when Mien opened her eyes and no longer saw the rays of light filtering through the cracks of Bon's roof, she wondered, dazed, if she was dreaming or awake. It was only when little Hanh woke up, nuzzling closer to her thigh to sleep, or whining for his breakfast, that she dared believe that she was now home for good. But this life here, that she had so often claimed to be her own, now swayed and pitched like a boat without a helm.

"Would you like me to prepare some tea for you, Madame?"

Mr. Lu stood behind her, speaking as always in a soft, serene voice. Without waiting for Mien's reply, he continued, "This clock's melody is beautiful. Mr. Hoan is a real connoisseur."

Mien turned to him. "Do you know many varieties of clocks?"

"Yes. I've worked for many different bosses. Some richer than Mr. Hoan, though none as shrewd."

Mien didn't know what to say. In fact, she couldn't add anything. She had never traveled to any other town, never known other vistas than those that had been traced for her. Hoan had been her entire universe, her protector, and yet he remained elusive.

Sensing Mien's confusion, the manager said, "Would you like breakfast now, or later, when little master wakes up?"

"Oh don't worry about me. I'll manage on my own."

"Please, don't even contemplate that, Madame."

"But you're directing all the construction work at Little Stream and for the school."

"Everything is in order. I've delegated the work. The foreman is in charge. But I'll pay only if the work is done correctly."

Mien covered herself with a shawl before going out into the courtyard. She still hadn't regained her strength. That morning, upon waking, she had picked up a tuft of her own hair off her pillowcase. She had a humming in her ears that lasted a long time, and sometimes she even heard a terrifying scraping sound. After she had given birth to Hanh, she had never had such symptoms. But this time . . . But how can it be compared?

I detested Bon. I hated him. But now it's over. I rejoiced with all my heart when I saw him suffering, but now . . .

She pulled at the hem of her shawl to cover her ears and neck as she crossed the empty, windswept courtyard. When she reached the kitchen, she saw that Mr. Lu had started the charcoal fire to warm her feet. He had her sit down in a chair and brought her a bowl of soup. The smell of beef broth flavored with five-spice powder whet her appetite, and raised a question for her: *What is Bon eating? He's probably spent the money I left him a long time ago.*

What had begun as just a vague question or a distant rumor slowly became clearer and more insistent. When Mien had finished her soup, Mr. Lu brought her a cup of ginger tea. She drank it in small sips, and each time she swallowed she saw Bon's face more and more vividly.

No, I don't hate him anymore. He himself took no joy in it, he knew he was humiliated . . . If I had been in his place . . .

And she remembered the terrible morning when she had thrown herself against the door to expel the fetus, right in front of Bon. She had felt a cruel joy in a way she never had in her entire life, a barbaric, ferocious joy that she had never imagined possible. That day, Bon had gotten down on his knees and begged her in front of Auntie Huyen. And in the days that followed, he had looked at her with the cringing eyes of a criminal, his back hunched, his face ashen. Often, he seemed breathless, panting like an old man. From that day on, he no longer dared climb into bed with her. He paced back and forth from the house to the courtyard, and then from the courtyard to the house, waiting until she had gone to bed. Only much later would he slip in next to her, curling up in a corner of the bed like a cockroach. She remembered having trouble sleeping, and as she lay on her back, her hands covering her face, she would watch Bon in silence. A bit of indifference, a bit of surprise, a bit of pity. Since the night of his unbridled lust, he was empty, just the shadow of a fetus that he had sown in her body.

One morning, when she woke up as the rooster crowed for the second time, Bon wasn't sleeping. He was crouched at the foot of the bed, clutching his knees to his chest. The lamplight cast its glow on his dark, shadowy eyes, those empty sockets. Mien didn't dare move. But she couldn't help watching him with an anxious curiosity. She saw him whispering, as if he were speaking to someone, but whether it was to the lamp, or to the shadows in the courtyard, or just to himself, she didn't know. A low murmur, more like the murmuring of a ghost than a human being. Tears trickled slowly from his eyes, glistening in the light of the flames. Bon didn't wipe them away with his sleeve. He probably wasn't even aware that he was crying. The tears rolled in silence down his cheekbones toward his chin, falling on the old soldier's uniform that he had worn to bed. Suddenly, Mien was moved, just as she had been when Bon had handed her the perfumed soap, the only gift he had managed to bring back from fourteen years of war.

Poor Bon . . . If I were a man in his situation . . .

This thought suddenly kindled a bit of compassion in her. The next morning, the compassion disappeared with the curses that Ta hurled at her daughter: "Ah, you little whore, get up and get to work if you don't want to eat shit!" Ta said in a croaking voice. "Go see if there's some rice stuck to the bottom of the pot. If not, go out to the fields and see if there are a few grains of paddy or some rotten manioc left and bring it all back here. Do you think all you'll have to do is spread your legs to stuff your belly with expensive food? Do you think fate has set you on some throne, that you don't need to suffer to fill your rice pot?"

With Mien's charity now cut off, they fell back into their former misery, a not-too-distant past that they had too easily forgotten. But Mien was the real object of Ta's rage because she knew that the villagers took it for granted that a rich aunt would provide for her indigent nephews.

But Ta didn't wait for the silent pressure of public opinion; she herself began the curses. And Mien replied with silence, contempt, and this new, cruel joy. She would open her door and from where she was seated, calmly watch this filthy, emaciated woman hunched over in the courtyard. Was it her gaze, her haughty attitude, the color of her hair, or the fairness of her skin that so provoked Ta's rage? When Ta saw that her vicious insults didn't even touch her sister-in-law, didn't so much as scratch her soul, it was as if her razor-sharp words had been hurled back in her face. Mien watched as she took it out on her kids, grabbing one or the other by the hair or neck and unleashing on them all the pent-up rage and hatred in her savage, filthy soul. And she remembered, too, how Bon had said nothing. How he had just turned to the wall and pretended to sleep, or flipped through one of his old, dog-eared comic books. But during meals, he lowered his head, avoiding the courtyard where his nephews had squatted around a pot of boiled potatoes.

I once rejoiced thinking that the hussy deserved her wretched life, that she deserved her fate . . . But I'm not rejoicing anymore . . . Now I've forgotten . . . I've forgotten . . .

Had she really forgotten these painful memories? Yet now she remembered as if it were yesterday.

I had forgotten the hatred.

She had forgotten that when she saw Hanh's puffy, red eyes she had wanted to crush those brats' heads one by one, then push them into the well so she could watch them wriggle and gasp before drowning, their swollen bellies floating to bob at the surface. She had forgotten every violent and painful act that her mother's tortured, vengeful heart had imagined.

But in the end, she realized that none of this made sense, that even these wild children were human beings, that they too felt pain. They didn't yet know what humiliation was. In that family, Bon was still the one who had the deepest capacity for that. That's why she had spared them, those vicious children, the real culprits, and concentrated her blows on him, knowing that she would hit her target . . .

These memories flooded back to her as clear as the hills in autumn, with their sharply outlined features and distant, looming sadness.

A dry, silver-gray grass grew on these hills, as thin as arrow reed, and its tiny flowers were covered with a fine down, so fine that it was hard to see with the naked eye. And when this down flew up in the wind it stuck to her hair and clothes. Sadness seemed to saturate the very air she breathed, as suffocating as the downy grass, piling up in invisible drifts in the corners of her heart.

Why did I go back to Bon? Why?

When she had lived under Bon's roof, hatred had mingled with pity. Sometimes she was so moved by it that she vowed to grit her teeth and live the rest of her life with him. But day after day, and month after month, these moments of pity grew few and far between, until all that was left was disbelief and rage.

How many times had she imagined throwing herself off a cliff as a quick, practical solution? She had even prepared her final words for Hanh, Auntie Huyen, and for Hoan. In her mind, she had rehearsed it a thousand times: She had wept for herself and her fate, following her own coffin to the cemetery, throwing the last few handfuls of dirt onto the burial mound. And she had taken note of the villagers who wept the most, who suffered the most. And then these imaginary scenes dissipated and she would return from the chasm, go back to Auntie Huyen's house and clasp Hanh in her arms, hugging and kissing him. Then she would take him back to play in his former home, cook his favorite dishes, and dream of a man who lived in the city. She couldn't die yet; the heavens wouldn't allow it. Behind their infinite harshness stood a man in flesh and blood, with a radiant face and an enchanting lock of hair, with passionate lips and tender eyes. Each time she came back, she would go and lie down on this bed, with Hanh in her arms. While the little boy babbled to himself, she would close her eyes, sift through her memory, and relive their past love. Sometimes she would take Hanh up to the rooftop terrace to look out at the skyline, dreaming of the day when they would both travel east, to the place where her sun rose, where the city held a beloved prisoner. And a mute cry would rise from the bottom of her soul.

We'll be together again, we'll live our old life again . . . in spite of it all . . . and nothing will be able to separate or estrange us.

And these silent cries piled up inside her, like so many pebbles, leaving tangled, painful scars on her soul. Each day pushed her farther and farther away, to a place where she knew the clouds were gathering inside her. And she waited with both fear and anticipation for the flash of lightning ... It had come the morning Hoan arrived at Bon's place holding little Hanh by the hand. The morning of her destiny. She had stood up like a spring at the noise of her boy kicking at the door. Mien was about to raise her voice to scold him when she saw Hoan. He bent over to walk through the door and then looked up. As their eyes met, Mien crumbled like a broken banana bush, and broke down, sobbing. In one leap, Hoan caught her in his arms. The thunder had started. Then the lightning had swept away the clouds that had been gathering for months. Tears too long held back streamed forth. All the sadness and humiliation and hatred she had repressed burst forth in jagged, incoherent sobs and painful, childlike cries.

Mien didn't know, afterward, how long she had wept. She knew only that it had lasted a long time, as if to compensate for all the suffering she had endured. At the beginning, Hanh began to cry too. No doubt the boy had guessed that behind his mother's tears lurked not just pain but joy. For the first time in ages he saw his parents together; this was the first, most important sign that things were going to change for the better. Despite the gaggle of children who stood gawking at the door, he kept silent by Hoan's side, as if he were not a boy but a serious old man. Some strained their necks or stood on tiptoe, while others stuck out their tongues. Mien cried until her sobs gently subsided. At that moment, Bon entered the room, set down his teapot at the foot of the bed, and walked over to stand facing Hoan. "This is my home."

Hoan nodded. "I know. I have no intention of taking your home."

"And Mien is my wife."

Hoan laughed and held up a piece of paper in his hand. "We'll see about that. Can you show me the marriage certificate?"

Bon paled and wheeled around to glare at Mien. She had stopped crying. Measuring her words, she spoke in a clear, icy, almost cruel voice: "We burned the marriage certificate with the rest of your old clothes the same day we commemorated the first anniversary of your death. Anyone in Mountain Hamlet can testify to that."

Bon looked frantic. A threatening light suddenly flared in his desperate eyes and he grabbed the piece of paper in Hoan's hand, ripped it to shreds, and then threw it on the floor. Mien leapt forward to pick them up, but Hoan stopped her, saying calmly, "You just tore up a photocopy. The original and a pile of other copies are at my house. Take a close look. You'll see that the stamp is black. On the original it's red."

Bon couldn't say anything more. His eyes glazed over. His body began to tremble uncontrollably, starting with his arms and shoulders, and finally his chin and all the muscles of his neck and his eyelids. His dull gaze turned and settled on Mien, like a last ray of sunlight before dusk, the hand of a drowning man emerging one last time from the water. Mien was unmoved; she felt only exasperation.

She was the first one to break the silence: "Let's go, Hoan."

Hoan turned to her and replied, "Yes, I've come to take you home."

"Wait, let me get my clothes."

Hoan shook his head. "No, leave everything."

Mien rose and took Hanh by the hand. The three of them moved toward the door. Hoan stopped for a moment before turning to Bon. "Mr. Bon, we are both men, we have neither hatred nor debts between us. I understand your situation. But life has imposed its own course of events that neither you nor I can alter or oppose. Believe me, I will always be ready to help you if you are in need. If, at any time, you feel you can no longer live here, please go over there to live. Henceforth, it's Mien's private residence."

Bon's pale lips twitched slightly as he spoke. "I'll live under my own roof."

Hoan crossed through the door, but he turned back. "Just think about it. Good-bye."

The curious brood of children gathered in front of the door

stepped aside to allow Hoan passage. His motorcycle stood in front of the gate.

"Let's go," he said to Mien. "And cover your head." Without a word, Mien covered her head with a shawl, as obedient as always. As Hoan drove the three of them back to the house, he was watched by curious eyes hidden behind the hedges, doors and windows of the neighborhood.

Seated behind Hoan on the motorcycle, Mien breathed deeply, as if she were suffocating. And like a prisoner who had just escaped from her jail cell, she didn't dare look back. Never again would she walk back down that muddy lane toward the rickety bamboo gate. All that was behind her now. Nothing in the world could force her to go back. The days and months of exile had emboldened her, made her courageous and obstinate. She had learned to sharpen her fangs and nails to defend herself, and she was ready to pounce on anyone who dared attack her. She vowed to be the first to jump into the ring if the enemy presented himself.

After they had returned to the old house, Hoan, Mien, and Hanh all ate lunch in the familiar kitchen, around the huge table. Mien thought that they would resume their old life, that she would go back to her old routine. But at the end of the meal, Hoan announced, "I've got to go back to town. Tomorrow, I'm taking the plane to Bao Loc to settle some business. You stay here with the boy."

She stared at him, dumbfounded. Hoan just smiled mysteriously and leaned over to muss Hanh's hair. "You stay at the house with Mommy and be good. This time, I'm going to buy you a game of numbers and letters."

"When will you be back?" Mien asked. She looked at him, both sad and irritated. But he didn't look at her, just squeezed the little boy's head in his arms to avoid her reproachful gaze. "Take care of your health, Mien . . . I've given instructions to Old Lu, too."

Turning his face toward the courtyard, he placed a warm hand on

Mien's back to bid her farewell. She stiffened, silent, and tried to hold back sobs.

He brings me back here and then goes right back to town. I'm not the pure woman I once was. We will never be able to live as we used to.

She waited until the noise of Hoan's motorcycle had faded into the distance, then went back to her room to cry. When she had sobbed to her heart's content, she consoled herself by saying that after all she could live her real life under this roof. But this life did not come as easily as she had imagined. Somehow, she felt as if she were just a guest and that the real masters of the house were her son and Mr. Lu.

Mien had prepared herself to fight back against the curious, the naysayers, the ill-intentioned, and the envious. She had braced herself for the onslaught of the ghosts that she knew were still lurking inside her, those all-powerful, ancestral voices that had reigned for millennia on this earth and whose influence had compelled her to return to live with Bon . . . She had even rehearsed for the day the president of the commune, the Party secretary, and the president of the Women's Union would come and ring the bell, ready to lecture and condemn her with some interminable, theoretical speech. She knew they would appeal to her conscience, or to her sense of civic duty and responsibility, as they invoked all the traditional Vietnamese values. And from her anguished soul and raging heart came a flood of words, in a language that was no intellectual's but rather the scalding hot lava of an indignant woman. Like a warrior sharpening her sword, she honed her arguments against the world, ready to defend her right to live the way she wanted to.

But her enemies did not reveal themselves. The president of the commune, the Party secretary, and the president of the Women's Union never came knocking at her door. And the shadowy ghosts of tradition never reappeared in the morning mist or in the chilly moonlight. One day someone did ring the bell, but it was only a neighbor come to pay her a visit. Other times it was someone asking for a bit of

balm, or a teaspoon of sugar to make a sauce, or to borrow her coffee
grinder.

It was strange. In their conversations, they never made the slightest
reference to her life with Bon, as if it had never happened, as if she had
never left this house, left her neighbors to live under another roof,
with another man, near other neighbors. The enemy was dead. And the
survivors had affected a serene, indifferent attitude, as if they themselves had never thronged to gape at her the day that Bon came back,
never stared at her with spiteful, accusatory eyes, never lectured her on
morality or fed the rumor mill. The ghosts, too, had vanished, probably drowned en masse crossing the river of Hell . . . But Mien's anxiety
had not vanished in the company of her enemies. No, the anxiety had
replaced the ghosts, taken the place of the invisible crowd, this power
that they called public opinion. And it was this anxiety that now
haunted and tortured her heart.

"Madame, please, drink up while the tea is hot," Mr. Lu urged.
"Ginger tea is very good for women who are getting over . . . illness."

Mien understood what he meant: childbirth. But he had avoided
the word just in time. She was grateful to him, but she felt sad.

*It's the truth. Everyone knows it, whether they say it or not. I carried Bon's child.
Even if it wasn't fated to live, to become a man, it was still a drop of lost blood. I
didn't even get to see it, the mass of flesh I carried in my belly for almost nine months.*

She remembered Bon's distraught face when the midwives had finally chased him out of the delivery room—no longer a human face
but a grave where joy and hope had been snuffed out. She remembered
his pale, trembling lips, how the words had tumbled from his mouth
and scattered like so many pebbles down a hill. Bon had called to it,
called the little fetus that would never know a human life, in a horrified, distant voice. The voice of a ghost. To Mien, Bon was like a ghost
cursed by the little soul who could never take a human form. Bon was
both its creator and its torturer because even before he had saved the
soul of this human, he had condemned him to a world of ghosts. The

little heart of this unfinished human being would be condemned to suffer eternally the pain of a headless, wandering soul.

Why didn't I look at him, if only for an instant? I'm a ruthless, unworthy mother . . .

Out in the courtyard, a gust of cold wind began to blow, lifting the dead leaves, scattering swarms of butterflies and hurling them into another corner of the courtyard. The dry, yellowing leaves recalled the garden in summer, when they had danced in the breeze, as lively as the birds, casting thousands of shards of green light toward the sky. Like the springtime of her youth . . . and everyone had once had youth. Everyone. Even Bon. He had been a young, vigorous, warm-hearted man. Mien remembered one summer morning, when Bon had invited her into the forest to gather firewood. They were falling in love, and had left early to avoid the curiosity and teasing of their friends. Mien had forgotten that she was about to get her period and hadn't brought any sanitary napkins. Like all poor country girls, she used pieces of crude fabric to soak up the blood, washing them discreetly when no one was watching. This time, in the middle of the forest, she was horrified to realize that she had nothing, not even a scrap of fabric. When the blood began to flow, she had to set down her bundle of firewood and squeeze her thighs so that her black pants would absorb the blood. Behind her, Bon saw her standing in this strange, uncomfortable position, incapable of speaking.

"What's the matter?" he asked her.

She didn't reply, but her eyes were brimming with tears.

Bon burst out laughing. "Such a feudal mentality! No one's modest about this stuff anymore."

He pulled off his shirt, tore off the sleeves, and gave them to her. "Here, take these. I'll sit here, my back turned, while you get changed."

At that moment, he had seemed mature, imposing. His eyes sparkled with delight and confidence. Bon wasn't handsome, but his black eyes were seductive, with a gaze so intense it seemed to reflect the land and the forests. The villagers used to say, *Who knows, perhaps he had Cham ancestors. He has the eyes of the Cham from Thuan Hai province.*

Mien had never been to Thuan Hai, nor had she ever met any Cham. But she had always loved Bon's eyes, their sad, wet darkness that glinted under thick eyelashes. She missed those eyes, that expression...

Why now? Why only now am I remembering that morning, that path, and his youthful laughter?

While she lived with Bon, she had tried many times to persuade herself that she still loved him, and that this love obligated her to stay with him until death. Many times she had tried to summon her old love, sifting through the ashes of the past to try to revive the flame. But the more she tried to revive it, the more the old images scattered into the dust of a sky already murky with smoke and fog. And now the sky itself seemed to crumble and fall. It was only now that she had come home that she knew she would never have to live with Bon again, that it was all in ruins behind her, that she would never have to see it again... And yet precisely at that moment of separation, all these images seemed to come back to life, each memory calling forth another, her past life unraveling like a ball of string, not very long but long enough to trouble her heart and mind.

No, I've paid my debt. No one in Mountain Hamlet could call me an ingrate.

And this is how Mien persuaded herself. She knew that for the people of Mountain Hamlet, her attitude toward Bon was an exception; no woman had ever had the financial means and the generosity to feed a sick husband as long as she had. The villagers valued money, but for Mien, submitting to intercourse with Bon had been the real price she had paid for the slice of her life that she had sacrificed on the altar of traditional morality. And yet she knew, when she left with Hanh, that she had freed herself. Why then, now that she was seated safely in her own luxurious home, did that miserable hovel come back to haunt her?

It's starting to get cold. Bon can't get by on just a bowl of rice gruel. Did he go to see Xa? Xa has a good heart, but he isn't rich and he's got three kids to feed. Why am I worrying about all this? Bon has to take control of his own life.

Finally Mien grew exasperated with these nagging thoughts and she turned toward Mr. Lu. "Please hand me the teapot. I'll serve myself."

The old man brought her the teapot. Mien poured herself a cup of tea, swallowed it, poured another, and gulped that one down even though she had had enough. She wanted to fill her stomach with the hot, gingery liquid to help her forget all these thoughts. Then she covered herself with her shawl and went back into the house, where Hanh was fast asleep. She sat down next to him and gazed out at the garden. The orange trees had changed color since their leaves had fallen, and the branches now seemed shriveled.

This moldy brown color. How it resembles the bark of the flame trees. The redder the flowers, the moldier the bark.

This idea suddenly called forth the memory of the row of flame trees along the path leading to the entrance of Mountain Hamlet, the trees that had witnessed their first kiss. She remembered, too, the intoxication of flesh caressing flesh, the red marks Bon had left on her neck and that she had hidden from the rest of the world with a scarf. Unbridled passion at age seventeen, as dazzling as the flame trees, as burning as the summer sun. Now, everything seemed so close, like the light on the veranda the previous evening and afternoon . . . a miracle or an evil spell? Mien didn't know. She knew only that now that she was no longer obligated to go back to Bon, that she had finally rallied the courage to live her life, this frantic, impotent, totally powerless man had suddenly stirred memories of her youth.

Could I still love him?

Just thinking about it made her scream in terror.

Never, never, never.

Even if some evil power forced her to go back, nothing would change. Every night she would go to sleep laid out like a corpse, her hands pressed against her forehead, the left half of her body permanently stiff. Night after night, her eyelids half-closed, she would watch him, this reincarnated ghost, crouched at the foot of the bed, with his desperate, humiliated eyes, his stinking breath, his body that no longer aroused her desire, only her revulsion.

Never. Never. Never.

Her soul screamed again, not just in fright but in rage. She was sure that if anyone forced her to live with Bon again, she would either kill them, or commit suicide.

What do I want? I can't live with Bon. I'd rather die. But I can't abandon him in this state either.

These thoughts hounded her, driving her nearly mad. Exhausted, she fell onto the bed and fell asleep.

When she woke up late that afternoon, Mr. Lu had left and Auntie Huyen had taken the little boy out to play. Mien ate the rice that Mr. Lu had kept warm in the box that held the teapot. He had made her a special dish of beef nerves stewed with *nuoc mam* and lots of ginger. Almost a whole piece of ginger for two pieces of meat, and lots of black pepper. The smell of spices filled the kitchen. Mr. Lu was a bachelor, but he knew how to cook dishes specially prepared for women recovering from childbirth.

She wondered whether he hadn't invented this story about being a bachelor to hide his past. Once, feigning indifference, she had asked him suddenly, "Was your wife from the same village?"

Mr. Lu was preparing tea. Without turning to her, he replied in a calm, gentle voice, "I told you. I've never been married."

"Ah yes, a long time ago. I had forgotten. But you loved a woman once, no? In your youth?"

"Madame, everyone suffers and endures hardship." He sighed. "It's just different for everyone, different from man to man."

He always spoke in the same calm, measured voice. Mien didn't dare ask any more questions, didn't dare pursue her curiosity any further. He had very strange eyes. Thin, wrinkled eyelids over deep irises, eyes that were almost motionless, with an attentive, poignant air about it, and a certain softness, too. Ever since Mien's return, he looked at her with a gentle questioning, or consolation, even a patient expectancy.

What does he expect from me? Those clever eyes seem to hide so many clues, hint at so much I can never guess. One thing is certain: it's all somehow linked to Hoan. He is Hoan's most trusted, most faithful servant. It's as if the heavens created the two men to meet . . .

She suddenly felt secretly jealous of Mr. Lu. He seemed closer to Hoan than even she was. He was like an appendage of Hoan, knew his innermost thoughts, executed his desires, his secret plans. She was outside all that. The recent past had dug a chasm between them. They still loved each other, but they couldn't share everything as they once had.

But why would I demand to share everything with Hoan when I live under his roof, eat in his kitchen, cover myself with the shawl he bought, and yet still seem to pity Bon, the man standing on the other side . . . ?

She saw her situation clearly: a woman standing outside the world each man inhabited, and yet burned by both sides, by two suns that were equally searing though fueled by a different fire. Like the horrific ancient torture of being drawn and quartered.

I chose to leave Bon's hovel. That action was reasonable and just. I must forget Bon. It's the only thing to do.

And thus she ordered herself. She concocted projects around the house to fill the time—cooking a new recipe, knitting a new hat for Hanh. But after a while, she would always see it again, the deep blue sky, the heavy, incandescent crown of the flame trees curving toward the heavens, the path lined with swaying, rustling arrow reeds. She would see the stream again, gurgling and singing, rushing over slippery moss-covered boulders, as she flailed helplessly, drowning, while a seventeen-year-old man with sad eyes stretched out his hand to her.

And Mien counted each evening that she spent this way, drowned in memories, her spirit divided. Two weeks passed. Her health improved by the same measure that her heart was torn asunder. She wanted to find out how Bon was, but didn't dare inquire. The neighbors were discreet; they avoided all subjects that might have a link to Bon or his family. Mien knew that they were all waiting for the new school, the place that would give their children access to all the material goods that the city kids dreamed of, the place where they could at last dream of a brighter future. Hoan's donation had gone beyond everyone's wildest imagination, and he now wielded a power that was utterly beyond their reach. He was virtually untouchable.

Poor Bon. Now his hands are truly empty.

Her heart groaned. Suddenly she hated the whole lot of them. The day that Bon had come back, they were on his side, but now they all admired and deferred to Hoan. Mien finally began to see, even in her confusion, that the villagers had no moral conscience, that the crowd always submitted to the strongest. When Bon returned, he had been the strong man, the heroic veteran. His martyred, ghostly body had recalled a tragic era of sacrifice for every family, for every man or woman who wanted to claim his or her share of the pride and glory. But now Bon was devalued. The hero of the new era was Hoan.

To think that I left because I was afraid of them, that I went back to Bon not out of love, but out of blind obedience. Oh, what a fool I was.

She wanted to do something to strike out at the invisible crowd, to avenge herself for that foggy morning. And though she didn't yet know what it would be, she vowed to do something to stand up to them, to expose their cowardice.

Five days after market day, Auntie Huyen came to the house as usual. She played with Hanh somewhere in the courtyard, while Mien drank tea with the manager. After they had finished, Mr. Lu went out to oversee work on the construction sites. Auntie Huyen waited until he had left to go into the kitchen and speak to Mien. "I hear that Bon is very ill."

"Since when?"

"For about ten days now, apparently. Yesterday, I saw Ta's eldest bring him a bowl of rice porridge. What a pitiful sight. Except for a few scraps of meat, it was nothing but water and a few onion leaves. Xa has gone off with the rest of the woodsmen into the forest. Soan is the only one back at the house taking care of Bon, to the extent she can."

I must feed him. I can't let him die a slow death in that hovel.

This thought had surfaced instantly in Mien's mind, followed by a torrent of others.

If I had an elder brother as unlucky as Bon, would I leave him in poverty like this? No. Never. I have to help him as if he were a brother, especially now that he is powerless and alone, forgotten by the world . . . If Bon dies in misery and solitude, I'll never be able to live with myself. He's a part of my past. Whether I like it or not, I can never erase Bon from my memory. But will Hoan accept my decision? What if he stopped loving me because of this? Then I would be truly alone on this earth. No, Hoan came back to get me, and he accepts the woman I have become. And if he doesn't accept it, he doesn't deserve my love, as he once did . . . and if we lost regard for each other then our separation would be inevitable and painless.

All clear, lucid thoughts. But they terrified Mien, who couldn't fathom how she had suddenly been able to think so quickly and with such resolve. Like an artist steps back, light-headed, to look at the work she has just finished, Mien stepped back to examine the thoughts she had just formulated.

Why such haste? I endured such suffering to come home and now I'm going to get myself into even more trouble? I'm going to tie my own hands. And what if Hoan were to stop loving me, how would I live with that?

Though she feared losing Hoan, a stubborn, willful voice still murmured to her: *I must act according to my conscience. It's like my father told me: Man is weak, but he becomes human only if he has a moral conscience. The heavens will decide whether Hoan accepts or rejects my decision, whether he loves me or not. Only the heavens know where the winding roads of our lives will lead. We mothers live like duckweed, drifting at the whim of the current . . . wherever fate may carry us . . .*

Her mind was suddenly as clear as the sky after a sudden rain. She turned to Auntie Huyen. "Please go catch a chicken from the roost and make me a rice porridge with it. I still don't dare plunge my hands in cold water."

The old woman raised an eyebrow and cast her a hesitant, questioning glance. Mien looked her in the eyes and said in a cold, decisive voice, "Do this for me right away, please. I'm going to take the whole pot over to Bon."

Auntie Huyen left the kitchen. Mien watched the old woman for a few seconds, then knotted her shawl under her chin and went out into the courtyard to play with her son. She had just thrown herself into a river. She would either reach the other side or be carried off by the current, but she could no longer turn back.

23

It was past noon when Mien entered the room. As if ordained by the heavens, Bon sat up suddenly, kicking off the covers. He kept silent. Mien did too. She set the pot of rice porridge down on the table and began to look around for a clean bowl. Ta and her kids had taken away the small cupboard and all the dishes. Mien walked toward the earthenware jar that had once held the rice even though she knew there wasn't a grain left. A dirty pair of pants was slung over the side of the jar. A few pairs of underwear and dirty shirts had been balled up and set on top of a padlocked trunk—probably the only piece of furniture that had survived Ta's looting and pillaging. The table and the floor were littered with dried potato peels and mouse droppings. Two of Ta's kids were crouched behind the door, staring at her. It was already cold out, but they were naked, their dark little penises touching the dirty brick floor. Behind them, right on the sidewalk, in the middle of squashed debris, was a half-finished basket of boiled potatoes. It was just as she had thought: Nothing had changed. In fact, the situation had degenerated. Since Mien had left, all this poverty and filth had pushed Bon over the edge, back into his sister's world. She walked into the kitchen. Her dishes had been stuffed into Ta's tiny, dirty cupboard. They had taken over Mien's old cupboard to store the kids'

clothes in. Mien found a bowl, washed it, filled it with porridge, and carried it back to Bon.

Bon didn't say a word, just took the bowl from Mien and ate. The porridge was scalding hot. Mien had kept the pan hot by wrapping it in a cotton cloth. A thick steam rose from the bowl. Bon's forehead and temples began to glisten with sweat. Mien took the towel that hung from a string and handed it to him. "Wipe your face. Sweating a bit will do you good."

Bon wiped his face. Mien looked at his gnarled, trembling hands and thought of the tiny plot of land that the commune had allocated to him, how it was still covered with weeds.

When she had come back to live with him, he had gone to clear the land twice, both times full of enthusiasm and hope. But each time he had come back and collapsed on the bed for an entire week. He had told her, "Okay, let's wait until I regain my strength. In any case, we need time. We're still young and soon . . ."

And soon . . . That's what Bon used to say, and each time he said it his eyes glistened as if lit by a flame. But the flame had died out. Not even the smoke was left since the midwife had shown him the headless fetus. Mien remembered the scene, how Bon had grabbed her legs when the nurse left with the bucket; his arms had been icy, his eyes frantic, and he had kept frantically mumbling, "Mien . . . where is the child? Where is the child?"

And she had given him no answer. Exhausted by the birth, she had felt lost herself. But behind this feeling of emptiness, she was finally at peace, and even deeper in her heart she felt an unspeakable, secret joy.

Poor Bon. I didn't want it to happen, but it couldn't have been any other way . . .

After he had finished the porridge, Bon set the bowl down on the bed without looking at her. Mien carried away the bowl, washed it, and then brought it back and set it on the table.

"I made you enough porridge for dinner, too."

Bon made no reply, just looked listlessly out the doorframe at the bare lilac branches swaying in the wind. There was no sun. Out in the courtyard, his nephews played naked in the dirt. Mien watched Bon as he stared at the lilacs, then got up to leave. "I'm going now."

Bon jumped. His eyes suddenly looked panicky. "Where?"

"I'm going back to my home," Mien said calmly.

Pain flashed across Bon's expressionless face, as if someone had just stepped on his finger, or twisted his flesh. "Mien is going back home," he repeated after her.

It was neither an answer nor a question. Just an echo, like the one that resonates when you shout into a valley surrounded by rocky cliffs. Mien looked at him, recalling her youth, the days when she had gone to gather firewood with her girlfriends, how they had competed to see who could shout the loudest, who could make the longest echo. Standing on the banks of the stream, they had thrown stones across to the opposite side, trying to see who could hit the wild tea bush. They had gathered wild myrtle on hill after rolling hill, their laughter echoing, their young lips stained red, smelling of ripe fruit. She didn't understand why Bon's soulless voice had brought back all these sounds and colors. But these memories moved her and helped her forgive Bon's silence. She pulled her chair closer to him.

"Bon, come back with me."

"No."

"It's my house now. It belongs to me. Hoan has built another house by Little Stream."

"I live in my own house."

"Our love has already run dry. We can't be husband and wife anymore. But we have shared a bed. Even if it had only been once, it would still be a debt. I can't love you as I once did, but I can take care of you as I would a brother."

"No."

"Bon, listen, I cannot live here. Sister Ta can't help you, and Xa's got a whole brood to look after. Your health is worse than when you came back from the war."

"Leave me alone, Mien."

"Please think it over carefully," she said patiently. "We may not have a living child, but we do have a dead child in common... I still feel grateful to you..."

Mien stood up after that and left. She didn't want to stay any longer. She was afraid to see Bon cry. She remembered the night when she had seen him crouched on the floor, his face bathed in tears. She kept walking, her temples pounding, her heart racing, partly from relief, partly from pity.

The next morning at dawn, she returned to Bon's place to bring him another pot of rice porridge and a few sticky-rice cakes. He had always loved her sticky-rice cakes stuffed with meat. They didn't talk. Mien had to go back to watch her son.

"Try to eat everything. Tomorrow, I'll go and find the medicine in town."

He didn't reply, just looked at her, consenting but resentful.

The following day, Mien brought him rice and a few meat dishes. She waited until he had finished eating to bring back the crockery. Ta's children had already carried off the pot she had brought the previous day, dragging it out into the courtyard to use as a fishbowl. They had even twisted her spoon to make a small shovel.

Bon looked ashamed and mumbled, "Sorry. Sick and bedridden like this, I couldn't stop them."

Mien said nothing. She waited until he had finished eating and then spoke. "At the moment, I can still bring you meals. But in a few days, I've got to go out to the fields to stand in for Mr. Lu. He's got to oversee the workers at the construction site."

Bon remained silent. Mien continued, "If your family had means, it wouldn't be a problem. But at the moment, you can't count on anyone... Think about what I proposed."

He didn't reply. They sat for a long time in silence, each looking out into the courtyard, watching the milky light of a sunless dawn spread through space. The courtyard was deserted, except for the

neighbor's cat, which sat on its haunches scratching the cracks between the bricks in search of crickets. Ta's kids had left to go play
somewhere, discarding a bowl with a few pieces of cooked potato by
the door. Not a single sound echoed in Bon's room aside from the
clicking of the lizards' tongues, or the scurrying of mice in search of a
few grains of rice. Mien listened attentively to all these sounds, finally
noticing them for the first time.

I once lived here. Is that possible? It seems like someone else's life...

She asked herself how she had managed to pass all the time in this
room, with this man seated here on the bed, within arm's reach. His
vacant eyes had turned murky. What was he thinking? She stayed
silent, waiting for him to speak. Time passed. She could hear the hum
of a conversation in the distance. And then the wind changed, carrying
with it cooking smells and the smell of smoke mixed with the savory
aroma of garlic browning in oil. Suddenly Bon said in a faint, tremulous voice, "Who is frying duckweed?"

"You like duckweed?" Mien asked, surprised.

Bon nodded. "It's my favorite dish. During the war, when it was our
turn to cook, the sergeant and I used to try to find garlic to make
sautéed duckweed. It was his favorite. The officers used to ask for it
every time they came to see us."

He smiled for a moment at someone, somewhere out there amid
the lilacs. A ray of light flashed through his dull eyes. Mien waited for
the end of his daydream and then said, "I like duckweed sautéed in
garlic, too. But the young squash leaves or cabbage leaves sautéed in
garlic are even tastier. If you like it, I'll make some tomorrow. There's
a pot of leftover fish stewed with ginger. All we have to do is make a
sweet-and-sour soup to have a full meal."

"Yes... yes."

"When do you want to come over?"

"I... I don't know... Whenever you want, Mien."

"Today. There's no sun and the wind is gentle... I'll take your
clothes."

"Oh, let me handle it," Bon grumbled. He looked at her, embarrassed. But Mien quickly turned and walked toward the corner where his knapsack lay. She picked it up, dusted it off, and packed his clothes. Suddenly, a tear fell, rolling down her cheek and the ridge of her lip, hot and salty.

This is it. Bon's entire fortune after fourteen years away from home . . . If it weren't for the bar of scented soap he saved for me, I'd think this was a beggar's sack.

24

The days and months came and went, events floating by, some bobbing lazily like bindweed on the waves, others swept off in the current
of life. For one whole day Mountain Hamlet had echoed with the
sound of firecrackers inaugurating the new primary school. Cars, big
and small, were parked on the hillside, as all the district and provincial
authorities flocked back for the ceremonial cutting of the red silk ribbon. People were delighted and they scurried about, the young mixing
with the old. The hamlet's schoolchildren, dressed in new hats and
clothes and sporting new school-bags and notebooks, came and went,
giddy with excitement. Drums thundered and a strange, festive atmosphere pervaded, like in some legend or fairy tale that would never fade
or end . . . But that day had passed, a long time ago now, and the quiet
monotonous flow of life returned to the remote mountainous region.

Gone were the crisp, dry autumn nights when the villagers sat outside popping sticky rice under the stars, when they gossiped around
their sputtering teapots and water pipes, huddled over flickering oil
lamps, everything cloaked in a dreamy, safe tranquillity. Gone too were
the winter nights shuddering with wind, when the fields sank early
into darkness, when men staggered home down the sides of the roads,
reeling like storm lamps, when the quiet was broken only by the distraught, muffled wails of a lost doe.

Then one morning spring would come as tiny white sprouts un-
furled from gray tufts of dead grass, and the beating of fledgling
wings somewhere in the trees revealed a crack in the sky that yawned
open over the vast blue sea.

For the people of Mountain Hamlet, the family clubs were no
longer the gathering place of choice; now it was the shade of the trees
where they paused to drink or have lunch. Afterward, they would
sprawl on the dry grass or on their bundles of straw or bamboo, the
young people taking a short nap, while the old men just rested their
backs. When they woke, conversations would begin to simmer, noisy
and lighthearted. And their discussions always ended up creating a
courtroom atmosphere in which everyone got a turn to play judge at
least once in their dull, uneventful lives ... Suddenly, the most frequently defended character now was Hoan, the boss of the plantation
at Little Stream and benefactor to the commune's entire population.

"You know, all in all, no one has suffered as much as that Hoan.
Another guy comes and squats in his estate, forces him to build a new
home. He's separated from his wife and child. Every morning he has
to travel miles and miles to come and get them, and at sundown he
travels miles and miles to take them back. What's clear to me is that
it's not the heavens, but men who are to blame for this. I'd call Hoan's
life prison without a trial."

"Yes, but it *is* a strange situation. Why doesn't Mien set up house
with him at his new place in Little Stream?"

"If she did, how would Bon justify living under her roof?"

"Have justifications ever fed a man? It's the truth, the blinding
truth. Bon spends his days tagging along after Mr. Lu. The two of
them eat together noon and night ... though sometimes, exceptionally,
Mien sits at the table for a few minutes."

"Well, everyone has to keep up appearances. Now, take Auntie Huyen.
She lives in Little Stream with Hoan, but she keeps her own house locked
up and refuses to sell. It's her fallback solution. The same goes for Bon.
It's as Mien's husband that he's able to stay on at the old house."

"Can't really say they're husband and wife. His cannon's been shot for a long time."

"Oh, his dick may not stand straight anymore, but he still needs to hold his head high. He's got to have some reason to be able to look people in the eye."

"Nonsense. Even a child can see that Mrs. Mien provides for Bon out of obligation. How humiliating! In his place, I'd commit suicide."

"Oh yeah? Just try. It's not so easy to die. As long as the moment hasn't arrived, the heavens won't let you leave, and the earth won't open up to host you."

"Are you insulting me?"

"No, I'm not insulting you at all. But if you want to talk you've got to get to the bottom of things."

"Come, come! Have you all so much energy to spare that you need to quarrel like this? Do they pay you to argue?"

"No one paid me, but my tongue itches when I hear such irritating arguments."

"Everyone's tongue itches. But it's not so easy to see where justice lies. At the moment, Hoan is as powerful as a hatchet faced with a sprig of bamboo. There aren't many of us who haven't already gone begging for his help. Defending him is like congratulating the king on his lovely attire. Only those who eat meat know how to pity cats. Only those who fall into poverty really know what misery is like."

"Oh, so you're insinuating that I'm indifferent to Bon's suffering? That I'm not capable of empathy, or generosity? Why, the day Bon came back to this village, who else but my own son rallied the young folk to go and build him a new wall and roof? I don't recall seeing you and *your* son at the time!"

"Hey, gentlemen, why are you all arguing like a bunch of kids? You're graying at the temples and you still have to have the last word?"

"I don't want the last word, I just want to show where the dragonfly really has his nest."

"Oh, please, I beg you. Whatever they say, you've got to admit that

Hoan is a generous man. Rich people usually tend to act like misers and bastards."

"You're right. But he *has* been very lucky. Remember when he married Mien? They weren't rich back then. Why, they had to toil all day in the fields just like the rest of us, torn old conical hats on their heads. But the heavens do protect those two. In their hands, gold and silver seem to grow into ingots and bars. You can count people as lucky as Hoan and Mien on one hand. The rest of us eke out an existence as best we can, or fall into poverty and hard times."

"That's true . . . In life, you've got to know how to aim for the summit, while never losing sight of the bottom. One shouldn't forget the taste of a poor man's *voi*, even if you've grown accustomed to savoring a rich man's flavored tea and candies."

"Now you're starting to insinuate again . . . What bush are you going to hide in next to spy on me?"

"How dare you accuse me of spying? I've never spied on anyone in my life, let alone behind some bush. I was walking down the main road in broad daylight when I saw you go to Hoan's on the backseat of the president of the commune's motorbike."

"That's true. But I'm not the only one. Tons of people go over to take tea on Hoan's terrace. It's not because I've had a few cups of his tea that I'm praising him. Would you let some other guy live in a beautiful house that you'd built? Especially when the guy has slept with your wife?"

"Each to his own. Our lives are not comparable. You can't ask Bon to earn his living with his own hands and strength, like we do, because he simply couldn't. I myself once went along with him to clear the land and was there when he collapsed after half a day's work. I had to carry him into the shade, douse him with cold water, and call for help to lug him home on a stretcher. In this world, who doesn't want to live as well as his neighbor? But the heavens don't distribute their gifts equally. It's better not to be envious of others."

"Now you listen to me. I've neither children nor grandchildren, but

I'm the only one here who's not beholden to Hoan. And I've no family ties to Ta. So I've got no link to either party; I'm impartial. Bon's predicament is terrible. But hundreds of other veterans in the same situation took to the streets, homeless, or had go live in the charity camps. So among the unlucky ones, he pulled the lucky card. As for Hoan, even if the heavens have endowed him with advantages, he's a rare honest man in this world. Let's suppose a thousand men in this country had his luck. I'm not sure you'd find another who would have acted as honorably."

These open-air clubs in Mountain Hamlet brought a bit of diversion and poetry into the long, busy days, making the labor a little less exhausting. The weeks passed so quickly that no one paid notice. Then, suddenly, one morning, the distant call of a hunting horn echoed from the depths of the forest. Wild sounds rang out, seemed to carry the cry of the does; the heavy cawing of ground eagles; the clumping of the hooves of ibex, roebucks, and she-goats in heat; the devilish grunting of the wild boars as they uprooted the trees with their muzzles, reveling in their destruction. People came out of their houses, left their plantations of pepper and coffee, and went out into the open fields or climbed to the summits of the hills to gaze toward the Truong Son Cordillera. Under the vast sky, they dreamed of paths where butterflies swirled out from the crevices of gray boulders, where velvety purple flowers grew, where springs trickled as clear as crystal. The nostalgia for the forest spread as imperceptibly as the tremulous sound of the hunting horns.

And one morning, the drizzle would come, sliding in from the east like a dusty white veil, as light as virgin grass. And this vapor seemed to seep into the skin and flesh, making the blood boil in the veins of the hunters—men who had just reached maturity and old men alike, and all who were still filled with a yearning for the forest and a passion for the hunt. Even before the head of the guild gave them the green light, the hunters had gotten out their rifles, polished them, and checked their ammunition. That night, when the sun began to fade, they gathered at the chief's house to drink tea. His wife brought out a basket of steaming hot honey cakes, still wrapped in banana leaves. The hunters unwrapped and ate them, shaking and blowing on their fingers to cool them. When they had finished the cakes, as they sipped tea and smoked, the conversation began to flow. The most important topic was Xa's absence. The previous year he had killed a bear-horse, and the year before that the only wild boar of the whole hunting season. He had once had every chance of becoming the future head of the guild since the chief was pushing sixty.

The chief spoke first: "It's a shame about Xa ... He deserves this role more than any of you. Truth be told, my legs are starting to fail me."

If Xa didn't replace him, then someone else would have to try to fill this position, one that was glorious and yet hard to qualify for. Ordinarily, in every guild there were a few huntsmen who had roughly the same level of skill, and the competition between them enhanced the atmosphere of the hunting season. For many long years, the candidates had invested all their efforts, praying for the chance to climb onto the chief's seat. But for Xa, everything had happened differently. He hadn't even had time to aspire to the position when people were already saying that it was his for the taking. He hadn't even had the chance to forge his chieflike stature when everyone was already loudly declaring that he was born to be one. Everyone, including the respected, incumbent chief, had to admit that he was so talented it was as if he had been chief of a tribe of hunters for at least his past ten previous lives. Xa's talents couldn't be attributed to his long years of war experience, since there were nearly twenty other veterans in the guild, but he seemed to have the kind of luck that they could only call a gift from the heavens. And yet, Xa had refused this glory right within arm's reach, declined the most exalted happiness of his life ... The hunters couldn't even imagine it, although his absence had brought joy and a new chance to compete to at least five huntsmen, all lightweight candidates who were secretly preparing to vie with their rivals during the hunting season that had just begun.

Seeing no one react to his announcement, the chief continued, "I'm really disappointed by this, but what's done is done. No one can choose for his neighbor. Now, it's up to you all to prove your talents. I don't want to carry the flag until the day I fall off my horse. So you had better hurry up . . ."

Then he fell silent. The candidates and the other hunters kept silent, too. So the proclamation was official: Xa had stayed behind. Now they could talk about him as they would any other neighbor.

"So his wife's been in bed for a week now to prepare for the birth?"

"Oh, more than that . . . Let's see, it's been eleven . . . ah, twelve days now."

"Poor guy! He must be in quite a state worrying about her."

"What did you say? It's his penis that's in a state. And a state of joy!"

"I don't believe it. In these times, having three kids is already exhausting. And now he has a fourth on the way? The commune authorities are going to make him pay!"

"Oh, you do love to comment on everything! He's not going to pay a thing. He respected the family planning policy to the letter. No president or Party secretary is going to dare reproach him. He took his wife to the medical unit right from the first day to get an IUD put in, but it fell out a few months later and then Soan got pregnant. Well, that's fate. Who knows what happened in that dark tunnel? I heard Xa teasing her about it the day he brought her back from the medical unit: *Miss, can you believe the bravery of my dick? Why it went and expelled the government's IUD! Now that we have four sons, we can walk tall around this village. No one can compare. Even an old goat like Phieu, who stuffs himself year round with gelatin and goats' testicles, managed to spawn only four sons and a bunch of girls, whereas my trigger shoots off four sons in just four shots!*

"What a joker!" The hunters were convulsed with laughter. After their fits had passed, they smoked and drank tea, chatting about all sorts of problems. One minute later, a man spoke up. "Hey there, that scoundrel Xa should have at least taken the time to raise a glass with us and say good-bye. Even if he is taking care of his wife and kids, a man has to make time for his buddies. He can't spend the entire day with his face pressed up against her warm oven!"

Again, the men all burst out laughing. Xa's neighbor spoke up now. "Don't be vulgar . . . Xa doesn't even work in the village anymore . . . He's got a job selling hardware and construction materials in town."

"Who hired him?"

"No one. He's his own boss now. He took over from one of his cousins. For the last few years, Xa had helped her hire workers to repair her house or to keep accounts. Xa graduated from college, you know, and even though he spent a long time in the army, he hasn't forgotten everything. And he's smart, so his cousin used it to her advantage. Last year, she went to Saigon and fell in love with a Chinese guy twenty years her senior, but still frisky. Turns out that the guy's loaded, with five houses in Saigon and in the provinces *and* he's a widower. So he was delighted to find this beautiful woman and proposed to her immediately. After the wedding, Xa's cousin left for Saigon and Xa suddenly got a free two-story house with a shop on the ground floor."

"So they're right to say *the right star brings good fortune.* . . . When it's not the right, auspicious moment you can bust your ass working and still not fill your belly. But when the moment is right, riches just fall from the sky right on your head."

"The heavens aren't responsible for everything! What's important here is that Xa has a good heart. He helped his cousin out royally for her to repay her debt when she got rich."

"That's true. Look at how Xa helped Bon. If he's that generous with a friend, what's it going to be like with someone who shares your blood! Like they say, one drop of your own blood is worth a whole pond of clear water."

"It's a big shop, apparently. They say he has to get help to keep it going. It would have been a good job for Bon if he had been lucid and in good health. Too bad Bon's lost it. I hear Xa had to hire Binh. That guy is just full of good will for his friends. As for his relatives back in the village, well, he doesn't care. It's actually not like that famous proverb about the drop of blood..."

"Well then, he's stupid."

"Who can say what constitutes stupidity and what constitutes intelligence? What you think is smart, others may think is stupid, and vice versa."

"What logic! Bon has lost his wits then? I thought he was doing better recently. He stays at home all the time, sheltered from the rain and the sun, well fed and well cared for with medication and herbal remedies. He looks more robust."

"A happy body isn't necessarily home to a serene soul. Man is like a machine. If you don't use your body regularly, you end up getting rusty."

"Well, Bon's pipe is beyond rusty—it's totally shot."

"I don't know about that. He's still young. Who knows where the female dragonfly hides her nest? If he's well fed, the kidneys are still warm. Why, he must be feeling a tad frustrated! Unfortunately, Mien's door is kept tightly padlocked. Not to mention the live-in guard. Can't really get into his wife's pants, can he?"

"His wife, so to speak... She doesn't love him anymore. She's in bed with Hoan. Everyone can see her belly's as big as a drum. Who doubts that that's Hoan's work? But she keeps feeding Bon as if he were her aging father. Very generous of her. Not many folks would do that."

"So when did he start to lose it? When I saw him he was chatting away happily about this and that."

"That was before Mien gave birth to the freak. They say it was a boy, with all the limbs and genitals, but no head. It had a big, thick, long neck. And at the end of it a kind of bubble, like a pig's bladder, filled with worms and blood."

"How do you know?"

"My sister-in-law in Vinh Quang was in the same hospital that day. Her husband heard the nurses talking about the monster. He got a peek at it when they carried it out in a bucket to bury it."

"That's strange. We've seen deformities like too many fingers or toes, or harelips, or even deformed noses, but I've never heard of a headless freak."

"From what they said, it wasn't really headless, but there was no skull or face. I think those white things, like worms, must have been the brain. Ever eaten pig brain?"

"Come now, let's not talk about it anymore. It's horrible."

"Hey, about Bon, my kids say that when they take the goats out to pasture, they often see him wandering around the cemetery. Is it true?"

"Yes, sometimes with a machete. When I went to see him, he greeted me politely and even offered me a cigarette."

"How was he?"

"Oh, I spent only a moment with him, just enough time to smoke a cigarette. He chatted politely and lucidly enough. But sometimes, in the middle of a conversation, he would start to smile, kind of vacantly, as if he were dreaming, and then he'd pick up the conversation as if nothing had happened."

"Why does he go around with a machete?"

"Maybe he wants to cut down some wild pineapple bushes?"

"He's no witch doctor, so why would he be cutting down wild pineapple bushes? My God, I hope he doesn't go and dig up any tombs. That would be a real catastrophe."

"How can he dig up tombs built out of brick and cement with an old machete? He'd have to have a jackhammer to do that! They may be rich or poor, but people in Mountain Hamlet all build their tombs to last. Only Bon's family graves aren't—not to mention the three graves that have gone untended for generations. All that's left are a few clumps of grass and weeds. Bon isn't going to go and dig up his own parents' graves! He may be crazy, but even madmen don't dig up their own parents' graves."

"When you've lost your mind, you aren't aware of anything."

"Bon hasn't lost his mind yet. He's just grieving after losing the baby. And if part of his spirit has gone astray, well, you can be sure the souls of his ancestors will guide him. I believe that."

"Poor Bon! When he was young, he was such a good student. He often helped my younger brother with his homework."

The chief of the guild brought two storm lamps out into the courtyard since the sun had set and faces had begun to blur in the darkness. He set the lamps on the railing of his porch, then turned toward the kitchen and barked, "Well, are they done, that new batch of cakes? Bring them as soon as they're ready."

A bevy of voices responded—his wife, his daughters, and his daughter-in-law. Less than two minutes later, the two daughters brought out a basket of steaming hot cakes, and as the water dripped from the tray it traced twisting lines on the ground.

"What kind of work is this?" the old man shouted. "Why don't you put them in a basin, then?"

His daughters, their faces flushed red, hadn't had a chance to defend themselves when his wife shouted out from the kitchen, "Here's the basin, here, here . . ."

She hurried out with a large copper basin and set it in the middle of the courtyard so her daughters could set the basket of cakes in it. The three women quickly retreated to the kitchen, which was really the safest, most pleasant place for them. Satisfied, the patriarch declared, "Brothers, let's eat the cakes and drink the tea. This year, the sky and the earth seem to have favored us. I'm trying to figure out the best time to launch the hunting season. Oh, I almost forgot . . . I've got good news for you. We may have lost Xa, but this year the guild has gained two new huntsmen, the president of the commune and Mr. Hoan, the boss of the Little Stream plantation. In fact, they came to sign up together."

"That's not surprising. The president takes tea every day on Hoan's terrace. It's normal that they would sign up at the same time. It's got to be said, that rich guy knows how to behave . . ."

Again, the hunters returned to their discussion of the cast of characters in this triangular marriage that was like a game of musical chairs. The first husband, the second husband, and the beautiful woman who had bewitched them.

Mountain Hamlet was too small. And in this small, closed world, joy passed like a fleeting ray of light, a slight breeze, while sadness and anxiety hovered like a poisonous vapor, the venom from a magic potion, an opium that both intoxicated and paralyzed the souls of men. For each of these weak, isolated, barbarous souls spread the germ of a disease, an envious, secretive affliction that rendered them incapable of understanding or accepting these tragedies that had struck like a tempest. For the envy of the villagers was in fact coupled with terror, a fear that stalked them as relentlessly and as insidiously as a fellow traveler.

25

Since his return to the village, Bon no longer looked at the mountains along the Truong Son Cordillera. He would never go back. The vast green expanse of the jungle terrified him. Like a man who had come back from hell, he didn't dare turn back to contemplate the shoreless, bottomless river that separated the human world from the underworld. He didn't want to see the primitive forest again, that unparalleled monster, that vampire of a thousand shapes that had sucked away his blood, drying up all his youth and vitality. He wanted the jungle to become an eternal grave to his past. Everything linked to it terrified him. He had categorically refused the invitation of the veterans to join their hunting group. Every time the hunting season came around, the sound of the horns made him shudder. In this sinister sound, he could hear the faint cry of the vultures, the murmur of wandering souls, the whistling of the night snakes and vipers, the howling of the wind in the caves. He could still see these same trees twisting and falling, their sap boiling in the napalm flames; he could still see pieces of dismembered arms and legs, scattered, skulls and shattered white brains, as gluey as sticky-rice porridge. Neither his body nor his soul could bear the memory of everything he had lived and endured. Sometimes it seemed to him that he had entered into the war in the shape of a young man and been spat out as a kind of soft-shell crab, a broken envelope, totally empty. Bon hated the jungle, both hated and feared it. For him it was too vast, too powerful, too sacred, too unpredictable. He yearned to live by the sea, and whenever he had a moment he would turn east, to that place where the sun rose, where the ocean lay with its waves and brawny fishermen, those tanned, muscular young men who breathed fresh, clean air and spoke in booming voices as loud as the roar of the waves. No doubt these men made love to their women without ever tiring . . .

If only I had been born in a fishing village, I'd be . . .

This daydream came and went frequently in his mind.

If, if . . . he imagined he had rich, healthy parents. He imagined them being there for him at his wedding, there waiting for him when he returned from the war. He imagined how they would have killed a cow and a few pigs and even goats to celebrate his return, inviting the entire village over to feast and share their joy. And they would live with him and his wife in a large, luxurious, tall house, just like Old Phieu's children. They would have helped him go on to university to fulfill his youthful dream, which was shattered by the war, while Mien would stay at home to tend the plantations and bear him smart, lively children. If only the pepper fields that had belonged to his parents had been green and the fields of coffee red when he had come back from the war, he wouldn't have to dig the hills, he wouldn't be dependent on Mien, wouldn't have to provide for his sister and her wretched kids. If only this dream had become reality. *If . . .* but he knew that there were no "ifs" in life.

His parents had been good people, but they lacked real talent. They had toiled like ants to feed their family, pinning all their hopes on Bon, ever since he was a little boy. "You'll honor your ancestors, you'll bring glory to the family." They survived on manioc and corn so he could eat rice. On festival days or Tet, they made do with a bowl of shrimp marinated with chili pepper and lemongrass so he could have a bowl of tiny fish from the stream or a small piece of pork. His parents had chained him to them with their immense love. What a grandiose dream he had been for them! Terrifying. All throughout his childhood, he had been bent under the dead weight of it, this immense fiery inferno of hope that still consumed his pure heart. He had broken his back carrying firewood to pay for his studies, had buried himself in his books, renouncing all other pleasures in life. And the doors of the future had opened. One morning he set off for town to take the entrance exams to the best provincial high schools. His teacher and the director of the high school had both smiled confidently as they bid him farewell. The vision of them—smiles on their pale, gaunt faces, their teeth yellowed by cigarette smoke—was like a talisman glued to his forehead that had stayed with him throughout all the long years of war. He was sure that after the war, when he threw away his soldier's fatigues, he would put his white shirt back on and stride back through the gates of the university—a bit older perhaps, but still bursting with ambition. Then fourteen years had passed. When he finally returned to Mountain Hamlet, he had lost his old energy, but was still full of hope, still following the grandiose dream. His parents had had many illusions, but the legacy they had given him had brought him moments of great joy and exhilaration. Instead of dreaming of the university, he had dreamed of becoming the boss of a plantation with the woman he loved. He had dreamed of the day when he would be rich enough to build solid tombstones for his parents, to travel the country and meet the families of his war buddies, both the living and the dead, especially the sergeant's family. Bon dreamed. In fact, he did nothing but dream . . . Could a man live without dreaming? Yet when one dreamed, it was impossible to live in peace.

The morning Hoan had walked into Bon's little room, Bon knew that the dream was over. The sight of this tall man with his fair skin and rosy lips, whose thick, luxuriant hair fell onto his forehead like a woman's, had knocked the breath out of him. There was no doubt that this was the owner of the gray underwear. In a flash, Bon's face had darkened and his whole body began to shake, sweat pouring down his spine. Yes, it was him. This man resembled something Bon already knew, and that terrified him. Something grandiose, mysterious, all-powerful . . . Bon stood speechless in the middle of the courtyard for a long time, as if he would never speak again, and when he finally got his breath back, he realized who this was, this tall, imposing, seductively gentle man: a second Truong Son Cordillera, an all-powerful reality, a ruthless God behind a kindly mask. This was the man who had taken the place of the ruthless jungle, who would annihilate all that remained of his life, like a vampire sucking away the last drops of his hope, his will to live.

It was all over.

What had the days that followed been like? He couldn't remember. Now that Mien was gone, his room was no more than an abandoned hut, pillaged by Ta's kids and mice, a place where ghosts of the past came and went—sometimes the sergeant, sometimes his parents or his veteran friends. They were all in a hurry. And they all stared at him in silence with their green and yellow eyes. They greeted him at the door, their bones in hand. He had tried to speak to them many times, but no one ever answered, not even the sergeant. Why? Bon didn't know. Perhaps the ghosts couldn't talk in places too full of life. Ta's children and the neighborhood kids kept them silent. He should probably have gone off to the cemetery or some deserted hill to talk with them. But he was sick, and he lay there day in and day out, feeding himself as he could—either with some rice porridge that Soan or her kids brought over, or cooked potatoes from Ta. These days the patch of sky in his doorframe was clouded with smoke. He saw neither the color of the sky nor the clouds, nor the faded blooms on the lilacs that usually eased his sadness. He remembered the enthusiastic young man who had left for town to receive the prize for the college exams. How his face and his temples had flushed from excitement. But everything had left on that train, faded into the distance, leaving him on the quay of an abandoned station.

I missed my chance. That train will never come back. Grass and dead leaves. That's all that's left in the courtyard outside the station . . . I made a mistake. The train of life makes only a one-way trip; and it never comes back to a station it's already left.

Bon had hoped too much, believed too fervently in that flickering light that comes and goes with the watery current, that he had pursued in vain, that had slipped from his grasp as he reached out his hand. Fourteen years of war. Doors that have been closed for fourteen years rust over; you can't open them anymore.

I missed my chance. My hands are empty. I can't lie to myself anymore.

He had been so eager to see his son, his last hope, the last bridge that could have linked him to the future. He was convinced that they had traded him in for another newborn to satisfy someone who wanted an heir, that they had laid a trap for Bon, a sweet, innocent boy from the mountains. "Where is my son? Where did you hide my son? Which baby did you exchange him with?" he had shouted, grabbing the midwife's arm, his heart racing with both fury and hope. But the burly midwife had turned and given him an icy stare. Shaking her head, she said, "What are you talking about?"

Bon didn't reply, just repeated, "Where is my son? Let me see my son . . ."

"You really want to see him?" the midwife replied, exasperated. And she grabbed him by the arm, pulled him toward the delivery room, a place as white and clean as a mourning armband. She dragged a pail across the tiled floor and pulled off the cover with a brutal gesture.

"There he is, your son! Lean over and take a look."

Bon leaned over. That thing. That thing. That fetus. His son. All that remained of his future . . . He didn't want to believe it. A piece of reddish blue flesh floating in sticky blood, the arms and legs huddled together. A brain in a pouch, like the ones in formaldehyde, preserved in laboratories in the city high schools. A swollen neck as big as a watermelon. And nothing else. God, he had dreamed of a son for so long, secretly hoping that he would have his eyes and Mien's nose, skin, and lips. Bon knew that his eyes were his only asset. He had waited a long time for the moment when the child would open his eyes, when he could see himself in his son's gaze. Those little eyes were the only source of light that could illuminate his future, that would be able to restore his lost horizon. Those eyes would be his strength, his reason for living. But this child had no eyes. He didn't even have a face. He had nothing at all.

When there's nothing more to live for, why doesn't a man just die?

He had asked himself this question many times. Each time, he had given himself a silent order.

I must die. I need to die. The quicker the better. All I need is a rope. The beam in my room would be strong enough for that . . .

But each time he tried, he stayed pinned to his bed. When Soan brought him rice porridge, he sat up, wiped his face with a dirty towel, and ate the hot porridge that this generous woman had prepared. As he wiped away his sweat, he felt a vague sense of well-being permeate and sustain his body.

A frail, shimmering thread still attached his life to a world of distant fog in which he could make out the form of a woman. His mother? Mien? Thoong? Or was it one of those young women volunteers he had slept with in a fleeting encounter on the roads of the war? He couldn't say. But he knew it was a woman. He recognized her scent, whiffed that magnetic perfume, the sweaty smell of her skin and hair, the mysterious warmth of her body. And this fragile link was the only thing that held him back.

The morning that Mien had returned to give him a steaming pot of chicken porridge, he had looked at her as if she were a stranger, a new woman, both the woman who had shared his bed and a new being from another world. Sad and humiliated, happy and indifferent, he had eaten the porridge, not understanding why Mien's face no longer caused him fear or excitement.

It's Mien, and it's not Mien . . .

This thought no longer hurt him. His heart no longer reared in pain as it once had, each time he felt the love or anger.

It's Mien, and it's not Mien . . .

He reformulated this thought, more calmly, more clearly, until the heady smell of the porridge carried it off. Beads of sweat gathered on his face and neck. He set the bowl down, took a towel, and wiped his face. The more he wiped, the better he felt. His body was now as light as cotton, his soul peaceful. The tide had receded.

Mien came back a third time and asked him to return to her place. Bon grumbled, but in his heart of hearts, he had replied immediately.

Why not? Mien is no longer the woman she once was. But she's still a woman. A world of softness and warmth. A smooth, sandy beach by the edge of the sea, when the tide has gone out . . .

As the wind carried the smell of the bindweed sautéed with garlic, as all the memories of his mother flooded back, he took his knapsack and followed Mien home—or rather, he followed the image of a nameless, ageless woman who held him to life. He didn't care about the curious looks and stares he got from the neighbors, or the people he encountered along the way; the smell of the bindweed and the garlic had soothed him, lulled him with an indescribable softness, and he smiled as he walked.

And his mother seemed to smile back. She didn't say a word, just pulled back the flap of her blouse and showed him her left breast, with its beauty mark no larger than a grain of rice. He reached out his hand, touched the breast, this place he had once loved to suckle, and he felt his childhood come back to him.

Mama, I miss you . . .

His mother stroked his hair and then vanished like steam rising off a pot of rice.

Now he would live under the same roof as Mien like a guest, like a relative, like an old friend.

Yes, what harm can it do? We loved each other, we've been husband and wife. Now we're friends. Time changes with the seasons. This house lies in Mien's magnetic field, a woman's place . . .

Slowly he grew accustomed to his new life. He took breakfast, lunch, and dinner with Mr. Lu. After dinner, he heard a motorcycle stop in front of the gate. That would be Mien, back with her son, and after she climbed the steps to the house she would ask him if he had eaten.

Sometimes it was Mr. Lu and sometimes it was he who replied, "We ate a fish soup with cabbage and grilled peanuts." Or "We killed a chicken to make rice porridge."

Then Mien would get out a few pieces of fruit she had bought in town, a package of candies or sweets, and set them on the table. "Uncle Lu, why don't you put these away for me. They're for your tea."

After these formalities, she would take her son into the bathroom and wash and change him. She would do the same for herself. Then she would go into her bedroom. She always took an enameled chamber pot with her so she wouldn't have to go out at night. She would push the latch and lock the door. Bon could hear the latch click into place, the key turning in the lock. These sounds pierced his heart, but he neither wanted to remember nor understand why he suffered. In the morning, Hoan would always come back to get his wife and child before Bon woke up. Most of the time, when he got out of bed, the roar of the motorcycle engine would be fading in the distance.

Mien has gone. She'll only be back at nightfall.

He would then go down to the kitchen to have some tea and a chat with Mr. Lu. This old man, who was as thin as a stork, always had something to say; his wandering eyes seemed never to tire and no noise escaped his ears. It seemed to Bon that the old man could divine his innermost thoughts and that through his gentle silence he showed affection for Bon. He would prepare Bon's infusions and the traditional medicines that Mien had ordered in town with his own hands. In this spacious house and vast garden, friendship grew easily between these two lonely men. As Bon slowly regained his strength, he would sometimes accompany the manager when he went out to the pepper and coffee fields. One day, Mr. Lu asked him, "Do you still want to establish your own plantation?"

Bon stuttered something, incapable of replying. The hill that the commune had given him had lain fallow for a long time. A young couple had cleared the land and were cultivating it, even though officially it was only a loan. The couple was young, of an age they could break a buffalo's horns with their bare hands. Their ambition was to "drain the eastern sea of its water" and they worked day and night. The pepper trees had grown and now stood over a yard high. There was no written contract but, even if he had wanted to, Bon couldn't claim back land that had been irrigated with someone else's sweat, that would soon start to turn a profit. Noticing his embarrassment, Mr. Lu continued, "Madame is very generous with you."

Realizing that the manager had guessed his thoughts, Bon replied, "I know."

The old man nodded. "You've gone through many ordeals, and you understand life, no doubt. There's no paradise reserved for men of flesh and blood like us. But there are hospitable lands and hostile lands. When a bird's wings are stunned by fatigue, the bird must alight on hospitable ground to rest."

"I know." Bon repeated the reply. He knew that the manager was just a mouthpiece for Hoan and Mien, that this is what they wanted. They had said they were ready to provide for him until the end of his life, like a brother, a friend, or a second-rank manager who would help Mr. Lu take care of the plantations and the house. In short, his presence under this roof would be accepted until his death on the condition that he respect the terms of this unwritten contract.

Once a husband, now a friend. I can eat Mien's rice and live under her roof, but we will each live at opposite ends of the house, like two banks of a river. But between those banks is not water but boiling oil . . . What does it matter? Life has forced me into this grotesque situation.

"It's beautiful weather today," Bon said suddenly, not even looking at the sky. He stared at a few bunches of coffee grains that hung under the leaves.

The manager blinked his lids and replied, "Oh, yes, the autumn sky is really beautiful. The weather is favorable, and the harvest will be a good one."

Then they fell silent.

And this is how the contract had been sealed.

Many moons had passed since this conversation between the two men. Bon thought he had adjusted to his new life. But suddenly, his body rebelled. He couldn't sleep. Waves of fury seemed to unfurl in his very flesh and blood. Waves that couldn't be appeased, that reared, ever more insistent, that invaded his heart and spurted forth in his brain, erasing all the images except for one vulgar, sensual image: naked women. This erotic vision seemed to grow huge and distorted, as in a circus mirror, blocking all paths of retreat. He pressed his burning temples, pressed his face into the mat, clenching his teeth so he wouldn't moan, rallying all his strength to dominate his lust. But it was all in vain. The waves of fury turned red, the crimson of coagulated blood, and then to the menacing violet of storm clouds at dusk. His veins no longer flowed with blood, but a molten lead so scalding that it paralyzed him, body and soul. But it was from his tortured body that the sudden cry burst forth: *Mien, Mien . . . You're mine, you're mine.*

He sat up, squeezing his knees between his arms to resist the urge to run into her locked room, to break down the door that was secured with a latch and a lock no larger than his hand . . . He knew he was big enough to break any lock or door . . . Time had given him back his strength. He was still young. He was now in his mid-thirties . . . But he kept his knees tightly locked in the clutch of his arms, for he knew he was bound by their unspoken contract.

But another, even more powerful voice, more ferocious, more insistent, retorted, *But I love Mien, and I've searched for the road back, followed the moon at the price of my life, dragged myself through the jungle, resisted thirst and hunger, survived the mosquitoes and the leeches, the enemy ghosts . . . I had to endure everything for you . . . You have no right to chase me from your heart . . . I staked my life on you. Either I get my due, or I'll die . . .*

His gaze blurred, sweat pouring down his chest and shoulders. He pulled open the door to his room with a decisive, violent gesture, and went out.

"You can't sleep?" It was Mr. Lu. "Come have some tea with me. Tonight, I can't sleep either."

The manager was seated right there, facing his door, a tray of tea in front of him. The oil lamp was brightly lit. They had foreseen everything.

"Ah . . . you're already up?" Bon stammered, his temples still burning.

Mr. Lu got up and added some boiling water to the teapot, and replied calmly, "I haven't felt sleepy yet . . . Old people don't sleep much." Not waiting for Bon's reply, he continued, "This year's jasmine tea is very fragrant. Come have some while it's hot."

Bon couldn't speak, just moved forward, pulled out a chair, and sat down facing the manager.

This old guy is just a guard dog for Hoan. One day I'm going to send that bastard Hoan to find his ancestors.

Bon sipped the tea, realizing that the sympathy this old man seemed to have for him was just a banal, generic sort of empathy for one's fellow man. The most important thing for this devoted jailer was to block his access to Mien's bedroom. Bon gulped down two more cups of tea, groaning in silence, *You dirty guard dog . . . have you never loved? You too were young once. Did you never even know the torture of lust?*

The manager emptied the teapot, added another handful of tea, and filled it with boiling water. Relaxed, he watched the teapot attentively, but Bon knew that not a single movement escaped the old man's scrutiny. The oil lamp that usually sat on the tea chest had been carefully placed on the table right next to Bon's room and the wick visibly lengthened. Judging from his face, the old man had been awake for a long time. He must have heard Bon panting and writhing in his bed. His demeanor, his gestures, his pensive, tranquil eyes betrayed him; he had thought of everything in advance to cover himself. Even if Bon had used physical force, he knew he didn't have a prayer of fulfilling his desires.

Am I really totally powerless? Am I really condemned to live here like a ghost?

His heart continued to moan, and for an instant he thought he might lunge across the table and strike a blow to the old man's head with a flashlight or the copper candelabra. But what remained of his lucidity made him tremble at the thought. Sometimes, when Bon went to stroll in the village cemetery, a gaggle of kids would follow him. At first he thought they were also out for a stroll and he had tried to chat with them. But he began to notice the curiosity and fear in their eyes. They might follow him, but they also were prepared to turn 180 degrees and flee. It was natural to fear people who hung around the cemeteries because they opened a path to ghosts and demons to come and torment the villagers. But another vague idea hid behind this thought, and it frightened him.

Maybe these curious kids are right? Have I gone crazy?

An enormous night moth flew through the window of the house and danced around the lamp. The light of the flame passed through the moth's translucent wings, making the veins and colored spots shimmer with a rare beauty. Bon set down his cup and watched, fascinated, remembering a distant spring when as a boy he and Big Toan and Hai the Dark One had watched butterflies dance in a crevice of the mountain. Thousands of butterflies flew up, giddy, excited, trembling, irradiated with the light. The three of them had jumped for joy. Years later, the sparkling colors of the butterflies in springtime no longer fascinated them. Instead, they scoured the grass for signs of butterflies who had fallen to copulate there. Later, as soldiers, they used to watch monkeys copulating. Once they had surprised a couple of orangutans, large monkeys that so resembled human beings, even in their lovemaking positions. Drunk with pleasure, the orangutans had kissed each other for so long that the soldiers were filled with admiration and envy. Bon remembered the scene clearly, how the male's face had covered the female's, his grunting, his lips peeled back over white teeth . . . And in a flash, the blood boiled in his body. He squeezed his thighs, emptied his third cup of tea, and then said to the manager, "Continue . . . I'm going to sleep."

The old man nodded. "Go ahead. I probably won't sleep a wink tonight."

Bon went back into his room and pulled the latch, as if to prevent himself from going out. He climbed into bed and immediately plunged his face into his pillow, his fists clenched.

Enough. Enough. Enough.

But it was impossible. His penis stiffened, as taut as a vigorous stallion's waiting for the stable door to swing open. He could think of nothing else. But the only image still etched on the screen of his brain was one from the jungle of his past: the orangutans copulating.

Why do I have to suffer like this?

He suddenly hated the piece of skin that hung between his thighs, that tortured him so mercilessly, so insistently. When he had needed its strength, he had coddled it, tried to heal it with all sorts of medicines and fortifiers, but the organ had hung as limp as the banner used by the boy who watched the ducks. And now, when he wanted it to be gentle and resigned to a peaceful life detached from desire, it stood up, demanding satisfaction.

Son of a bitch! You son of a bitch!

He cursed himself as he had once cursed the vultures that had come to tear at the sergeant's guts. He cursed to spit out the anger and the hatred that lurked in his heart. But this cynical, stinking bit of flesh didn't want to hear anything. It just stood up, stubborn and cruel. Resigned, Bon slipped a hand into his underwear, did what he could to appease the organ that had metamorphosed into a strange, almost autonomous monster.

The next evening, Bon waited for Mien's return. He pretended to want to play with little Hanh, though the little boy was always distant and suspicious around him. When Mien moved toward the bathroom, he followed her, the little boy in his arms, and then blocked her path right in front of the door.

"Mien, I've got to talk to you about something."

Mien turned and looked at him. He knew that she had understood. She spoke first.

"Bon, I already told you. I'm ready to consider you as a brother. But there can be nothing else."

He nodded. "I know. But I don't want to go on like this. I know that you have another man. But I still love you. I still want my share."

She looked at him, stunned. "I don't understand."

He swallowed hard, repressed his humiliation, and continued, "It's simple, really . . . Once, a man could have five wives, seven concubines. We could all peacefully coexist here in the same manner . . . I'm not asking for much . . . But I should have my share."

Mien flushed. She glanced quickly toward the kitchen, afraid that the manager had overheard everything. Her face hardened and a terrifying light flashed in her eyes.

"Never repeat that again, to anyone. You must be mad. No respectable woman would do that."

He didn't dare look her in the eyes, but he continued, "I'm not a eunuch . . . I can't live like this forever."

"Well then you can leave!" Mien snapped.

"No. I don't want to."

He set the boy down, went back into his own room, and shut the door. Mien didn't call him back, didn't add a single word. She took her child in her arms and called into the kitchen, "Uncle Lu, would you go and see if the pot is ready yet."

The manager always seemed to be in the wings, ready to accomplish whatever Mien desired. Bon watched from a window as the old man carried the pot of boiling water with fragrant herbs across the courtyard, his robust shadow elongating on the bricks. Mr. Lu was not just Hoan's faithful guard dog; he was also Mien's trusted adviser. Bon was isolated in this house.

That night Bon had a beautiful dream, a dream that brought him a feeling of perfect happiness, a joy as intense as any he had ever felt in real life: An enormous tidal wave engulfed the world, washed over the continents and all the countries. Everyone died. Yellow people, black people, white people. Bon was the only one who had been given a raft by the All-Powerful. And in his raft, which he guided over a churning expanse of water bobbing with millions and millions of the dead, among the bodies that writhed on the flotsam and jetsam of the waves, he had found Mien. She held out a trembling hand to him, her eyes supplicating him. Once again, he became the hero who had saved her from death. He took her in his arms. As she trembled with fear, he was the one who caressed and consoled her, twisting her hair to squeeze out the water before handing her his own shirt. He guided the raft through the ocean of corpses toward the only island that still rose above the water. The place the All-Powerful had reserved for Bon and the woman he loved, where they would breed a new humanity. On this wild, deserted island, surrounded by water, their love was reborn, a hundred times stronger than it had been. He made love to Mien on the grass, under the stars, in the dawning sun, longer than even the monkeys and orangutans, as if the blood of all species mixed together flowed in their veins. When Bon awoke the next morning, he felt dazed with regret. He reached his hand down to his damp pants, trying to remember the supreme happiness, the supreme pleasure he had just tasted . . .

And the days passed. He went out to the fields, down the hills, drank tea and ate cakes, busied himself cooking rice porridge or noodle soup with vegetables, and generally led the idle life of leisure that many people in Mountain Hamlet only dreamed of. But at night he was tortured by desire, and he would summon his old dream, imagine the season of love among the monkeys, relieving himself as he could from the tortures of the flesh. He never stopped wanting to break down the door to her room, to break the lock.

And what if I just left? If I tried to go to that state plantation that Xa told me about? More than two hundred volunteers, past the marriageable age. I would have a huge choice. It would be better than living this humiliation. And I would also free Mien. She could go and live at Little Stream with Hoan or bring him back to this place. Mien would certainly give me the money I would need to start a business. That man doesn't lack money, and he wouldn't haggle over the price of total happiness. One day, I too could have a happy home, a child with a new woman whom I would choose from two hundred, all longing for a husband . . .

At first, the idea of being able to choose from two hundred women made him happy. He somehow realized that it would give him the power and the pride he lacked. But this flash of pride passed, and he realized that these two hundred women were just a cloud of dust, a dark, nameless, shapeless mass without a clear face that could attract him. Two hundred women was no extraordinary number to him. He had met thousands of them during the war. And none of them had moved him . . . Perhaps his heart was truly bound to only one woman, a first, catastrophic love. And now that he had staked his life on that woman, he couldn't extricate himself. Even now, some dark, stifling residue of it remained.

No. No. No. I can't drag my knapsack to some remote, unknown place and rummage through some crowd of strangers for a woman to love.

Just imagining a road stretched out in front of him was enough to make his muscles go slack, his skin and flesh go cold, his hair stand on end as if he were going to confront the air of the jungle, the poison wind of the ravines, the misty rains . . . No, he no longer had the strength to throw himself into a new adventure like this. Why should he accept this humiliating defeat after so much suffering, so many efforts? Slowly, somewhere in the bottom of his heart, a faint hope began to glimmer.

Who knows? Maybe . . . if one day . . .

But what day and what event that hope was for he didn't know.

One morning the distant sound of the hunting horns no longer made him shudder. The mournful, monotonous, sometimes shrill, sometimes moaning sounds shook the peaceful sky in his heart, reminding him of his childhood sobs. Seated on a deserted hill, his arms crossed, he listened to them for hours. One night, these sounds echoed from the forest more loudly, as insistently as a march. Bon suddenly saw a clear blue patch of sky, fields of corn flowering in the evening sun, thick stands of purple sugarcane, higher than his head, all slowly covered with a white powder, a pure, silent space where bees hummed.

Where does this sky come from? And these cornfields? I've seen this somewhere before . . . But where?

He fumbled through his memory, and the past opened like a huge, smoky cavern. Cold. Desolation. Terror. Nostalgia. Everything dissolved, everything crumbled. He couldn't see anything more than that. Seated, he stared at the horizon as the sun fell slowly over the mountains. As it flickered out behind the Cordillera, to the west, the sun of his memory rose over the shadowy jungle, sweeping aside the curtain of smoke, illuminating this masked cavern. "Kheo Village!" he suddenly cried out.

His cry echoed through the fields of pepper and coffee. A few shepherds, who were bringing their herds of cows and goats back from their grazing, were startled and looked up at him, but Bon didn't see them. He just stood there, repeating the name he had found over and over: "Kheo Village . . . it's Kheo Village. Kheo Village. Kheo Village. Kheo Village."

In the echo, he heard the creak of a wagon drawn by a water buffalo; the sputtering of sap in the bonfires; wild honey bubbling away in a pan, birds chirping, affectionate, sweet laughter in a strange language that he didn't understand. And he could almost taste the sticky rice and grilled meat on his wedding day. He remembered how the clan headsman had prayed and offered his blessing, how his bride's elder brother's eyes had sparkled with joy. And illuminating all these images, a tall, glowing flame on a hearth where logs thicker than a man's thighs burned all day and all night. The eternal flame of Kheo Village.

He closed his eyes and saw himself naked, bathed, perfumed, on a mattress embroidered with bright colors next to the naked body of a woman. And a few yards away, a blazing fire in the hearth spreading its light and warmth. He remembered how Thoong had pressed her heavy breasts against his chest, how his hands had caressed them, as he drifted on a tide of pleasure. And with these memories, his desire flooded back.

I knew happiness with this woman. Why did I leave her, abandon her there?

A frenzied regret tore at his heart. His penis snapped erect in his pants. The more this odious monster reared its head, the more clearly he began to remember Thoong. The embroidered patterns on the linen mattress suddenly took the shape of the Laotian woman's breasts or his organ thrust between the iron thighs of this mountain woman. He had made a woman out of her when he saw the blood spreading on the mattress, when she sat up to point to it. And at that moment, she was no longer ugly. At that moment, her eyes danced with the light of the flames, transforming her into a mountain goddess whose long hair spread on her shoulders.

Was I an ingrate to the woman who loved me only to run after something that was beyond my reach?

He remembered Mien's icy look when she had rebuffed his prayer, when he had begged her for something as small as a crust of burned rice at the bottom of the pan, a consolation prize. He remembered Thoong's puffy eyes, her stammering supplications, her disheveled hair, how she had kept watch at the base of the ladder to their house. She wasn't the only one; her elder brother's entire family and all of Kheo Village had stood guard. These people who spoke another language, who lived according to other traditions, had held him back, imprisoned him, not because they were evil, but simply because he was indispensable to the happiness of an unlucky woman in a hut built on stilts. Bon remembered his home there with her, how sacks of corn, sticky rice, and jars of honey had been stacked on bamboo shelves beside piles of banana leaves and old pumpkins. The sky above Kheo Village was clear. The dirty smoke of the war didn't reach as far as that remote village, that lost patch of land. Why was it only now that he saw that peaceful life, how it was enough to satisfy his painful existence? What had made him flee that cozy cabin on stilts?

Bon thought about all this for a long time, a very long time, without finding an answer. He stayed seated on the hill until night fell, lost in his memories, tortured by lust. All of his suffering merged and churned inside him. And time passed. The grass all around was damp with fog. Bon's hand moved to rub himself. He pulled the sleeves of his shirt down and buttoned it at the wrists and neck. He couldn't remember the way back. Chilled, he hugged his legs to him as he looked up at the darkening sky. The moon appeared, rising slowly over the mountains to the west like a silver ball, a serene, peaceful face...

Hang Nga...

A name sprang out of the void, like a fish jumping, breaking the motionless surface of a lake. A flash illuminated the dark tunnel in Bon's brain.

He sat up and shouted, "Hang Nga... it's the moon... it's her."

Now he remembered. Between the two mountain slopes, like wings of a lark, the moon had risen just as it had that night back in Kheo Village. It was the moon that had seduced him, led him astray, poured her magic potion into his soul, paralyzing his brain. And he had left Kheo Village to follow her. He had abandoned the sweet, unhappy woman who loved and adored him as if he were the reincarnation of some tutelary genie. It was the moon that had poisoned his spirit, dragged him into all these misfortunes. He would destroy her. Without bow and arrow, he would use a rifle or dynamite to avenge himself against the deceitful moon.

But it was Mien... Behind the silver arch it was Mien's face... the woman I love...

This thought extinguished the anger that had flared within him. Bon lowered his arms and sat back down. The grass, now drenched in dew, had wet the seat of his pants. A murmur grazed his ear. He squeezed his knees between his arms, listening, waiting. He was the only one left on this hill shrouded in darkness. All around, nothing but fields, gardens, and hills of pineapple bushes that still hadn't borne fruit. The wind rustled softly, seductively. Somewhere in the distance, he thought he heard the rats or the foxes running, crushing the grass, the bushes, and he heard dead branches falling . . . Patiently, he waited for the murmuring . . . and then it came to him again.

It's Mien and maybe it's not Mien. You are my moon and that man is your moon. You were the one who called me to leave Kheo Village, and he was the one who made you leave me . . . A game of musical chairs . . .

His heart froze. His brain was stunned, shattered. A moment passed before he could continue.

Wait, it's so simple, why didn't I think of it sooner? Poor Thoong couldn't kill that seductive moon . . . But me, I'm going to kill yours. Then nothing will be able to take you away from me ever again. And we will live together again, really live together . . . always . . .

In that instant, Bon was overcome with joy. This time, he didn't shout. He lowered his head, blew on his hands to warm them, and muttered to himself, "Bon, oh, Bon, how could you be so stupid, so slow to see it? I should have thought of this long ago, long ago."

His mind cleared and sharpened as he devised a complete, detailed plan of action: *Tomorrow, I'll go to Xa's house to borrow his hunting rifle. I'll tell him that the hunting guild in the neighboring commune is short on rifles, that their chief is a relative so I can't refuse to help them out. Xa is in the clouds at the moment. He won't suspect a thing. Then I'll make a detour via the Valley of the Red Chilies. I'll wait for him at the edge of the forest, on the other side of Great Stream . . . the terrain is perfect. Since he's the tallest of all the hunters, he'll be an easy target. Once upon a time, I wasn't such a bad shot. No sharpshooter, perhaps, but better than some city boy businessman . . . Tomorrow, that Hoan is going to live the last day of his lucky life.*

Bon got up and made his way back to the village, down dirt paths that he knew by heart. And as he walked, quickly as a cat, he saw himself as a man on the road to regain his former happiness. And he smiled a winner's smile . . .

26

Mountain Hamlet was truly unlucky that hunting season.

All contrary to what the chief of the guild had predicted in the course of that raucous, happy party on the eve of the season's opening, when they had smoked fine tobacco, drank good tea, and enjoyed those piping hot honey cakes. No one had actually said it, but everyone dreamed of the game that they would haul back to the village. But the first victim of the hunting season was not a wild boar, a bear, a deer, a doe, or a monkey. It was a pregnant woman. She lay on a wide-mesh stretcher hammock that they had brought in case anyone was wounded by the charge of a wild boar or a swat from a bear paw. The hunters padded the hammock with their shirts and lay the wounded woman on top. The wound wasn't serious. A bullet from a rifle had taken off her index and middle fingers. But she was seven months' pregnant, had just run a long way, and was now in the throes of early labor. Two bare-chested men carried the hammock—Xa and a twenty-one-year-old man who had been admitted into the guild the previous season. Mien's first husband walked on the left side of the hammock and her second husband on the right. Both looked lost, their eyes distraught.

The president of the commune and the chief of the guild had decided to call an end to the hunt to bring Mien back to the village. When they reached the edge of the forest, they sent one of their men off on a motorscooter to get a car to take her to the hospital in town. Then they settled Mien in the house of one of the hunters to wait. There, at least, they could make a proper bandage before taking her to the hospital.

Mien lay on a bed, her face ashen, her forehead drenched in sweat, but she wasn't moaning. The president approached the bedside and asked her, "Was it you or Bon who fired the shot?"

"It was me... Curiosity just got a hold of me... I must have touched the trigger by mistake." She smiled weakly, her black eyes glinting with an odd light.

The president seemed to want to ask another question, but he restrained himself. The chief of the hunters' guild said, "Come, let's let her rest. She's lost a lot of blood."

No one said a word more. They waited for the car. A crowd of men piled into the small brick house at the edge of the forest, the closest place they had been able to find a bed for Mien. The owner was a young man who had just been admitted into the hunters' guild with Hoan and the president. He bustled about boiling water and making tea, because his wife had taken their child to visit her parents, who lived about twenty miles away from Mountain Hamlet. There were only four cups in the house, so the hunters had to take turns drinking. It was difficult to keep calm as they waited anxiously for the car to arrive. After emptying a cup of scalding hot tea, the president could no longer contain his impatience and strode out the door to the patio.

Bon was seated on a bench right outside the house. His head bowed, he looked down at the ground of the courtyard, as if to count the bricks or the blades of grass between them.

"Tell me, Bon," the president asked quietly.

The first husband looked up, his eyes vacant, his face as empty as an old gourd. He said nothing. The president spoke again, his voice harsh. "Was it you who held the rifle or Mien?"

Bon shook his head. "I didn't shoot at Mien... I didn't shoot her... I didn't shoot."

"Are you joking?" the president exploded. "I asked you if it was you or Madame Mien who held the rifle?"

"I didn't shoot . . . I didn't shoot at Mien . . . ," Bon repeated in a low murmur, almost as soft and gentle as the whispering of lovers. His face was vacant, devoid of emotion, uncomprehending.

The president sighed and went back into the house, frowning.

"I didn't shoot . . . I didn't shoot at Mien . . . I didn't shoot at Mien."

This endless refrain irritated the men, and their exasperation only increased as they waited. Finally, the chief of the guild, the eldest among the hunters, couldn't contain himself any longer and screamed at Bon.

"Shut up! Just shut up!"

Everyone jumped. Bon looked up at the old man, his eyes haggard, and stopped instantly, like a machine whose current had been cut. Silence reigned again, except for the vague hum of the bees in the garden. The host came back with a pot of boiling water and filled the Thermos. The men could be heard sipping tea, without speaking. The second husband sat down calmly by Mien's bedside. He held her hand, the left hand that was still intact. The crude bandage was Xa's work. He had been the first one to grab Bon when the tragedy happened. He was the one who had wrestled the rifle away from Bon, who had caught Mien in his arms, who had torn a sleeve of his own shirt, fashioning a bandage out of tobacco leaves. And he was also one of the men who had carried the hammock back to the village. Ever since, he had stayed as silent as a grave. Mien opened her eyes and, seeing her husband there, smiled weakly. She closed her eyes again. Her good hand held Hoan's. The second husband's face had gotten its color back. His frantic eyes were calmer and his lips moved slightly as he whispered something softly to his wife, something only the two of them could hear. Xa tapped the back of the man next to him in a silent request for a cup of tea. The man passed it to him and he lowered his head, drinking his tea, totally concentrated, as if it were the only thing that mattered.

Finally, the car arrived. The horn honked noisily from the street. The second husband got up and approached the president, whispering in his ear confidentially, "I'd like you to drop this whole incident. It is my wife's wish . . ."

He turned toward the bed, lifting Mien in his arms as easily as if she were a child.

"I'm going now. Thank you everyone . . . ," Hoan said suddenly as he walked swiftly across the courtyard with his wife in his arms.

The driver had already opened the door of the command car. Hoan slid inside, Mien still in his arms, hunching his wide, bearlike shoulders as he tucked his head inside. Everyone noticed his efforts to avoid any sudden, jerky movements so as to spare his pregnant, wounded wife any pain. Every married man there, even the old men, looked at him with a mixture of respect and envy.

The car sped off, the sound of the motor fading in the distance.

The small house fell back into silence.

The people who remained were transfixed, and didn't dare move.

The chief of the hunters' guild poured himself some tea and drank it.

The president, seated outside the house, looked over at the water pipe.

Leaning against the door, the host crossed his arms. He seemed to be waiting for something else, lost in his scattered thoughts.

Suddenly Xa woke up. He slid off the wooden bed inside the house and walked outside. Bon was still seated, swaying, on the bench. Hearing the sound of Xa's footsteps, he looked up. The footsteps were familiar to him. They were sounds that he had grown accustomed to hearing, to waiting for in the most unhappy moments of his life.

The two men looked at each other.

Xa raised his hand, his lips twitching uncontrollably, and slapped Bon hard in the face.

27

The next day a drizzling rain floated toward the village. It came from the eastern horizon, bringing humid air and the threat of a rare, late-spring tempest. In the slanting layers of white dust, you could still feel the mist of a distant winter, heavy with the weight of memories stirring beneath the ashes of time.

The corridors of the town hospital were packed, crowded with patients and their families coming and going. At that time—according to the lunar calendar, it was the day the silkworms left their cocoons—everyone seemed to be sick. The line in front of the examination room was long. White silhouettes seemed to glide along the buildings as the orderlies, flanked by nurses, carried people on stretchers the length of the porches. In the back of the hospital, the morgue was overflowing. From time to time, a hearse would leave, moving slowly toward the cemetery behind the market, another soul leaving for eternity.

Hoan had already smoked more than half a pack of Dunhills that morning. He sat on a bench in the waiting room, watching the curls of smoke, incapable of taming his anxiety. They had just taken Mien into the operating room. The doctor had decided to perform a cesarean, fearing that she wouldn't be able to give birth normally. The previous evening, when they changed her bandage, they had taken her blood pressure and checked her general state. She had been fairly strong, but they weren't sure she had the stamina to go through with the birth. They had done all they could to delay the labor until the morning. Mien had remained calm. She had smiled every time Hoan had come to see her. And her smile had seemed to say, "It's nothing serious. Don't worry."

But Hoan couldn't stop worrying. Mien was his other half. If he lost her, he would lose half of himself. He had done everything he could. He had made sure to give money to everyone in advance—the director of the hospital, the head of the maternity ward, the surgeon's assistants, the nurses, and even the old midwife with the pockmarked face who had shamelessly demanded her share. But Hoan wasn't entirely reassured. He knew from experience that the success of human enterprises only half depends on their efforts. The other half depends on a mysterious power, and he didn't know how to prostrate himself to pray to the tutelary genies. All he could do was chain-smoke cigarettes, like a man gone mad who could no longer smell their scent nor feel their heat at the end of his fingertips. The rain continued to fall and float about. The white blossoms of the plum trees that surrounded the hospital blurred and merged with the drizzle. Hoan suddenly thought of a sharp, pointy blade ripping into Mien's skin, cutting her flesh, of blood flowing.

You're going to suffer alone. I'm powerless to help or share your pain, and yet you continue to smile, and encourage me.

The previous evening, Mien had said, "I've lost two fingers. I'll never have the hand I once had. Will you still love me anyway?"

"You'll always be the most beautiful of all women to me, the one woman who belongs to me, the one woman I'll always love."

She had looked at him wistfully with sad eyes. "You can meet other, younger, more beautiful women than me."

Hoan had shaken his head. "We've overcome ordeals together. We've lived far apart, at a great distance. We survived that separation."

Mien had been about to speak, but the nurse had come to take her temperature. And their conversation had ended there, when they asked Hoan to leave so that Mien could rest and sleep soundly before the operation.

Now Hoan suddenly remembered that conversation. He couldn't explain why Mien, faced with such imminent danger, hadn't worried about her own life or the life of their child, but rather had tormented herself about her lost finger, fearing she would lose his love. There was something similar between this attitude and her behavior toward Bon. She had exonerated him of his crime—attempting to murder Hoan—by claiming to have touched his rifle out of curiosity, an awkward lie that wouldn't fool even a child. And yet everyone had listened to her, everyone had accepted the lie in silence, first Hoan, the victim of this attempt; and then the president of the commune, who represented the State; then the chief of the hunters' guild . . . All of them. No one had dared contradict her.

A woman is a mysterious, incomprehensible world. She isn't interested in ordinary logic, and she listens only to the voice of her heart. That's why a man can never measure up.

He reconstructed the chain of events: Bon went to Xa's house to borrow the rifle. Xa lent the rifle to his friend enthusiastically, and then jumped on his motorcycle to go buy food for his wife. A moment later, Soan got up and learned the news by accident while chatting with her eldest son. Without even taking time to dress or comb her hair, she ran over to Mien's house to warn her. Mien herself didn't even take the time to change, or to call Mr. Lu. She just ran through the fields of pepper and coffee, caught up with Bon, and grabbed the rifle just as he was aiming a bullet at Hoan's head. Neither of these women had the slightest evidence of what Bon planned to do—only their intuition. How had these two women, who led vastly different lives, had the same thought, come to the same conclusion? Hoan couldn't fathom it. Now, all he knew was that Mien had been ready to sacrifice her own life to save his. And so he had accepted her wish to spare Bon.

She had squeezed his hand and her pale lips had moved slightly, murmuring, "Let this whole thing drop . . . for me, I'm asking you to let it drop."

And if I hadn't done as you wished?

If he hadn't, the powers-that-be would have done their duty. Bon would have gone to prison if they found him to be sane. If not, they would have almost certainly locked him up in an insane asylum. Hoan knew that kind of hospital only too well. The kind of hospital where they treated sick people like wild animals, locked them in rooms with bars in place of windows. The kind of place where the "patients" slept on mats on the ground and ate from plastic bowls filled with a mash of rice and soup mixed together like pig feed. The kind of place where the inmates made love in secret, where, when a woman got pregnant, they tied her up to perform an abortion. Rarely did any of the "sick" people get better; in fact, they usually got worse. The psychiatric hospitals were in reality internment camps to isolate the mentally ill and reduce the risk to society. The doctors and unhappy souls who worked in these remote, suffocating places received a pittance for a salary, which of course destroyed all charitable feeling, turning it instead into a venom that tortured both them and the unlucky patients in their care. Inside these crude, dirty walls carelessly smeared with paint, behind the windows and doors set with heavy iron bars like cages for wild animals, fits of madness grew more and more violent as the days passed. All this usually led to the sick person's death.

Hoan knew all of this, and Mien did, too. Locked up in a prison or an asylum, Bon would end up in the village cemetery in no time. And that is why she had tried to protect him.

Was it her conscience or the last remains of her love for him? I didn't have the heart to ask her, and I'll never again have the courage to . . .

Hoan sighed and got out a new cigarette. The man seated facing him, on the other side of the hospital porch, fumbled in his shirt and got out a crumbled Hoa Mai cigarette, smoothed it straight, and then approached Hoan to ask for a light. He tried to strike up a conversation, "Are you waiting for your wife to give birth, too?"

He had a crooked tooth that lent a bit of charm to a mouth that had been yellowed by cigarettes. Hoan nodded and asked, "You here for the first time?"

"No," the man replied immediately. He took a few puffs before continuing. "This is my second love song, dear brother."

The second love song . . . Well, he's a romantic. He looks like a village chief and he has this flowery language?

Hoan smiled to himself, flicking his cigarette stub out the window. The man laughed and continued, "You think it's funny that I speak with such romantic verve, no?" He chuckled, proudly but somewhat bitterly, too. Hoan noticed the wrinkles on his cheeks and at the corners of his eyes. He had to be fifty years old—the hair had started to gray at his temples and behind his ears. After this gaiety, he began to recite some comic verse, almost as a challenge to Hoan.

"So, you're a storyteller," Hoan said.

"It's not me. It's life. There are so many interesting stories."

Hoan laughed. "Well, tell me some then . . . I need to kill time and so do you. Is your wife in the delivery room?"

"No. She's waiting for the operating table. The hospital has only one and another woman's on it at the moment. A beautiful one, too, apparently. And they say she has had an extraordinary love life."

So you and I have become characters in some bawdy story to amuse everyone . . .

Hoan suddenly felt bitter, and his ears and neck burned. Nevertheless, he pretended to be surprised. "Really? What's so extraordinary about it?"

Just then, the midwife with the pockmarked face showed up and called out loudly, "Hey, sir, your wife just gave birth to a boy. Five pounds nine ounces. He looks really cute, very lively. But you can't come in yet. The anesthesiologist is still waking her up."

"Thank you."

The midwife turned and ran off, looking satisfied, as if she had just accomplished the task for which Hoan had paid her handsomely the night before. The gray-haired man looked at Hoan again. "Oh, so it's you, the central character in this story? Well, excuse me, I'd never have guessed."

"No need to excuse yourself. A strange story always piques people's curiosity. It's just a fact. Banal, really."

The man's voice suddenly turned harsh. "No, no . . . it's banal and it isn't. People's curiosity is not as innocent as you think. It always comes with prejudice and cruelty. Sometimes it can even kill a man, or a love story or even a family without even paying the price of going to court or to prison. Curiosity doesn't even have a face you can spit on . . . What we call curiosity, opinion, the rumor of the crowd, is something invisible and yet terrifying. I've been its victim. I was once the main character in a story just as extraordinary as yours . . . that's why I'd like to offer you my sincere apology."

He spoke in a grave, serious tone. Dark wrinkles creased at the corners of his mouth. His eyes clouded over and his entire face suddenly seemed gaunt, gray, old, and faded. Hoan felt disarmed; he didn't confide easily in someone he had just met. Neither did he have the gift of consoling or encouraging others. This joking man had suddenly turned somber—which only added to Hoan's confusion. Fortunately, the midwife reappeared at the other end of the porch and waved to him.

"I must be going," Hoan said.

"So your wife's finished? Well then, mine will have her turn . . . I must be going, too."

He followed Hoan toward the operating room and the postoperative recovery room. The midwife guided Hoan all the way to a private room that had been reserved for Mien. A tiny room, just twenty-six square feet, with two iron beds painted white and a tiny bedside table in the middle. Other women had to share common rooms made for eight or twelve people. Hoan had had to pay a large sum of money so that Mien could be alone in these twenty-six square feet. The midwife pointed to the second bed.

"You can stay here tonight with your wife."

"Thank you."

He approached Mien and his new baby son. The baby was lying by his mother's side, swaddled in white cotton linens as if he were in a co-coon. He looked at Hoan through half-closed eyes. A calm, serene, friendly look, filled with friendship. The baby moved his lips as if to laugh. A tiny, proud pout. His tiny little eyelashes fluttered. Even this fluttering seemed to have the mark of a mature man about it. Hoan gazed at him, stunned. This boy was utterly different from his elder brother. When Hanh was born, Hoan had gone in to greet his son as soon as he had left the delivery room. He had met a newborn who looked like all newborns. Little Hanh had been seven pounds nine ounces. His face was bluish, his forehead creased with little wrinkles, his nose dusted with tiny white pimples. He was born at full term, but his look and his gestures were fragile, dizzy, and even a bit silly. But this boy, born prematurely, looked like a miniature old man. He seemed to know the ways of the world by heart already, as if he were returning someplace for the second time to see familiar faces and landscapes that held nothing new for him . . .

The midwife's voice echoed at Hoan's back.

"We've never seen a seven-month baby as mature as your son. We put him in the incubator, but after a half hour he started to wriggle like a fish. When that kid grows up, only the heavens will be able to handle him."

As if she feared Hoan might still doubt her word, she added as she left, "I've worked here for almost twenty years. I'm not just trying to humor you."

Hoan leaned over and smelled the baby's skin. His nose grazed the baby's face. A light, warm breath caused a tiny shiver on Hoan's cheek. And the shiver spread.

My son, in spite of everything you've come into this world. You're not just my son, you'll be my friend and my fellow traveler, a man I can lean on. You were born in the midst of an ordeal and like a fruit that grows ripe in the stormy season, you know how to hold tightly to the branch, to mock the rain and wind.

The child continued to stare up at him with a contented look.

Hoan put forward a finger to touch his tiny face, to trace the arch of his eyebrows, the bridge of his nose all the way down to his upper lip. The little guy looked exactly like him, a perfect copy. Virtually every feature. And in that way he was different from Hanh, who was such a mixture of his face and Mien's. Hoan remembered what Mien had said when she was just four months' pregnant with this one: "This one is going to look so much like you he'll be your reincarnation."

"How do you know?"

"Because I'm his mother," she had replied curtly. Then she had turned to some household task, and he couldn't ask her for any further explanation.

"I'll call him Hung," she had suddenly announced.

"Why?"

"Because I like the name. 'Hero.' "

"I'd prefer he not become a hero. There's no happiness in a hero's life."

"But this boy must be called Hung. Without a hero's courage, how would he dare enter this world?"

"You don't want our child to be happy?"

"Of course . . . but to each his destiny. It's different from when we conceived Hanh . . . now."

Mien didn't finish her sentence, but he knew what she meant.

I'll call you Hung, as your mother wished. And when you grow up, you will be the pillar of this family and this whole lineage.

The little baby blinked, looked up at him. Still the same tranquil, serene look. His arms were swaddled in the cloth, which covered him entirely in a white cocoon. Only his face expressed his feelings. Hoan was amazed by his features: the tiny, fragile muscles that seemed to communicate with such finesse. Either he was imagining things, or this newborn was an extraordinary being. No sooner had he formulated these thoughts than those tiny red lips began to move again, the arrogant little eyes twinkling as if to say, *Don't worry, my friend. I know my fate. Tomorrow, I'm going to bear the weight of the world on my shoulders. You can enjoy your happiness into old age.*

And the baby winked, a wink that seemed to replace words brimming with confidence and generosity.

Stunned, Hoan wondered, *Have I gone mad? Did I just imagine everything?*

As pride submerged his father's heart, Hoan suddenly felt embarassed. He tucked a tiny wool cover to one side of the baby, even though it was wedged between Mien and the wall. He left, closing the door behind him. Once outside, he sat down in a deserted corner of the porch and continued to roll cigarettes. Tobacco . . . This exasperating habit had suddenly become an efficient way to hide his embarrassment. The drizzle continued to fall. Hoan looked out at the plum trees, which seemed to melt in the misty rain. The nurses and midwives, the relatives of the patients, women waiting to give birth— everyone came and went, each pursuing their tasks and objectives. Hoan looked at their faces. He suddenly understood how alone a man is. All his life he had tried to free himself from the quest for a soul mate, and yet this quest was for the most part hopeless.

It's you, you are my soul mate, my fellow traveler, my beloved son . . .

A strange, unexpected happiness intoxicated his heart. Who could have imagined that this tiny boy would elicit such a wonderful feeling? His elder brother was just a son who needed tenderness and protection from his father. But this little one, on the contrary, had crossed through the door, given Hoan the feeling of finally having a companion; from the very first look, he had felt protected and supported.

The veranda suddenly became more animated and boisterous.

"Come, step aside, let him past . . . step aside," someone shouted.

Hoan turned around. At the other end of the veranda, four white blouses pushed a stretcher toward the operating block. The only man in the group kept shouting, "Step aside, clear the way, please."

A short, chubby doctor bustled about. He was one of the best surgeons at the hospital, and had been recommended to Hoan when he was arranging Mien's operation. He had probably agreed to operate on the wife of the man Hoan had been chatting with.

Where does he find the money to pay all these people?

When the family of a patient didn't dole out money, the patient was often at the mercy of a lottery whereby he became a guinea pig for interns, or newly promoted doctors. It was absolutely critical to have money, so it was normal that it drove men crazy. The stretcher rolled past Hoan. The short, chubby doctor glanced at him indifferently. Hoan smiled. The previous evening, when Hoan had paid him a visit at home, the doctor's round face had bloomed, those thick, sensual lips dripping with sympathy when Hoan had set a beautiful gift on his tea chest. His wife, a woman as petite and as plump as he was, had offered Hoan a cup of tea, and welcomed him with an exceptionally polite voice.

That's life.

Hoan flicked his cigarette butt to the ground, remembering the gray-haired man, his wise, caustic words, his cynical, bitter laugh.

Who is he, this gentle, yet edgy man? Has his soul been crushed? I'm sure that . . .

Hoan didn't have to wait long. The man was walking right in front of him, a few yards away from the stretcher. A few paces behind him, the midwife with the pockmarked face was shaking a small, brightly colored bag. The man watched the doctor's back and passed in front of Hoan without even noticing him. You could see the tension in the twitch at the corners of his mouth. His wrinkled shirt flaps were pulled out over his belt. He must have spent the night on the bench on the porch outside.

Poor man.

Somehow this man whom Hoan had just met was for him the precise image of the human condition. The midwife walked toward Hoan, smiling her wide, irritating smile.

"You're not waiting for her to wake up, are you?"

Hoan shook his head. "I'm going to let her sleep."

Hoan watched the jiggling flesh of the old woman's crude face. Suddenly, unable to restrain his curiosity, he asked, "Tell me . . ."

"Yes?"

"The wife of that thin guy over there in the gray shirt, is she being operated on?"

"Yes. Her hips are too narrow and her blood pressure is much too low. For a first child, it's very unfortunate."

"Where are they from?"

"Oh, you don't know about them? He's Professor Thong, the best history teacher at the high school in town. His wife teaches biology. They came north before the war. They say that the two of them were well-respected; the Party secretary even gave him an award. But after the liberation of the south, one of his female students made him drink a potion and he left his wife and kids to follow her. In the end, he had to resign, leave the city, and go live as a dyer in Son Quang. His new wife has had some difficulties giving birth, so they brought her here. What an idiot! A rich, respected man and he suddenly becomes some unknown pauper in a nest of leeches."

The woman held up the plastic bag for Hoan to see. "Look at this bag of cakes, fit for dogs, that he just handed me. Still, I can't throw it on the sidewalk, can I?"

Hoan looked at her cruel, shameless face and remembered his father's words.

That's life, that's life . . .

Suddenly these words seemed to haunt him. The sky outside seemed even cloudier and colder than before. The stand of red flowers planted the length of the veranda had been showered by the rain and they now shimmered like some ornamental plant. But their crimson color didn't add any warmth to the atmosphere. On the contrary, this false flame bothered him.

What if I hadn't obeyed Mien yesterday? What if I had let them put Bon in prison or an asylum? Her conscience would have tortured her and that poison could have destroyed our love, our future together. But by obeying her, I am also putting our future in danger. So that's the way it is. Happiness is just mortgaged property.

Hoan lit another cigarette as a new question rose in his mind.

But if Mien had urged me to send Bon to prison or to an asylum to kill this threat to our love? . . . If . . . would I still love her?

He didn't know. He didn't dare reply. He knew that the human soul was twisted, that love is extravagant and uncontrollable. All he had lived through had taught him that. He knew that he respected and obeyed Mien because this seemingly frail woman was in fact strong. She heeded only her own conscience and she was willing to pay for her choices. People could free themselves from all the jailers on earth, but not from the prisons of their own souls. And they could destroy all the courtrooms in the world, but still have to face those they had built in their own hearts. He knew it all too clearly now. But at the bottom of his own heart rose a mute moan, an unending refrain.

Why? But why?

Through the veil of drizzle outside, he could make out a blurred horizon, a line of demarcation between life and death, happiness and unhappiness, similar to a spider's web flapping in the wind.

If this is the way it is, then I have the talisman everyone dreams of. I've found my companion, my fellow traveler. Oh my son, hurry, grow up. I will create history for you myself, and you won't have any debt to pay to the past.

He imagined how quickly the time would go by, how the baby would soon be a five-year-old boy that he could set in front of him on the motorcycle, how they would go and survey the fields of coffee and pepper. And he would take his son to go see the city too, sit with him in cafés and fancy restaurants. He would sit facing him and talk with him as he would a friend with the same experience in life. The boy would be his equal.

Hoan suddenly felt small and fragile next to this tiny child. He felt confident, consoled by his presence in the world. He closed his eyes and saw in his mind's eye this tiny hero traveling everywhere with him, perched on his motorcycle. He tossed his cigarette aside and went back into the room where his protector lay sleeping. A smile of happiness on his lips, Hoan didn't notice that the men seated on the veranda were staring at him, both curious and perplexed . . .

In the meantime, in Mountain Hamlet, Bon is also laughing with joy. Rain falls on the cemetery. A rain that both shelters and assails him.

Shepherds with their cows and goats give him doleful looks. He is alone, at peace. Cold water soaks his hair and skin, the water snuffing out the bonfire of fury that once roared and howled inside him. How beautiful they are, these white droplets, gently slanting through the sky. They remind him of the rains of his youth, the ringing laughter of young girls. And of the rolling green hills shrouded in fog. There was a plant here that resembled a reed; they called it fox's tail. Its flowers seemed to have been woven out of millions and millions of droplets. If only he too could melt and become rain, he would scamper down the leaves, the blades of grass, the lips of the young girls. He would slide between women's breasts, dive into their belly buttons, glide into their most intimate flesh. If only he was young enough to dance, to strum his penis like you would strum the strings of a guitar—that game he and the other soldiers used to play as they waited for the next campaign. If only he had magical powers, he would leap in a single bound onto the tips of the trees and swing there like a kite . . . But what good was hoping or dreaming?

Childish nonsense.

The sergent was standing behind him. How long had he been there? Bon couldn't say. He laughed nervously, embarrassed. "I ramble on like this . . . nothing but nonsense."

The sergeant sat down beside him. "God, the rain is beautiful! Just like up north!"

"So they have drizzle like this in your village?"

The sergeant nodded. "Just like this. But even more beautiful. It's cold up north. If you go to the banks of Quang Ba Lake or Nhat Tan, you'll lose your way in field after field of peach trees in full bloom."

He stopped, a distant air about him. No doubt he was dreaming of the peach trees of Quang Ba or Nhat Tan.

Bon didn't dare question him. He put his arm around the sergeant's shoulder. A moment later the sergeant said, "Do you have a cigarette left? With the weather like this, a cigarette would be so perfect."

Bon fumbled in his pocket. "I've got a whole pack." And he handed it to the sergeant.

Bony, transparent hands deftly peeled off the wrapping and tore a corner of the pack. "You have one first."

"Oh no. You first."

"Stop this politesse. Take one, quickly, or the rain is going to dampen your tobacco. Come on now, get out your lighter . . . Wait, let me shield it with my hat."

The sergeant lifted off his hat and helped Bon light his cigarette. Afterward, it was his turn.

He lights his cigarette the same way he always did, his head slightly tilted, his hand on the rim of his hat.

The silvery blue flame flared up over his translucent hands, flickering in the wind.

"Are you okay, Elder Brother?"

"I'm fine. Put out the flame . . . ah, would you pass me that lighter? Every time I want a smoke, I've got to find a light."

"Here, have this."

The sergeant stuffed the lighter into his pants' pocket with the same old gesture: After he let go of the lighter, he smoothed the opening of his pocket back into place. His pants were thin, as if woven of threads from witch's pineapple, a variety that grew only in the cemeteries. Bon was going to ask him why he wasn't wearing his new uniform, but the sergeant tilted his head and said, "It's strange. Even with the drizzle, you can still hear the wind howl."

"Maybe it's the echo of the wind whistling through the gorges."

"Yes, almost sounds like the wind we had on Hill A46 in Chien Khan . . . Do you remember that base?"

"Yes, I remember."

"I go back there often."

"Do you remember the night we roasted that beef?"

"Yes, Quang made that delicious sauce for the barbecue. He died, you know, two and a half years after me. His bones are still on the battlefield in Military Region K."

"Quang was really good to me. Every time he was on kitchen duty he always put aside a huge crust of grilled rice for me. And Thieu, from Thai Binh, do you remember him, sergeant?"

"Oh yes."

"Well, the day the chief of the division came to congratulate us, while the guy is speaking, Thieu goes and lets out this horrible, noisy fart!"

They both laughed.

Bon looked at the sergeant's face, so close to his. His skin was transparent. The clump of freckles on his left cheek wasn't there anymore, nor was the scar on his chin. And the long, thick, curly black hair he had once tucked behind his ears was gone, too. His face was blurry, indistinct, without eyebrows or lashes. A smile without lips, revealing only white teeth. What did it matter? . . . This was still the face that was dearest to him, the only one that belonged to him, that would now accompany him . . .

Behind that face stretched the fields of pepper and coffee, the villages and hamlets clustered on the rolling hills, and, farther in the distance, the curving rice fields that linked them to the narrow, sandy beaches along the sea to the east. But for Bon, from now on, all this was a desert, a land of absence. A WORLD WITHOUT HUMANS.

> November 23, 1998. Hanoi
> Duong Thu Huong

©Timothy Karr

DUONG THU HUONG was born in Vietnam in 1947. A vocal advocate of human rights and democratic reform, Huong was expelled from the Communist Party in 1990 before she was arrested and imprisoned without trial. Though her novels are banned in Vietnam, where she continues to live in internal exile, she remains one of Vietnam's most popular and controversial writers both at home and abroad.

Translators **NINA McPHERSON** and **PHAN HUY DUONG** live in Paris. They have also translated Duong Thu Huong's *Paradise of the Blind, Novel Without a Name, Memories of a Pure Spring,* and *Beyond Illusions.*